DARK RISING

BOOKS BY BRIAN ANDREWS & JEFFREY WILSON

TIER ONE

Tier One

War Shadows

Crusader One

American Operator

Red Specter

Collateral

Dempsey

Ember

TIER ONE ORIGINS

Scars: John Dempsey

SONS OF VALOR

Sons of Valor

Sons of Valor II: Violence of Action

Sons of Valor III: War Machine

THE SHEPHERDS

Dark Intercept

Dark Angel

Dark Fall

Dark Rising

OTHER NOVELS

The Sandbox

Four Minutes

TOM CLANCY'S JACK RYAN SERIES

Act of Defiance

Defense Protocol

W. E. B. GRIFFIN'S PRESIDENTIAL AGENT

Rogue Asset

BOOKS BY ANDREWS & WILSON WRITING AS ALEX RYAN

NICK FOLEY

Beijing Red

Hong Kong Black

BOOKS BY BRIAN ANDREWS

The Calypso Directive

The Infiltration Game

Reset

BOOKS BY JEFFREY WILSON

The Traiteur's Ring

The Donors

Fade to Black

War Torn

Julian's Numbers: A Ghost Story

DARK RISING

ANDREWS & WILSON

BLACK STONE PUBLISHING

Published in 2025 by Blackstone Publishing
Cover and book design by Candice Edwards

Printed in the United States of America
Originally published in hardcover by Blackstone Publishing in 2025

First paperback edition: 2025
ISBN 979-8-8748-6859-8
Fiction / Thrillers / Military

Version 1

Blackstone Publishing
31 Mistletoe Rd.
Ashland, OR 97520

www.BlackstonePublishing.com

For Ashley—our prayer warrior

AUTHORS' NOTE

We want to thank our readers for their patience. So many of you have reached out to us asking about when, or if, the next books in this series might be coming. A lot has happened the last few years that impacted the timing of this book, but please know that these stories and these characters have a very special place in our hearts. It was hard to wait—for us as well as for you—but we trust that His timing is perfect. And we thank you for going on this journey with us.

PART I

Watch out for false prophets. They come to you in sheep's clothing, but inwardly they are ferocious wolves. By their fruit you will recognize them. Do people pick grapes from thornbushes, or figs from thistles?

—Matthew 7:15–16 (NIV)

CHAPTER ONE

CTRA. EL COPEY-PEPILLO SALCEDO

TWO MILES EAST OF PEPILLO SALCEDO

DOMINICAN REPUBLIC

1440 HOURS LOCAL

Sani Marcelin squirmed in her seat but kept her head down, focusing on the pages of her math book despite the noise from the boys laughing and tossing a soccer ball back and forth behind her. She understood: These boys had never owned their own ball, and now they had a new shiny blue one to play with. She had no doubt the sun would set on them playing soccer on the field they always talked about, by the clinic just a block from the Saint Fleur Orphanage, where they lived in Pepillo Salcedo.

Sani had never seen the field or the inside of the orphanage. Hers was a poorly kept secret of deception that had allowed her to ride the bus to the Mount Hope School in El Copey these last two school years. Sani knew Granmè had called in favors so Sani could attend Mount Hope, and they would both die of broken hearts if Sani lost her spot. The school in Fort Liberté Sani had attended closed when she was still barely able to walk. Granpapa had died only a year later, and since then it had been just her and Granmè, the most amazing woman she would ever know. Not only was Sani not an orphan nor a resident at Saint Fleur, but she wasn't even Dominican, which might have kept her from the Mount Hope School for orphans. But Granmè somehow took care of everything.

Granmè always took care of everything.

Her grandmother worked two jobs to keep her fed, clothed, and to even give her the occasional baby doll. She earned enough to keep gas in the old pickup truck that spewed black smoke behind them when they drove from Fort Liberté to Pepillo Salcedo five mornings a week. The twelve-mile drive took them over an hour on the poor roads of northeastern Haiti, and Granmè had taken a job cleaning dishes and tables at D' Dulce Empanadas, one of the only restaurants in Pepillo Salcedo, on the Dominican Republic side of the border. This way she only made the round-trip drive once a day and saved money on gas.

Sani smiled, then squished up her face, trying to make sense of the math problem on the page despite the chaos around her in the old, rumbling bus. She was in class with older kids now, some fourteen or fifteen years old, because the American teachers from the church in Ohio who ran the school told her she was gifted. But as she looked at the strange formula, where you had to figure out what the letters stood for in an equation, she didn't feel gifted. Why would you put letters in math?

The bus jerked suddenly to the left and then back to the right, spilling her book and binder out of her lap and onto the floor. Another pothole, she assumed, reaching for her book. But then the bus skidded to a stop, tossing her onto the vehicle's floor beside her books. Her backpack with the large blue cross stitched above the words *Mount Hope Christian School* fell on top of her.

"Stay on the floor, children," the kind old man who drove

their bus shouted, fear in his voice, she thought. In the two years she'd attended Mount Hope, Mr. Toussaint had been at the wheel of the bus every single day, and he had never once sounded frightened before now. "Stay on the floor and don't move."

She heard the gears grind, and the bus jerked backward a few yards. The other kids around her hollered in panic and confusion.

Then she heard a gunshot.

The sharp crack resounded around her, and she heard glass breaking. Children began to scream and cry. Sani opened her eyes and saw the terrified face of Alexis Laquerre under the seat. The six-year-old had tears on her cheeks, and her chin trembled. Sani beckoned the girl with her hands, and the little one squeezed under the seat and crawled up into her arms, sobbing.

More glass broke. The children's screams that followed urged Sani to hold the young one even tighter.

Sani felt fear all around her.

But she felt something else too. Something dark and unfamiliar, like an invisible presence. It terrified her. Sani closed her eyes tight and mouthed a memorized prayer, then made a *tsk* sound to herself when the memorized words would not come to her.

She heard heavy boots pound up the stairs of the bus, then another, softer gunshot. She didn't know how she knew their driver was dead, but she did.

And when she *knew*, she was never, ever wrong.

God protect us. Jesus, keep us safe and be with us. And Jesus, please take Mr. Toussaint home to be with you. He is a good man.

"This one," a man's voice barked.

Sani turned her head around, looking under the seats toward the front of the bus. A large hand reached down and grabbed Little Mary—little because she was tiny, though, at eleven years old, Mary was almost a year older than Sani—by the cardigan she wore every day. Mary screamed and kicked, but she disappeared off the floor anyway.

Two sets of feet moved farther back, and Sani could see them now, clods of mud falling off the unlaced work boots. The road was always muddy between El Copey and Pepillo Salcedo. The boots paused at each seat, their owners apparently looking at each occupant, and Sani felt Alexis tremble in her arms. She wondered how they chose who to take. Why didn't they just take them all? Children were stolen for many horrible reasons in both Haiti and Dominican Republic, from slavery to other far more terrifying purposes. Why take only a few?

Perhaps they have only so much room?

As the reality set in, she felt fear begin to build. It was always like this—fear bubbling slowly to the surface, where she could decide whether to let it be part of her or not. It had been like this when her parents had died, but then God had brought her to live with Granmè and all had been well, as His Good Book promised. But this was different. Because that voice inside, that voice that told her things, now told her she would be taken.

She decided not to be afraid. Was David afraid when he faced the giant? Was Daniel afraid in the lions' den? What about Noah? Joshua? No, because God was with them.

"This one."

Sani looked up from the floor and felt Alexis's face burrow into her neck now. She looked, trying to be brave like Daniel, at the thin, filthy man staring down at her with dark, menacing eyes. He had a pistol in his hand, a rifle over his shoulder, and he stared back and forth between the two girls, a paper in his other hand.

Was he looking at a picture, maybe? Was that how they chose? Did they know the children somehow?

"This one," the man with the pistol said again and gestured to his partner in the front of the bus.

"No," Sani said, sitting up on the floor and holding Alexis, who cried louder now, closer. "You can't have her."

"I will take whoever I want, and you can do nothing to stop me," the man growled at her, a flicker of orange shining in his eyes. "But it is not her we are taking. It is you."

Sani felt tears well in her eyes, and Alexis held her even tighter. She had already known, somehow, but hearing the man say it made it real—into more than just another nightmare that turned out to be true.

"No, no," Alexis said. "Please don't go."

"It will be all right," Sani whispered to Alexis with a courage she felt ebbing away. "God will be with us both."

A hand reached down and grabbed Sani by the arm, just below her shoulder, and lifted her in the air. She grabbed for her little bag, the one Granmè had given her for Christmas, but couldn't reach it.

Then she was hoisted over a man's shoulder, flopping up and down painfully as he took her from the bus. As they went down the stairs, she looked up and was immediately sorry she had. She would have preferred to remember kind old Mr. Toussaint without part of his face missing and his blood and brains on the side of the window. She said another prayer for him and his soul and felt peace, like God answered that He already had him.

But what about me? About us? She prayed silently.

But there was no answer.

And then she was in the back seat of a large black car—dirty but with weirdly clean windows. There were bars, like a cage, separating her and the two other kids from the front seat. Mary was beside her on the left, and a boy named Amede was on her right. Amede was big for his age, always laughing and clowning around. He teased her on the bus in the mornings, which she hated—until Granmè had told her boys did that when they liked a girl. That was the dumbest thing Sani had ever heard, but it had made her less angry.

But Amede wasn't teasing her now. He stared straight ahead, in shock maybe, his cheeks wet with tears. His mouth hung open, but at least he wasn't making the soft babbling sounds Mary made on Sani's other side.

Amede turned suddenly toward Sani. "Where are they taking us?" he asked. His voice sounded far more childlike than she had expected.

"I don't know, Amede," she said gently. "Perhaps we can pray together?"

The driver's door opened, and a man slipped into the seat; then another—the man who had carried her over his shoulder—got in on the passenger side. The driver wore dark sunglasses, but when he took them off, she recognized him as the one who had pointed at her after looking at his paper. He reviewed the papers in his hand once more, then looked up at her, Mary, and Amede, then back at his papers.

"This is them," he said, tossing the papers on the bench seat up front and dropping his dark sunglasses back over his eyes. "Let's go."

The other man, who wore a ball cap—a dirty blue cap with *NY* on the front, like the American baseball team—nodded and closed his door. "You children don't be giving any trouble now and no bad things be happening to you." He didn't turn around or look at them when he spoke. "We taking you to a nice lady to be in a new home, is all."

"Like a new orphanage?" Mary asked, her voice a tight sob.

"Yeah," the man with the sunglasses said as he put the car in gear. "Like a new orphanage."

"Pray with me, Amede," Sani whispered.

"No," Amede choked back softly. "I don't want to pray. I want to go home."

Sani smiled sadly. She'd heard Amede correct kids hundreds of times for calling Saint Fleur their home. He always insisted that an orphanage couldn't be a home because being an orphan meant you had no home. He usually laughed when he said it, like he was kidding around as usual, but Sani always felt the pain in him, the pain behind the words.

Sani bowed her head as they headed away from the bus, a cloud of dust surrounding the car. Her granmè would be terrified when she didn't arrive at Saint Fleur. How long would it take her to notice the bus was late? How much longer until someone from town or the school went and found it? Where would Sani and her friends be by then?

As if in answer, the car veered left onto an even smaller and bumpier dirt road off the main road heading into Pepillo Sancedo, which Sani could see now in the distance. The orphanage was several blocks north, near the water, too far to see from here. With the bad roads and frequent flooding during the rainy season, no one would think a thing of them being even an hour late.

And an hour from now, they would be far away from Pepillo Sancedo, wouldn't they? And just where would they be?

Sani continued to mouth a prayer of petition to Jesus but concentrated now on where the car might be going. It was possible, maybe, that the information could be useful if she had an opportunity to tell someone who could help them. Or perhaps she could escape, and then she would need to know which direction to go in to find her granmè. Granmè would be waiting for her, she knew, at Saint Fleur, no matter how long it took.

A few minutes passed and they drove over a rickety bridge across a narrow river. This must be the Rivière du Massacre—but then, that meant they were across the border and back in

Haiti. Who smuggled orphans *into* Haiti? Haiti had too many homeless kids already and certainly didn't need anymore.

Sani remembered her teacher, the young American woman from Ohio, telling her that the river was named Massacre because of the killing of thirty French buccaneers by Spanish settlers. How odd that an American from Ohio, wherever that was exactly, had to come all the way to Haiti for Sani to learn about the naming of a river only eight miles from her grandparents' home in Fort Liberté. But then, few in Haiti today cared much about French buccaneers or Spanish settlers and their arguments almost three hundred years ago.

How much stranger that she would be thinking of this, of all things, now.

Across the bridge, they turned south on another terrible road. Perhaps fifteen minutes later, they emerged onto a slightly better road, still heading south. By this time, Amede looked nearly catatonic, and Mary now lay in Sani's lap, still sobbing, a thumb in her mouth. Sani couldn't remember ever seeing her suck her thumb before. The road improved as they continued south. Sani tried to imagine how far, in miles, they had traveled, but realized that she had no idea at all how time translated into distance. She couldn't see the speed of the car because the man's shoulder blocked her view, but maybe she could figure out how far they had gone if she knew . . .

Oh, wait—that's why you do those crazy math word problems, right? A train leaves the station and goes ten kilometers an hour for two hours . . .

If only I knew how fast we were going.

And had a watch.

She counted instead, figuring she could turn seconds into minutes and at least be able to guess how long they'd been traveling south.

As the road got better, they went faster. Eventually, she saw a big town out of the left window as she looked over Mary's sobbing body. So they'd gone at least to the first town south of Pepillo Salcedo, she thought. Moments later, they turned left onto a paved road and headed into the town, which she could see was at least three or four times the size of Pepillo. How strange that this large town was so close, only a half hour or less, by her counting estimate, away from home—and she'd had no idea it was here or what it was called. She realized she knew more about the rest of the world than about her own little corner of Haiti.

They turned off the good, wide road only a few moments later and again weaved on dirt roads through poor little shanty-style neighborhoods. The car passed people walking along the road, but no one seemed to pay any attention to them at all, and she wondered if this town was where the men came from.

Perhaps it would be easy for Granmè to find her after all. She was so close, less than an hour away, she thought. But any such hope was dashed when the filthy car weaved onto a paved road that led them up and then out onto a sprawling field. The road circled around, toward a big metal building, and she realized that this wasn't a field at all.

It was a runway.

Sitting beside the metal building was a fancy silver-and-white airplane with two big engines and propellers on the wings. Its door was open, and a little stairway led up into it. Another car, silver and covered in rust, sat beside the plane. As they pulled up, Sani felt Mary hug her leg. She looked over at Amede, whose gaze was fixed, tears still streaming down his cheeks and dripping from his chin. She took his hand in hers, and he squeezed it gently.

The car came to a stop, and a cloud of dust surrounded them for a moment and then settled onto the windows. The rough-looking man from the passenger seat got out, his rifle slung over his shoulder, and opened the door beside Amede.

"Get out," the man growled.

"I want to go home," Amede said, still staring straight ahead. "Please, can I go home?"

Instead of answering, the man slapped the boy. Sani heard the sharp open-hand slap and felt both the pain and fear rise up in Amede. She squeezed his hand as he began to sob, but then he turned and climbed out of the car, still firmly holding her hand. Sani reached behind her and took Mary's hand as well, shooting a tight smile at the shell-shocked girl.

"Come, Mary," she said, her own voice shakier than she expected. "We must go now."

The girl said nothing but followed her out of the car.

They approached the plane in a little line, single file behind the bad man who cradled the rifle, linked by hands with Sani in the middle. At the stairs, the thin man with the rifle gestured up the steps with his left hand, gripping the weapon now with his right. He didn't smile or frown, but he also wouldn't look at Sani.

But as it often did, the gift she kept secret told her more. She felt no conflict in him, but she felt anger and she felt shame. The man believed that what he did was someone else's fault—not his own.

Amede led them up the stairs on trembling legs. Inside, the airplane was nicer than anything she had seen before, nicer even than Granmè's living room. The seats—there were eight of them—were wide and plush and covered in a tan, shiny leather. They were set in groups of four, two facing back and two facing forward, with little tables between the sets on either side of the aisle. A man in a suit sat cross-legged on an additional bench seat beside a door at the rear. There were two other girls, both older—perhaps fourteen or fifteen—sitting on the left, holding hands across a table. Across the aisle from the two teens sat another little girl—perhaps eight or nine years old—her lower lip quivering as she rocked back and forth and cried in the forward-facing seat.

Sani released Mary's hand and turned to her classmates.

"Sit with Amede," she said to Mary.

The girl did, taking the seat facing backward and now holding both of Amede's hands in her own. Sani took the seat across from the other little girl on her right.

"I'm Sani," she said softly.

The little girl looked up at her, soft brown eyes staring from between braids that framed her frightened face. She wore a blue dress with a logo Sani didn't recognize, identical to the ones worn by the two teenagers, and tears were glistening her light brown cheeks. Sani could feel the fear but also the longing in the girl. She saw images of a woman—the girl's mother, she thought.

"What is your name?" Sani asked.

"I'm Emelin," the girl said, her voice cracking. "I'm nine. They took me from my mom. I want to go home."

Sani's chest tightened as she thought of Granmè, probably sick with worry by now.

"Me too, Emelin," she said, taking the girl's hands in hers. "I'm scared too. You are from Azua—where is that?"

"How did you know?" the girl asked, her voice now a conspiratorial whisper.

Sani shrugged. "I sometimes know things. Where is Azua?"

"Far away from here, I think," the girl said.

Emelin jumped as the door up front was closed by the pilot, who then slipped back into the cockpit.

"So, we are all here," the man on the bench seat now said.

He uncrossed his legs, though he didn't get up, and Sani saw how shiny his black dress shoes were. He was not one who walked in the dirt, she imagined.

"Now listen to me, children," the man said, smiling with bright white teeth as he adjusted the cuffs on his starched white shirt. "I want you to know that nothing bad is going to happen to you. Nothing bad at all. I know that you are frightened, but we are taking you to a better place. Some of you are orphans who have no home at all, and one of you comes from a very, very poor family. The places you come from want to help you, but they are poor and unable to give you what you need, no matter how much they wish they could. You are all very, very blessed, children. You have been chosen for a new life—a better, richer, happier life. We are taking you to a new home where you will be taught, fed and clothed, and given nice things. You will have someone who loves you there in this new home. Someone very special, who wants to help you become something better than where you came from. We are headed there now, and soon you will see your new home. Each of you will have your very own room. You will have your very own clothes and things. You will eat well, and you will go to school. Soon, you will have the most amazing lives you could ever imagine. Isn't that wonderful?"

Sani sensed that his smile was not genuine, though his happiness was real.

"Why?" Amede asked, but then cowered as if he thought he might get in trouble.

"Because you are all very special. Your new mother knows this and is already proud of you. She wants to help you become even more special—and more powerful. You have a very blessed and comfortable life waiting for you. Soon, you will meet Manbo Athaliah, your new mother. She is mother to many, but she will love you just as much as any. She is excited to see you.

"Now please put on your seat belts, and Miri will get you anything you would like to drink or eat. We have sandwiches and fruit, and we also have snacks—even Hershey bars. Please ask for anything you want. It is Manbo Athaliah's desire that you be happy and comfortable."

The man snapped his fingers, and a woman who must have been Miri appeared from beside the cockpit door. Sani had not noticed her before, but this new woman smiled at them. Her hair was perfect, and she was dressed in a dark blue dress and comfortable black shoes. She had a gold bracelet on her wrist that sparkled. Sani looked over at Amede, whose eyes were wide, but no longer with fear. He even had a touch of a smile on his face. She was reminded of the lost boys she'd read about in the book about Pinocchio.

Sani put her seat belt on, smiled at Emelin, and pushed hard against the dread she felt growing at the mention of their new "mother's" name. Manbo, she knew, meant priestess. Her granmè had talked often about the Voudou priests and priestesses and how they perverted the teachings of the Bible.

"I know things too . . ."

Sani looked up at the scared face of Emelin across from her.

"What?"

"You said you sometimes know things. I have that gift too. And I know that man is a liar. And"—she leaned in and looked over her shoulder at the man at the rear of the plane—"I know, somehow, that this Manbo Athaliah is something very, very bad."

Sani stared at Emelin in her little blue dress, tears drying on her cheeks, and nodded.

Little Emelin was right, she knew.

Sani could tell too. And not just because she could now sense that even the well-dressed man in the shiny black shoes was terrified of the Voudou priestess who would soon be their new mother.

This Manbo Athaliah was, indeed, something very, very bad.

CHAPTER TWO

OFFICE OF THE DIRECTOR

SHEPHERDS NORTH AMERICA

TRINITY LOOP COMPLEX

WEST OF NASHVILLE, TENNESSEE

0830 HOURS LOCAL

Former Navy SEAL Jedidiah Johnson—who headed one of the most secret, direct-action, covert operations teams in the world, and who had quite literally saved the world only a few short weeks earlier—slunk down in his chair like a high-school sophomore waiting in the principal's office. The very thought made him smile. He'd been a decent high-school student and had been the straight arrow of his little trio of musketeers with David and Rachel. If he'd been in the principal's office, it was likely to read announcements or get some sort of attaboy award. But he'd *seen* the members of the football team sitting in chairs, slumped down like he was now, waiting on prosecution for some prank.

Well, look at me now . . .

After all that had happened in their senior year, Jed had

since found his place in the world for a decade as a Navy SEAL. There, he had become a rock-solid mass of a man who would put any high-school ball player, other than maybe a young Dwayne Johnson, to shame.

But he wasn't sitting here in Ben Morvant's office because he was in trouble.

In fact, he didn't know why he was here, but he hated waiting more than almost anything.

It was a SEAL thing.

"So sorry to keep you waiting, bro."

He looked up to see Ben Morvant, the head of the Shepherds North America, walk into his own office like a tardy guest, a backpack over his shoulder and a coffee in each hand. He handed one to Jed.

"But I brought gifts as an apology," he said, his nod indicating the steaming beverage now in Jed's massive paw. "Double-shot caramel macchiato, right?"

"Yeah, baby," Jed said, inhaling the aroma of the steaming brew.

"Jeez, Jed, my teeth hurt just ordering that sugary mess."

Jed took a long pull on the creamy coffee concoction and made an exaggerated *ahh* sound.

"How are you healing up, Jed?" Ben asked, his tone still light but his face now more serious.

The question made the healing wound on Jed's right flank itch, but he resisted the urge to scratch at it. The laceration above his right eye had healed nicely and no longer pulled at all, but the long, deep cut on his side—created by the impossible, animallike talons from Victor in their final showdown—had been jagged and irregular and had taken nearly a hundred stitches to close. That one still drove him crazy.

"Five by," he said instead of complaining about the itching.

"Lucky that they treated my spleen injury without surgery, I suppose, or I'd be taking a longer time to heal."

"Anything else to be done for the facial fracture?" Ben asked, leaning back and kicking his booted feet up on his desk.

"Nope," Jed answered. "Just keep looking pretty, I guess. And I'm back to full PT now as well."

"Docs said that's okay?" Ben said, eyeing him carefully.

"Yes, Mom." Jed laughed.

Truth was, the docs had told him to advance at his own pace but to be careful for six weeks about any heavy lifting because of the spleen laceration. Those six weeks were up, and Jed had dived headfirst into the pain of rehabbing his battered body. Much as he hated running, he was doing three to five miles daily but now got most of his aerobic workout from the low-impact laps in the Olympic-sized pool in the gym complex on Trinity. Even as a SEAL, swimming had never been his go-to PT, but he found he enjoyed it more now than when he was younger.

It's the quiet. And the solitude . . . Alone with my thoughts was never somewhere I liked to be until recently.

"Great," Ben said. "The rest of Joshua Bravo is on the mend as well, I hear."

"Yes, sir," Jed reported.

It seemed like this was just a status report on the team, which Jed hoped meant they were heading into a training phase to get back in fighting shape—and then back into the fight. Victor was gone, but there was plenty of evil still out there. Sarah Beth was right—the devil would always find another Victor. They needed to be ready when that happened.

"Eli was on extended light duty because of the head injury, as you know," Jed said, filling his boss in on his team's status. "He's coming to the end of that now. Repeat CT scan and MRI of his neck were good, so I expect him to be cleared for full duty soon. Johnny is the miracle, but then you know that, don't you?" He gave a smile and nod to his boss. "You performed that miracle."

Jed's youngest Shepherd teammate had been mauled nearly to death by a Dark One at the gate of St. George's. In fact, he should have died—everyone said so, including Bex, one of the best and most experienced Special Operations combat medics he'd ever known. Jed had seen the glazed, sightless look on Johnny's face and the arterial blood shooting out of his operator's torn-out throat with his own eyes.

But then, apparently, Ben had laid hands on him . . .

"I don't perform miracles, Jed," Ben said, running a hand through his shaggy hair. "God does that when and where he chooses. I'm glad Johnny is recovering well from his injuries."

"Me too," Jed said. "He's a great part of the team. He's already cleared and working hard in the gym and on the range. The rest of the team is five by as well. Grayson works out twice a day like most Green Berets, Nisha does that brainy stuff that Nisha does and then ventilates it out on the rifle range. Bex is doing very well, despite all she saw and did, and she and Hyeon just got back from the 18-Delta refresher course we sent them to at Bragg. Mostly, I think the team is ready to get back to work."

"I'm sure," Morvant said and took another long pull on his coffee, his gaze at the middle distance.

After a moment, Jed spoke again.

"So can we?"

Ben Morvant turned to him, his face suggesting he'd been somewhere else and lost the thread.

"Can you what?"

"Get back to work?" Jed asked. *That's why I'm here, right?*

"Yeah, of course," Ben said and smiled. "We'll get to that

in a sec. How's David? I keep close touch with him and Rachel, after everything, but am wondering from a team perspective."

"He's great," Jed said, but wondered if that was true. Honestly, David seemed more like the David he remembered from their youth than ever—but in a better, more productive way somehow. Still, almost losing his daughter—again—had taken a toll on both the Yarnells. But David had seemed to rally and was more invested in the Shepherds than ever. That was good, right? "He seems solid. And I heard you're looking for a role for Rachel as well. I think that's a great idea—for her, but also for him."

"I agree," Ben said. "Discovering her gifts—and the shock that there may still be some residual gifts left for her—was a pleasant surprise but also explained a lot, don't you agree?"

"I do," Jed said, squirming uncomfortably.

This wasn't a conversation he wanted to have. He was deeply haunted by the new knowledge that not only did Rachel have gifts when they'd been together as teenagers but she had been targeted by the Dark Ones back then as well—by Victor himself, it seemed. It changed everything and filled Jed with deep guilt that he'd not been there for her . . .

"God placed David there for her, Jed," Ben said.

Jed smiled and nodded. He knew Ben was right, but it still annoyed him when Ben read his mind without permission.

"I hate it when you do that," he said, half joking.

"I know," Ben said and laughed. "I hate it when I do that too." The director of Shepherds North America leaned forward on his elbows at his desk. This was it, maybe: back to work. "So, it sounds like you think the team is as good as ever."

"Better," Jed said without hesitation.

"How so?" Ben pressed.

"We're tighter," Jed said. "These last few missions, but

especially all that happened at St. George's, brought us together and made us a real team—a brotherhood. I've seen it many times when I was in the Teams—that tough, bloody mission that makes your bond something unbreakable. We have that now. And we have lessons learned, both tactically and spiritually, I believe. David has been key in fleshing that out in our weekly team meeting. I feel Joshua Bravo is better than ever—the best in the Shepherds, quite frankly."

"I agree," Ben said and leaned back again. "And that's why I want to take Joshua Bravo in a different direction."

Uh-oh . . . What the heck is this? If Ben wanted to make Joshua Bravo into some sort of training cell, he was making a terrible mistake. They were best in the field, the best at fighting the evil in the world . . .

"Not what I'm planning at all," Ben said.

Jed snorted.

"I hate it . . ."

". . . when I do that, yeah, I know." Ben rose and began pacing. "Jed, since we started, or at least since I've been here at the Shepherds, the teams have run pretty much on equal footing. We've always known when one team might be better suited for a particular op than another, of course, and we rely on the Holy Spirit and prayer on those rare occasions we move the order around. But other than that, the teams are pretty much interchangeable. Joshua Bravo, we've decided, is different."

"How so?" Jed asked.

"Well, partly because of you, Jed. You have gifts that are unusual for an operator, as we discussed."

"So do you," Jed said, not sure why the statement made him feel defensive.

"Yep," Ben agreed. "And when I ran a team, it gave us an edge, but one we never took advantage of institutionally. In addition, after all you've been through together, I agree that Joshua Bravo now has a special bond—something we try to replicate with training but can only come so far in achieving. And add to that the special role David plays in the team dynamic and the obviously very unique relationship he and Rachel have with the Watcher program through Sarah Beth—well, there's a lot of things now in play that make Joshua Bravo different."

"Okay," Jed said, not sure what else to say and not sure where this was headed. So much for his own gifts . . .

"You also have a very unique relationship and bond with Sarah Beth, Jed. That's played out to our advantage more than once now. So"—he took his seat again—"we've decided that Joshua Bravo is coming out of the rotation. You will instead be redesignated as the Special Missions Unit for the Shepherds North America."

Jed nodded, taking it in. In Special Operations, Special Missions Units were generally the Tier One units that fell under the auspices of Joint Special Operations Command. In terms of counterterrorism, they were the very best of the best—handpicked, specially trained, and given unprecedented autonomy and responsibility.

I like that sound of that . . .

"So, what does that mean?"

Ben smiled. "It means that in two weeks, we're going to start training hard to make Joshua Bravo the SMU for Shepherds and task you with both investigative and autonomous direct-action authority. We all know that the void left by Victor will be filled quickly, and we need to know what that threat will look like and be ready to respond. Victor was deadly, but we at least knew who he was. Now, we're starting over. We need a special team to gather intel on what the Dark Ones will be up to next, how they'll regroup—and be able to respond."

Jed watched his boss a moment as Ben's mind churned. "What is it you expect will happen next?" he asked. "I mean, with Victor gone . . ."

Ben sighed.

"The truth is, we just don't know what emerges next, Jed," he said. "Victor was at the helm of the Dark Ones for hundreds of years. And it was hardly a democracy, was it? He ruled with an iron fist, but he also compartmentalized to keep his operations fragmented as a defense against the Watchers. We know, from our Watchers intel, that the individual cells are in chaos. Without Victor, they have no direction, which gives us a breather, maybe. But it will be short. The void will be filled . . ."

"How does that work, exactly?" Jed asked, intrigued now.

Ben shrugged.

"I wish we knew," he said. "What we have is history—and ancient history at that. We know there is an inner circle of sorts, but we have very little on the who or where. This is where the Watchers are focusing their attention now. In the meantime, having an SMU in the field for more conventional intelligence gathering would be highly beneficial until we find threads to follow. You think Joshua Bravo is up for that mission?"

"Hell yeah," Jed said, pumping a fist enthusiastically. "I mean, I'll meet with them shortly in the team room and make sure we're all on the same page, but I believe the team is ready and willing. You said in two weeks, though. Why two weeks?"

"Two reasons," Ben said, smiling and sipping his coffee again. "First, we'll be meeting with some connections at JSOC over the coming week for advice on both structuring and training. And second, I want you and your team to take the next two weeks to get healthy . . ."

"We are healthy," Jed protested. "I just told you that. We're all cleared and ready to go."

Ben pursed his lips and nodded.

"Yes, I heard you. And I believe you. But this is a new direction, and I need you all to be one hundred percent. Yes, your team is recovered enough to begin a training cycle to get back on the horse. But I want you to be mentally and spiritually refreshed and ready to go before we launch this new direction."

"What does that mean?" Jed asked, but he felt he already knew.

"It means a *mandatory* two-week vacation. It means beaches or mountain cabins, reconnecting with family, doing something *fun*. You remember fun, don't you, Jed?"

"Yes, I remember fun," Jed shot back, aware his voice took on an irritated teenager quality that made him cringe. "But I don't need a vacation."

"Well, I disagree, and I'm the boss," Ben said, ending the conversation. "And your teammates need one for sure. Let them know today, and let's get them rested. This unit will be officially redesignated two weeks from Monday. Sara Beth gets out of school soon, and I'm going to encourage Rachel and David to take her on a real getaway vacation. Get your teammates to do the same—together, individually, I don't care. Grayson will want to take Barbara away somewhere just the two of them, I imagine. Eli will do his usual 'escape to the mountains alone' thing, maybe. Christy and I are going to take Jason and Elizabeth to the Beaches Resort in Turks and Caicos. We've been talking about it forever. Jason is finishing seventh grade and Elizabeth starts first grade next year, so we're finally doing it . . ."

"That sounds great, Ben," Jed said, and meant it. But he just wasn't a vacation guy. What was he supposed to do? He could head to Florida and visit his parents. That was long overdue, and they'd be at their condo in Bradenton for at least another few weeks before heading north—the life of the snowbird. Or maybe he really would go somewhere tropical. Maybe he could talk Eli or Johnny into a dive trip or something. Maybe they could get Nisha and Bex on board and go as a group . . .

"That's the spirit," Ben said. "Get with your team, give them the vacation marching orders, and then plan a trip. If I see you in the greater Nashville area, I'll have you arrested. If I see you on Trinity Loop over the next two weeks, I'll have you shot."

Jed laughed.

"All right, I got it, I got it."

He rose and reached out a hand to his boss, mentor, and friend.

"Thanks for the opportunity, Ben."

Ben shook his hand, and Jed felt the strength—and something else—in the man's grip.

"For the vacation opportunity?" Ben said with a chuckle.

"*Also* for the vacation opportunity." Jed laughed back.

Ben nodded.

"This is what I strongly believe that God is calling us to do with your team, Jed."

Jed nodded. "Understood."

Jed left and closed the door behind him, looking at his watch. He had a meeting in their team room in a few minutes, and he imagined everyone would be thrilled—both by the new assignment and by the vacation orders.

Jed shook his head and laughed at himself.

He hoped he was up to both.

CHAPTER THREE

OFFICE OF THE DIRECTOR
SHEPHERDS NORTH AMERICA
TRINITY LOOP COMPLEX
WEST OF NASHVILLE, TENNESSEE

Ben Morvant sat back in his chair, kicked his booted feet back up on his desk, and marveled at how easy it was to feel both content and pensive at the same time. His contentment, he knew, came from the powerful God-given belief that Jedidiah Johnson was proving to be all Ben had prayed he would be. Ben had no doubts whatsoever that God had led Jed to this place, at this time, to serve with the Shepherds in their ages-old battle against the dark forces intent on keeping Man far from God. Jed was a gifted operator, obviously, and a battle-blooded warrior, but it was his natural leadership, combined with his growing, simple faith, that made him perfect to lead Joshua Bravo into this new role.

And there were Jed's gifts—gifts that seemed to grow stronger each day, even as Ben worried his own might be fading.

Those gifts, and his relationship with both David and his daughter, Sarah Beth—arguably the most gifted Watcher they'd seen in generations—all pointed to success in this new mission for the team. Keeping God at the center of their growth would be absolutely critical, and David had grown rapidly into his role as tactical spiritual leader for the team—had in fact bonded with the unit like Ben had only ever seen his own personal TSL, Pastor Mike Moore, do previously.

So, after hours of prayer for guidance with Mike as well as with his leadership team and the head of St. George's, they all agreed that they felt the spirit leading them to the same decision: toward the formation of a Special Missions Unit, with Jed leading, David providing spiritual guidance, and Corbin Worth assigned as Watcher with Sarah Beth at her side, growing into her own role. He'd spent hours in prayer with David and Rachel Yarnell as well. They all felt that, with the proper safeguards in place, this was God's plan for their family. Rachel being brought on to the staff at St. George's as an adviser and liaison for the Shepherds—specifically the new SMU—made the decision that much easier for the Yarnells, and Ben truly believed that Rachel was called to that role by God. Rachel still had gifts of her own, it seemed, though the extent of them was unclear. That she had them at all at her age was highly unusual.

And God never gave gifts without purpose.

And, of course, Sarah Beth—being so powerfully gifted and at such a very young age—would benefit from having a parent close. He should have seen that sooner, perhaps.

So, there was much to be content about.

Ben glanced at the picture of his own family on his desk and smiled. Little Jason wasn't so little anymore—eighth grade next year. And soon Elizabeth would be in first grade. He stared at the smiling face of Christy, the woman who'd been at his side from the beginning—since his own gifts had come to the front of his life and had very nearly killed him before he'd grown in his faith and come to understand them and the responsibility that came with them. Without her, the love of his life, could he have made it through this, the last—good grief, was it almost fourteen years already?

So, why did he feel such pensive unease at the same time? He'd spoken with Mike about this strange sense of foreboding, something he'd learned more than once never to ignore. He'd prayed about it, he'd thought about it—and had no real answers. He knew what it *wasn't*, though. Whatever the discordant worry was, it wasn't concern about his family. It wasn't concern about Jed and his team or about the direction Ben intended to take that team or the Shepherds organization at large. He felt that calm, peaceful confidence he'd learned came from the Holy Spirit and meant he was on the right path. And he wasn't worried about himself. If the gifts faded, it only meant he no longer needed them—that there was someone coming to relieve him of that burden. The responsibility and calling that came with the gifts had been burdens he felt honored to shoulder, called to serve under, but they had taken a toll nonetheless. He knew, after all these years, that God led you where you needed to be and that the fulfillment of being on God's path was better than anything he could seek for himself. Whatever came next for him, and whoever filled the shoes he'd worn at the Shepherds—Jed perhaps, one day—Ben was content with God's plan for his life.

So, what was this feeling—this vague discontent that felt nothing like premonitions he'd had before, but instead just like he was ill at ease?

He had to admit that the slow fading of his gifts did make him feel more unsettled. Not that he had any concern over losing them, only confusion over what he *received* from them now. For years, he had trained himself to differentiate with ease between his own desires and discerning visions from God, thoughts from others placed in his head, premonitions about things to come or where to be, and of course, an almost prophetic sense of what Victor was up to.

Was the explanation for his dysthymia, or whatever he should call it, really that simple? Was it simply that, with Victor gone, the clear connection to the plans Victor had made to create barriers between Man and God was less obvious?

Maybe.

But little Sarah Beth was right. He'd heard and felt her conversation with her "uncle" Jed the night of the attack on St. George's.

It's never over, Uncle Jed. There will always be another Victor. The devil will always find another lost person to empower and fight in this war . . .

True words from a young girl with a close connection to God, the Holy Spirit, and her own faith. The Yarnell girl never ceased to amaze him. Finding out what the Dark Ones serving Satan had in store next was, indeed, crucial.

So, where were the threads he was used to sensing with his gifts, and then following to learn the truth? He sure didn't see or feel them. He felt only . . . chaos.

The chaos felt much like he remembered from the early years of this journey. When his gifts had first appeared after a SEAL Team mission fighting al-Qaeda terrorists in Africa, he'd been able to hear the thoughts of others. But he had no control over that gift then, which at the time felt more like a curse. He remembered being on a plane with Christy—on the way to their honeymoon, in fact—and the cacophony of voices in his head, the thoughts of others that he couldn't block or drown out, had been overwhelming and confusing. It had been a useless din of white noise, impossible to organize into useful information.

Just like those early days, *chaos* was the right word for what he sensed now. He felt and heard only a cacophony of chaos.

Ben sighed and looked at his watch. Mike would be in his office by now, his meeting with David Yarnell probably over. Mike would have some thoughts on all of this, he suspected. Mike Moore was nothing if not straightforward and pragmatic.

It occurred to him that he should consider checking in with Pastor Dee as well. If the Watchers were receiving information as usual, then this disquiet was just him and his fading gifts, nothing more. But if the Watchers were facing similar struggles, that might be a bigger problem. There was no doubt in his mind that the Dark Ones were out there, in the shadows, planning the rise of whoever the next Victor would be. And someone sure as hell better be able to get a read on who the players were, or they would find themselves in very real trouble.

He glanced at the family picture again before rising from his chair with a middle-aged grunt. After talking to Mike, he'd surprise Christy with a lunch out—off base, even. They deserved an impromptu lunch date. Soon enough the kids would be done with school and that would be harder to do. And they could talk about their own upcoming Caribbean vacation.

Maybe he just needed to enjoy the lull. After a decade and a half of war, he was feeling the toll. Lunch was, for a moment at least, peace.

There was plenty of time for war after.

CHAPTER FOUR

CALLE EL CONDE

ZONA COLONIAL

SANTO DOMINGO, DOMINICAN REPUBLIC

A FEW DAYS LATER

1731 HOURS LOCAL

Walking on the narrow sidewalk along the cobble street in Zona Colonial, Jed thought about how vacation means different things to different people—a chance to get away from it all, a break from the daily grind, the chance to experience a new place, with new people, new culture, and new flavors. For many, it was just a chance to relax and pamper themselves and recharge.

For Jed, a lifelong operator, the word *vacation* had always felt almost like a punishment, forcing him away from his brothers and the work he loved. Sure, in the Teams he'd earned plenty of leave, but he'd never used it for the military's generally intended purpose: to spend time with family or for rest and relaxation. Things like sightseeing, going to fancy restaurants, or wasting hours away in a spa at the Ritz-Carlton simply weren't his jam.

So, when Morvant *ordered* him to take a vacation, he honestly hadn't had a clue what to do with himself.

He wasn't sure why he'd chosen the Dominican Republic. It wasn't for the beaches. As a SEAL he'd practically spent a lifetime in the surf. It wasn't to escape the cold because Nashville was positively perfect this time of year, and Santo Domingo was hot and humid. And it wasn't for the food because he didn't know what kind of cuisine they were famous for here. So, why did he come? Maybe it was because Nisha and Bex had said they were going to the Caribbean, and in doing so he'd kind of copied them without meaning to.

He shook his head. Truth be told, he'd have rather gone with Nisha and Bex to the Bahamas, but they hadn't invited him. He was always better off with teammates—on or off duty—and if he was being forced to vacation, then diving in the Bahamas with teammates seemed like it might be tolerable. But it hadn't happened. Nisha and Bex had missed or ignored his hints. Eli, predictably, went off to a cabin he owned in the Blue Ridge Mountains—alone. Grayson was doing a late anniversary trip with his wife to Arizona—definitely not something he could tag along on—and Johnny and Hyeon were both headed to visit family. He knew David and Rachel were planning a getaway with Sarah Beth after her exams.

So that left Jed as the odd man out.

The Dominican Republic had just sort of popped into his head, and he went with it. *Maybe Sarah Beth put the idea in there,* he wondered. He thought about asking her via a quick Watcher snapchat, but she was probably busy with finals and end-of-the-year school stuff.

A small shop on his side of the street caught Jed's eye. He glanced over at the plate glass, where he saw the number *21* written in yellow paint across the top of the window. Moving closer, Jed could see that inside the display window was a row of beer bottles, each with a lit candle, glowing in front of a bowl of fruit behind which was a painting of what looked like a Catholic saint. To the left of this strange altar sat a ceramic monkey, and on the right side was what looked like a human skull, an unlit candle secured to the top with melted wax. Hanging upside down from above, just over the unlit candle, was a white dove—fake or real, Jed couldn't tell. As he stared, a small snake slithered out of the mouth of the skull.

What the heck is this?

Jed had no idea what the 21 on the window meant, but the display had a distinctly creepy voodoo vibe he remembered from being inside a shop in New Orleans—the makeshift altar, the skull, the discordant shout-out to a Catholic saint. His eyes were drawn inside, where a large man sat in a chair beside a bright-colored table, a book of some sort in his hands, with rows and rows of vials on a shelf behind him. The man shot him a big smile.

Jed nodded, then continued his way down the sidewalk. He decided to look it up later, but the shop looked very much like the voodoo shops that tourists frequented in the French Quarter. He didn't know if Voodoo existed here in the DR, though he knew it was prevalent in next-door Haiti.

His mind went home for a minute and to the kids at St. George's. It was going to be a strange summer for the Watchers and the rest of the St. George's student body and staff, he reflected. The Dark Ones' attack on the school had shattered everyone's paradigm of safety. Until that night, St. George's had been a spiritual and physical refuge for everyone who called the campus home—a safe space where Victor and the Dark Ones couldn't intrude. But Victor had shattered that illusion, and even now, after the Dark Ones' defeat, a great many things were being reconsidered by the Shepherds and the St. George's security—as well as many parents, he imagined. And yet, despite all the feelings of uncertainty and vulnerability, there was great, collective hope. Victor was gone. Forever. He'd been defeated by a coalition of Shepherds and Watchers working together in a final battle in which they'd pooled their courage, their faith, and their gifts to slay a legion of demons and the Dark Ones' most recent commanding general on Earth. That had earned them all an excuse to relax.

Hadn't it?

A raindrop plinked him on the head.

Jed looked up at a blue sky being quickly gobbled up by rain clouds—rain clouds which were growing so fast that they looked like a storm in a movie being played on fast-forward. During the flight down, he'd chatted with a young Gen Z couple who told him that the Dominican Republic had a rainy season and a dry season, and the former season ran from May until September. They told him to expect pop-up afternoon showers pretty much every day except for along the eastern tip of the island. When he asked them if they were visiting on their honeymoon, they'd laughed. When he'd asked what was so funny, they'd informed him that after getting married three years ago, they'd never stopped honeymooning.

"After the wedding, we went to Bali and had so much fun we decided that traveling is what we want to do together for the rest of our lives. Vacationing is our job now," the woman, Harriet, had said.

"Your job?" he'd asked with a cocked eyebrow.

"Yeah, we have a YouTube travel channel with 2.1 million followers. *The Ozzie and Harriet Roadshow* . . . get it? We travel, film all our adventures, and live off the ad revenue. Plus, Derrick kept his side hustle as a freelance IT consultant, but he can do that job from anywhere so long as we have an internet connection."

"I thought you said his name was Ozzie?" Jed had said.

"That's just his nickname for the channel. But if you give me your number, I'll send you a link so you can like and subscribe."

"Thanks, but I don't give out my mobile number," he'd said.

Strange world we live in, he thought, reflecting on the dichotomy between what they did for a living and what he did.

A second raindrop hit him, this time on the bridge of his nose, and he surveyed the street for shelter from the expected deluge. A nearby café with outdoor seating and giant table umbrellas caught his eye, and his stomach grumbled almost as loud as the thunder. The blue awning had the words *El Conde* written in white, and minutes later Jed was seated outside El Conde under an umbrella, listening to the soothing drumbeats of the rain. He leaned back in his chair and took in the lovely view of the tree-lined square with a statue in the center.

After only a moment, he realized he was bored. He just wasn't the sightseeing type. He glanced at his watch and sighed, then forced himself to learn something about his surroundings by checking the map app on his phone.

The square was called Parque Colón, or Columbus Park. The bronze statue, which had long ago gone green, was of Christopher Columbus, his outstretched arm presently serving as a perch for pigeons, even in the pouring rain. Jed had learned from "Ozzie and Harriet" that Santo Domingo was the oldest European city in the Americas, founded just six years after Columbus landed on the island. Jed stared across the park at what his map told him was the Cathedral of Santa María la Menor. He decided this would be his first tourist stop of the trip once his stomach was full and the rain let up.

Santo Domingo, the island nation's capital, was also a much larger city than he'd expected. After seeing the sprawl from the air on the flight in, he'd been surprised to learn that the city and metro area were home to three and a half million people—triple the size of Nashville.

Nisha had told him that to get to know somewhere and really *feel* the soul of a place, you had to go to its beating heart. That was a bit flowery, but he got the gist and had booked a Vrbo in the Zona Colonial neighborhood near the city center. Here most of the buildings were two stories tall, constructed from stone, and had white stucco facades, and power lines zigzagged haphazardly overhead, strung from building to building as if the electricians had just tapped into the lines wherever was most convenient. But the small bed at his rental barely held his gigantic operator body, and Jed figured he wouldn't get much sleep tonight. He'd go see the church, but what the hell was he going to do for the rest of the weeklong vacation?

The server brought him a menu and rattled off something in Spanish. Jed had a limited working vocabulary in the language, but he'd never heard anyone speak Spanish with the rapid-fire speed that they did in Santo Domingo.

"I'm sorry," he said with a smile. "Do you speak English?"

"Yes, yes," the man said and smiled back. "Would you like something to drink? We have many fruit drinks to choose from, but also iced tea, iced coffee, Coca-Cola . . ."

"I'll try a fruit drink," Jed said.

"What type of fruit?" the man asked. "Papaya, melon, pineapple, mango, banana–passion fruit, lemon . . ."

"Whatever you think is good," Jed said awkwardly, realizing he was out of his league just ordering lunch. He quickly scanned the menu for the word *burger* as he did. *Bingo . . . there it is. The Conde Hamburger. Quarter-pound beef, cheese, bacon, caramelized onions, lettuce, and tomato with french fries.*

"And I'll have two of these," he said. Ordering lunch in a

new place was usually an easy decision for Jed, who was on a lifelong quest to find the perfect hamburger.

"It's big," the man said.

"So is my appetite," Jed said with a grin.

The waiter looked up and down Jed's thick and muscular six-foot-four frame, nodded, and went to put in the order.

Across the street, a trio of men appeared with instruments and began playing a lively but nerve-grating tune he didn't recognize. The musicians—a generous title—played an accordion, a tambourine-type thing, and a drum. A quick glance at the diners at the other tables confirmed that Jed was not alone in his irritation at having an otherwise pleasant afternoon soured. *Hopefully, they'll get tired and move along to another corner . . .* The server delivered his fruit drink, and Jed sipped on it and people watched, trying to savor the experience of being in Santo Domingo—to find its heart and soul, like Nisha suggested.

"*Dos hamburguesas con queso para el señor,*" the server said with a smile as he placed two burger-and-fry platters in front of Jed.

"*Muchas gracias,*" Jed said, and his stomach growled in accord.

Jed wasted not another second before digging in. It rained while he ate, but the giant umbrella kept him mostly dry, and the drumbeat of rain on canvas was far more relaxing than the noisy musicians, who abandoned their efforts as the rain increased. He also noticed a woman holding a sign, seemingly making the rounds of Parque Colón. She looked desperate. She was no street peddler, that was for sure, and something about her appearance—hair plastered to her face, holding up her message to passing cars now that the pedestrians had thinned—tugged at his heartstrings.

Turning back to his burger, Jed reflected that some people probably felt self-conscious or lonely eating out by themselves. Not him. In fact, he wondered now if he might actually prefer it. Making conversation, especially with women, wasn't his strong suit. Banter, he could do. Meaningful conversation, not so much. Ever since he lost Rachel as a young adult—or ran away from Rachel, if he was going to be completely honest about it—he'd struggled to talk to women. With Maria Perez, he'd been proud of himself for relaxing and talking more easily, but now he knew that those conversations didn't count. He'd been her mark. She'd been trying to seduce him, which meant he could have talked about the pros and cons of using chicken manure versus horse dung and she would have feigned interest.

He shooed the thought away.

You're on vacation, dude. Just live in the moment.

In a blink, the two thick burgers were gone, his belly was full, and he glanced at his watch. There were a lot of hours left to kill before searching for a juicy steak and crawling into the too-small bed at his Vrbo.

Jed left enough cash to cover the bill and a generous tip, pushed back his chair, and headed into Parque Colón. He walked south, through the park's middle. Instead of grass, the entire plaza was bricked over—red bricks laid in a herringbone pattern, glistening wet from the rain as rays of sun now struggled from behind the thinning clouds. He gave the statue of Columbus a look as he walked by, scanned the row of street vendors set up under the trees, and glanced ahead at the single cross-bearing spire of the Cathedral of Santa María la Menor as it reached heavenward toward the blue sky he could now see behind the parting clouds.

Jed knew nothing about architecture, so to him the stone church just looked old—historic, maybe. It cost him the equivalent of a dollar fifty US to enter, and he took his time exploring the inside, which was much more ornate and interesting than the exterior. He silently congratulated himself on doing something touristy. If only Ozzie and Harriet could see him now, strolling through the sights, hands clasped behind his back, taking it all in. Bone-white stone columns lined the nave and supported a truly magnificent vaulted ceiling with rib-shaped arches that intersected to form a series of curved triangles. *Gothic design*—the phrase popped into his head from somewhere.

He walked up the side of the nave to check out the main altar, which was roped off, and had a momentary flashback of the church in Nashville where he and his team had prevented an attack by the Dark Ones. In some ways it felt like it was yesterday, and in others a lifetime ago. He couldn't resist the urge to scan the small crowd for threats, then forced himself to instead study the paintings and statues depicting Christ, the Virgin Mother, and the disciples at various key moments in their lives.

Soon he'd seen enough. He made a cash donation in a collection box and left the way he'd come in, via the north entrance. When he stepped outside into Parque Colón, he noticed again the Dominican woman with the sign, now pacing back and forth, showing a picture to passersby. Fresh tears ran down her caramel-colored cheeks, and her wavy chestnut hair hung loose and unkempt about her shoulders.

Their eyes met, and perhaps seeing a kindness in his eyes, she headed his way, approaching cautiously but deliberately.

"*Señor, por favor*," she said when she got close to him. Jed towered over her by more than a foot, but she did not seem intimidated by his size like so many people.

"I'm sorry . . . *no habla Español*," he said, meeting her tear-rimmed eyes.

"Sir, look at this," she said, switching to accented English and holding up her sign—which, he now saw, contained a grainy blown-up photograph of a young girl. "This is my daughter, Emelin. She is nine years old, and she is missing. Have you seen her?"

Jed stared at the picture and committed the face to memory. Then, he tried to recall if he'd seen this girl on his morning walk through the streets of the old town.

"I'm sorry, but I've not seen her. How long has she been missing?"

"*Tres días,*" the woman said. "She is so little and must be so frightened. She does not know this city . . ."

"Don't you live here, in Santo Domingo?" he asked, confused.

"No," she said, shaking her head. "But my heart told me to come to this place, on this day. Maybe I am supposed to meet someone who has seen my Emelin. Maybe I am supposed to meet someone who can help. I don't know why, but I believe God works in mysterious ways."

Now, as sometimes happened for Jed, her unspoken thoughts came to him like a soft breath.

"You're from Azua?"

"*Sí*, yes, how did you know this?" she asked, her expression surprised and hopeful.

"It's a gift I have," he said, "but it only works sometimes and with certain people."

"Can you use your gift to find my daughter?"

"I'm sorry, but it doesn't work that way," he said, feeling the weight of her disappointment.

Locating, he knew, was a Watcher gift. Even on his best day, he doubted he could even sense this woman's daughter. For that to happen, Emelin would have to reach out to him and give him a signal to follow, like Sarah Beth had when she was taken—a *thread*, the Watchers called it. But he'd never met this woman's daughter, and the girl would need to have Watcher gifting herself in order to reach out.

"Try, *señor*. Try, *por favor*," she said. The woman began to reach out to touch his arm but stopped herself. She'd taken in his confession of his gift with remarkably little surprise.

Jed's heart ached for this poor mother, but his gifts were still an enigma to him. In the presence of powerful Watchers, like Corbin or Sarah Beth, he could sort of piggyback off their abilities and get dragged along for the ride. In the kill house training evolution, he'd followed Ben's thread, but that was only because Ben had found him first and was actively infiltrating his thoughts.

It made Jed sick to rebuff her, but the reality was what it was.

"I'm sorry," he said. "I really am. I wish I could help, but there's nothing I can do."

"Then take this," the woman said. She handed him a pamphlet-sized version of her sign. "I have no *teléfono*, but the number on the paper is for the priest of my church. His name is Padre Lopez. If you see Emelin or find any information, I beg you to call him."

Jed nodded and took the paper. "I will. You have my word. And I will keep an eye out for her, I promise you."

"*Muchas gracias, señor.* She must be so frightened. She has had nightmares that someone wants to make her into a zombie. It is crazy, but it made her so scared. Maybe now these nightmares are coming true."

"If I can think of any way to help, I'll find you," he said.

"*Dios lo bendiga,*" she said and bowed her head to him.

"God bless you too." He took a picture of the pamphlet she'd given him with his phone before stuffing it in his pocket.

With the weight of this woman's stare on his back and a nagging guilt in his heart, Jed set off to try to enjoy the rest of his day in Santo Domingo. But the truth was, the idea of helping this poor woman find her missing daughter seemed far more appealing than wandering the streets until his next meal. Not much of a vacation maybe, but the task seemed to Jed far more relaxing. He was built to be on mission. Or maybe it was just the SEAL in him, always ready to protect those who couldn't protect themselves.

Either way, little Emelin's face was burned now into his mind, and he knew he wasn't going to find it easy to let her go.

CHAPTER FIVE

CALLE EL CONDE

ZONA COLONIAL

SANTO DOMINGO, DOMINICAN REPUBLIC

1912 HOURS LOCAL

Jed stood at the railing of the rooftop terrace, looking out over the old town toward the Cathedral of Santa María la Menor. The owner of his Vrbo rental had decked the small place out with an outdoor furniture set and a firepit, as well as a fully stocked mini fridge on the terrace, which was the highlight of the property. If he'd traveled here with Eli and Grayson, or even Bex and Nisha, he imagined this would be where they'd spend every evening, taking in the sounds of the city to the north and the view of the ocean to the south.

But instead of enjoying a cold beer while reclined on the outdoor sofa, he'd spent his time pacing. He'd tried desperately to put the woman from Parque Colón and her missing daughter out of his mind and enjoy the rest of his day, but it had been impossible. Like a paper cut you can barely see but which makes itself known with every movement, the image of the missing girl had nagged him wherever he went. Now, unable to take it anymore, he pulled his mobile phone from his pocket to call Ben.

But instead of calling the Shepherds' commander, his disobedient fingers dialed David Yarnell.

Why am I calling David of all people?

As the phone rang, Jed considered hanging up until David answered a split second before Jed could press the red icon.

"Hey, Jed," David said. "What's up? Aren't you supposed to be on vacation?"

"I am. I'm calling from Santo Domingo."

"Is everything all right?" David asked, his tone shifting from upbeat to concerned.

"Yeah, everything's fine. It's just . . . something happened today, and I needed somebody to talk to about it."

"Sure, I'm all ears."

"I was touring the Cathedral of Santa María la Menor in Old Town, and I was approached by a woman in the square outside. She was holding a sign with a picture of her missing daughter, Emelin. She's nine . . ."

"Okay, go on," David said.

"She said Emelin's been missing for three days, and she asked for my help to find her," Jed said. It was sort of true.

"That's horrible," David said. "Obviously, I can relate and empathize with this poor woman personally." After a beat, he added, "Do you think she's telling the truth?"

Jed had wondered that, of course. There were a million scams in a country like this, preying on tourists and other foreigners. But the woman hadn't asked for any money or anything else other than that he keep an eye out for her daughter.

"I do," Jed said simply.

David knew of Jed's gift for reading people and would

probably chalk his assurance up to that. But Jed *wasn't* sure. Could it be he just wanted her to be telling the truth so he could be back to work?

"Okay. In that case, what else did she say? Why does she think an American tourist can help?"

"I think she's just desperately looking for anyone who might have seen her little girl," Jed said. "But she's not even from Santo Domingo. She lives in a different town, Azua, but she said that God told her to come to the Cathedral of Santa María la Menor today. It seems possible we crossed paths for a purpose, David."

"Interesting," David said. "And do you believe that?"

"I don't know. I've been debating all day whether I should try to help her."

The truth was that Jed had never once been able to walk away from someone in need. That had led him to want to be a youth pastor as a kid, and later—after everything that happened his senior year—to want to be a SEAL. He should hardly be surprised at his inability to ignore this woman in need now.

A long silence hung on the line, and Jed thought the call might have dropped, but then David spoke.

"Jed, I don't want to sound callous here, especially considering that Rachel and I basically *were* that woman barely a year ago, begging you to help find our missing daughter . . ." David paused. "But you're an American tourist on vacation in a foreign country. And not just a foreign country, but a third-world island nation that shares a border with Haiti. Poverty, crime, suffering—you're going to find them everywhere you look. I reckon there's somebody who could use your help on every street corner in Santo Domingo, but you didn't travel to the DR for mission work. You traveled there for vacation, and not just any vacation. You're taking time off because physically, spiritually, emotionally, and psychologically, you not only deserve it but desperately *need* it. What happened at St. George's that night was powerful and traumatic and soul-wrenching. You saved our kids, but you almost died in the process, Jed. It's okay to rest. It's okay to recuperate. Even Jesus found time to be alone, away from the crowds who needed him, and recharge. It's throughout the Gospels, in fact. You don't have to bear all the world's burdens all the time. That's God's job, not yours."

"I hear you, David, I really do," Jed replied. "But how often did Jesus walk away from a crisis?"

"Jed, I believe that God, the architect of the universe, is an efficiency expert and not prone to wasting eternity trying to fit square pegs into round holes. You have your gifts for a reason, and God will call you to use them when it's *His* time."

"Yeah," Jed agreed. He let out a long sigh.

"Look, Jed, I don't want to dismiss anything out of hand. We've seen some crazy things this past year, and we both know God has His own way of getting our attention when He needs to. What if we both take the evening to think and pray on it, then touch base tomorrow after a good night's sleep? How does that sound?"

"That sounds like a plan. Thanks, David."

"No problem," David said. "Oh, and Jed?"

"Yeah?"

"Thanks for reaching out to me specifically. It means a lot that you thought to call me about this."

"Yeah, man. I knew you'd get where I was coming from on this better than anyone else. And you are the Joshua Bravo TSL, after all."

"I am," David agreed, and Jed could hear the satisfied grin on the man's face even from all the miles away.

"Talk to you tomorrow, David."

"Sounds good, Jed. Talk tomorrow."

Jed ended the call and wasn't sure if he felt better or not.

See, this is why I hate vacation, he thought to himself. *At least when I'm working, there's always a plan. Always a chain of command—and no damn guilt involved.*

But as he walked to the mini fridge to grab himself a cold beer, Jed realized that he did feel better. Talking seemed to have lightened the anxiety and guilt he was feeling about walking away from the woman. David hadn't shared anything Jed didn't already know, but hearing it from someone else still helped. With a deep cleansing breath, he forced himself to recline on the outdoor sofa. After kicking his heels up on the edge of the unlit firepit, he cracked open his beer.

With nobody to raise a glass to in person, he lifted his beer toward the heavens.

"I just need to chill, right? You've got a plan, and all I have to do is let it happen . . ."

CHAPTER SIX

THE WHITE ROOM

ST. GEORGE'S ACADEMY

OUTSIDE OF NASHVILLE, TENNESSEE

0820 HOURS LOCAL

Sarah Beth felt guilty about using the White Room as her own private study hall. She really did. Just not enough to stop. Technically, there was no official policy that said she couldn't study here. Students with access privileges to the White Room were free to come and go and use the sanctuary as they pleased. No teacher or Keeper had told her she couldn't study for final exams in here, and a couple of other kids were doing it too.

But it *was* kinda, sorta unfair.

Pastor Dee's words echoed in her mind from the first time she stepped foot in the Watcher Sanctuary ten weeks ago:

The Sanctuary is not a break room or common space, Sarah Beth. This is a special place intended for intense meditation, prayer, and learning. Only a select group of students, like Corbin and yourself, are given access privileges.

She supposed that studying *was* learning, but she knew in her heart that she was testing boundaries. The White Room was arguably the most beautiful, well-appointed space on campus, and it was definitely the most spiritual. To use it as a study hall might be an abuse of her privilege. While the rest of the kids tried to carve out a quiet spot in the common spaces, library, or their dorm rooms, she was able to disappear into a quiet sanctuary where it was impossible to be interrupted. Did this give her an unfair advantage over the other students?

Definitely.

If only she could stop wasting all her time agonizing over it.

And there's the irony of the situation. If I'd just gone to the library, I'd probably have gotten more done!

That thought made her chuckle . . .

She knew what her dad would say about it.

In life, Sarah Beth, advantage is fleeting. Time, probability, and people's natural desire for fairness have an uncanny knack for leveling the playing field.

She'd always thought her dad was a pretty smart guy, but it wasn't until she started boarding school and living away from home that she appreciated just how smart he was. The thing about Dad was that he hid it really well under a layer of easygoing kindness and compassion. Since she'd been at St. George's, she'd realized that lots of people make the mistake of thinking that when someone is nonconfrontational it must mean they're weak, dumb, insecure, or some combination of those things. That's what people thought about her dad.

Everyone underestimated him.

Even Mom and Uncle Jed.

Supposedly, her dad had been a hotheaded wild man in high school, but she'd always had trouble believing that. Because the dad she knew seemed always so cerebral and collected. She could count on one hand the number of times she'd seen him lose his temper. He'd never been the type of dad that bossed her around and told her what to do. Instead, he'd always given her information and choices, then guidance and encouragement to make decisions for herself.

Sometimes that meant letting her fail.

When she was forced to face Victor, the entire time she had been praying for Uncle Jed to come and save her. But now, in the aftermath, she'd come to realize something very important about herself and her dad. If not for her dad, if not for all the years he'd encouraged her to think for herself, to take chances, and to make decisions, she would never have had the confidence to rally the other Watcher kids and face Victor without the grown-ups.

Without the Shepherds.

Without Uncle Jed.

She'd thanked her mom and Uncle Jed multiple times for coming to her rescue that night. But in many ways, it was her dad's decade of training and leadership that had really saved the day. Without all she had learned about herself from him, it would have been over before Mom or Jed arrived.

A guilty knot formed in her stomach as she wondered how her dad felt about everything that had happened.

Probably terrible . . .

The sofa cushion next to her let out an impressive fart sound as Corbin plopped down beside her.

"Hey, sis," Corbin said with a smile. "That wasn't me, by the way."

They both giggled.

"I know," Sarah Beth said. "How are finals going?"

"Not sure. Math was awful. I felt like I flunked it, but I always feel like that on math tests. On the flip side, I feel pretty good about AP English. Those are the only two I've taken. How about you?"

"I've only taken Theology so far, and it was okay. I'm worried about Spanish. It's not really gelling in my head, you know?"

Corbin nodded. "Language is one of those subjects that you either get, or it's, like, so painful. I suck at foreign language."

Sarah Beth nodded and looked with frustration at the Spanish notebook in her lap.

"Spill it," Corbin said. "I can tell there's something on your mind."

Sarah Beth hesitated at first but decided to come clean. "I'm feeling guilty about studying here when everyone else can't. Are we even allowed to study in here?"

Corbin bobbed her head from side to side. "It's a gray area. Nobody is going to kick you out, but . . ."

"What do you think? Do you study in here?"

"Sometimes yes, sometimes no. I guess the way I look at it is—I've put my life on the line, more than once, with the Shepherds," Corbin said and tapped the spot on her chest where the metal spear had run her through. "I kind of feel like I've earned the right to use this place whenever I want. That's how privilege is supposed to work, in my opinion. The adults have left it up to us, so you need to decide for yourself. Are you using this place as it was intended or taking advantage? You have to do what's right for your conscience."

Sarah Beth nodded. It was the exact guidance her dad would have given.

"But I have a feeling you're not camping out here just to

study," Corbin said, flashing her a squinty face. "Pretty much every time I've come up, you've been here."

"And your point?" Sarah Beth asked with a flair of defensiveness.

"I'm just asking, as a friend, if you're okay. Maybe you're spending all your time here because it makes you feel safe?"

"No. Well, maybe."

"Dude, we both almost died. We fought freakin' Victor, and it was horrifying. So, I'm not throwing shade, promise. Just asking if you need to talk," Corbin said. She reached out to squeeze Sarah Beth's hand.

"It's weird," Sarah Beth said, holding her friend's hand. "I thought I would have lots of nightmares about Victor and everything that happened that night, but I haven't."

"That's a good thing, Sarah Beth."

"Yeah, but I'm still afraid. And I'm having a different kind of nightmare now."

"Do you want to talk about it?"

"It's hard to explain. It's not like my normal dreams. They usually make some kind of sense."

Corbin chuckled at this. "Well, for me at least, most dreams don't make sense."

"Right, but what I mean is that this dream isn't like a movie—I'm not in it as me or a character or anything. And it's not like a vision either. It's hard to explain . . ."

"You don't have to if you don't want to."

"I do, it's just," she said, getting frustrated with her tongue-tiedness. "It's like I'm in this big room, but I'm there as air, not as me. I'm everywhere, but I'm nowhere. And there's all these faceless people. They have faces, but when I try to look at them, they go completely blurry. And they're so angry and hungry, and they want control."

"What do they want control of? Control of you?"

"No, no," Sarah Beth said, shaking her head. "Control of each other, I think."

"Yeah, that sounds weird. But I think everyone's dreams are different. And I think after . . . everything . . . we should expect a few weird dreams."

"Maybe," Sarah Beth said with a shrug. But just talking about the dream brought back some of her anxiety. "The worst part about it is even when I wake up, the feeling doesn't go away. It's terrible. No matter what I do or where I go, I can feel it, like, clawing in my mind. The only place I don't feel that is in the White Room. That's the real reason I'm spending all my time here. I even snuck in after lights-out and slept on this sofa last night so I could get a good night's sleep."

"That sucks, Sarah Beth," Corbin said. Her face—and the way her fingers again went to the healing wound on her chest—suggested that maybe she suffered her own private nightmares from that night as well. "Look, I think that if being in the Sanctuary lets you study and get away from whatever dark thing you've tapped into lately, then you don't need to feel guilty about that, okay?"

Sarah Beth nodded.

"Have you talked to Pastor Dee about any of this?"

"No."

"What about your parents?" Corbin asked.

"Definitely no."

"Okay, well, maybe you should think about it. Your parents are awesome—and your mom was a total badass." Corbin blushed at the word. "Sorry. But for sure you should consider telling Pastor Dee."

"What if she tells me I can't hang out in here?"

Corbin smiled. "I don't think you have to worry about that."

"All right, I'll talk to her, but not until after my Spanish final," she said. "That would stress me out even more."

"Yeah, I get it." Corbin smiled. She gave Sarah Beth's hand a parting squeeze and got up from the sofa. "Talk later."

"Later," Sarah Beth said. Feeling a thousand pounds lighter, she opened her Spanish notebook and, with a clear head, got to studying.

CHAPTER SEVEN

SANTO DOMINGO, DOMINICAN REPUBLIC

0819 HOURS LOCAL

Jed slept in late—which was something he never did—and woke with a clearer head and lighter conscience than he'd gone to bed with. David's advice had been, surprisingly, exactly what he'd needed. Jed's job with the Shepherds was to save the world. But that did not mean saving the world single-handedly, one person at a time. As a SEAL he knew full well the importance of a team. No one SEAL kicked in a door and rescued an HVT Rambo-style in real life. It took a team, both in the field and in the TOC, to do that. He would keep an eye out for the girl, whose face he'd burned into his memory from the woman's sign and pamphlet, but there was little else he could do on his own.

After dressing, he grabbed a bottled water from the kitchen and ate one of the fifteen remaining protein bars he'd brought from home. At his size and level of fitness, a single protein bar barely put a dent in the amount of daily protein he needed, but that's what two-burger lunches were for. At home, he'd boost with daily protein powder shakes, but no way he was messing with shakes on vacation.

Feeling like a run would do him good, he laced on his Nikes, slipped his mobile phone into a fitness armband, and headed out the door. Old Town Santo Domingo was definitely not ideal for training, but if he stuck to the waterfront, he could run the three-mile stretch of sidewalk between the beach and George Washington Avenue and enjoy the shade and sea breeze.

Minutes later, his feet pounded the pavement into submission and his muscles urged him to push harder. He wasn't built for speed, to be sure, and he'd been trying to listen to his body during the healing and recovery period after the battle with Victor. But today he felt good. After a long warm-up, the miles clicked off almost effortlessly and his pace increased with each.

It felt great.

It felt magnificent.

And as he slowed to a walk and knitted his fingers behind his head to catch his breath, he grinned to himself. At this very moment, Colonel Jericho was barking orders and insults at the latest class of Shepherds candidates pounding the pavement in Jericho Basic back at Trinity Loop. *Well, Colonel, you might have your nuggets to torment, but I've got the beach,* he thought with great satisfaction. He chuckled, imagining that some might think starting the day with a five-mile run wasn't much of a vacation, but it was just what he needed. Still, he forced himself to take a breath and enjoy the view of the tree-lined beach for a moment.

Besides, it's late morning. I slept in. Maybe I do *know how to vacation after all . . .*

To his right, a little peninsula jutted out into the surf, and he heard the unmistakable commotion of kids having fun. He pulled his phone from his armband and checked Google Maps: Plaza Juan Barón—a seafront park with fairground rides, go-carts, a Ferris wheel, and open-air karaoke. He chuckled and decided "open-air karaoke" was something he had to see for himself. As he got closer, a distinctive aroma that can only be created by a mélange of street food vendors flooded his nostrils: fried dough, grilled meat, and caramelized sugar—the culinary trifecta of carnivals and outdoor fairs the world over.

Mopping the sweat from his brow, Jed meandered through the fairground. Most everyone was smiling, especially the parents watching their little ones squeal with delight—and sometimes fear—on various mechanical contraptions designed to spin, sling, or rapidly raise and lower human cargo. At six feet, four inches tall and 225 pounds, his kiddie carnival ride–hopping days were long over, but that didn't mean he couldn't remember the joy of it. His thoughts drifted back to this one time in high school when—

"¡Sebastian! ¡Sebastian! *¿Dónde estás?*"

A woman screaming interrupted Jed's nostalgic rumination. He turned to find a young Dominican woman, no older than twenty-five, frantically searching for what Jed assumed was her son. The look in her eyes—equal parts panic and dread—was the same look he'd seen yesterday with the woman in Parque Colón. Despite this woman's desperation, almost everyone was ignoring her.

"I'll help you find him," Jed said, approaching her. "What does he look like?"

"*Él es* . . . I mean, he is this tall," the woman said, holding her palm at the height of what Jed would guess was a kindergarten-aged child. "His hair is brown, and his name is Sebastian."

"Where did you last see him?" Jed asked.

"I was buying ice cream. He was there, beside me. Right beside. I don't know where he could go," she said.

"Okay, he probably saw the Ferris wheel or one of the rides

and ran to it. Kids go where other kids are having fun," Jed said. "Why don't you check the rides, and I'll check the food stalls again and make sure he's not wandering toward the busy street."

"*Sí, sí,* let's do this."

"What is your name?"

"Paloma," she said.

"Okay, Paloma. I'm Jed," he said. "Don't worry, we'll find him."

The woman nodded and then set off toward the carnival rides, calling her son's name, while Jed headed the opposite direction. Because he towered over everyone, Jed had good visibility, but the fairground was extremely crowded, and kids were everywhere. He moved with methodical precision through the area where the street food vendors had their carts and tents set up. "Sebastian?" he shouted, head on a swivel as he moved through the crowd. "Sebastian . . ."

But when he reached the far end of the food area, a cold, foreboding dread seemed to worm its way into his brain.

"*The boy's gone,*" a voice said in his head. "*Walk away.*"

"*Big mistake,*" he fired back at his unseen adversary as an adrenaline spike supercharged his body. He knew the voice of a Dark One.

Vacation's over, he thought to himself. *Back on mission . . .*

Jed felt his senses sharpening, his awareness of his surroundings focusing. Instead of scanning for a little brown-haired boy in a sea of little brown-haired kids, he shifted his scan for adults moving away from him with purpose. Nothing suspicious caught his eye immediately, but he started moving north anyway, out of the fairgrounds toward the major thoroughfare of George Washington Avenue.

"*Close your eyes, I will help you,*" a new voice, young and unfamiliar, said in his head.

Closing one's eyes while pursuing a Dark One was ill-advised, but Jed's gut told him to go with it. The instant he did, he was looking through Sebastian's eyes, though how he knew this he couldn't explain. The boy was being dragged across the street toward a tree-lined sidewalk. Sebastian, if it was really Sebastian who had reached out, must be a Watcher. But how was that possible?

"*C'mon, give me something more, kid,*" Jed begged in his mind.

The view shifted as Sebastian looked left at a white obelisk painted in murals . . .

That's Obelisco de Santo Domingo, Jed realized, eyes popping open. *Gotcha!*

Jed took off in a full sprint, vectoring west. He shot the gap between the go-carts and a hamburger stand before angling right to cross the street that separated Plaza Juan Barón from another park. Brakes squealed and car horns blared as he juked and weaved his way across four lanes of traffic. A voice in his head—this time his own experience and instinct from years of combat—told him to leap up and twist right, and he rolled across the hood of a black sedan that would have run him over otherwise.

He was on mission—his senses tuned, the world crystal clear—only it was the Holy Spirit and a strange child's voice in his head, instead of a teammate in an earpiece.

Impossibly, he made it across the heavy traffic unscathed, then scanned left and right. He acquired his target in the near distance: a medium-height, medium-build man with long black hair was moving through the crowd, untucked shirt perhaps concealing a firearm in the waistband of his jeans as he dragged a small boy by the wrist. Jed wasn't carrying or kitted up, but he knew he would be able to dominate the engagement without too much difficulty—unless there was a gun that leveled the playing field.

As if sensing Jed's presence, the kidnapper looked back over his shoulder and locked eyes with the Shepherd. Without missing a beat, the kidnapper scooped the boy into his arms and kicked into a sprint.

Jed cursed in his mind and took off in pursuit.

Muscles still warm and limber from his run, Jed pushed himself to the limit. Arms pumping and legs churning like a locomotive, he ran the kidnapper down over the next hundred yards as the man tried to escape to the north. Jed caught up along a massive reflecting pond with a tiered stone fountain at the far end, lengthening his stride as he arrived in striking distance. He grimaced at the thought of tackling the man carrying the boy, risking serious injury to the kid. Instead, he grabbed the kidnapper by the back of his shirt and jerked the man backward and down so that he landed on his back with Sebastian on top of him. The impact knocked the wind out of the man, stunning him and allowing Jed to easily wrestle the child from the kidnapper's arms.

"Your mother, Paloma, sent me to help you," he said to the boy.

"I know this," Sebastian said in Spanish aloud, but in English in Jed's mind.

"Sebastian!" called a woman's voice. Jed turned to see Paloma running toward them in the park.

"Go! Run to your mom," he said. "I'll take care of this man."

"*Gracias, señor*," the boy said, a knowing sparkle in his eyes. "*Dios lo bendiga, señor.*"

God bless you, sir, he heard in his head.

Then the boy darted away toward his mother while Jed turned his attention back to the would-be kidnapper, who still gasped for air on the ground. Not willing to take any chances, Jed hammered a fist into the man's nose, breaking it instantly and taking the thug out of the fight. He prepared to roll the man over, pinning him to the ground until the police arrived.

That's when the fight shifted suddenly, and without warning, against him.

Jed grunted in pain as something crashed into his side, blindsiding him with the force of a linebacker. The impact knocked him off-balance into the fountain, where a foot of water cushioned what would otherwise have been a brutal landing on stone. Disoriented and drenched, he got to his feet and spun to face his assaulter.

His eyebrows raised in surprise when he saw who his attacker was—a thin and attractive woman, crouched like a tiger ready to pounce, on the granite curb that ringed the reflecting pond. A malevolent smile spread across her light cocoa-brown skin, and orange light danced in her eyes.

He'd seen that flame before, in the eyes of demon-possessed Dark Ones, and it no longer brought fear and panic, but instead anger and resolve.

But was it the glow of the Dark Ones, or just a trick of the light? Was he seeing what he expected to see after all he'd been through?

"Jedidiah Johnson, you should not have come here," she said, her English heavily accented. "Especially not alone."

"And *you* should not be kidnapping children," he said, scanning to see if the dark warrior was alone. He knew better than to assume he had the advantage over the small but ripped woman. All the Dark Ones he'd faced these past months possessed superhuman strength, quickness, and stamina. Challenging a Dark One unarmed was a dangerous and difficult proposition, even one-on-one.

"Get out of the water," she said with a vulpine grin. "I want to dance with you."

Fists balled, he stood up and marched toward her, sloshing through the water.

She waited, patient and unperturbed, balancing on one foot atop the raised granite. But before he could throw a punch, she exploded upward, twisting in the air to land gracefully in a forward-facing fighting stance just feet away.

With a bemused grin, Jed stepped over the edge of the fountain and into the stone courtyard. He glanced at the man he'd beaten, not wanting to find himself in a two-on-one battle.

"Don't worry about him," she said, reading his concern—or perhaps taking the thought from his head. "He's about as dangerous to you as he is useful to me."

Probably true, he thought. *That dude is no Dark One.*

Jed shifted into a close-quarters combat stance and drifted toward her as she began to circle counterclockwise. She moved with a fluidity and grace he'd not yet seen in the devil's warrior ranks. Dark Ones usually relied on ferocity over finesse, but this creature seemed different. She moved like a human-animal hybrid—a cross between a serpent and a ballet dancer.

Jed ducked her first strike, a roundhouse kick to his head, and parried the second, a driving kick to his midsection. She spun clear of his counteroffensive and did a backflip, this time with a half twist, shifting left to maneuver behind him. She immediately hammered his lower back and kidneys with a series of rapid-fire blows before he could react or defend. His spinning elbow to her face whiffed, catching nothing but air.

"Too big, too slow," she said, laughing and swaying in sync with some inaudible rhythm, "but so, so beautiful . . ."

A siren wailed nearby, and the dark woman's gaze ticked to the sound like a stalking lioness interrupted by an intruding hunter.

"I have to go now, but I'll see you tonight," she said, turning back to look at him.

Then, in a single fluid motion, she pulled a blade from a horizontal sheath on her belt and threw it.

Jed spun reflexively to avoid the incoming dagger, but he'd not been her target. The blade, thrown with preternatural precision, had embedded itself so deeply into the kidnapper's neck that it all but disappeared. Eyes wide, Jed whirled. But the woman was already sprinting away at eye-blurring speed.

"*¡Levanta las manos y no te muevas!*" an angry male voice called in Spanish from Jed's right. The voice repeated the order in heavily accented English: "Put your hands up and don't move!"

Jed groaned an exhale as he raised his hands over his head.

Wonderful . . . they're going to arrest me while the actual killer gets away.

"You've got the wrong guy," he said as a pair of Santo Domingo police officers converged on him with pistols drawn. "I didn't do this."

"We will see what the witnesses have to say. Until then, you are under arrest . . ."

Jed glanced left, down the road where the woman had fled, but he saw only curious tourists staring at the big American being handcuffed on the sidewalk. He looked for little Sebastian and his mother, Paloma, hoping they were still in the crowd to back up his side of the story.

But they, too, had long since disappeared.

CHAPTER EIGHT

MORVANT RESIDENCE

15 NAZARETH CIRCLE

TRINITY LOOP HOUSING COMPLEX

Ben felt the calming warmth of Christy's hand in his as he watched his thirteen-year-old son, Jason, push his baby sister in a swing in their backyard. Elizabeth had absolutely refused to let Jason lift her into the enclosed "baby" swing, insisting she was a first grader now and could swing in a big-kid swing. And so Jason, the big brother that he was, was helping her pump her legs to get higher on her own, all the while remaining close enough to grab his sister if she fell off.

A natural-born protector, that one.

Ben felt a twinge of guilt that they continued to homeschool Jason. It was an unspoken truth that this boy, with complex gifts rivaling Ben's own, belonged at St. George's. Advocating strongly for St. George's as the best path for David and Rachel's daughter, Sarah Beth, had made him revisit their decision again. They had prayed so long and hard about it, and he did believe it was the right thing. But not only was he keeping his son from meaningful relationships, social learning, and a sense of purpose, he also was cheating him out of the wisdom of amazing people like Pastor Dee and Jean-Baptiste Allard—not to mention amazing kids like Sarah Beth and Corbin.

But it's not that simple, is it?

He had spoken early on to Jean-Baptiste, who believed they could help prepare Jason for whatever lay ahead, but even he admitted that it would be complicated. Jason wasn't just "not like the other kids": He was also not like the other Watchers. He had gifts of second sight, the ability to read people both mentally and empathically, and he was becoming an expert at locating. But he also had so many other gifts that the staff at St. George's were in no way prepared to help him with. Gifts of healing, for example. When he was only three, he had brought a frog, mangled on the sidewalk, back to health—maybe even back to life.

But he also had different, more dangerous gifts, ones that needed complete control before he could be out in the complex world of teenage angst.

Jason Morvant had all the gifts his father had—maybe more. Christy was amazing with Jason, helping their son grow into his abilities—and his faith in God—just as she had for Ben so many years ago. But whatever God was preparing his son for, it was obvious that only someone with similar complex and multifaceted gifting could really help him. Someone like Ben, who was the only one anyone at the Shepherds had encountered with such gifting.

Well, at least, that had been true until Jed arrived.

"Jay-Jay, I wanna play stuffed animals," little Elizabeth whined from the swing, leaning back to look at her brother.

"No, Lizzie, I don't like to play with stuffed animals. I'm too big. Just let me push you in the swing."

Ben smiled. Somehow, through it all, Jason remained a

normal, big-hearted middle schooler. And with summer baseball coming up, and the youth group at church, he had plenty of friends.

Ben looked at Christy, feeling her smiling eyes on him, and he smiled back.

"We're doing something right," Christy said as if reading his thoughts. He nodded, squeezing her hand in his.

"At least come up in the tree house with me, Jay-Jay," Elizabeth said. Her brother gave a good-natured eye roll, but his smile was unmistakable. He loved being a brother.

A chirp from the phone beside Ben brought him back, reminding him that the Morvant family vacation was still a week away. Of course, in his line of work, you were never more than a call away from a ruined vacation.

Not again. Not this year's vacation . . .

He picked up his work phone and looked at the number, which was the switchboard back at the TOC. He clenched his jaw and pressed the green icon.

"Morvant."

"Yes, sir. It's Peterson in the TOC—I have the watch today. I have an overseas call from one of our guys—Jed Johnson from Joshua Bravo. Says it's urgent he speak with you, sir. But the man on the phone wasn't Johnson."

Ben let out a sigh. What was it about vacation that Johnson found so repugnant? He was about to tell Peterson to advise that Jed have a drink and lie on the beach, and that he'd talk to him next week, but then he felt his own spidey sense tingle. Not a supernatural gift, just that tingling instinct from his years as a Navy SEAL before everything changed one day on a mission in Africa.

What did Jedidiah get himself into now?

"Put it through," he said.

Christy raised her eyebrows in question, and he shrugged

his shoulders in reply. "It's a call coming in from Jed," he said, not really answering her question.

"Jed Johnson? I thought you sent him on vacation to the Bahamas or something."

"Dominican Republic, and yes, I did."

There was a click and a strange hollow sound, and then a new voice. "Is this Mr. Ben Morvant speaking?" asked a thick island accent.

Ben felt his chest tighten.

Hopefully Jed is all right . . .

"It is. With whom am I speaking?"

"I am Captain Arturo Ramos of the Santo Domingo Police Guard," the voice said. "Are you knowing a man named Jedidiah Johnson?"

"Yes," Ben replied quickly. If something bad had happened to Jed, he would have known about it—he would have felt it, right?

But then, my gifts are changing—fading, perhaps . . .

"Is Jed okay?"

"*Sí*, señor Morvant," the voice said, seemingly satisfied. "*Sí*, but he is in very much trouble. He is here with me in jail in Santo Domingo. It is very serious, I am afraid. He is acting much like, eh, *ratería*—you are knowing this word?"

"No, I'm sorry . . ."

He heard the man muffle the phone, speaking to someone else.

"He is like criminal. He is—how you would say—up to no good."

"What has he done?" Ben asked, rubbing his temple with his free hand and feeling Christy's hand on his arm. She was no doubt curious what was going on.

"Well, to be starting our story, he has killed a man with a knife."

"What?"

"He will tell you himself *un momento*, but a man has died. He is telling us this man was kidnapping a child. We are still talking to witnesses, but we have found no child yet . . ."

"May I speak with him?"

"*Sí*, of course. If he was to be helping someone, then we will—you call it, clear it up, yes? But if not . . ." The man made a *tsk* sound. "Here is señor Johnson, and he will have a few minutes to speaking in privacy."

There was some shuffling around and then voices in Spanish in the background.

"Ben?"

"Jed? What happened? Are you all right?"

"Yes, yes, I'm fine—well, I mean I am in *jail*, as you just heard."

"You killed someone?"

"Actually, no," Ben said; his voice was soft, and he didn't sound to be under duress. "But a man was killed, to be sure—just not by me. Not sad he's dead, though. He was trying to kidnap a young boy, and I intervened. His mother flagged me down as it was happening. I stopped the kidnapping and saved the boy, but there was someone else—they attacked me and then killed the first kidnapper."

"Someone . . ." Ben thought carefully about how to word this. Jed was in jail in the DR, not Nashville. There was almost no chance he was being given privacy for real. "Someone . . . *dark*, Jed?"

He cringed at how that probably sounded to anyone listening in, but he didn't know how else to put it.

"I'm not positive, boss," Jed said after a pause. "But probably. They were both bad people, I can tell you that. The second person may have been . . . um, dark."

"Anyone else hurt? And you said you're not hurt, correct?"

"Yeah, I'm good," Jed said. "But I'd sure like to get out of here sooner rather than later, if you know what I mean."

"Yeah, of course," Ben said. "I'll reach out to our connections at State and also, you know, other agencies. I'll get you out as quickly as I can. But it might take a minute, okay? Not a lot going on down there right now that our connections would be involved with, so . . ."

"What about our people?" Jed asked. "Do we have any . . . um . . . business dealings down here?"

Ben chewed his lip. This might not be a Shepherd situation—time would tell—but either way, he could certainly get people there to help a brother. The problem was, the Shepherds didn't have a formal base of operations in the area. Ben knew of assets in the DR that he could call—but maybe not the kind of direct-action team Jed was looking for. It would take time to connect with them. They weren't "organic" to the organization, but operated more like managed assets and were undercover in an NOC. The Shepherds had never really needed a major presence in the DR.

Or at least not before Jed vacationed there . . .

"Sit tight, Jed," he said. "We'll get you out of there as quick as we can, but just be prepared to spend at least a few hours there—maybe even overnight."

"Oh, lovely . . ."

"I'll make clear that you're not a criminal and not to be screwed with, then I'll get a call in right away. Lay low, get along, and I'll have you out as soon as I can. Once you're secure, we can talk more. And I'll send you contact information on some . . . connections we have in country," Ben added, already searching for the contact information for the husband-and-wife team who worked as assets for the Shepherds in the DR. "Not company people, but two folks who work with us from time to time. I'll forward you their contact information for once we get you out."

"Thanks, boss," Jed said. Ben thought the head of Joshua Bravo sounded like he was all right.

"So, other than that, how's the vacation?" Ben asked, unable to resist.

Jed chuckled—a good sign. "Very relaxing. Sorry about all this, but I have some things to catch you up on as soon as I'm out."

"Can't wait for the debrief."

There was some shuffling again, then Captain Ramos was back on the line.

"Captain Ramos, I appreciate and respect your need to conduct a thorough investigation."

"Oh, I assure you, we take these things very seriously . . ."

"Of course, and I'm sure you're quite good at your job. Follow the facts, but I need you to know that Mr. Johnson is a member of an elite American Special Operations counterterrorism unit and was on vacation when this happened. He is a man of honor and courage, and I assure you he is not a . . . *ratería.* Did I say that right?"

"You did. I thank you for sharing this, but we must conduct our own investigation into this matter."

"Of course, and you will get no interference from me," Ben lied, already laying out in his mind the series of phone calls he needed to make to the State Department and then to the CIA. "But I just want you to know who he is so that you can be sure he is treated well and kept safe until you find he is telling the truth."

"Of course," Ramos said, and Ben couldn't be sure if he had perhaps insulted the man with the implication. The man's next words were more reassuring. "I had thought he might be an American agent or military. He carries all his self like honorable man, but also like man of action. I will personally see to his safety while all is being sorted out."

"Thank you, Captain. That's more than I have a right to ask," Ben said, feeling a sense of relief. "I am in your debt. Mr. Johnson works for me, but he is also my friend."

"Of course."

"May I give you my number and ask you to keep me in the loop as your investigation unfolds?" Ben asked. He had no intention of leaving Jed in jail long enough for any updates, but you never knew.

"Yes, please," Captain Ramos said, and Ben gave him the number to his encrypted work cell. "He is safe with me, I assure you."

Ben clicked off the call.

"I won't ask if everything is all right," Christy said with a tight smile and another squeeze on his arm. "Kids, come on inside with me. Elizabeth, do you want to help Mommy make the dinner?"

"Yes, yes," their daughter said, running to the wood deck they sat on.

"I can help too," Jason said. As he passed by, he gave a reassuring nod to his dad. "He didn't hurt anyone, Dad."

"I know, son. Thank you."

"It was a woman, I think. She's kind of scary."

With that, his thirteen-year-old followed Christy into the kitchen, the sliders closing behind him.

A woman? Why had Ben not seen that himself? It wasn't unusual for Jason to see things Ben couldn't, but this was about his teammate—someone he was well in tune with.

He shook the thought off and pressed the speed dial for the TOC.

"Peterson."

"Hey, it's Morvant."

"Yes, sir?"

"Gayle James is our new CIA liaison," he said. "Can you get her on the phone for me, ASAP?"

"Right away, sir," Peterson said.

"You can just pass my number and have her call me directly. And as soon as you get me connected, start working on finding Meredith Pinellas over at State. I need to talk with her next."

"You got it, sir," Peterson said and hung up.

Ben tapped his finger on the armrest of the Adirondack chair. Perhaps he should get a team down to the DR? Not that he would ever authorize any kind of rescue of Jed—not in this situation, anyway. State and Gayle James would have him free by morning if not in the next few hours.

But perhaps Jed is seeing something I'm not—something Jason seems tuned in to?

"Can I bring you a beer or glass of wine?" Christy called from the sliding door to the kitchen.

He smiled back at her over his shoulder.

"Iced tea, for now," he said. "But I'll probably have a glass of wine with dinner."

She smiled—engulfing him in those gorgeous eyes of hers—and closed the door.

He'd wait for now. No sense mobilizing everyone and then having them pass Jed in the air while Jed flew home. He'd wait to see just what Jed had gotten mixed up in. It sounded more like his operator was just in the wrong—or maybe the right—place at the wrong time.

His phone chirped again.

"Hello?" he said, looking at the 202 area code. "Gayle?"

"Hi, Ben. Yes, it's Gayle. Is everything all right?"

"I think so," he said, "but I could use your help . . ."

CHAPTER NINE

LUXURY VRBO APARTMENT

CALLE EL CONDE

SANTO DOMINGO, DOMINICAN REPUBLIC

0402 HOURS LOCAL

The woman known as Calypso paced the tile floor beside the wall of glass that overlooked the Atlantic Ocean. The energy she felt was fueled by a mix of excitement, anger, and curiosity. She did not doubt that the man who had intervened was a Shepherd—or, at the very least, he was a man of action who had the faith in God needed to be a Shepherd. She still had much to learn about him, but she knew that for certain.

What he was doing in Santo Domingo was another matter.

If Manbo Athaliah's enemies were aware of her plans, then it made no sense that they would send a single Shepherd, and this man had clearly been alone. No one else had intervened, and his surprise at the event felt genuine.

No, this had been a chance encounter.

Or destiny, she thought, a vulpine grin spreading over her face. This man was so filled with good. Such a counterpoint to the dark arts she had dedicated her life to. But therein was the excitement, right? To corrupt one so righteous was the ultimate challenge and, therefore, the ultimate excitement . . .

But that was not the mission. Not the primary one, anyway.

Manbo Athaliah had been furious. The boy she had failed to capture had particularly well-developed gifts, and now the opportunity to use them might be lost. Calypso's benefactor and leader claimed she needed to keep these gifted children from finding their way to the Shepherds, where their gifts could be exploited in the battle that raged in the shadows. But Calypso suspected there was more to Athaliah's plan than that. Otherwise, why not just dispatch these dangerous children instead of adopting them and giving them a relatively luxurious life?

Calypso was not as thickheaded about the world as Athaliah believed.

But she also didn't care that much about the world. She knew who she served. But she found the temptation to corrupt this delicious man overpowering.

Calypso had now been tasked by Athaliah to use her assets to surveil the one called Jedidiah, to determine whether he was a Shepherd and might need dealing with, or if he was just in the wrong place at the wrong time. She had mobilized her personal network to do just that, but as long as he was in jail, there was little for them to do, and little did it matter.

She stopped her pacing and stared out across the lights to the sea. Then she smiled again.

Perhaps she would visit him tonight. There might be something of value to learn, but the visit would also be great fun.

CHAPTER TEN

POLICIA NACIONAL

F4F6 C. EL CONDE

SANTO DOMINGO, DOMINICAN REPUBLIC

0420 HOURS LOCAL

Despite his difficulty sleeping in the relative luxurious comfort of his Vrbo, Jed—in typical Navy SEAL form—fell instantly asleep on the narrow cot of his small jail cell, feet dangling off the end. He woke a few hours later and relieved himself in the lovely toilet–water fountain combination—the only thing in the cell other than his narrow cot and a tiny metal sink—and fell back asleep in seconds on the musty, wafer-thin pillow.

He'd slept inside hollowed-out logs, underneath fallen trees, in caves beside bat guano, and in the desert underneath a helicopter. He never, ever had any trouble sleeping while in the field. Once in tactical mode, it was as if his body understood that rest was a weapon, quieted his mind, and pushed him deep into needed sleep. Despite the nightmares that visited him during his down time, when he was on mission he always slept like a baby.

Perhaps, after his battle in the streets of Santo Domingo, his mind and body knew he was again in tactical mode because the first few hours he'd slept a deep and fretless sleep, free of dreams.

The second half of his night, not so much.

It began with nightmares of the night at St. George's, a rather trite nightmare these days, a nightmare that then morphed into a few oldies but goodies he'd not visited in a long while from his time in the SEAL Teams: dark, disturbing, but familiar memories of the horrors of war, the cost of violence, and teammates lost. Not the kind of nightmares that left you feeling exhausted the next morning—at least not anymore.

Then came the new one. He had no idea if it was just a nightmare spawned by the others and placed in the context of his current situation, or if it was something more—maybe the promise the woman had made that she would be visiting again soon.

In his dream, he lay quietly, stretched out on a wooden chaise longue covered in dark blue cushions. He was on a beach that wasn't familiar, but he knew (the way you do in dreams) it was in the Dominican Republic. That quiet narrator who sometimes narrated his dreams in his own voice asked if this didn't look like the beach he'd seen online at the Paradisus Punta Cana Resort, the resort where he had reservations for the second half of his vacation in just a few days.

Yes, it does, he agreed in his dream.

He lay there stretched out, booted feet crossed at the ankles, a pink tropical drink, complete with umbrella, in his hand. It was strange that he was in 5.11 cargo pants and boots, shirtless with his custom assault rifle on his chest, but the sun felt good on his skin and the drink cool in his throat.

The beach was eerily empty except for right at the water's edge, where a familiar young woman—Paloma, he remembered—sat in a low beach chair beside her son. Sebastian, the boy he had saved, sat on the sand, using colorful plastic shovels and a blue bucket to create an extraordinary sandcastle. As Jed sipped his drink, Paloma looked over and waved. Jed raised his drink in reply.

Thank you, she mouthed at him, glancing at her boy playing in the sand.

Jed gave her a humble nod. He'd done a good deed. He had stopped a terrible thing, a horrible crime separating mother and child, and whatever evil plan the Dark Ones had for the boy. He'd won. If a night in a tiny jail cell in Santo Domingo and losing what was left of a vacation he didn't really want to take anyway proved to be the cost he paid for doing the right thing, then so be it.

He smiled, watching with satisfaction as the boy and his mother chatted, Sebastian excitedly explaining something about the massive sandcastle he'd built.

Then Sebastian glanced up from his castle, suddenly rigid, and dropped his two plastic shovels as he looked out at the calm turquoise water. Jed's body tensed. He followed the boy's gaze, just as Paloma rose to her feet, leaning forward and cupping a hand over her eyes to block the glaring sun.

Jed saw it—the strange motion of the water, the growing ripples in the calm surf suggesting something enormous moving at very high speed, just below the surface, headed toward the shore. Jed went to get up but found he couldn't. His body was paralyzed—or most of it, anyway. He could move his head, but he couldn't sit up; his legs were completely useless. He could feel the rifle that he now gripped in his right hand, but his arm ignored his plea to raise the weapon and sight on whatever creature approached.

Strangely, though, his left hand worked fine and brought his fruity drink up, the straw slipping between his lips.

He spit the straw out in irritation, an irritation that morphed into fear as the creature now broke the surface. He'd expected a shark—a large one based on the displacement—but the scaly yellowish-green back with a single rippling dorsal fin along its entire length looked more like some mythical sea creature, writhing through the water with great power.

"Sebastian—Paloma—Run! Run to me!" he screamed.

But as so often happens in dreams, the words came out as a barely audible whisper. Mother and son both remained frozen, staring at the strange creature rapidly approaching.

Jed dropped the drink, which splashed onto his forearm as it hit the sand, and planted his left hand firmly on the edge of the wooden chaise. He pushed with all of his considerable might, trying to raise himself up from the lounger, but it was like pressing into a cement wall. His left arm screamed with pain, but he didn't budge. His brain screamed at him to raise the rifle, but his right hand just lay there, the gun's grip firm and familiar in his hand.

Jed watched in horror as the creature breached the surf. Finally, he saw the head for the first time. It was a serpent's head, triangular and massive, mouth open and forked tongue licking across humanlike lips. Jed somehow knew immediately, from the orange eyes and the smile, that this was the same woman who had pounded his kidneys and thrown the knife almost through the other man's head with expert precision. The creature rose into the air, towering over the motionless boy, smiling down at him with rows and rows of razor-sharp teeth. The creature looked up from the boy, smiling now at Jed, still paralyzed on the chaise longue, his heart pounding in his chest, his mouth dry cotton.

"You've stopped nothing. You prevented nothing. You've only delayed the boy's future and are powerless to stop what is rising

against the Shepherds. You are powerless, just as you are here in dreams . . ."

The serpent stared at him, the rows of gleaming teeth glistening in the moonlight. The eyes—the woman's eyes but with the vertical pupils of a snake—glared at him . . .

A scream stuck in his throat.

A lightning-fast strike from the serpent snatched the boy from the beach, his legs flailing, the rest of him now inside that horrible maw. The serpent tilted its head back, opened its throat, and then swallowed the boy whole. Sebastian's mother screamed. Jed finally found his voice, and his own cries mixed with hers.

Then the serpent turned to the mother and attacked. Instead of swallowing her as it had the boy, it tore her to pieces as Jed continued to scream. Moments later the beach was soaked with blood and body parts, the boy was gone, and still, Jed couldn't move.

The serpent stared at him with the woman's eyes, then slithered toward him, dragging a deep divot in the sand as it moved with impossible speed, mouth open. A child's toy shovel fell from its mouth onto the beach as it approached. Jed should have been terrified, but instead, he felt only pure rage.

"Let me up, then we'll see who's powerless," he snarled.

As the serpent moved toward him, teeth gleaming in the sun, the creature began to morph, shrinking rapidly in size and changing until it slithered over his boots and then moved up his body. Human arms appeared, and delicate, soft hands caressed his body as the serpent's head changed into the woman from the street, scales turning to soft cocoa skin, hair sprouting from her head and framing her thin, attractive face. The fingernails dug painfully into his side as she moved up his body, bare breasts dragging across his chest and pelvis grinding into his as she lay on top of him now in a fully human form. Only the eyes remained those of a snake, set in her pretty face. When the woman spoke, a forked tongue flicked out of her mouth, licking across full lips.

"You've lost, Shepherd," she said. "So why don't we have some fun?"

Her mouth descended toward his, lips parted, and her eyes closed.

Jed turned his head, the only thing he seemed able to move.

In response, the woman shrieked in anger. Her sharp teeth tore through the flesh of his neck, and he felt hot blood spray onto his chin and chest—

Jed sat bolt upright on the narrow bunk, shifting to his right, his weight tipping the small cot and dumping him painfully onto the floor. Immediately, he rolled up and into a crouch, eyes scanning the dark cell for any sign of movement, fully expecting the female assailant from the street to be in the corner, ready to attack. His body was a coiled spring, his mind sharp and his focus clear despite the pounding pulse in his temple. His breathing was deep but came in long, slow breaths from years of training and combat.

Slowly, he allowed his readiness to abate as the cell echoed back at him, empty except for the overturned cot. Jed rose, hands still balled in fists, scanning outside his small cell into the narrow section of hallway, where five other cells, three to a side, stood empty.

He ran through four cycles of four-count tactical breathing, felt his pulse slow almost immediately, righted his cot, and took a seat on the edge, pulling on his face with rough, tired hands.

A sound brought him back to his feet. He heard the heavy door at the end of the hall swing open, and braced himself: arms at waist level, rolling onto the balls of his feet. It could be a barrage of bullets or another expertly thrown knife.

Instead, it was a uniformed police officer who gave him a nod and slipped a key into the lock of his cell.

"*Ellos están aquí por usted, señor,*" the man said with a rather passive smile.

"What? What does that mean? Someone is coming? Do you speak English?"

If the woman from the street was here, or any of her colleagues, Jed needed to know—and be ready for the threat.

"They are here for you?" the man said slowly and questioningly, his English accented.

"Who?" Jed demanded, straining to see past him.

The man just shrugged and swung open the door, gesturing for Jed to exit the small cell.

One thing was for damn sure, he could not risk having this man put handcuffs on him. He debated whether he should try and "acquire" the 9 mm pistol the police jail guard wore on his belt, but the man made no move to cuff him, instead leading him down the hall without much concern for his own safety. He opened the heavier door at the end of the hall, and Jed followed him into a small antechamber—almost more like a small foyer—with a desk at the end.

A woman stood at the desk smiling, and Jed felt his mouth drop open.

"Hi, Jed," she said with a bemused grin. "Seems like you're having a great vacation."

He chuckled and shook his head.

"It's great to see you, Gayle," he said, feeling his muscles relax. He let out a long, whistling sigh. "Thanks for coming to get me."

CHAPTER ELEVEN

ADMINISTRATIVE BUILDING, ROOM 304

ST. GEORGE'S ACADEMY

OUTSIDE OF NASHVILLE, TENNESSEE

0830 HOURS LOCAL

Sarah Beth sat on the long bench in the hall outside Pastor Dee's office, kicking her feet back and forth. She loved, but also kinda hated, her talks with Pastor Dee. Loved them because by the end of the talk, she always felt better. Hated them because getting to the end of the talk was emotional and stressful. Pastor Dee was one of those grown-ups who had a way of pulling stuff out of Sarah Beth's emotional lockbox even though Sarah Beth hadn't given her the key. And she was very, very good at it.

"Hi, Sarah Beth," Dee said, sticking her head out of the partly open office door. "C'mon in."

Sarah Beth forced a smile and got up from the bench. A trip to Pastor Dee's office wasn't exactly like getting called to the principal's office, but it still always felt that way. She had planned to make an appointment to see the woman who served as her Keeper anyway, but Pastor Dee had beaten her to it.

Oh well, it is what it is.

Today, Dee's office smelled like vanilla. Her Keeper liked to use the little jars full of aromatic oils with wicks sticking out of the top, whatever those things were called. It smelled nice, but Sarah Beth could see herself feeling nauseated after probably fifteen minutes of the smell.

"How are finals going so far?" Dee asked as Sarah Beth followed her into the office and took the familiar seat facing her desk. Dee fixed Sarah Beth with what she liked to call a *pleasant* smile—a smile without judgment but also without substance.

"I feel pretty good about Theology, but not so good about Spanish. Those are the only two I've taken. I have Algebra later this afternoon," she said.

Dee nodded. "When I was your age, I used to get so stressed out about finals that my hands would shake."

"Really?" Sarah Beth said, surprised. She always thought of Dee as unflappable.

"Oh yeah," Dee said with a nostalgic squint. "I've never been much of a test taker. I'm good at listening and talking, but being quiet and writing down my answers with a time limit . . . well, let's just say it was never my cup of tea."

"Yeah, me too," Sarah Beth said, although it wasn't exactly true. She was a great test taker in subjects she liked and understood, but she didn't want to rub that in. "Is that why you called me in, to talk about finals?"

Dee laughed. "Good heavens, no. I called you in to see how you're doing."

"Oh, in that case, I'm doing okay. I mean, I'm a little stressed about finals, but who isn't?"

"How are you sleeping? Are you having nightmares?"

Sarah Beth bristled. "Who told you about that? Have you been talking to Corbin?"

"Sarah Beth, honey, I have not been talking to anyone about you behind your back, and that includes Corbin. I wanted to visit because you have been through an incredibly traumatic event. And I would not be doing my job as your Keeper and your friend—much less your teacher and counselor at this school—if I didn't give you an opportunity to talk about how you're dealing with things after everything you've been through."

"You mean the night that Victor came?"

Dee nodded.

"It's over and done with . . . and I've probably talked about it *too* much, if you know what I mean," Sarah Beth said. Then, for good measure, she added something she hoped would sound very grown-up. "It's really not healthy to dwell on these kinds of things."

Dee smiled and shook her head.

"Is that so?"

"What?"

"Sarah Beth, when a person experiences trauma, it can take a long time to sort out all the emotions and feelings. That process of healing can be difficult, and it can also be quite time-consuming. Have you ever heard of the term *posttraumatic stress*?"

Sarah Beth nodded. "PTSD. Like what Navy SEALs and veterans get after they retire."

"That's right," Dee said. "Although now it's simply called PTS. Do you know why?"

Sarah Beth shook her head. "Why?"

Dee smiled. "Because we now recognize that it is not, in any way, a disorder. It is not only natural and normal, but a *healthy* response to severe trauma, whether physical or emotional—or even spiritual. You mentioned that many Navy SEALs experience it after they retire, and that's true, but only partially. The symptoms of PTS exist while they are still serving, but in the setting of repeated trips to the same environment that causes the trauma, the brain isolates the response, locking it up where it festers and grows. When they leave the repeated stressor—when they retire, for example—the symptoms of PTS can explode out in very dangerous and damaging ways. We know that this must be avoided, and the military now engages very early on with Special Operators, like your uncle Jed, to give them the help and support they need even while they are still in the fight and to allow them to process the traumas they experience in healthy and adaptive ways. Does that make sense?"

"I suppose," Sarah Beth said with an uncomfortable shrug. She did not like where this was going—not at all. She was content to keep her trauma locked up on the top shelf of the closet in her mind, thank you very much. Avoidance was working very well for her at the moment, and she had exams to study for.

"We also know now that it's very common for Shepherds and Watchers to experience PTS too. It can manifest in different ways. Most people experience anxiety, nightmares, fear, and even depression after a traumatic event. So, if you're experiencing one or more of those things, I want you to know you can talk to me about it. I'm here for you anytime, night or day."

"Thank you. That means a lot to me," she said. Then she hesitated a moment. "Is St. George's doing this for the others as well? For Elizabeth and Darilyn? For Josh and all the kids in the basement—especially those who saw . . . who saw . . ."

The image of Mr. Baker shooting himself in the head when Victor arrived filled her mind and made her stomach churn.

"Everyone here at St. George's is being given the help, counsel, and prayer they need, Sarah Beth. Every Keeper is doing just what I am doing for you, and every student is receiving counseling."

"Even Corbin?" she asked, narrowing her eyes. Corbin was so together, such a total badass Watcher. She was everything Sarah Beth hoped to be; she never, ever seemed rattled. But Corbin had been stabbed with a spear. She'd needed a tube in her chest . . .

"Of course," Dee said and seemed disappointed in her, which felt awful. "Sarah Beth, I can't discuss other students with you, just as I wouldn't discuss you with them. But I assure you that whatever you are experiencing after all you went through, whatever difficulties you may be having, we are all having similar issues. Even those of us who weren't here, but feel we should have been . . ."

Sarah Beth stared at Pastor Dee as the wonderful woman she admired and loved gazed off in the distance, then shook her head.

How selfish and clueless am I . . . ?

Maybe it really was PTS, just like Pastor Dee suggested. The images in her head were kept mostly at bay now, at least when she was awake. But all this *had* affected her, hadn't it? And if even Corbin needed help . . . well, maybe it was time to share.

"Well," she said softly, "I *am* having nightmares, but not like the kind I'm used to having. These feel . . . different."

"Different in what way?"

Sarah Beth told Dee the same thing she'd told Corbin in the White Room—about the nightmares of faceless people, vying for control—hoping that maybe Dee would have more insight or thoughts on it than Corbin had.

"If you had to pick one word to describe the feeling you have the instant you wake from the dreams, what would it be?" Dee asked.

The question caught Sarah Beth off guard but also intrigued her.

"Chaos," she said. It was the first thing that came to mind.

"Interesting," Dee said and jotted down a note—her first handwritten note of the session.

"What do you think the nightmares could mean?" Sarah Beth asked, crossing her arms. "Do you think it means I have PTSD—I mean PTS?"

Dee smiled and then leaned in, a conspiratorial look on her face. "Do you want to know the truth? I believe everyone on this campus is suffering from PTS in one form or another after what happened that night. I know I certainly am."

"Wait, what? You?"

"Yes, me. In my dreams, I'm trapped in the Bullpen and powerless to help you and the rest of my kids. It's awful—having to relive that night over and over again," Dee said, and the expression on her face told Sarah Beth her Keeper meant every word. "Because of what happened, we're changing our protocols. It's one of the reasons your mom was hired to work here."

"Yeah, about that," Sarah Beth said, pursing her lips. "What exactly is my mom's job supposed to be?"

The truth was, after all that had happened, there was a part of Sarah Beth—the leftover little-girl part, maybe—who had been relieved when she learned her mom would be working on campus. Being away from Mom and Dad had been the hardest, very worst part of coming here, especially that first semester. But she'd adapted. And now she'd made friends, finally, after feeling like an outcast because of her accelerated gifts. She loved her mom, but she didn't want to lose that feeling of belonging, the feeling of being . . . the same as the other kids. Even if, she supposed, she really wasn't.

"Her primary function is to serve as a liaison between the Watchers and the Shepherds, but exactly what that looks like is something we'll have to figure out over time."

"But I thought talking to the Shepherds was the Keepers' job?"

"In the past, it has been each Keeper's job to coordinate with the Shepherds, but that was always an ancillary responsibility. My primary job, as Keeper, is to mentor you. Your mom's job is to unburden all the Keepers from acting as individual liaisons and to streamline communications. We've needed a centralized point of contact to manage the relationship for a long time, but we didn't realize how much until now."

Sarah Beth felt her face flush.

"Wait, wait, wait," she stammered, "you're saying my mom's going to be the person interfacing between us and the Shepherds? Like, she'll be in the Bullpen when I'm there working? When I'm working with my friends?"

"Yes," Dee said with a surprised expression.

"At least promise me she won't be allowed in the White Room."

"As far as I understand, she has unrestricted access to all spaces on campus. Does that upset you?"

Are you kidding me; it's mortifying! Sarah Beth thought with a heavy sigh. *Sorry, God, but really? Why does it have to be my mom?*

"It's just that . . . I . . . I mean I just started making friends and, you know, making it here on my own, and now my mom's going to be, like, walking the halls and checking on me all the time. Being away from home and family is, like, one of the things that we all share—the one thing that makes us equal."

A horribly embarrassing image of Mom finding her in the cafeteria and telling her to brush her hair or giving her a hug and a kiss in front of everyone popped into Sarah Beth's head. She must have pushed the thought to Dee because her Keeper chuckled.

"I don't think you have to worry about your mom hugging you in the lunchroom. Not only is she a professional, but she's also not so old that she doesn't remember what it's like to be a teenager. I think you can relax, Sarah Beth. Everything is going to be fine."

"But what if she *does* embarrass me?"

"Then you can always talk to me about it, and I'll coach her as one adult to another without mentioning a word of our conversation. How does that sound?"

"You'd do that for me?"

"Absolutely. I'm your Keeper, and that means I'm always, always on your side, even if that means talking to your parents."

"Thanks," she said, feeling a little bit better. But only a little.

"Is there anything else you'd like to talk about?" Dee asked.

Sarah Beth glanced at her Apple Watch. She was ready to get out of here: She only had an hour and fifteen minutes until her math final, and she really needed to study. She did want to talk more to Pastor Dee about the dreams. It wasn't really their content—they always felt so vague, like eavesdropping on the conversations of hundreds of people at once through a wall—it was how she felt after. And it was the anger she heard or felt in those dreams. Not her anger, but others'.

Anger, and *hunger*.

But she had an exam in her weakest subject. "I'm good, but I do want to talk again. Maybe even tomorrow morning?"

"Of course. And in the meantime, I'll think and pray about your faceless chaos dreams. I'll also ask some of the other Keepers if any of their kids are reporting something similar. How does that sound?"

"Sounds good," Sarah Beth said and pushed her chair back as she stood. A flash of something, something unsaid, from Dee came to her. For some reason, it filled her with anxiety. "Is there something else you need to tell me?"

"Yes, but I'd like it to wait until after finals," Dee said. "I don't want to distract you."

"Is it something bad?" Sarah Beth asked, dread flaring in her gut.

"Nope, quite the opposite. You're doing great, Sarah Beth. You've impressed just about everyone there is to impress."

"Oh, good," she said, wondering what it could be. Maybe the Shepherds were going on a trip to Italy, like Corbin had gone on a few months ago, and taking Watchers with them. That would be awesome.

"Thanks for visiting with me, Sarah Beth. Good luck with the rest of your finals, and remember, my door is always open. You don't have to wait for me to request a meeting to talk with me. You know that, right?"

Sarah Beth resisted the urge to roll her eyes. *I know! You literally beat me to it by ten minutes.* "I'll try to be better about that. I'll stop by after my last final so you can give me the good news. Okay?"

"Sounds perfect. Good luck with that math final. And Sarah Beth . . ."

Sarah Beth raised her eyebrows in the universal *Yes?* expression.

"Sweetheart, I think we should meet over the summer as well. I know you have a vacation planned soon, but after that we should meet regularly, okay?"

"That would be awesome," Sarah Beth said and meant it. "To be honest, I was worried about the summer. I'll be glad for the break from classes, but can I continue the training I'm doing with you and with Corbin?"

Pastor Dee smiled her amazing, disarming smile—the one that felt like a warm blanket right out of the dryer on a cold winter's night.

"I'd like that. We've talked about it some already. Corbin will be traveling for a short time with her family and then she'll be back for some summer work herself. I'll speak with your parents, but I think that's a great idea, Sarah Beth."

"Great," she said, feeling buoyed that at least one of her worries was being addressed.

With a smile on her face and an unburdened heart, she left Dee's office. Instead of fretting about her math final, she suddenly and inexplicably found herself wondering about Uncle Jed and how his vacation was going. She'd not Watcher snapchatted with him in almost a week. *Maybe I should check in with him?* she thought, then shook her head.

No. Math final first . . . then, I can say a quick hello.

CHAPTER TWELVE

SANTO DOMINGO, DOMINICAN REPUBLIC

0507 HOURS LOCAL

Jed tried to stop, but he couldn't pull his gaze away from Gayle as she drove him back to his Vrbo rental.

"What?" she said through an awkward laugh, glancing at him sideways from the driver's seat.

"It's just so surreal—you being here," he said.

"Surreal good or surreal bad?"

"Surreal good. I'm happy to see you."

"Ah," she said with mock sweetness, "I bet you say that to all the girls who bail you out of jail in a foreign country."

He chuckled at that. "True, but they don't have your style. I mean, look at you—khaki suit, white linen blouse, and fancy trainers."

"Thanks, and they're HOKAs. I don't *do* heels."

"Why'd you change that pixie cut you were rocking in Peru?"

"My boss said that haircut made me too *recognizable.* Told

me I needed to go with something generic and boring, so this is the result."

"Well, you could shave your head and you'd still look pretty."

She shot him another sideways, quizzical glance. "Dude, you're awfully complimentary and chatty for five o'clock in the morning. Did you hit your head or something?"

He laughed and shook his head. The truth was he *was* happy to see Gayle. Maybe not in *that* way, but happier to see her than made sense. And not just because she'd bailed him out of jail—she'd been ordered to do that—no, this was something else. The *idea* of going on vacation alone and the *reality* of going on vacation alone had been two very different things. It turned out that Jedidiah Johnson—the guy who could go an entire day and say fewer than fifty words—was dying for somebody to talk to. And Gayle not only fit the bill but was someone he liked being around.

"Do you prefer me silent and brooding?" he said with a crooked grin. "I can brood if you like."

"No, no, definitely not," she chuckled. "I remember you as a master brooder, but I like this better."

"Too late, I'm officially brooding the rest of the way back to my Vrbo."

"Okay, well, while you brood, do you mind filling me in on why you were arrested and thrown in jail?"

"Did you not get the download from the head shed before you came?"

"I did, but I'd like to hear the unsanitized version from you."

As the CIA's official-unofficial liaison, Gayle was cleared to be read in on pretty much anything Ben and the leadership team felt comfortable sharing. She had worked hand in glove with Jed's team in Peru and Hong Kong as they'd unraveled the mystery of Victor's energy weapon. Consequently, she'd seen and experienced some freaky stuff firsthand—like glowing eyes and people getting vaporized to ash.

But how much about the Dark Ones did she really know—or understand? Was she aware that a supernatural war between good and evil was being fought in the shadows, a war that transcended nation-states and that had been raging for millennia? And if so, what were her beliefs on the matter? With her ability to leverage the US intelligence community apparatus, Gayle made a powerful ally, but how far she was willing to stick her neck out for him and the Shepherds was still an unknown, he supposed. Did her arrival in Santo Domingo mean she was here to work as a partner or to serve as his babysitter?

Hopefully the former, he thought, *but I probably should try to figure that out before I share too much.*

"There's something strange going on down here," he said, dipping his toe in the proverbial water to check the temperature.

"When you say *strange*, do you mean like villages-getting-vaporized-from-above strange, glowing-eyed-bad-guys-with-superhuman-strength strange, or just, like, regular strange?"

"Before I answer that, can I ask you a question?"

"Sure. Anything," she said.

"Remember in Cusco, those people we fought in that courtyard?"

"You mean after you jumped off the balcony at dinner and charged off into the night by yourself like a crazy man?"

"Yeah, after that," he said with a grin.

"I remember," she said, her tone hedging.

"We never really talked about what you saw," he said, "but now that you're our agency liaison, I think it's worth revisiting."

She nodded but kept her eyes on the road. "Yeah, that was some *X-Files* level stuff . . . with the glowing eyes and superhuman fighting ability they had."

"We call them Dark Ones," he said.

"I know. Please understand that, since its early days as OSS, the CIA is no stranger to things that fall outside of the ordinary. From ESP experiments to other things outside of the explainable. My predecessor read me in on your organization's worldview."

"My organization's 'worldview'?" he said with raised eyebrows. "Is that your way of saying that you and the CIA have a different take?"

"My predecessor was a believer, if that's the right word. He made that pretty clear."

"What about your boss, Steve Schmidt?"

She flashed him a close-lipped smile. "I'd categorize him as a strategic but cynical pragmatist. Steve's a man who sees the utility of partnering with Trinity rather than butting heads, but also the type of person who'd prefer to withhold judgment until the eleventh hour and fifty-ninth minute."

He nodded. "I could see that about him."

"But Jed, it's not Steve who you need to worry about. The rank-and-file CIA would not embrace your activities or interpretations of the world events you react to. That's why my little group keeps this stuff highly compartmentalized. It's why my new position exists, I suppose. But understand: It exists to serve the purposes of the CIA, not as some philanthropic support system. It assumes we are all on the same page—on the same team."

"And aren't we?" he probed.

She glanced over, then back at the road.

"I certainly think so," she said. "Am I right?"

Jed smiled and nodded.

"If your team and page are about fighting back against evil in the world, then yes," Jed said, watching her face closely.

"Well, that's a relief."

He hesitated a moment. "You said your predecessor was a believer. What did you mean by that?"

"Well," she said slowly, framing her answer, perhaps. "I mean that he is a man of strong religious conviction. That he believes very much in what you are doing, but also that he believes in the . . . stranger aspects of working with you."

Jed nodded. "And what about you, Gayle? What do you believe?"

She sighed and pulled the car into an open parking spot along the curb half a block from his rental. "I still haven't worked out how all this fits with my personal beliefs and faith."

"That's okay. I'm still working through some of those issues myself. It is quite a lot to wrap your head around," he said. "But how do you explain what you saw in Peru? What do you think the Dark Ones are?"

"My predecessor believed they are the demon-possessed," she said, her voice cracking as she did. "I can't believe I actually said that out loud."

"And what about you? What do you believe?"

She hesitated a long moment before answering. "I think what I hear you asking me is whether I believe that a battle between the agents of God and the agents of the devil is raging all around me—and whether you can trust me, not only with that knowledge but also with the delicate responsibility of safeguarding your organization and your mission."

"Yes," he said and blew air through his lips. "And thank you for articulating that so I didn't have to."

"You're welcome," she said and reached out to give the top of his knee a pat. "The truth is, Jed, I'm still on the fence, but I'm open to the possibility that we live in a supernatural world."

He nodded, glad to have finally crossed this particular Rubicon with her.

"That said, I want you to know that you can trust me. You can trust me not only with your safety and your mission but also with your faith and beliefs . . . and all the potential liabilities that both create when dealing with secular law enforcement and the intelligence community."

"Thank you for saying that, Gayle. And I'd like to make the same vow in return. I promise you that I will never knowingly or intentionally put you in a compromising or reputation-jeopardizing situation within your community," he said, patting the back of her hand, which was still on his knee.

They locked eyes and smiled at each other.

"This is where you're staying, right?" she asked, pulling her hand away and ending the moment.

"Yep," he said and turned to let himself out of the car. "Do you want to come up? I've got fresh fruit and coffee."

"Absolutely, but if there's someone out there targeting you now, we need to clear this place first. You booked in your name, right?"

He shrugged. "No reason not to. I came here on vacation."

But she was right, and his desire for company aside, it would be good to have a wingman when he arrived back at the apartment he'd rented.

"Okay, well, hold on a sec." She turned and grabbed a duffel bag from the back seat. "Brought you a present," she said, producing a Wilson Combat SFX9 short-barrel compact from the bag's main compartment.

"Ooo, nice," he said, accepting it with a grin. He pulled the slide back to chamber a 9 mm round. "Thank you."

"Figured you might want this after last night," she said.

"Indeed. Hopefully we don't find any *friends* waiting for us inside."

She pulled a slightly less compact HK for herself. "No argument there."

"I'll lead," he said. "On entry, I'll clear left, you clear right. Cool?"

She nodded.

They exited the vehicle, and Jed led her up an exterior flight of metal stairs to the second-story rental unit. At this dark and early hour, the streets of Zona Colonial were quiet and deserted. Despite stepping with care along the edges of the stairs, their combined weight and movement made the metal staircase creak and groan as they ascended. Stealthy they were not. Jed scanned the wall of the roof deck overhead, looking for signs of a shooter in waiting, but he didn't see a suppressor or rifle muzzle hovering over the edge. He glanced over his shoulder at Gayle. On making eye contact, he pointed to his eyes with two fingers then at the rooftop. She nodded, and he saw her gaze tick up for a sweep of her own.

Weapon up, he advanced to the landing at the top of the staircase. It wasn't big enough for them both, so Gayle halted behind him near the top. In his peripheral vision, he saw that she was keeping an eye on their six and the rooftop.

There's a future Shepherd in this girl, he decided, seeing her move and think like an operator. He'd worked with many CIA officers over his years in the SEAL Teams, and outside of Ground Branch, he'd met only a few who took much of tactical value away from their training at the Farm.

Jed checked to see if the door was locked and shut as he'd left it. It was. Next, he looked for signs of forced entry—pry bar marks or damage to the lock or handle—but everything looked intact. Instead of providing renters with physical keys, the apartment owner had installed a digital lock with a keypad. Jed didn't like digital locks for civilian applications because if the property manager wasn't diligent about changing the code with each new renter, then previous tenants and anyone given access in the past could enter the apartment at will. He didn't know how many people in Santo Domingo knew the code to this place. On top of that, the keypad beeped with each button press.

Muscles primed and ready for action, he looked back at Gayle.

"Ready?" he mouthed silently.

She nodded.

He entered the code, and a split second after he heard the dead bolt shift, he depressed the handle and entered the apartment. Leading with his weapon in a two-handed grip, he swept left. Gayle's footsteps reverberated off the metal stairs and landing and then became barely audible thuds as she glided into the apartment behind him, clearing right. Their pistols were not equipped with optics, so he had no red dot for his eyes to follow as he scanned the darkened apartment for threats. But that was okay; he had hundreds of hours operating with iron sights and his aim was equally deadly.

His mind conducted a silent assessment as he finished his sweep left and swiveled back to center: *No one hiding behind the door . . . no human-shaped figures crouching behind furniture or corners . . . no movement other than Gayle.*

"Clear," he said, his voice a hard whisper.

"Clear," she echoed a second later.

Jed quickstepped back into the lead and advanced on the kitchenette, which was separated from the common room by a half wall.

If I was a bad guy, that's where I'd crouch in ambush.

Moving silently, he swept low around the corner and cleared the alcove. Finding it empty, he immediately advanced on his bedroom. Without looking back at her, he gestured with his left hand for Gayle to clear the apartment's lone bathroom. As he drifted past the bathroom's shut door on his left, he quickly cleared the cased opening on the right, which had steps to the roof deck.

Clear.

With the staircase dark and empty, he kept advancing.

Suddenly, however, a powerful, unsettled feeling told him the bedroom had been violated. He felt an almost magnetic pull from the room. Heart pounding and nerves on fire, he quickstepped through the open door—clearing left, then right. Finding no immediate threats, he advanced on the closet and pulled the left bifold door open and cleared it too. *Nobody hiding in here.* Next, he dropped to hands and knees and cleared under the bed, which was something he'd normally never do. But the nightmare was still haunting his subconscious, and he wouldn't feel satisfied until he was certain no monsters lurked under his bed. Literally.

But there was nothing there.

"Bathroom's clear," Gayle called from the hallway.

"Bedroom clear," he called back. "Last thing to check is the roof deck."

"Roger that," she said.

He moved out of the bedroom back into the hall where the staircase leading to the roof deck was located. "Ready?"

"Yep. Let's do it," she said.

"Same as last time; I'll clear left, you clear right."

"Roger that."

The door to the roof deck had an old-fashioned thumb-turn dead bolt lock and twist doorknob. Jed quietly turned the manual dead bolt—shifting it smoothly and without even a click. Then, he twisted the knob, pushed the door open, and burst out onto the roof deck in a low tactical crouch sitting over his pistol.

A startled pigeon cooed and took flight from where it had

been perched on the ledge above the door. His heart skipped a beat at the disturbance, but his brain quickly disregarded the bird and resumed scanning for actual threats. His iron sights glided over every piece of furniture and across every potential hiding place. In his peripheral vision, Gayle moved away from him, scanning the other half of the roof deck. Five seconds later, they had the roof cleared and could stand down.

"Well, that was fun," she said, disappearing her compact pistol into a small-of-the-back holster under her linen jacket.

"Always nice to *not* get shot when you come home from jail," he said, lowering his pistol but keeping it in his hand since he didn't have a holster.

"Pretty nice view from up here," she said, turning east to where a pink glow on the horizon hinted at what would undoubtedly be a beautiful ocean sunrise.

"Yeah, we can have breakfast up here if you like?"

"Sounds good."

"Let's head back down. I just want to give the place a quick once-over to make sure nobody's been snooping."

"No problem," she said and gestured toward the stairwell.

Taking the lead once again, he descended into the apartment and made his way into the bedroom, where he had the strongest feeling that something was amiss. The room had a dresser, but he typically lived out of his suitcase and didn't unpack into drawers unless he was staying somewhere for at least a week. In this case, his default laziness worked to his advantage. He walked straight to his suitcase, which he'd left unlocked but zipped closed on a luggage stand along the wall.

"Looks undisturbed," he murmured, noting that the zipper pulls were dangling in the exact location he'd left them. He unzipped the bag anyway and inventoried the contents inside.

"Anything missing or messed with?" Gayle asked.

"I don't think so," he said, finding everything seemingly in order and exactly as he remembered it.

"Hmm," he murmured. He turned to face Gayle, who was standing at the foot of the room's queen-sized bed.

"What?"

"I don't know," he said, scratching at his neck. "Nothing appears out of place, but I can't shake the feeling that someone's been in this room."

Gayle suddenly twitched.

"What?" he said.

She laughed at herself.

"Nothing," she said, running a hand through her hair. "Leaky roof, I guess." She stepped away, and he heard the *plink* sound of another drop hitting the floor.

But when Gayle looked down at her hand, her eyes widened in horror. She held her crimson-smeared fingertips up for him to see.

"Oh, God, Jed— It's blood . . ."

Jed followed Gayle's gaze to the ceiling. A white dove, the poor creature's wings fully extended, had been affixed there, belly side facing down, nailed to the beam with penny nails, its feet tied together. There was a large hole in its chest, like a stick or stake had been used to kill it. Jed watched in horror as another drop of blood formed along the edge of the gaping wound, broke loose, and dropped to the floor at his feet.

Plink.

CHAPTER THIRTEEN

AMOUR ET ESPOIR CHILDREN'S HOME

#4 RUE LAULIEN

PORT-DE-PAIX

HAITI

0730 HOURS LOCAL

Sani Marcelin looked at the door to her new bedroom at the sound of an enthusiastic woman coming down the hallway. "*Vini timoun yo! Se yon gwo jou!*" the young Australian woman named Harper called out, clapping her hands, her voice filled with real excitement. "Come on! We have a big day!" the teacher repeated in English.

Sani smiled just a bit. The foreign missionaries always worked hard to teach kids English at the schools run by charities and churches, believing—perhaps correctly—that a real future would require language skills other than Haitian Creole or Dominican Spanish at Mount Hope. Sani had only been here a couple of days and was grateful to have learned English at the last school because her English was *much* better than Miss Harper's Haitian Creole.

Sani took a long, deep breath, something Granmè had

taught her to do, and said a short prayer—something Granmè always *insisted* she do . . .

Lord God, keep these children safe and find love for their lives. Be with Granmè and help her know I'm all right. Keep me from being scared and show me what you want me to do . . .

A feeling of calm descended on her, just like in the car and again on the plane, and she almost smiled—almost, but not quite—and pulled on her maroon jumper. On the chest was the logo for the new children's home and school where she and the other kidnapped children—because no matter how nice this place was, that's what they were, kidnapped children—now found themselves. Their new home was called Amour et Espoir—Sani would have pronounced it *Lanmou ak Espwa* in the Haitian French-Creole. *Love and Hope.* She supposed whoever had the money to build the place had thought the fancy French sounded better.

"Are you doing okay today, Sani?" Harper asked, arriving at her door and placing her hands on her knees, leaning down, and smiling.

"Yes, Ms. Harper," she said.

Sani liked Harper. She had thought perhaps she might be someone she could tell about her grandmother—someone she could tell that a terrible mistake had been made. She wasn't sure why she'd not told someone already. Even with Sani's prayers, her grandmother must be worried sick by now, several days after they'd been taken. Granmè would be frantic, but then Sani supposed the staff at Saint Fleur must also be worried sick about Mary and Amede as well. They would surely be looking for them, but wherever they were now was very far from Pepillo Salcedo since they had taken an airplane to get here. Shouldn't she tell someone a mistake had been made?

They will never find you here.

That voice inside her head was never wrong, she knew. It was the same voice that had warned her not to tell the teachers and the staff of the new "Love and Hope" orphanage and school about her grandmother. She had learned early to never, ever ignore that voice.

Nine-year-old Emelin had talked on the plane about her mother. Sani had learned that, like her, Emelin was not an orphan—and Sani had not seen Emelin since they landed.

All the other kids at Amour et Espoir, however, were orphans. All of them had come here from somewhere else—from other orphanages all over the island comprised of Haiti and the Dominican Republic.

All of them.

How strange . . .

So, Sani had kept quiet. Everyone here must have believed she was an orphan too—after all, she rode the bus from Saint Fleur Orphanage to the Mount Hope School with everyone else each day, right? That must be why she had stayed together with the rest of the orphans while Emelin had gone somewhere else.

Sani desperately wanted to stay with Mary and Amede. Mistake or not, this place seemed beyond nice—nicer than anywhere she'd been in her life, and even Mary was beginning to come around. As for Amede, he had never been happier. It had taken only a day for him to settle in—and no wonder. Unlike the run-down home at Saint Fleur, Amour et Espoir was one of the most beautiful places any of them had ever seen. It was like something out of a dream. Instead of two huge dormitory-style rooms with cots which the kids at Saint Fleur had shared, here they all had their own rooms. Their *own* rooms—with no one else allowed in and their very own sink and mirror. Her hallway had five other rooms—six girls—and yet it still had two bathrooms, with private toilet stalls and even private showers, one for each girl. The walls were covered in bright fresh paint; there was a cafeteria with amazing food—as much as you could eat! When they had been told that they could go back for more, she had not believed the other kids at first—until Amede had gone back for seconds, and then thirds! He'd eaten so much his belly had ached all night, he told her. They had fresh vegetables, like Granmè grew in her garden, as well as meat, fish, chicken. They had french fries, something she'd had only twice in her life, every night if they wanted them. And dessert. Every night. Pie, cake, fresh cookies.

No wonder Amede was happy. Sani was happy for him—and for Mary, who still seemed scared but ate well and even smiled yesterday. It was like Saint Fleur was fading away for them. But it was different for Sani. Yes, Amede and Mary missed their friends from Saint Fleur, but that wasn't family. Granmè was Sani's real family—all that was left of it—and she needed to get back to her, no matter how beautiful it was here.

Sani was here by mistake, right? *But then what about Emelin? Was that also a mistake? And why is she not here with us?*

Sani knew something was very wrong, despite the soccer field and wonderful air-conditioned gym, the warm and friendly teachers, the new clothes, and the great food. Something was wrong. But, until the voices told her otherwise, there was little else she could do but wait.

So, wait she did.

She smiled at Harper, still at her door, waved to her, and picked up her brand-new toothbrush and bubble gum–flavored toothpaste.

"Okay, see you in a minute!" Harper said happily, then headed down the hall for the other girls.

But Sani felt something else from the young teacher also—a worry, maybe even a fear? Confusion, perhaps?

She had tried to reach out to Granmè in her mind, the way

they did sometimes, but it hadn't worked. Maybe it was because she was so far away. She had tried to reach out to Emelin too because she felt like the girl had the same gift—but again, nothing.

Sani had no problems hearing thoughts from Amede and Mary and the other kids, though. Maybe because they were all here and close by, or maybe for some other reason she couldn't figure out. And Harper too. Sani liked Harper. Harper's thoughts literally flooded to her. Sani knew Harper had a boyfriend named Kip back at university in Australia, and that she thought someday they might get married, and that she missed him terribly. She knew Harper wanted to do mission work—like she was doing now, Sani guessed—but only if she and Kip could be together next time.

And she knew that Harper was deadly afraid of something, but Sani just couldn't figure out what. How strange to be so afraid and have no idea why or of what.

"Come on, Sani," Harper said, back at her door. "Special day."

"Coming," Sani said, wondering just what Amour et Espoir had in store for them.

The cafeteria buzzed with excitement, but no one seemed to know what the exciting thing was, at least not from the cloud of thoughts Sani waded through. She sensed that the exciting thing might be a visit—a visit from someone very special—but had no idea who or why. She ate pancakes, freshly made, with strawberries and whipped cream on top. She'd had whipped cream for the first time yesterday and had instantly decided that whipped cream was the very best food on all of the earth. She was sipping her apple juice when Mary came and sat beside her.

"*Buenos días*, Sani," Mary said and smiled at her—Mary's second smile in as many days.

"*Bonjou*, Mary," she said, sliding over to allow her more room. She smiled at Amede too, who was approaching with a tray literally packed with food. "How about we speak in English? Would you like that?"

Pepillo Salcedo was only a few miles from Sani's home in Fort Liberté, but it was across a border that separated not only countries but cultures and languages. Other than poverty, Dominican Republic and Haiti had little in common—except perhaps a love of family and faith in God. But she supposed maybe that was everywhere in the world, right? She imagined the dark magic of Voudou was something else the Dominican Republic and Haiti shared, but her granmè had once told her they called it something different in the DR—21 Divisions, or something like that.

"Okay," Mary said. "How are you, Sani?"

Sani's smile broadened. Sani had decided not to call her "Little Mary" here like they did back home. The fear driving her into some weird state where she acted almost like a toddler had begun to fade, but was not gone entirely, Sani could see. Sani believed she might be some really important lifeline for Mary and had prayed hard for her friend. It seemed to be working—Mary smiled back as she began to eat her own stack of pancakes and cream.

"I love it here," Amede said, sliding into the seat across from them. "Look at all of this wonderful food, Sani!"

Sani did look, then laughed.

"Don't you miss your friends?" Mary said, her voice dropping to a whisper and her eyes darting around to see who might be listening. "And don't you wonder why we're here?"

Amede shrugged and began shoveling food into his mouth.

"Yeah, I miss my friends, but I'm making new friends in class and even in my hall," he said. "And this place is amazing, isn't it? It's so clean and so big and there is so much for us here." Amede swallowed the bite that he chewed while talking, then took a long slug of apple juice. "They keep saying that they are preparing for our future, Mary. What future do you think we had at Saint Fleur or in Pepillo Salcedo? I think God rescued us. I think He saved us and brought us here."

Was that possible, Sani wondered? Was this place God's plan for her?

"I don't know, Amede," Mary said, her face clouding. "I . . . I feel something here. Something not right. It scares me . . ."

Sani looked at her friend, her eyes widening. Did Mary have the same intuitions she did? Did she hear thoughts too?

"Don't be afraid, Mary," Amede said, reaching out to take the girl's hand. He wanted to be a protector; Sani could tell from the feelings emanating from him. "And we're here together. We can keep each other safe. This place will be wonderful, you'll see."

Sani pursed her lips but nodded. Certainly she *wanted* that to be true.

"Children, good morning!"

Sani looked to the front of the room where an older woman stood, with Harper and several other teachers beside her. She'd seen the woman before—the first day they'd come, she thought. Harper was smiling too, but her face seemed different from earlier that morning—worried about something, maybe.

"Good morning!" the children of the room replied with a loud, collective voice.

"As most of you, except perhaps our newest family members, know—I am Ms. Wilshire, the head of this school. This morning, before we have chapel and then begin classes, we have a special treat," the woman said, clapping her hands together. "As you know, the wonderful staff of teachers and caregivers at Amour et Espoir have come to help you find a better life, a brighter future, and overall happiness. The staff are all so grateful to be here and to have such a beautiful home and school for you kids. All that we have to give you, all that we want to share with you—all of this—is possible only because of our special guest. Today, we get to say *hello* and *thank you* to Madame Athaliah."

The staff around Ms. Wilshire clapped. Unsure what else to do, the kids in the room clapped and cheered as well—including Sani, Mary, and of course Amede, who added a big "Whoop!" to his applause.

I don't like Ms. Athaliah. I don't know why, but she terrifies me . . .

The voice was Ms. Harper's, inside Sani's head.

Then another voice came to her, and she remembered where she'd heard that name before. They'd been on the plane just a few days ago, and the man had said that Manbo Athaliah would be their new mother. She'd not heard the name again since they arrived, but the memory of what nine-year-old Emelin had said on the plane came to her now.

I know things too . . . That man is a liar, and I know, somehow, that this Manbo Athaliah is something very, very bad.

Ms. Wilshire was speaking about a foundation that had money to care for them and give them a future, but Sani could barely hear her over a familiar voice in her head.

"She's coming. She's gone from here so she can't hide my thoughts now, but she might be quieting mine. I've been looking for you, Sani. Can you hear me?"

"Yes. Yes, I hear you!" Sani thought, *"Is that you, Emelin? I've been looking for you too. Are you safe? Are you . . ."*

"We only have a moment, Sani. She will hear you so don't use your thoughts when she comes in the room. I am at her house—her palace or whatever—and when she's near you she can—"

The voice in her head cut off like a phone suddenly hung up.

She looked up and saw a woman who must be Madame Athaliah.

The woman walked in with the style and grace of royalty—or

a runway model, maybe. Sani had seen videos of the supermodel Aube Jolicoeur on Granmè's phone. She was from Haiti, and Granmè showed her pictures because she wanted Sani to know anything was possible. This woman moved just like that, like Aube Jolicoeur: beauty and grace, but especially confidence.

And power . . .

Sani shushed the familiar voice in her head and stared at the woman—as the whole room fell silent. Her face with the high, chiseled cheekbones and full lips set in creamy, cocoa-colored skin, the perfect hair falling to her shoulders, the beautiful silk suit, the way she stood, her smile, and most especially her pale, penetrating blue eyes—everything about Madame Athaliah was mesmerizing.

Sani reminded herself to breathe.

There is no way this beautiful woman is bad. She is using her wealth to care for children . . .

"*Bonjou—Buenos días*—Good morning, my lovely, wonderful children," the woman said, her voice wrapping around the room like a warm blanket on a cool, stormy evening. "It is such an amazing and exciting pleasure for me to see all of you." She clasped her hands in front of her, clearly delighted to see them.

"Good morning, Madame Athaliah," Ms. Wilshire said, apparently just as mesmerized as the children.

Beside her, the younger Ms. Harper stared at her feet.

"Good morning, Madame Athaliah," the children recited in reply, Sani included. Amede positively glowed with excitement. Mary, however, took Sani's hand and squeezed it.

"I know that change is hard, children," Madame Athaliah continued, her voice soft and compassionate. "I know the way in which many of you came here was difficult and, at times, scary. I am so sorry for that, that it was confusing, but all of it was done only for your safety—for your protection—because you are the most valuable things in the world to me. So, please know you are here, in this wonderful place we have built for you, because we love you so much. *I* love you so much, children. You are here so that we can give you the very best—the best clothes, the best food, the best home, the best playthings, and with the help of our church partners, the very best education. Why? Because, as I have said, I love you as my very own children. And when a mama loves her children, she wants the very best for them, of course! What I want to give you more than anything—other than the love I give so freely—is a future. A bright future of happiness, of security, of love, and even of wealth. It is my dream for each and every one of you. We will teach you many things, and some of them may seem strange, but they are the skills that will give you power—power to control your future."

She raised her hands over her head. Beside her, Ms. Wilshire clapped her hands together like a child just meeting Santa Claus.

Ms. Harper still stared at the ground, hands behind her back.

What does she know about Madame Athaliah that Ms. Wilshire doesn't?

"Today is a celebration," Madame Athaliah continued. "We have new members in our growing family, which means I have new children to love and to grow and to care for. Those of you who have been here for a time I have met with already, and I hope to see you and hug you today. But I want to be sure that our new brothers and sisters get special attention, as you did when you arrived. So, first, can we give a big clap for the seven new children who joined us the last few days?"

The room exploded with applause, the children and adults all rising to their feet. Sani couldn't help but feel infected by the excitement—and happiness—in the room. She got to her own feet, pulling Mary up with her. Sani clapped, and her smile grew bigger. She felt Mary's nervous eyes on her and turned to the smaller but slightly older girl.

"It's okay, Mary," she said.

A strange, almost hypnotic peace suddenly washed over her.

"I think it's really going to be okay."

A faraway voice whispered urgently that this wasn't true at all, but Sani had trouble listening . . .

"Are you sure?" Mary said, but she also began to smile and then to clap.

Sani nodded.

"We're where God wants us to be," Amede concluded, clapping loudest of all.

Moments later, the applause died down as Madame Athaliah raised a hand.

"Such a lovely family we have here at Amour et Espoir," she said. "Such wonderful children here and in our other homes as well. You are all truly a blessing on me, and I will make sure you are blessed as well."

The adults sat, followed by the children. Ms. Wilshire and the handful of teachers around her remained standing behind Madame Athaliah.

Manbo Athaliah, Sani's voice reminded her, using the Voudou title for a high priestess. But it didn't seem right, not in this moment, for some reason. She found herself still smiling, the little voice inside her fading to background noise.

"Manbo Athaliah is very, very bad," the voice shouted at her from the distance, this time in Emelin's voice, but Sani barely heard.

"Now, enjoy your breakfast," Madame Athaliah said, smiling and waving like a celebrity. Sani supposed, to the people gathered in this room at least, she was the most important celebrity in the world. "Please enjoy your meal. I will make an effort to say hello to as many of you as I can. But first, it is time for me to meet our newest family members."

Soon everyone was eating again. Sani could see Ms. Wilshire grinning broadly beside Madame Athaliah, and she noticed that Ms. Harper was still staring at her hands.

"Let's begin with"—Ms. Wilshire turned, her eyes looking right at Sani—"Sani Marcelin, our very special new child from Pepillo Salcedo!"

Everyone gave a few claps, but the tide had turned in favor of breakfast. Sani rose, almost against her will, or like she was outside of herself and just watching. She walked to the front of the room where Madame Athaliah held out a hand to her. Sani took it, feeling a strange and hypnotic jolt at the touch.

Tell her nothing. Don't let her know about your granmè. And keep your mind closed like Granmè taught you . . .

Sani followed Madame Athaliah toward a door to a small, more private office that sat behind where Athaliah had addressed the children. She could feel Ms. Harper's eyes on her as she followed Manbo Athaliah inside, then she felt an overpowering fear struggling for control of her against a strange sense of peace and contentment growing inside her at the touch of Madame Athaliah's hand.

She couldn't help but smile, for some reason.

"Please have a seat," Madame Athaliah said, gesturing to a comfortable leather chair in front of a small desk. The lovely, stylish woman poured two cups of tea and slid one to Sani.

"Sugar, Sani?" she asked.

"Yes, please," Sani answered, feeling herself slipping into an almost trancelike contentment. But as the smiling woman dropped two sugar cubes in her cup, the other childlike voice in her head shouted for attention.

"Stop, Sani!" Emelin's voice hollered inside her head. *"Don't let her in. She will . . ."*

In that moment, Sani saw a flicker of fire—a literal orange

flame—flash in Manbo Athaliah's eyes and at once felt the woman worming into her head, like a snake slithering under the covers of her bed. The childlike voice she knew to be Emelin was cut off like a dropped phone call.

Instantly, she built the wall around her mind, just like Granmè had taught her, as she took a sip of tea with a shaking hand.

Madame Athaliah leaned back in her chair, pursing her lips.

"Is everything okay, Sani?" she asked, as those penetrating eyes bored through her.

"Oh, yes, ma'am," she answered, forcing a smile. "I love it here."

There was a long pause as the woman stared at her. Then she smiled, as if all was resolved.

"Let me tell you about my vision for Haiti, Sani," she said. "And the amazing part you and my other children can play in it."

CHAPTER FOURTEEN

JED'S VACATION VRBO

SANTO DOMINGO, DOMINICAN REPUBLIC

Jed clenched his jaw, more in anger than disgust, at the message of a white dove—a symbol of peace, a symbol of the Holy Spirit—being killed and nailed to the ceiling of his apartment.

The white dove had descended from heaven to rest on Jesus when he was baptized by John. And now this one had been executed and nailed, crucifixion-style, to the ceiling. There was no missing the symbolism—and no missing the message, presumably from the Dark Ones: Stay away. His mind went back to the eerie shop that he'd seen on his walk during his first day in Santo Domingo; the shop literally dripped with Voodoo creepiness, not far from where they were now.

"Yeessh," Gayle said with shudder. She stepped back to avoid being dripped on again. Jed imagined her linen suit was probably ruined from the few bloody drops that already stained it.

Jed frowned. "I knew it. I knew it."

"Knew what?"

"That she came here last night."

"Who came here?" Gayle said, shifting her gaze from Jed back up to the bird.

"The woman I fought in the park."

"The police said you attacked a man in the park. Nobody said anything about you fighting a woman."

"That's because she ran away," he said. "Those cops only saw what she wanted them to see."

"In that case, do you mind reading *me* in on the whole truth?" she said.

After a heavy exhale, Jed recounted everything that had happened to him since his arrival, including the details of his altercation with the woman he'd fought by the fountain and the bizarre nightmare he'd had while in jail.

"She had the . . . special fighting abilities, like you saw when you worked with us before," he said.

"Good Lord, Jed," she said when he'd finished. "That's all beyond disturbing. And a helluva lot more than just wrong place at the wrong time."

"Yeah."

"And she had the . . . glow in her eyes?"

"I think so. It happened pretty fast. And every Dark One I've ever faced has always had the glow in their eyes—that telltale ring of fire around the iris always gives them away. Regardless, her speed, strength, and agility all scream Dark One. And now this," he said, looking up at the dove. "She's clearly sending me a message."

"How do you think she got up there?" Gayle said. "That ceiling's got to be twelve feet at least."

"Who knows," Jed said, shaking his head. "Maybe she levitated. The things I've seen them do would blow your—"

"Jed, look out!" Gayle screamed.

His gaze followed hers and he saw movement by his left foot. An enormous crimson snake, as thick as his forearm, slithered across the bedroom floor. Jed instinctively leaped onto the bed as it passed by his boot.

"Where the hell did *that* come from?" he asked, looking from the snake to Gayle, who had joined him on the bed, leaping over the footboard like a high jumper.

"From under the bed, I think," she said and clutched his arm. They stared at each other for a moment and then both started laughing.

"If my team saw me like this," he said, "I would never hear the end of it."

"Don't worry, your secret is safe with me," she said. "I'm terrified of snakes."

"They've never bothered me before, but that thing definitely took me by surprise." He leveled his pistol at it.

"Don't," she said, grabbing his wrist. "That snake is not venomous."

"How do you know?" he said, lowering the pistol.

"The CIA travel advisory brief. There are no poisonous snakes here. That's a red mountain boa. It's harmless to people."

"It doesn't look harmless—it looks like how the devil would appear."

"I know, but I promise it can't hurt us," she said. "Whoever put it here is just trying to scare us."

"For someone who is terrified of snakes, you sure are concerned about this one's well-being," he said, stepping off the bed.

As if on cue, the snake looked at them, then stopped slithering and coiled its body into a defensive mound.

"You have to admit, it's striking and kind of beautiful in its own way."

Jed walked to the corner where a woven wicker laundry

hamper sat. He picked it up, turned it upside down, and used it to trap the boa. Gayle watched, hands clasped in front of her.

"Got him," Jed declared victoriously. Gayle slowly walked over to him, her eyes on the hamper. When she got next to him, she grabbed his arm again, and Jed savored the touch. Then, suddenly, the snake moved inside, causing the hamper to shift a few inches, and Gayle squeezed tighter as she jumped. Jed laughed, then grabbed his suitcase and set it on top of the basket to add some weight.

"There," he said definitively. "He ain't getting out now."

"Should I call animal control?"

"Assuming they even have that here . . ."

He looked up again at the miserable creature on the ceiling. "What about the dove?"

"You should probably take it down," she said. "I wonder if there's a ladder around?"

"I'll use the dresser," he said and dragged it away from the wall. He set his SFX9 down, stepped up on the bed frame, then stepped from there onto the top of the dresser. He stretched his long arms and was just able to reach the dove, despite the high ceiling. Taking care, he pulled the penny nails from the ceiling and out of the dead bird's wings. Cupping it in one hand, he dropped back to the floor. Jed couldn't help but marvel at how light and insubstantial it was.

So delicate, he thought, staring down at it in his open palm. The bird's head was lolled to one side, the eyes glazed over and dry, its beak hanging open. Jed felt warm blood on his hand. The stake used to kill it must have passed all the way through the pitiful thing.

An upwelling of pity for the little creature blossomed in his chest and spread like electricity to his hands. As he cradled the dead bird, he felt sad that it had died because of him. If he could undo its suffering, somehow give it back its—

The dove's feet twitched, and he almost dropped it.

"Whoa, did it just move?" Gayle said, flinching away from Jed.

"Yeah," he said, flabbergasted.

He felt an invisible tug in his chest from the little creature. Then its wings fluttered.

"It's not dead," Gayle said, her eyes going wide.

"I don't understand," he said. "It was cold . . ."

"Oh my God, Jed, look at the wound on the chest. It's closing."

The dove's eyes blinked clear, and it tried to shift its feet. Gayle rushed to Jed's side and, with deft fingers, worked to untwist the strand of metal wire binding the bird's feet. The instant she got the wire undone, the dove flipped over in Jed's palm, glanced up at him, and then spread its wings, which, like the chest, now showed no visible wounds, and took flight. The dove darted back and forth a moment, then settled into a graceful glide, narrowly avoiding the walls and ceiling as it circled and looked for an exit.

Jed darted to the bedroom's only window and raised the bottom pane. With a flurry of wing strokes and feathers, the little white bird made for the opening and disappeared outside.

Mouths open, Jed and Gayle both turned and looked at each other.

"What just happened?" Gayle asked slowly.

"I don't know," he said.

"Did you do that?"

"Do what?"

"That!" she said, shaking her head in disbelief. "Did you somehow . . ."

"I . . . I don't think so," he said, afraid to contemplate the possibility that he'd—what?

No way. Impossible.

"Jed?"

"Yeah?"

"Should we clear out of here? Take your stuff and find a safe place? If someone is sending you a warning . . ."

He thought about that a moment. Yes, they were sending a warning. But whoever was behind this clearly didn't want to raise attention, or they would have ambushed him as he came to the Vrbo instead of nailing a bird to his ceiling. And Jed wasn't one to back away from a threat.

"I think we're safe for now," he concluded. "Otherwise, they would have sent a bullet instead of a bird."

Gayle let out a long, shuddering sigh and took his hand.

"Can we agree to not talk about this, or the snake, over breakfast?" she said.

"Mm-hmm," he said, nodding vigorously.

He thought again about the dead bird that had come to life in his hand. *Did I do that?* He had seen Ben do miraculous things to heal teammates with a touch, but he'd never contemplated having such a gift himself.

Gayle tugged at his hand, leading him through the bedroom door toward the kitchen. "You promised me coffee, and I want it. Right now. Let's go. Coffee before I pass out."

The apartment had a K-cup machine, but Jed didn't care for coffee made that way. Even though it took a little longer, he brewed them each a fresh cup using the moka pot he traveled with. He then sweetened both coffees with cane sugar and added a splash of cream. While he made coffee, she washed and cut fruit. They both performed their respective tasks in silence and finished at the same time. They loaded a serving tray with two fruit medleys, two cups of hot steaming coffee, silverware, and napkins.

"Let's go watch the sunrise," Gayle said with a smile.

Jed carried the tray and followed her up the stairs to the roof deck and the four-seat outdoor dining table. They angled their chairs to watch the sunrise and enjoyed their coffee and fruit breakfast in relative silence. As he sipped from his mug, he looked at Gayle, her face bright in the morning sun and beautiful beyond words in that moment. She stared off into the distance, deep in thought, then a subtle smile crossed her lips, and she took a sip from her own mug. Jed watched, mesmerized, and realized how often he'd thought of her since they'd last been together.

And that she was even more striking than he remembered.

As if suddenly back from wherever she had gone in her mind, she turned to him and held his eyes a moment. Then she broke the gaze, and he thought she might have blushed.

"I didn't say we couldn't talk," Gayle said and looked into her mug of coffee. "Just that we couldn't talk about the bird or the snake."

He chuckled. "I'm normally not so chatty," he said. "You happened to catch me in a weird mood earlier."

"Ah, I see," she said. "So back to brooding?"

"No, I'm not brooding. Just still processing."

"Well, while you've been processing, I've been thinking about that woman you fought, and the bird, and the snake, and your dream, and the kidnapping you foiled, and the mother of the missing girl outside the church with the sign. They must all be related, right?"

"I think that's a safe bet."

She exhaled through pursed lips. "This is going to sound weird, but weird has pretty much been the vibe since I bailed you out of jail, so hear me out."

"Sure."

"Voodoo."

"Voodoo?"

"Yeah, Voodoo. It was a big part of the country brief I received before coming here. Then seeing that bird nailed to the ceiling like that . . . I don't know, it just makes me think about Voodoo. What do you know about Voodoo?"

He considered the question. "I know it's a *thing* in Haiti, but that's about it. There must be something like Voodoo here in DR as well. I saw a shop when I got here. It had, like, a little altar of candles in bottles beside what looked like a human skull. There was a dove—I don't know if it was real or fake—hanging upside down over the skull and a snake slithering around. Inside the shop, through the window at least, it reminded me of the voodoo shops in New Orleans. It was super creepy. Do you know much about whether there is Voodoo here in the Dominican, like in Haiti?"

"Not beyond my brief," she said. "In the DR they call it *Las 21 Divisiones.*"

"Wait—21?" His mind went again to the strange shop he'd seen.

"Yeah. Snakes, doves crucified to ceilings, voodoo shops . . ." She looked at him again. "My gut tells me that Dominican Voodoo is connected to this case in some way, if only that the players here seem to have a connection to it. Or maybe they're just using it to frighten you—us—but either way, I think we both need to become quick studies on the topic if we're going to figure out what in the heck is going on down here."

A tentative grin spread across Jed's face. "You said *we*. You also said *case*. Does that mean we are officially working together now on this?"

"Yes, Jed. We are officially working together. I mean, I was sent to get you out of jail, obviously, but if your head shed wants you to work this thing . . ."

Jed wasn't clear just what Ben and the head shed wanted to do, so he decided not to broach that with Gayle just yet. But he felt surer than ever that he needed to pursue this. Would Ben trust that instinct? He thought so but didn't know yet.

"Do I have to wear a linen suit too?"

She gave his arm a smack. "I can already see you're going to be a very annoying partner."

"Ben told me we have two assets in country, apparently," he said, getting back to business. "I think it's time we made contact with them. I'm sure they'll know about gang activity, other bad players, and probably even local voodoo practices and whether those could be tied to the kidnappings. For sure they'll know something about what kind of presence the Dark Ones have on the island. Because to me, this is starting to feel like more than just local crime."

"Good idea," she said, spearing the last piece of mango on her plate with her fork. "If this is the work of these Dark Ones, it'll still be so much better to have someone with real local knowledge to fill in the gaps, rather than the two of us spending all day on Wikipedia comparing notes."

"I'll give it an hour, then reach out and set up a meeting," he said, checking his watch. "It's still early."

"Agreed, but when you do, you might see if your contact can do anything about the six-foot-long boa in your bedroom."

CHAPTER FIFTEEN

THE WHITE ROOM

ST. GEORGE'S ACADEMY

1040 HOURS LOCAL

Sarah Beth stirred gently on the white half-circle couch, fully aware she was dreaming. Her first thought was how nice it was to have an *actual* dream instead of the fragmented and schizophrenic parade of voices and faces that had bombarded her dreams the last few weeks. Tonight, she saw an actual dreamscape—a lovely beach with a gentle surf—and that was comforting.

Her second thought wasn't a thought at all, but a voice: an unfamiliar, childlike voice, telling her to pay attention. She felt her heart rate pick up because the voice could only mean one thing—this wasn't a dream at all.

It was some sort of vision.

She swallowed, aware in a distant, far-off way of the honors geography book page that was stuck to her cheek. She wondered whether this voice was an ally or some new enemy—some new Victor, even—disguised by the disarming voice of a child.

She shooed the thought away. It didn't matter. She was safe here.

Pay attention . . .

She walked the beach, the sand on her feet changing suddenly from warm to cool just as the scene turned suddenly from day to night. She shivered and wondered if this was just the real world sneaking in. Sometimes she got cold when the AC turned on in the White Room because there was a vent right over her favorite white couch . . .

Pay attention . . .

She shook off the thought.

She returned to walking the beach, looking for what she was supposed to see here. The beach was quiet, the surf gentle, a lovely moon reflecting on the sea. She glanced left, inland toward what looked like a hotel, where people milled about or sat by a pool with drinks, unaware of whatever was about to happen on the beach—something bad, her gut told her.

She stepped on something and looked down to see a child's plastic shovel next to a red bucket. In the moonlight, beside the shovel, she saw something else: a child's flip-flop sitting in a puddle of dark crimson in the sand. Beside that, she found part of a woman's hand, severed somehow at the wrist, rings still on two of the fingers.

"I think I want to wake up . . ." Sarah Beth heard herself say.

"One moment more. She can't see you, I think."

"You *think*?"

There were two palm trees close to one another, one with a thicker trunk that bent nearly horizontal before stretching upward. As the water just beyond the break began to churn with something—something living, she thought, like a shark—Sarah Beth scurried behind the thicker of the two palm trees, in case the voice was wrong and whatever was coming *could* see her. She remembered the time she had projected herself to the Ethiopian College at the Vatican for the first time. No one could see her then, right?

She looked up and found the beach was no longer empty.

Now dozens—maybe even a hundred—children had appeared. They laughed and chatted with one another, some in Spanish, she thought, and others in a singsong language she couldn't place. They seemed happy, but she wondered why they were all out here on the beach with no parents anywhere to be seen.

The water churned faster now, bubbles rising from somewhere deep below.

She watched as a giant serpent, a snakelike creature with a strangely human—almost feminine—face, slithered up onto the beach. Inside the strange mouth, rows and rows of razor-sharp teeth glistened in the moonlight. The creature towered over the children—at least thirty feet high, Sarah Beth guessed—and waited.

She turned to look at the children, who now stood frozen, staring at the beast, their mouths open and eyes wide. Then, as she watched, dozens and dozens of the children morphed impossibly from children into slithering, smaller versions of the creature at the water's edge—like a brood of serpents responding to the bidding of their mother. They slinked across the sand, joining the creature, who smiled with her mouth full of teeth.

The remaining children stood on the beach in terror. One girl, hands on her hips, stared defiantly at the beast and shook her head. In a flash, the serpent struck—like a rattlesnake attacking its prey—snatching two of the remaining children and swallowing them whole. The other kids immediately screamed and began running away from the water. A few turned into serpents and slithered to join the others, forming a living, squirming nest at the base of the beast, joining her as she attacked and ate the others, one by one, until only a single child remained. Sarah Beth looked at the horrible sight, the blood of children dripping from the oddly human mouth and onto the scaly serpent body as baby snakes crawled over her back and others lapped with forked tongues the puddle of blood in the sand.

The lone remaining girl stood and faced the beast, hands still on her hips, her dark face frightened but still defiant. Her braids were pulled back into a single ponytail, secured together with a red ribbon above a jumper of some sort—like elementary-aged kids wear at a private school.

"Help her if you can. Please . . ."

The voice in Sarah Beth's head was not the girl on the beach, she realized. That girl didn't seem to have noticed her standing behind the tree, invisible perhaps to everyone in the dream.

And then the serpent struck a final time, crushing its teeth-filled jaws onto the girl's body, biting her in half and swallowing her head and shoulders, dropping the rest to the sand in a bloody heap.

"She can't do it alone . . ."

Sarah jerked awake, sitting up on the couch and knocking her geography textbook and binder onto the floor.

"Are you okay?"

She looked over to see Corbin seated in one of the two oversized chairs flanking a small table, her own book open in her lap.

Sarah Beth nodded and bent to collect her book and the pages that had spilled from her binder.

"Bad dream?" Corbin asked.

She nodded again. Corbin closed her book and rose, joining Sarah Beth on the couch.

"The weird one again—the chaos dream, I think you said you call it?"

"Not this time," she said. She felt her breathing finally begin to slow, tucked a loose strand of hair behind her ear, and leaned back on the couch. She let out a raspy sigh and rubbed her face.

"Wow," Corbin said. "Looks like more of a nightmare. Want to talk about it?"

"Yeah," Sarah Beth said. "I think it might be important."

Sarah Beth described the dream as best she could, aware that—like always—it was hard to capture the visceral terror and emotions she'd experienced in her description. When she was done, she looked over at Corbin. "Ever have a dream like that?"

Corbin pursed her lips, her face thoughtful and her mind turning over the details of what Sarah Beth had shared.

"Not exactly, but I get it," she said. "Sarah Beth, I think we should tell Pastor Dee about this one, okay? It sounds important."

"I agree," Sarah Beth said. Her skin still crawled as the remnants of the nightmare slowly faded. "What do you think it means?"

"I have absolutely no idea," Corbin said, patting her leg and giving her a soft smile. "But I've learned not to dismiss much when it comes to you, sister."

Sarah Beth let out a small barking laugh. "Yeah, I guess."

"Want to go this afternoon?" Corbin asked.

Sarah Beth shook her head. "No," she said. "I think I should tell her now. It just felt so—I don't know—urgent."

"Do you want me to go with you?"

She gave her friend and mentor a sheepish grin. "Do you mind? I know you have an exam."

Corbin waved her hand as if shooing something away. "Don't be silly. We're a team. I'm pretty much ready for the British literature exam anyway." Corbin rose and held out her hand. "Did you recognize the girl's voice that spoke to you?" she asked as Sarah Beth rose beside her. "Do you know her?"

Sarah Beth shook her head. "No," she said. "But she seemed to know me."

Corbin nodded. "Come on. We'll go tell Pastor Dee and then get you back to cram some more for geography."

"Thanks, Corbin," Sarah Beth said. Now that the dream was fading, she was starting to feel a little silly. People with gifts still had regular old nightmares sometimes, right? Maybe that was all this was.

She followed Corbin toward the elevator door, leaving her books on the couch.

Team before self. Wasn't that what Uncle Jed liked to say? Pastor Dee would know what to do about the dream, and then Sarah Beth could concentrate better on her exam. Once that was over, she would finally be free to give all her attention to whatever voice was calling to her for help.

That was her job, after all, as a Watcher, right?

CHAPTER SIXTEEN

VRBO RENTAL
ZONA COLONIAL
SANTO DOMINGO, DOMINICAN REPUBLIC
0843 HOURS LOCAL

Jed rose quickly to his feet from beside Gayle at the sound of the knock, relieved that the Shepherd assets Ben had shared with him were finally arriving. The waiting had been killing him, even if only a few hours had passed since breakfast with Gayle. He hustled to the door and opened it.

He was surprised to find an unassuming middle-aged couple waiting on the landing.

"Marcello?" he said, focusing his attention on the balding, plump man who stood in his doorway, nearly a full foot shorter than Jed.

"*Buenos días*, Jed," the man said and flashed Jed a broad, genuine smile, showing off a mouth full of perfectly straight white teeth. "I am Marcello, and this is my wife, Kaprica."

Jed's face must have betrayed him as he summoned a smile

for the pretty, thin woman, who smiled at him from beside her husband.

"You were expecting a pair of warriors like yourself, *mais non*?" Kaprica asked. Her voice had a singsong quality and a strong French-Creole accent. Jed pegged Marcello as Dominican, and he guessed Kaprica might be Haitian.

"I'm not sure what I expected," he answered honestly. "My chain of command gave me very little information other than that you were married. But I want to thank you for coming on such short notice," Jed said, realizing as soon as he said it how *military* that sounded. He offered a self-deprecating smile in lieu of an apology and gestured for the couple to enter the apartment.

Gayle stood and, with a relaxed air, walked up to greet the newcomers. "Hello, my name is Gayle," she said. "I'm a friend of Jed's who works with the State Department."

"Very nice to meet you, Gayle," Kaprica said, stepping up to shake Gayle's hand first. The Haitian woman was as tall as her husband but lithe and delicate. She moved with a dancer's grace. Her flawless, wrinkle-free complexion looked like that of a twenty-year-old, but her ebony-colored hair was streaked with dramatic swaths of silver.

"Can I get either of you something to drink?" Jed asked, vectoring toward the kitchen in anticipation. "Coffee, juice, water?"

"We've both had our morning coffee," Kaprica said. "Water would be lovely."

The four of them took seats in the main room after Jed retrieved bottled waters from the fridge. The couple sat on the sofa while Jed and Gayle each took a chair on either side.

"It is okay, you can ask the question on your mind," Kaprica said to Jed.

Jed felt his cheeks get warm, but clearly the woman wouldn't let it go. He was curious, so he just spit it out. "Are you Shepherds or . . . local agents?"

"Shepherds come in many shapes and sizes, young man," she said. "We are not Navy SEALs, but we serve on the same battlefield. We have a flock to protect, the same as you."

"Don't mind her," Marcello said, speaking up for the first time since they entered. "She likes to play games."

Staring at his houseguests, Jed had an epiphany. His operator pedigree, his time in Jericho Basic, and the very tactical approach to how Trinity addressed the Dark Ones in the world had cemented in his mind certain notions about what defined a "Shepherd" and what didn't. His default paradigm was that Shepherds were operators because he was an operator. The team TSLs—pastors like David who provided spiritual guidance and support—were noncombatants, but they were still Shepherds. The other support staff—logistics, medical, cyber, intelligence, et cetera—at Trinity Loop earned the title of Shepherd, and two-thirds of them never left campus. Marcello and Kaprica certainly viewed themselves as Shepherds, and he reckoned they'd been in the business of keeping evil at bay since he was a little boy.

"I apologize if I offended you," Jed said with a deferential nod. "I'm relatively new to the organization and a door kicker at heart."

"No apologies necessary," Marcello said quickly, beating his wife to the punch. "We have witnessed tremendous change in the North American operation over the past decade. Under Ben's leadership, Trinity has become more organized, responsive, and tactical. These are wonderful things—"

"—but having a community presence is vitally important," Kaprica said, stepping in. "We have lived here our entire lives. We know the people, the culture, and the history. We know the cracks the Dark Ones try to exploit. We have our fingers on the pulse of the island's beating heart. As a former missionary, I'm sure Gayle understands the importance of this."

Jed glanced at Gayle who, to her credit, did not flinch at the comment. Either Kaprica had done her homework before this meeting or she had gifting for reading people. Jed hoped for the latter, because the former would mean that this couple had been surveilling them.

"I agree," Gayle said simply. "Which is why we're so grateful to have the two of you to call upon as local partners."

This answer seemed to please Kaprica. She smiled broadly and rested her hand on her husband's knee. Jed watched Marcello move his hand on top of hers and their fingers intertwine. The bond between this couple—their love, devotion, and trust—radiated from them in a way he could almost feel.

I wonder if I'll ever have that with someone.

"Jed, we are a bit short on time because we have another obligation in Dajabón this afternoon, which means a long drive ahead of us," Marcello said. "Maybe you can tell us how we can help?"

Jed nodded and recounted all the events of the past twenty-four hours—from the woman in the rain with the missing daughter to the attempted kidnapping he had thwarted and the battle with the mysterious woman. He ended with his arrest for the death of the man killed by the woman he believed might be a Dark One, and then the bizarre discovery of the sacrificial dove and the snake in his bedroom.

When he finished, the couple shared a knowing look.

"It would seem, through no fault of your own," Kaprica said, "that you have sailed your ship into a tempest while trying to navigate unfamiliar waters."

"I'd say so," Jed said with a chuckle. "Gayle and I were wondering if we might have crossed paths with a local Voodoo cult tied to the Dark Ones."

"Here it is called *Las 21 Divisiones*, and in Haiti it is pronounced *Voudou*. Haitian culture and Voudou religion are not something I can explain to you in twenty minutes over tea and biscuits—or, in our case, over a glass of water—but it is important for you to gain context. Will you indulge me a brief history lesson?" Kaprica said.

"Yes, of course," Jed said, nodding.

"*C'est bon*," she said and sat up a little straighter. "We have a saying in Haiti: eighty-five percent of the people are Catholic, fifteen percent are Protestant, and one hundred percent are Voudou. I tell you this joke because this is something that foreigners, especially Americans, need to understand about Haiti: Voudou is not a cult practiced by a small group of uneducated fanatics at the fringe of society. *Non*, Voudou is woven into Haitian culture and history. There are many, many misconceptions about Voudou. The first and most blasphemous is the notion that Voudou is a Satanic cult run by witches and witch doctors. This is false. In fact, vodouisants do not believe in a powerful antagonistic deity that opposes God."

"They don't believe in the devil?" Gayle asked.

"No," Marcello said, "but vodouisants *do* believe in evil—whether it be maligned men or maligned spirits."

Kaprica nodded. "Voudou is a religion that recognizes spirits, or Iwa. In Christian terms, Iwa could be angels or the spirits of saints. Iwa are typically regarded as intermediaries between man and God. Voudou practitioners believe spirits can offer help and guidance, but also that they can be offended and may choose to inflict misfortune or illness on a person. The canon around Iwa is complex and varied based on region."

"Interesting," Gayle said, leaning in. "So is it really just a unique cultural expression of some tenets of Catholicism, then?"

Kaprica shook her head.

"No. There is a mystical witchcraft to the practice which is most certainly distinct from Catholicism, or any other form of Christianity. Spells, charms, and even legends of zombies are still very much a part of modern Voudou. And, unlike Catholicism, in Voudou women are empowered to become priestesses and spiritual leaders, which gives them power and influence in their communities. This point is not something to gloss over. In Haiti, Voudou gives women strength in a culture that many would otherwise categorize as patriarchal and misogynistic."

"Wait . . . zombies? That's a real part of this religion? I thought we made that up for movies," Jed said.

"The belief in zombies is woven into the culture and the religion," Kaprica said.

Again, Jed's mind went back to the scared mother, searching for her daughter. She had told him that she'd had terrible nightmares about her daughter being made into a zombie.

"Also," Marcello added, "you need to understand that Voudou is not institutionalized like Catholicism. There's no Pope, no orthodoxy, no formal creed maintained and taught by a governing bureaucracy. Voudou is communal, not hierarchical."

"I'm curious: How is it that Haitians can consider themselves Christians but also practice Voudou at the same time?" Jed asked.

"It is because Haitians do not view Voudou and Christianity as mutually exclusive. It is perfectly acceptable to sit for Catholic Mass in the morning and attend a Voudou *dans* that same night. Voudou is syncretic—a melting-pot religion derived from West African tribal practices, Roman Catholicism, Freemasonry, and also the indigenous Taíno people's worship of ancestors. I know this doesn't make sense to an outsider—especially Americans, who like to put people in well-defined boxes—but this is the way it is. The best metaphor I can think of is culinary. In

America, you will happily eat Chinese food on Monday, Mexican food on Tuesday, Italian food on Wednesday, French food on Thursday, and German food on Friday, but put it all under the umbrella of American cuisine. Haitian Voudou is like this, taking many interesting flavors and ideas from different religions and accepting all of them," Kaprica said.

"And you?" Gayle asked gently. "How do you rectify this cultural belief system with your Christian faith as Shepherds?"

Marcello smiled.

"The Bible tells us much about false prophets and religions, Ms. Gayle," he said simply. "As Christians, we recognize the areas where Voudou works outside Biblical teaching and reject those practices, but we also accept that there are cultural truths we cannot escape. To be honest, this paradox is why this hybrid religion is so easily manipulated for evil, whether by Dark Ones or others. But most everyday practitioners are good people."

Jed realized that was a partial answer, but perhaps all there was. Certainly, the culture of the United States impacted how he expressed and practiced his own faith—didn't it?

"Okay. So, what about the Haitian woman I fought in the square and then the crucified dove and the snake? I mean, it was just like what I saw in the shop . . . Don't you think this sounds like a connection to Voudou?" Jed asked.

"Yes, it is very possible, if not likely," Kaprica said. "Voudou is very ceremonial. Spiritual possession and animal sacrifice are important thematic components of the religion. And listen to me very carefully when I say that this is a very natural and logical way for the Dark Ones to exploit and pervert Voudou for their evil purposes. The dove and the snake in your room were very likely a message to you from a vodouisant who has been corrupted by the Dark Ones."

"We have seen such things before," Marcello said, his

expression grave. "And much worse. It is a scare tactic. A means to intimidate you, to scare you into backing off from investigating whatever it is you seem to have stumbled on."

"Well, I'm not backing off, that's for damn sure," Jed said. "This island is your sandbox, I get that, but I believe God directed me here for a reason. And from day one of my *vacation*, the message has been loud and clear: Bad things are happening down here. First, my encounter with the mother who lost her child, and then the attempted kidnapping of another kid, with a Dark One clearly involved. I simply don't believe in coincidences. There are people and kids who need our help. No matter how hard I try, I can't stop thinking about the woman who confronted me at Parque Colón. She was terrified—not just that her daughter, Emelin, had been kidnapped, but that before, her daughter had been having nightmares about being turned into a zombie. That must be a Voudou reference. What was she talking about?"

Marcello and Kaprica shared another one of their silent looks. "The reason we were eager to meet with you," Kaprica said, "is because we agree that there is, indeed, something happening on this island. Exploitation of children—as forced workers, in the sex trade, for-profit adoptions where children are sold to agencies in America and Europe—these things have always happened here. But there is more going on now. Recently, children are being kidnapped at an alarming rate. We have started an investigation, and we believe the root of this diabolical operation is in Haiti, but we don't know for certain. The two children you told us about—Emelin and the boy you saved last night—are Dominican, so maybe it is happening in both Haiti and the DR. We need time to ask questions and task our network with collecting information. That is why we are going to Dajabón today, in fact: to secretly meet with a Haitian contact who is risking his life to talk to us."

"Would you like us to come with you?" Gayle asked, beating Jed to the punch by a millisecond.

"*Merci*, but no," Kaprica said with a smile. "I'm afraid your presence could spook our contact and may also telegraph our investigation to the enemy."

Jed understood Kaprica's concern, but he was tempted to insist that they tag along anyway. But as the outsider, he needed to trust them. They knew the culture and what was best for their investigation. Besides, this hadn't yet become an official Joshua Bravo tasking. When Marcello and Kaprica returned, they'd have more information to share—information which would be valuable to answer questions that Ben would undoubtedly ask when Jed pressed him to make this investigation into what was happening to these children official.

"Very well," Jed said. "All I ask is that we can reconnect with you after your meeting so you can share what you've learned, and then we can decide next steps."

"This is a good plan," Marcello said. "We are leaving shortly for the drive to Dajabón, which is up north and on the Haitian border. Our meeting is after sunset and will take a couple of hours—or we hope so, anyway. We can return to Santo Domingo, or alternatively, you are invited to stay with us at our home in Santiago de los Caballeros. It is a very beautiful city in the mountains, and we can meet you there after our meeting. We have spare quarters, and you would both be welcome to stay as our guests." He leaned in, his eyes serious and his tone now conspiratorial. "It may be safer for you than remaining here in Santo Domingo after the warning you have received. If all of this is connected, you are quite clearly on someone's radar, yes?"

Jed looked at Gayle.

"It's up to you, Jed," she said with a devious little grin. "It's your vacation, not mine. But no matter what, Marcello is right—you can't stay here anymore. You've been made, my friend."

The thought of sleeping here—after finding a six-foot snake under the bed—was considerably less appealing than when he had first arrived. Jed was not afraid of who may come for him—he was a SEAL and a Shepherd and could handle himself—but whatever investigating he might want to do would be hampered if they were being watched. And Gayle was right—the enemy knew this place, obviously.

I'm back on mission.

"I think I've had enough fun for a lifetime here in Santo Domingo," he said with a wry smile. "Santiago de los Caballeros sounds like a good idea."

"It's settled, then—you will stay with us," Marcello said, and Kaprica patted his hand in agreement. "We will meet you at our home tonight. We can easily be there by midnight."

"You'll be exhausted," Gayle protested. "We can meet you tomorrow, if you like."

Marcello laughed good-naturedly. "We are more spry than perhaps we appear," he said. "We are not operators like you, but we are accustomed to working late into the night. It is the nature of what we do. And you really should get out of Santo Domingo. We will meet at midnight, share a late meal and tea, and tell you everything we know about what is going on with these children."

"And we will better educate you on all we know about Voudou," his wife added, taking her husband's hand.

"Great," Jed said. "But before you go . . . is there any chance you can offer me advice on how to relocate a six-foot red mountain boa? Because it's trapped under a hamper in my bedroom."

CHAPTER SEVENTEEN

OFFICE OF THE DIRECTOR
SHEPHERDS NORTH AMERICA
TRINITY LOOP COMPLEX
WEST OF NASHVILLE, TENNESSEE
1400 HOURS LOCAL

Ben Morvant, Navy SEAL combat medic veteran and now head of Shepherds North America, sighed at his desk and rubbed his left temple with a thumb. He prided himself on never having a bad day. It wasn't that he didn't have struggles like everyone else—he did. Maybe *more* than most people in fact, given his unique line of work. But Morvant had spent years of study and prayer to bring himself to the point where he viewed difficulties not just as challenges, but as opportunities to grow, to overcome, and to strengthen his walk with God. After nearly dying as a Navy SEAL in his first direct combat with pure evil so many years ago, and after everything he had learned about the gifts God gave people like him and how to use them for *His* glory, Ben viewed struggle as a privilege. He'd spent hours in conversation with Mike Moore on the topic and had found in those conversations his life's verse in 1 Peter 5:10: "And the God of all grace, who called you to his eternal glory in Christ, after you have suffered a little while, will himself restore you and make you strong, firm, and steadfast."

Ben had endured loss and pain and suffering, but never once had he felt it was in vain or a burden. That mindset, he knew, was what kept him from ever having a bad day.

But today, Ben Morvant was having a bad day.

He leaned back in his desk chair and wondered just what was wrong with him today. Little things—like the looming possibility of delaying a family vacation because of whatever Jed Johnson had stumbled on in the Dominican Republic, feeling helpless that he couldn't seem to focus or find voice for his gifts, questions about the future of Joshua Bravo, and his confidant Mike being gone today, enjoying his own period of refreshment on a camping trip with his wife—none of these should be bothering him.

This is nothing. This is far from the worst day of my life—light-years away from it. So, what the hell is wrong with me?

His young teenage son, Jason, waking up from some weird dream about a snake eating children: That had been the first domino. But Jason had bad dreams sometimes, as he often did himself. Once his son had told him about this one, the almost fourteen-year-old had been fine—unburdened in the telling, as was so often the case. So why was Jason's dream sticking with Ben? What was he missing?

He picked up the picture of his family, brooding as he stared at it.

I'm just feeling . . . distant.

He placed the picture back on his desk. He didn't feel distant from Christy or the kids. He felt distant from God. But why? Had his gifts become some sort of idol for him, and in this season where they felt poorly focused, he could no longer focus on God? That felt possibly true, but how embarrassing that he'd become dependent on gifts and talents for his walk with the Lord. That was, like, Christianity 101, right?

Ben needed to sit and talk with Mike, but that wouldn't happen today . . .

A phone call jolted him from his pathetic brooding, and he laughed at himself as he raised the device to his ear, recognizing the number immediately. A sense of purpose chased most of the demons away.

Mostly . . .

"Morvant," he said.

"Ben, it's Jed," his operator and friend said.

"Glad to see you're out of the pokey," Ben teased. Talking to Jed, he felt more like himself already.

Maybe it's not the gifts at all—maybe it's just a need for purpose. With Victor gone, I should be celebrating instead of looking for the next fight.

"Nice," Jed said with a chuckle. "Thanks for sending Gayle to get me out, bro."

"Wait," Ben said, sitting up in his chair now. "She came down there? To the DR?"

"Yeah, did she not tell you?"

Ben was surprised, but he shouldn't be. Gayle James had proven herself a great ally and asset to the Shepherds. Of course she took care of this personally, rather than delegating it to someone on her team. It said everything about her.

"No, but I'm glad to hear she handled it personally. Thank her for me. Are you on a plane?"

There was a pause, and Ben knew what would come next. *Don't need gifts to read that one, though, do I?* He knew Jed.

"Not yet," Jed confirmed. "Look, boss, there's something going on down here—something relevant to our work."

"We're encrypted on my end, Jed," Ben said. "Are you secure on yours?"

"Yeah," Jed said. "Should be."

"Okay, so what's up?"

"Ben, what happened with the kid wasn't an isolated thing. We met with the team working down here—the ones you sent the contact information for—and they've been looking into the same thing. They only gave us a cursory briefing, but they have more they want to share. They believe this is more than just secular child trafficking, which is bad enough anyway in my book."

"Mine too, Jed, but . . ."

"There's more, Ben. This is right out of the Dark Ones' playbook, I know it. Think about it, boss. Using a hybrid religion full of dark magic, spells, and fear. Manipulating people to embrace the dark side of religion. The fear and anxiety of missing children, for whatever purpose, and the hopelessness that brings. You taught me that the primary mission of the Dark Ones is to keep people far from God through fear and doubt. This sure fits the bill . . ."

"But why take the kids, Jed? What are they doing with them? And are they targeting specific children for some reason?" Ben had to admit, the Joshua Bravo team leader made a compelling case. This had the feel of a Dark Ones op.

"I don't know—or not yet anyway. I think with Victor gone I have a harder time focusing my—you know—but I'm telling you, we need to look into this," Jed pressed. "Look, I'd like to stay just a little longer. I have a meeting with the couple you connected me with later tonight, and they'll share more then. I can brief you after, and we can decide—*you* can decide . . ." he corrected.

Ben smiled. "Jed, the new structure for your team implies—in fact *requires*—more autonomy from the team and from you. I trust your instincts here, even if mine may be a little cloudy."

"Thanks, boss," Jed said, sounding relieved.

"Of course. Do I need to mobilize a team to send you?"

Another pause as Jed considered that.

"Not yet," Jed said. "Let me meet with the . . . assets . . . tonight and then we can decide. I have to drive a good ways away from Santo Domingo to meet with them, but afterward, I think we'll know enough to make a decision."

"Sounds good."

"How much do we trust them? I know they're not—organic to the Shepherds."

Ben nodded.

"No, they're not, but I trust them completely," he said. "I consider them to be an extension of the Shepherds organization. Make your own assessment, but you can trust that they're straight shooters. They have been working with us for quite some time."

"That helps; thanks."

"Of course," Ben said, glancing at his watch. "What time are you meeting them?"

"Around midnight."

"Call me after, no matter which way you're leaning."

"Will do, boss," Jed said.

"Is Gayle hanging with you?"

"She is," Jed answered, and Ben could hear the confidence in Jed's voice. "She's good people too. I trust her."

"Me too," Ben said. "Keep me in the loop."

"Roger that," Jed said. The phone clicked off.

Ben set the phone down, feeling much better for some reason.

Purpose matters.

He made a note to make contact with all the members of Joshua Bravo, scattered as they were on their various vacations. He needed them to be aware of what was happening in the Dominican Republic and to be standing by.

CHAPTER EIGHTEEN

AUTOPISTA DUARTE (DR-1 HIGHWAY)

FIVE MILES SOUTH OF SANTIAGO DE LOS CABALLEROS

NINETY MILES NORTHWEST OF SANTO DOMINGO

SANTIAGO, DOMINICAN REPUBLIC

2335 HOURS LOCAL

A drive that would have taken two hours or less back home, even on the winding roads of western Tennessee, had now taken over three, and Jed was feeling the fatigue. Partly because his vacation so far had been anything but restful, partly because of the extreme attention required to maneuver the terrible roads outside of cities in the DR, and partly because Gayle had fallen fast asleep only a few miles outside of Santo Domingo. The Autopista Duarte highway, or DR-1, had been like an autobahn near the city, compared to what the same road had become with every mile farther outside of Santo Domingo. But even this late, he'd encountered frequent bottlenecks from slow-moving trucks and farming equipment. The drive was beginning to drag out.

Jed strained to see in the dark, not wanting to miss the exit for Ctra. Matanza, which would take them west just a mile or two to the Ctra. Santiago de los Caballeros-Baitoa, which Marcello had told him would wind them south and then west a few miles to a fork just before the small village of Baitoa. They would go right and then take the second dirt road, which would wind up the mountainside to the couple's house. Jed hoped the directions were good because even if the reception had been reliable it wouldn't matter. After the Ctra. Matanza, none of these roads appeared on his GPS app.

Gayle stirred in her seat and made a rattling snore he was sure would embarrass her terribly. The thought made him chuckle.

She was turning out to be a good partner in this—but also great company. They'd found a coffee bar in Los Alcarrizos, a suburb just north of Santo Domingo on DR-1, and had spent several hours doing their own research on Haitian Voudou and on its Dominican cousin Vudú—or Las 21 Divisiones to locals. It turned out, Voodoo as they knew it was only called that in New Orleans, and there was a somewhat commercialized version of the culture and religion. Unlike in Haiti, where Kaprica had told them some cultural form of Voudou was almost universal, here in the DR, Vudú was far less universally accepted and had in fact been formally banned—though the practice certainly still occurred. From what Jed had gleaned, the ban was largely about driving Vudú out of view of the economically essential tourism industry. They'd learned a lot, laughed a lot, and drank way too much delicious, strong Dominican coffee.

For Jed, at least, spending time with Gayle was finally making his trip actually *feel* a bit like vacation. Fun, good company, good drinks. They'd walked around Los Alcarrizos after, and he'd nearly taken Gayle's hand out of reflex. He caught himself just in time. If she'd noticed, she hadn't let on.

They'd enjoyed an enormous meal later in the afternoon at

Paladar de Mi Terraza, a local favorite recommended by their waitress at the coffee shop. Jed decided that the recommendation must have been divine intervention. While burgers were notoriously absent from the small but amazing restaurant's menu, he'd sampled at least four other kinds of meats and rice and had left stuffed and satisfied. Gayle, to his surprise, held her own, devouring almost as much fried and grilled meat as he had, and they'd both overindulged in whatever the light, flaky, fried bread had been called. They'd talked very little about the case, as she kept referring to it, but he learned a lot about who Gayle James really was—a small-town girl who grew up on James Bond books and movies. She'd thought about joining the Air Force to serve as an intelligence officer—even taking a year of ROTC classes while at George Washington University—but in her senior year she'd met a CIA recruiter at an on-campus job fair, and the rest was history.

"So, what, he was creeping around the event in a trench coat?" He managed to laugh.

"Worse," she told him. "Can you believe they just had a booth? Like a literal booth with a bowl of candy, free pens, and a banner that said *Central Intelligence Agency* and everything."

"You've got to be kidding me . . ."

"Swear to you." She laughed.

They talked about the Navy and the Teams. They talked about her growing up in the church, leaving, and finding her way back. They danced around his faith journey a little bit, and she blushed at having laughed when he told her he'd originally wanted to be a youth pastor.

"Why is that funny?" he said, feigning good-natured indignation.

"Jed, do you own a mirror? You scream Special Operations from across the room."

"Sure, but not then," he said, remembering the skinny kid he'd been.

Jed now looked over at the pretty woman beside him in the car, the woman who hours ago had consumed nearly her body weight in heavy, spicy Dominican food.

No wonder she's sleeping.

He smiled, and she stirred, just as the exit for Ctra. Matanza came up on his left.

As they moved farther west and north of Santo Domingo, he found the only thing worse than the roads was the road markings and signs. He drove painfully slowly until, finally, he saw the unmarked turn to the left that his GPS said should have been there a quarter mile sooner.

"This is us," he said.

Gayle blinked away the sleep from her eyes and oriented herself. Jed brought the truck through the turn, heading west just a hundred yards before Ctra. Matanza bent north toward "downtown" Santiago de los Caballeros, and he continued west on what instantly became a much narrower and poorly paved road, Ctra. Presa de Tavera.

"Sorry I fell asleep," Gayle said, yawning.

"Sleep is a weapon," Jed replied with a grin.

Though, it wasn't like they were headed into combat. He was looking forward to a nice late-night meal with their new friends, Marcello and Kaprica. It seemed impossible that he could be hungry, but it was nearly midnight, and he was not a small man. He was also hungry for both more information and more conversation from the couple they'd met this morning. There was something about them, a quiet strength and confidence balanced by humility and compassion. Jed had no doubt at all that they were doing the work that God had called them for.

"Think they'll be impressed with what we taught ourselves

about Voudou and Las 21 Divisiones?" Gayle asked with a deprecating grin.

"I doubt it," he said with a laugh. "I'm excited to learn more, but I'm dying to hear what they were able to learn about the disappearances."

"Me too," Gayle said, her voice turning serious. "I hate that it's kids. I just can't even imagine how terrifying that must be."

With Victor gone, they'd been told that there was chaos within the Dark Ones' ranks and no real leadership. Still, they knew that individual cells tended to operate with some autonomy. Perhaps the vacuum emboldened Dark Ones in the DR and Haiti to do things they'd not dared under Victor's reign.

Or perhaps new leadership had already emerged, and somehow, the Shepherds had missed it.

Gayle shrugged.

"They're evil, Jed. Isn't that the whole thing? If these Dark Ones, as you guys call them, are really demon-possessed, then I would expect nothing less."

Jed shook his head, both hands on the wheel now, peering out the windshield to carefully follow the narrow road winding up the side of the mountain, the switchbacks leading them higher and higher. He slowed yet again, the tight turns making him grip the wheel tighter.

"Evil, yes, but not just cruelty for cruelty's sake. The Dark Ones follow a dark path, and make no mistake, it is Satan who calls the shots. Victor may have been his most recent general, but it's the devil who is in charge. The problem is, with Victor gone, we don't really know what to expect now . . ."

"The devil you know," Gayle said, one eyebrow raised. Then she gave a tight smile. "No pun."

"Right," he said. "My point is we may not know the rules or objectives of what they're doing here, but the endgame doesn't change much: wreak havoc and shake people's faith by showing the horrors possible for mankind. But they *are* mission-oriented and results-driven. Kidnapping children just to scare them doesn't serve any purpose."

"So, they're—what? Demons with a conscience?" she retorted sarcastically.

"Not at all," he said, not taking the bait. "I'd use the word *pragmatic*. They have no guilt or shame when it comes to violence, cruelty, torture—you name it. But it must serve their mission objective and their war strategy."

He glanced over at her. She seemed confused but captivated.

"Which is?"

Jed smiled.

"The Christian's job on earth is to be the light, right? To spread the Good Word about Christ and touch as many people for the Lord as possible. I'm not talking about preaching, or forced conversion, or any of that. I mean, we are meant to show God's love, the way Jesus did—giving the truth, but always with love. Our mission is to share the word of God and bring as many people into relationship with Him as we can. Do you agree?"

She shrugged again.

"Sure, I guess," she said. He could see on her face, and also feel inside her, the questions.

"How each of us fits into that mission individually is very different," he said. "Paul said we're all different parts of one body. Can't have a body with just arms or just legs or just a liver, right?"

"I suppose," Gayle laughed. "And I remember that verse. Somewhere in Romans, right?"

"I think so," he said. "The point is that as Christians—the body of Christ Paul refers to—we can't all be preachers, or nurses, or social workers, or Sunday school teachers, or . . ."

"Okay, I get it, I get it," she said.

She patted him on the leg, and he smiled.

"So, if that is the mission for us, with many different jobs to accomplish that mission, then for the Dark Ones, it is the exact opposite. For the Dark Ones, the mission is to stand in opposition to the light. Their job is to fight for *their* boss and achieve his evil plan of keeping as many people away from Christ as they can. Just scaring the crap out of kids won't do that. They need to show people a dark, evil, fallen world where a loving God can't possibly be anything but a fairy tale. They sow division and infighting, making mankind focus on their differences instead of seeing themselves together, as one people, as the children of God. If they're taking children, we need to figure out how and why that fits into that mission. If we can understand it, we can maybe stop it. Make sense?"

He realized that all of that would be so much easier if they just knew who was in charge now that Victor was gone—or if there was no global leadership yet, who, if anyone, was running the show here in the DR.

Gayle nodded, but he thought she might only be partially convinced.

"Can I ask you a question?" she said and placed her hand on his knee again. "And it's not meant to be critical or judgmental—it's a real question."

"Okay?" he said.

He eyed her with curiosity before putting his eyes back on the winding road. They were coming to the fork where Marcello had said the better road went to the right, farther up the mountain, as the left road descended toward the large lake. He saw the turn and slowed to bear right, continuing their climb.

"I get everything you're saying, for sure. But I guess I'm wondering, well, how do people like you—like us—how do we bring light into the world? Does that make sense?"

He nodded. "Warfare and violence feel very un-Christian, don't they?" he said, gripping the wheel. "It's a question every Christian warrior struggles with. I sure did, and sometimes still do. But here's my answer for you: If we are all different parts of the one body of Christ, all doing different jobs, then ours is very, very important to bringing God's light into the world."

"And what is that job, as you see it?" she asked, her hand still on his knee.

"We bring light by blocking and defeating the darkness," he said, aware of the fire in his voice. "We're not the first warriors God created for this purpose. King David is a great example, Caleb and Jacob two others. Peter was a bit of a hothead himself, remember, but he's not really an example of what I'm talking about—I think I just identify with him. Look, God created me with a pretty unique and well-developed skill set for combating His enemies. I'm very content in my belief that I bring light into the world, God's light, by stopping the Dark Ones and their plan to block His light with their darkness. I allow God's love into the world by defeating those who fight against it. That"—he slowed as the road switched back again, then took the dirt road off to the left—the first dirt road he'd seen, just as Marcello had said—"is my purpose. It's why God made me as He did. It's why He gave me certain . . . gifts."

"Like hand-to-hand combat, handling firearms, and leaping off balconies to chase red-eyed demons into the night?"

He couldn't tell if she was agreeing, expressing cynicism, or just making fun.

"Yes," he said, swelling with confidence.

Among other things, he added quietly in his head.

"There it is," Gayle said.

Jed glanced up and saw the wood-frame mountain house lit up inside, the lights reflecting on the huge lake below them.

The house was modest in size, but more than generous for a single-family home in the DR. Dark wood gave way to huge panels of glass affording what had to be views of the mountains and lake from inside, views every bit as stunning as those from out here. A large deck wrapped around the rear of the house. The lights were on, signaling, he assumed, that Marcello and Kaprica had made it home safely. His stomach instantly growled at the thought of what they might be preparing for them to eat. He glanced at his watch and then pulled into the wide gravel drive, parking right behind the truck he assumed belonged to the couple.

"Thanks for sharing all of that, Jed," Gayle said, unbuckling her seat belt. "I know you're more of a doer than a talker, and I appreciate you being willing to tell me your perspective."

"My pleasure," he said, realizing he meant it.

Why did he find her so easy to talk to? It was usually not that way for him. He slipped out of the driver's seat, closed the door with a thud, and followed Gayle up the walkway from the drive.

In an instant, his relaxed, happy mood dissolved away, and he felt his body tense, his senses sharpening in anticipation of . . . something. He scanned around to see just what was screaming for his attention.

"Gayle, wait," he said, but at the same moment, she tensed as well, pulling her pistol from under her shirt.

"Jed, the door's ajar," she said, her voice a whisper.

Too late for that now—we drove up here on the gravel and slammed our doors. If someone bad is here, they know we've arrived.

There was nothing he could see to warrant his heightened state of alarm. Their new friends and hosts might well have left the open door—which indeed stood open a full foot, he saw—as an invitation to them to come on in, or in case they didn't hear a knock, perhaps. He saw nothing that explained his feeling of foreboding. Or Gayle's. But, after years of experiences where he didn't understand but had learned to trust that feeling—and a year of learning from Ben where it really came from—he knew all too well the perils of ignoring it. It wasn't just the cracked door, he knew. This was the gift that had saved him more than once in Iraq and Afghanistan, screaming warning when everything appeared to be just fine.

He pulled the Wilson Combat SFX9 from inside the waistband holster on his hip and shifted left, urging Gayle with a head nod to shift to the far-right side of the door.

She complied, rising softly and silently up the wooden stairs to the porch, to the right of the heavy wooden door, light streaming out onto the porch from inside. Jed's additional hundred pounds or more didn't allow for the same degree of stealth as Gayle, and he grimaced as the wood steps creaked under his weight. A second later, they flanked the door. She stared at him, looking for direction. She was an experienced CIA operative, but they were in his world now. He was the door kicker.

He pointed to himself, then indicated he would go first, clearing left, and then pointed to her and the right. She nodded, and he hoped she got it. Then he nodded his head in cadence to his silent mouthing of *three . . . two . . . one . . .*

On zero, he reached across the doorframe, pushing the door inward to widen the space, then he moved through and to the left, sighting over the pistol, his body floating over his fast-moving legs in a familiar combat crouch.

He cleared left, starting behind him in the corner, which turned out to be a small room—an office—with bookshelves and a simple desk, open through an archway. He felt rather than saw Gayle moving right, clearing her corner. He swung right, sighting over his pistol and clearing forward and then upward where the stair opened to a landing above them.

Nothing. No gunshots. No dark figures with glowing eyes falling on them from above.

But where were their hosts?

He surged forward quickly, glancing at Gayle to be sure she was keeping with him, something he wouldn't have done if a fellow operator was to his right. He paused at the short hall, glancing into the large, open room where he saw a wall of glass looking out onto the valley and the lights on the lake below. He saw no one.

Should he call out to Kaprica and Marcello? Were they simply on the deck, cooking on a grill around the corner?

His instinct told him to remain silent, so he did. He could apologize later if needed.

He moved forward, again shifting left, clearing his rear corner then sweeping across the room to his right where a fireplace sat cold in a stone wall and a large sectional-style leather sofa faced it. Beyond was a small dining table, and as he swept right, he saw Gayle, expertly clearing and scanning, moving slowly forward.

Look up.

He listened to the inner voice, as he always had, but especially now that he understood the source.

He wished he hadn't.

His mind was taken back to the white dove at the Vrbo, its wings stretched crucifixion-style, nailed to the ceiling.

Marcello hung from the thick, exposed wood beams of the high, arched ceiling. He was positioned thirty degrees, head up, along the slant of the peaked ceiling, but his head hung down. The body was naked from the waist up, covered in blood, his abdomen ripped open and his intestines forming a long irregular rope of bloody gray all the way to the wooden floor where they pooled in an enormous puddle of blood. He was nailed to the beams by his outstretched arms, heavy metal spikes piercing his mid-forearms twice on each side, securing his body to the ceiling. His legs were stretched open as well, similar railroad-spike nails piercing his legs at the ankles.

Jed clicked on the light he held in his left hand, shining it on the battered face, and found only dark, empty holes where the eyes had been.

"Oh my God," he heard Gayle sob from his right.

He clicked the light off and turned to his partner, who stared open-mouthed at the dead Shepherd.

"Gayle . . . Gayle . . ." he whispered harshly, trying to get her back in the fight. She ignored him and stared at the crucified corpse on the ceiling, her gun hanging at her side.

He was on his own, for the moment anyway. Jed shifted behind her, gun back up, sweeping the rest of the room. A hallway ran along the wall behind them, a light on from a bath at the end, it seemed. He saw no movement.

"Gayle, cover my six," he urged, shifting back left, crabbing sideways to peer over the breakfast bar into the kitchen.

Gayle blinked, then finally complied, her gun hand coming up, moving around the enormous puddle of blood and viscera, and turning to look away. She cleared up the hall, then angled back toward the entrance, letting her gun shift between the hallway and the archway into the foyer.

"We need to clear upstairs," she said, her voice a tight band of stress.

"Hold my six," he commanded.

Jed got to the bar and peered into the kitchen. The far wall had a door, partially open, that led out onto the expansive deck. He craned his neck, trying to see onto the deck, but the angle was wrong. Then his eye was drawn to something in the square of light on the floor from the refrigerator, whose door he now saw was open.

In the light from the refrigerator, he saw a small foot covered in a white shoe.

The foot rocked gently, back and forth.

"Hold and cover, Gayle," he said, more loudly now. "I think I found Kaprica."

He moved swiftly around the bar, cleared the narrow corner, and then stepped over the bleeding mess at his feet, clearing out the back door first.

"Gayle, cover me from the corner of the bar," he ordered. From there his teammate would have lines on both the front and over top of him to see the deck and out the rear door.

Jed took a knee beside the woman. Her eyes were wide, not with fright, he thought, but with urgency. Her lovely dress—no doubt donned because she and Marcello had late-night dinner guests coming—was completely soaked in blood. She had both hands to her throat, and blood oozed between her fingers. There was a pool of partly congealed blood in a halo around her head. Jed realized the poor woman had been lying like this, slowly dying in a pool of her own blood and staring up at her husband nailed to the ceiling, for a long time. Perhaps an hour or more.

Bloody bubbles formed at her lips as they moved, trying desperately to form words. She blinked her already-glassy eyes and stared at him. He leaned over, placing his ear near her mouth. She tried again, but he heard only a horrible, wet gurgling. He gently pulled her hands away from her neck.

"I've got you, Kaprica. It's okay," he lied.

It wasn't.

The slice in her throat was deep and wide, gaping open like a cruel second smile beneath her chin. He immediately placed his hand over the left side of her throat when a small geyser of blood came up from the wound in a little fountain, clearly arterial from a severed carotid artery, but the low-pressure spray suggested she was almost gone, most of her blood on the floor around her. The only reason she was still alive was that the other artery, on the right side, must not have been severed, and she had sealed the giant hole in her windpipe with her hands so she could suck little gasps of air into her lungs.

She tried again, her lips moving, but only wet gurgling and bloody bubbles came out.

Her face looked desperate—and annoyed, somehow.

Jed placed a hand on her shoulder and closed his eyes. He didn't know if he had the gifts to do this or not, but maybe she did—maybe, like with Sarah Beth, he could at least be a decent antenna . . .

"I'm here, Kaprica . . ." he told her in his mind.

"Dark . . . Ones . . ."

The voice in his head was Kaprica's, weak but clear even now.

He opened his eyes, but hers were now glass, staring off into space. Her face went slack, and he could literally feel her leaving. In her last instant, she sent one final thought to him.

"Amour et Espoir . . . Port-de-Paix . . . the children . . ."

And she was gone, like a gentle breeze that just fades away.

"She's dead," he said, his voice cracking.

He looked up and saw tears streaming down Gayle's cheeks.

"She told me something," he said, rising, his gun at his side. He let out a long, shaking sigh.

"What? When?" Gayle asked, clearly confused.

"I'll tell you in the car. We need to clear the upstairs and the back, but there will be no one here. Then we need to go. We need to go right away."

"We can't leave them here—not like this." Gayle sobbed.

He shook his head.

"We have to go," he said. "But we'll send help. Ben will send help."

Jed moved forward, back in his combat crouch, surging toward the foyer and the stairs.

"Where are we going?" Gayle said, her voice barely a whisper as she cleared her side and he began his ascent up the stairs.

"Haiti," he said, his tone now determined and strong. "Someplace called Port-de-Paix."

PART II

And no wonder, for Satan himself masquerades as an angel of light. It is not surprising, then, if his servants also masquerade as servants of righteousness. Their end will be what their actions deserve.

—2 Corinthians 11:14–15 (NIV)

CHAPTER NINETEEN

ST. GEORGE'S ACADEMY

EXECUTIVE SCIF IN THE CENTER

0802 HOURS LOCAL

Sarah Beth forced a smile onto her face and told herself not to be nervous. The stress of finals was finally over—and she now felt certain she had done great despite all of her worry—but it seemed there was something else going on. Pastor Dee had waited until after finals to tell her about the meeting—which Sarah Beth appreciated, she supposed—and had promised that Sarah Beth wasn't in trouble. What Pastor Dee had neglected to mention, however, was that both her parents had also been invited to the meeting, along with Corbin, Corbin's Keeper Pastor Margaret, and Corbin's parents.

To make matters even more disconcerting, this gathering was being held in the secure room known as a SCIF in the Watcher's secret basement ops center. Something big was definitely up, but she had no clue what it could be.

"Do you know what this is about?" Sarah Beth said in her mind, Watcher snapchatting with Corbin.

"Absolutely no idea!" Corbin said. *"Dee did a good job of keeping this a secret—and that's no small feat when it's from you and me."*

"Do you think we're in trouble?"

"I don't think so . . . nobody seems mad. I can tell my parents are nervous, though."

"First off, I want to thank everyone for coming," said St. George's headmaster, Jean-Baptiste Allard, as he breezed into the secure conference room and shut the door behind him. "And second, I see some worried faces around this table, so I want to put everyone's minds at ease—especially Corbin and Sarah Beth—that this is not a disciplinary session of any kind."

It probably should have been obvious considering the location of the meeting, but hearing the words from Headmaster Allard did make Sarah Beth relax.

"Everyone here knows I love to talk," Allard said with a sly grin, "but I was merely *invited* to this meeting just like most of you. So, without further ado, I'll turn things over to David and Rachel Yarnell."

What?

Mortified, Sarah Beth swiveled in her chair to stare at her parents, who, like Pastor Dee, had not told her anything about this.

"Thank you, Headmaster Allard," her dad said with a gracious and easy smile. "Rachel and I are very excited to speak with you, but we must confess, we're also a little bit nervous."

"You swear you didn't know about this?" Corbin asked in Sarah Beth's head.

"I swear!"

"That's right, David. Anytime God presents us with a new opportunity, it can be a little nerve-wracking," her mom said.

She realized in that moment that Mom actually seemed happier and more at peace than she remembered ever seeing her. This new job did, indeed, seem to suit her. "For example, I'm still trying to find my way in my new position as the Watchers' Shepherd liaison. But thanks to the kindness and patience of everyone here at St. George's and at Trinity Loop, I'm already feeling more connected, and everyone I have met has been tremendously helpful."

"And to further build on that point," her dad said, taking the verbal baton back, "I'm here as the TSL for the Shepherds' Joshua Bravo unit. Corbin and Sarah Beth, you both know the members of Joshua Bravo well, since you've worked with them multiple times."

"Is everything okay with Joshua Bravo?" Corbin asked, taking the words right out of Sarah Beth's mouth.

"Everything is fine. In fact, the entire team is on vacation, getting some much-deserved rest," Dad said.

"You're part of Joshua Bravo, but you're not on vacation," Corbin said with a grin. "How's that fair?"

Her dad smiled back. He looked at Sarah Beth's mom before saying, "The Yarnell family decided to postpone our vacation until summer. We didn't think it would be fair to leave Sarah Beth here taking finals while we go on a Caribbean cruise."

"We're going on a cruise?" Sarah Beth said excitedly. She'd always wanted to go on a cruise.

"We are, but that's a conversation for outside the SCIF," her mom said with an uncharacteristic wink and a smile. "What we're in here about is a big change happening with Joshua Bravo. David, do you want to explain?"

Her dad nodded. "First, for Mark and Ashley, I want to explain that Joshua Bravo is one of a number of direct-action teams that the Watchers' mission supports. They are the unit that was involved in an operation in Rome, which we can't share too much about, but also the team that rescued Corbin and our daughter—as well as many others—that terrible night here at St. George's. They defeated a great enemy that night—with the help of my amazing wife, Rachel, in fact. They are a top-notch unit within the Shepherds, and it is such an honor to be part of their team."

"And my uncle Jed leads the team," Sarah Beth couldn't resist adding, beaming with pride. She realized that, in the heat of exams, she'd forgotten to Watcher snapchat with Uncle Jed, something she would have to correct later this morning.

"Do you have questions we can answer about the unit?" Dad asked.

Mark looked at his wife, who gripped his hand tightly and shook her head.

"I think we understand, from all the family briefing that Pastor Dee and Pastor Margaret have been allowed to share, the gist of what the direct-action teams do," Corbin's dad said grimly.

"And the importance of what your daughter—and ours—provide to the team and all of the Shepherds units," her dad added. "Like Rachel and I, I have no doubt that you have both great pride—but also fear and reservations—about all our girls are doing with the gifts God gave them."

"That's an excellent summary," Ashley said with a nervous laugh. "We are certainly proud of our girl," she added, shooting a smile to Corbin, "and we've come to peace with her calling, but this meeting is making us a little anxious."

"It's okay, Mom," Corbin said, taking her mom's hand. "We got this."

Ashley nodded but looked unconvinced.

"Well, first let me reassure you that our girls will not be tasked to do anything that they haven't been doing already. The real changes come to the mission set of Joshua Bravo, but the support from the Watchers will be the same as always. Joshua Bravo is being given a new charter. Instead of functioning as one of the rotating alert Shepherd tactical teams, they will serve as a Special Missions Unit, or SMU. When you hear that acronym going forward, know it's referring to Joshua Bravo."

Does this mean Uncle Jed is going to be in even more danger now? she wondered, not loving the sound of this.

"What does a Special Missions Unit do exactly?" Sarah Beth asked.

"Good question, Sarah Beth," her dad said. "The Shepherd commander, Ben Morvant, believes that Joshua Bravo has proven themselves skilled, or dare I say *gifted*, at investigating secret plots by the Dark Ones. After the infiltration that happened here by Victor, Ben realized that the Shepherds have in some ways relied on you kids as a crutch. The Shepherds place a heavy burden on the school—and on Watchers in general—to see and predict threats before they happen. The feeling is that, by teaming so heavily with Watchers, the Shepherds have gotten really good at reacting, but at the same time we've lost some of our ability to be proactive."

"Hold on," Sarah Beth said. "Are you saying that Joshua Bravo is going to try to replace us? Because if you think they can do our job without us . . ."

"No, no, no, sweetheart," her mom said, jumping in. "That's not what Dad is implying. What he means is that Commander Morvant realized the burden he's asked the Watchers to bear has grown too heavy. Which is why Joshua Bravo is going to shift to more fieldwork to gather intelligence rather than just *reacting* to intelligence you provide. They'll work in tandem with the Watchers to identify threats earlier."

"So, I don't get to work with Uncle Jed anymore?" Sarah

Beth asked, knowing that the question made her sound selfish, but she didn't care. As far as she was concerned, not working with Uncle Jed was off the table.

"Actually, Sarah Beth, the reason we're having this meeting with you and Corbin specifically, and having it in the SCIF, is because Commander Morvant wanted us to extend the offer to you girls to become part of the SMU," her dad said.

"Wait, what?!" she blurted.

"Seriously?" Corbin added.

"Yes, seriously," David said. "Being out in the field more means they will need a dedicated Watcher team backing them up. And the members of Joshua Bravo, Jed in particular, feel strongly that the two of you will be important to their success and be valued team members."

"Wait, I'm not sure I like the sound of that," Ashley said, shooting a look to her husband.

"My reaction exactly, Ashley," Mom said with an understanding smile. "But actually, assigning the girls to support just one specialized team—especially one with"—she glanced at David and then Pastor Dee, who both nodded—"well, with certain gifts that the other units don't have, spiritually . . ."

". . . and tactically," Dad added.

"Yes, and tactically. Having them with just that unit will, I feel at least—and here I'm speaking as Sarah Beth's mom, not as the Shepherds' liaison—reduce their risk, and also perhaps their workload. They'll be responsible for only this one unit, instead of each team that comes up in the rotation."

"We also feel it will make both Joshua Bravo and Corbin and Sarah Beth far more effective and capable because they'll be part of the team and will have an ongoing relationship with one another."

Ashley seemed modestly satisfied with that answer from

what Sarah Beth saw—and heard in the woman's thoughts. But Sarah Beth had a more pressing question.

"Does this mean I get to go into the field like Corbin?" she asked, practically bursting with excitement.

"Someday, maybe, but not today," her mom said with no hesitation at all. "Corbin is older and cleared for limited fieldwork . . . unless, that is, her parents have changed their mind on that matter."

"We love this school. We love this program, but a few weeks ago, we had to go to the hospital because a metal spear had been thrown through our daughter's chest," Corbin's dad, Mark, said. "We're still processing that and, as a family, revisiting the question of fieldwork for Corbin."

"*Daaaad!*" Corbin said, with the irritation and condemnation that only a teenager can manage to cram into a single syllable. "I'm totally fine now."

"Yes, but you almost died," Ashley said, her voice a tight cord, tears welling up in her eyes.

"But that wasn't the fieldwork. It happened here at *school*," Corbin said.

"I know, so count yourself lucky you're still enrolled here," Corbin's mom, Ashley, fired back.

"This is an important and difficult decision," Pastor Margaret, Corbin's Keeper, said, speaking for the first time. "And one that nobody expects you to make today."

"That's right," David said. "The purpose of this meeting was to notify everyone about the change in operational charter for Joshua Bravo and explain what an SMU is. There's no rush. It will be several weeks, I imagine, before we get to work on our first case. At present, Joshua Bravo is on R and R, and when they return, they will spend a couple of weeks in training and preparation for their new role."

The conversation carried on for a little while longer with the grown-ups doing all the talking, like they loved to do. That worked out great, because it meant Sarah Beth and Corbin had a chance to Watcher snapchat about their reactions to the news they'd just received.

"This is awesome," Sarah Beth told her friend.

"Yeah, as long as they let us do it."

"They will," she reassured her friend. *"My dad says God only gifts us with talents for a purpose. This is what we're supposed to do, Corbin."*

"I hope so . . ."

Sarah Beth hadn't felt so excited since her parents had agreed to let her come to St. George's in the first place. She and Corbin would be working together constantly and exclusively with the best Shepherds team there was. Sarah Beth was so giddy, she had trouble sitting still for the rest of the session.

When the meeting finally ended, her parents held her behind to talk one-on-one while Corbin and her parents went to Pastor Margaret's office to have their family discussion.

"I assume your answer is *yes*?" her mom said with a big smile once they were alone.

"Yes, yes, one hundred percent yes!" Sarah Beth said, throwing her arms around both her mom and dad at the same time.

"We knew it would be," her dad said with a chuckle. "But Sarah Beth, this is a big step. Not just for you, but for us as a family. You're going to be interacting with me and Mom a lot more now. It's not just going to be you and Uncle Jed saving the world together. You understand and you're okay with that, I hope?"

"Absolutely," she said, pulling back to look at both of them. "My heart knows this is the perfect arrangement. It's going to be really good for our whole family and Uncle Jed. It's going to bring us together even more. Now it's like the family business, right?"

"We think so too, sweetheart," Mom said. "And we're proud of you."

"Thanks, guys, that means a lot to me," she said, but her mind was already racing ahead into a future filled with crazy adventures in cool faraway places, battling the Dark Ones with Corbin and Uncle Jed.

She was definitely going to snapchat Uncle Jed in a little while. Since he was on vacation, she'd let him sleep in—but he was going to be hearing from her very soon . . .

CHAPTER TWENTY

HIGHWAY RN 6

THIRTY-SEVEN MILES WEST OF DOMINICAN REPUBLIC BORDER

FOUR MILES EAST OF CAP-HAÏTIEN

NORTHERN HAITI

0835 HOURS LOCAL

Unlike during the trip to Marcello and Kaprica's home, Gayle had not slept until now, several long hours into the challenging drive in the dark. The roads west out of Santiago de los Caballeros only got worse the farther they traveled, winding through mountains, at times turning to dirt or crumbled asphalt, at others creeping along the edge of drop-offs, even more terrifying for how narrow they were. The town of Dajabón, on the border with Haiti—which they passed easily without even showing their passports—was poor and not much to look at compared to Santo Domingo, or even what they'd seen of Santiago de los Caballeros. But Dajabón had gas, which they bought, and would have had food too if they'd been there any time other than in the middle of the night. They bought water and snacks at the gas station and continued.

After passing through the Haitian town of Ouanaminthe on the other side of the Rue Massacre bridge, they left civilization behind and now were weaving through terrible roads of northern Haiti without having seen a single vehicle in hours. Jed glanced at Gayle, finally asleep, her head tilted back uncomfortably. Her gentle, almost cute, snore was much more soothing than the creaking of their truck on the brutal roads. He smiled, then his jaw set with tension at the thought of what he may have dragged her into. Sure, this was her job too, but what he believed might be waiting for them in Port-de-Paix was beyond what she had signed up for when she joined the CIA. Still, she'd hung with them in South America and again throughout the op to stop Victor and his Chinese weapon, so he knew she had it in her—right? She might still be wrapping her head around what she believed about the things they saw, but had he been so different just a few months ago?

His phone chirped from the center console. He popped in an AirPod so he could keep his hands on the wheel.

"Hey, boss," Jed said softly, knowing only one person would be calling him right now on the sat phone, which rested beside his basically useless cell phone. He turned the wheel left and then back right, weaving around yet another deep hole in the road.

"Hey, Jed," Ben said. "Tried you a bit ago but couldn't get through. All good?"

"Yeah, good," he said, glancing again at Gayle. "Even on the sat, it's a little spotty here. Tried you again an hour ago and couldn't connect. No signal."

"Yeah, well, we don't exactly have a dedicated satellite over the Caribbean right now," Ben said. "So, quick update. We have secured the site outside of Santiago de los Caballeros. It was a horror show, as you know, and I'm very sorry."

Jed let the silence hang, not sure what to say to that. It was horrible to see, but it was Marcello and Kaprica who had suffered it.

"It's a real loss to the Shepherds, but also to the community of believers."

"They were amazing people," Jed agreed, his throat tight around the words. This felt different from losing an operator, and not just because of the horrible manner of their deaths—a manner clearly calculated to send a message. It was because, as an operator, Jed always felt his job was to protect those who couldn't protect themselves—to fight for those who couldn't fight. Failing to do that for Kaprica and Marcello had, he realized, been haunting him the entire drive. "And we'll find those responsible."

Another pause.

"We agree that this is clearly the work of the Dark Ones, or some pawn of their plans in Haiti," Ben finally said softly in his ear. "Our intel shop is working the missing-children thing, and you're right—there has been an incredible uptick in abductions over the last six months. There is always a market in both countries, Haiti especially, for the exploitation of the vulnerable, but this looks different."

"Different how?" Jed asked, still keeping his voice low and his hands on the wheel.

"Well, for one thing, there is a growing percentage of kidnappings that seem less random. There'll be a hit on a school or a bus, but instead of taking twenty kids at once, they take only a few. Witnesses suggest they are targeting specific kids—searching for them. We're not sure what to make of it, but we have some partner agencies working with us to try and sort out similarities among the taken. Not much yet. We'll provide you real-time information as we get it. We're also locating and setting up a pickup route to get the rest of Joshua Bravo headed your way. But I need to know your plans. We have a satellite ping on you right now, obviously, and show you westbound in Haiti, about forty miles west of the border on highway RN 6, is that right?"

"Affirmative," he said.

"Any change in destination?"

"Nope," he said. "The only lead we have right now is the dying words of Kaprica, so we're headed to Port-de-Paix. Any luck with the other words she said?"

"Amour et Espoir," Ben said. "And yes, we think so. There is a school for orphans in Port-de-Paix by that name. It's the only reference we found in the area, in fact. It means 'Love and Hope.' The institution is like a boarding school for Haitian orphans. It's supported by a very wealthy—by Haitian standards especially—foundation focused on the out-of-control orphan population there. They partner with international charities to staff the facility—and a half dozen like it across Haiti—to bring caregivers and specially qualified teachers to the facilities."

Jed used his left hand to stroke at his beard, then quickly replaced it on the wheel as the road bent sharply to the left, then began a steep climb up the side of a rising hill.

"Did Kaprica tell you anything other than the name?"

"No," he said, gritting his teeth. "Unfortunately, she had only a few breaths left in her. She gave me the name of the town, those words—*Love and Hope*—and then just said *the children*. I'm not sure what it means, but I intend to find out."

Jed's mind raced back to the mother on the street in Santo Domingo, searching for her daughter.

She has had nightmares that someone wants to make her into a zombie . . .

"Do you have the feeling they might hit the school? Could it be their next target, whoever is behind this?" Ben asked.

"I don't know. What do the intel guys think?" Jed asked.

"Well, on the surface it seems unlikely, but there's so much we don't know. This facility—and the others run by the foundation—they're all very high-end, well-built, and have their own security in place, physical and armed personnel on site. They seem pretty serious about protecting these kids, so why take the chance when there are thousands of kids more easily targeted?"

Jed nodded, but something was beginning to take shape in his head now. It was shadowy and vague but there, in the distance and just out of reach.

"I guess it depends why the specific kids are targeted."

"Our feeling also."

"Are we getting any Watcher support on this?" Jed asked, hopeful that the answer would be yes, and that it would be Corbin and Sarah Beth assigned to dig into it.

"Getting that going this morning, I promise," Ben said. "Jed, when you get to Port-de-Paix, I need you to be careful . . . and also methodical."

"What do you mean?" Jed asked, but he already knew, he thought.

"Well, at this point, this isn't a direct-action operation, Jed. We have no idea what's going on or what to do about it. We have no clue the people involved or why. So, settle into Port-de-Paix and work with Gayle to gather intel, okay? This is a prime example of the new charter we have for Joshua Bravo, so figure out what's going on before you go storming the walls by yourself at some school for orphans. I'll need thirty-six hours to get your team assembled from their various locations and to you in the middle-of-nowhere Haiti, so try and get a sense of just what's going on by then."

"Will do, boss," he said. He glanced over at Gayle, who was now watching him carefully with awake and curious eyes. He gave her a reassuring wink. They were really on mission now, with the support of Trinity Loop and his team en route.

"I have the logistics folks setting up accommodations for you in Port-de-Paix. They'll forward information to you shortly, but I believe they are renting a house where the rest of the team can join. Keep a low profile. We'll send NOC information as well, to help you stay under the radar. The team is putting something together now, but getting documents will be a challenge, so just avoid needing them for me, okay?"

"Okay," Jed said.

His mind still danced awkwardly with what he'd learned. Children were missing, lots of carefully selected and targeted children, and Kaprica had sent them to a school for orphans across the border in Haiti. A dark thought came to him.

"Hey, Ben . . ."

"Yeah, brother?"

"What if the walls and security aren't to keep the kids safe and bad guys out? What if . . ." He glanced at Gayle, who raised an eyebrow, her face suggesting she already knew where he was headed. "What if it's to keep people—to keep the children—*in*?"

He let the silence hang in the air, knowing that Ben would chew on that a moment.

"Stay in the shadows until we get the team there, Jed," Ben said finally. "Learn what you can, but do it safely. I'll let you know what the Watchers come up with. We'll send what you need for your accommodations and NOCs shortly, and let's talk again when you get settled. How long until you arrive? An hour or two?"

Jed snorted and weaved around part of a tree lying in the middle of the road.

"Yeah, maybe in Tennessee," he said. "Don't worry until it's been more than three or four hours before we've called. The roads here are beyond terrible."

"Got it," Ben said. "Stay safe. Praying for you . . ."

And he was gone.

"Ben?" Gayle asked.

Jed nodded.

"Anything new to add?"

"We're on a sanctioned mission now," he said with more than a little satisfaction. Jed filled her in on what little he'd learned, especially about Amour et Espoir. "For now we're just ISR. We need to surveil this school and see what role it plays in whatever the hell is going on. We lay low, gather intel, and try to uncover who is behind all of this. By then, we'll have the rest of the team with us." He looked at her with hard eyes. "Then, we can take action."

She nodded.

"So much for vacation," she said with a tight smile. He imagined, like him, she was haunted by the images of the fallen Shepherd couple. Those images would likely be with them for a long time—forever, probably.

"I'm not much of a vacation guy anyway," he said with a smile and shrug. "Prefer to be working."

She looked at him with her lovely eyes.

I would love to one day vacation with you.

The thought he received inadvertently from her mind made him blush, and he turned away so she wouldn't notice.

"So, what's our plan, partner?" she asked, stretching her back.

"We get settled wherever they set us up in Port-de-Paix," he said. "Then we learn what we can and wait for any intel Ben can provide."

"We get something to eat . . ."

"We get something to eat," he agreed, looking back at her now with a genuine smile. The girl could eat. "Not sure we'll see much between here and there. We're coming up on Cap-Haïtien.

They're big enough to have an airport, so we can probably find something there."

"Sounds good," she said and stared out the windshield, lost in her own thoughts. Gayle turned to him again after a moment. "Jed?"

"Yeah?"

"What if we find out they're hurting children in that place?" she asked.

He clenched his jaw and clutched the steering wheel tighter.

"Then we won't wait," he said. "We'll make sure those kids are safe and that whoever is responsible pays for what they've done."

"Just the two of us?" she asked, but she seemed okay with that.

"If need be," he said and nodded. "But you need to remember the most important thing about the Shepherds."

"What's that?" she asked.

"We're never alone," he said, nodding to her and then returning his eyes to the road. "As long as we're listening to God's call and doing His work—we're never, ever alone."

CHAPTER TWENTY-ONE

AMOUR ET ESPOIR CHILDREN'S HOME AND SCHOOL

#4 RUE LAULIER

PORT-DE-PAIX

HAITI

0905 HOURS LOCAL

"Shut up, Amede," Sani said in a harsh whisper, her own leg bouncing up and down as she sat beside Mary and Amede—the two kids who'd been taken from the bus with her what seemed a lifetime ago—on a long bench outside the massive wooden door to the director's office. "You're scaring her."

"What did I do?" Amede asked, arms up in the universal *Who, me?* gesture. "I'm just telling you what I heard."

Amede had been regaling them all day with stories he'd heard about kids being turned into zombies. Like an old wives' tale meant to keep kids in line, the rumors at the school were about troublemakers who were punished by becoming zombies.

"There are no zombies here, Mary," Sani said, taking her friend's hand in hers.

"But why would kids make that up?" Mary said, her eyes wide with fear.

"Because that's what kids do," Sani said, giving Amede a sharp look.

Her grandmother had talked about zombies from time to time—the living dead, created by a Voudou priest or priestess, usually as a punishment for something. When she was little, Granmè had told her of a cousin from Gonaïves who had been turned into a zombie. The young man had come home terrified, telling of how the Voudou priest, whom his father owed money, had approached him in the street, blowing a powder in his face and then laughing as he sauntered off. The young man died a few hours later. They'd buried him and then, days later, saw him with the Voudou priest, serving as his slave. Most people in Haiti seemed to believe that zombies were real, despite what the Americans who came to teach and preach in their schools claimed. Sani didn't know what to believe about zombies, but she knew her granmè would never lie to her . . .

"Sani, are you sure?" Mary asked, her voice trembling.

"I'm sure," she said, knowing that it was a lie—a white lie, maybe, but definitely not a whole truth.

She was sure of nothing now, not after meeting with Madame Athaliah—*Manbo* Athaliah, she reminded herself. The man on the plane had used that title, the title meaning a Voudou high priestess. She had felt it—the dark confidence of a Voudou priestess—as they sat and chatted, or believed she had. She was so frightened she sometimes didn't know whether to trust her instincts. The thoughts that came to her could be her own frightened thoughts, or thoughts brought to her by her gift, the thoughts of others. How could she be sure they were not just the thoughts of the scared twelve-year-old girl she still was most of the time?

But it was more than a malevolence that she felt, wasn't it? While they had chatted in a lovely office and sipped tea, Madame Athaliah had shared with her a vision to rid Haiti of poverty and suffering and how that could only happen when people took control of their lives—that no one, no thing, no religion could do it for them. As she spoke, Sani had felt Madame Athaliah probing her mind, trying to get inside and steal her thoughts and emotions. It felt like a snake, slithering around her ankle slowly and gently, ready to strike and pour venom into her at any second. She had put up the wall, just like Granmè had taught her. She always pictured a wall made of thick trees, for some reason, and it seemed to work.

Athaliah had stopped talking when Sani built her wall, as if something had suddenly snapped her attention. Athaliah had put her hands in her lap, and, for just a moment, Sani thought she'd seen a flash of red-orange light—like the embers of a campfire—in the woman's dark eyes. After, she had smiled.

"You seem so frightened, Sani," Athaliah had said. "I know you have had a difficult life. I know it must be so hard to trust, after losing parents and growing up an orphan, but I'm here to help you. I want to give you a life you deserve—one of health, happiness, wealth, and even power. It will take time, but you will come to know me as Mother. And you will come to love me."

"Yes, ma'am," Sani had said, forcing a shy smile onto her face.

That her captor—and that was how she thought of Athaliah now, as her captor, despite Amede's enthusiasm for his new life—had called her an orphan must mean she had not been inside her head, right? That her wall of trees must have worked? Otherwise, Athaliah would have known about Granmè. Sani wanted to talk to Ms. Harper about everything, but it would have to be in private, and Harper had been busy—and frightened, it seemed. Sani had thought to go into her mind and learn why, but she was terrified to remove the wall of trees—terrified of what might come inside if she did. Later, perhaps she would try and reach out to the girl Emelin, but while Manbo Athaliah was at the school, she knew using her gifts would be far too dangerous. Was Athaliah still there? She'd heard that sometimes she visited for an hour, other times for several days . . .

"Why do you think they want to talk to us?" Mary asked, squeezing her hand and bringing her back into the present.

"I don't know," Sani admitted, but seeing Mary's worried face, she added, "I'm sure they just want to meet all the new kids and introduce us to all the teachers and staff."

Amede turned, and without even reading his mind, she knew he would say *and zombies*, so she shot him a stern look, and he closed his mouth and shrugged again.

"I bet Sani is right," he said, then looked at Sani for approval.

Sani gave him a nod and a smile.

"Ms. Wilshire will see you now, kids," said Ms. Fabiola, whom Sani knew from English class, as she poked her head out from the office door. The middle-aged woman was Haitian but spoke flawless English, making her a better teacher than the Americans with their broken Haitian Creole. Sani knew, from being near the woman her first night, that Ms. Fabiola had once been a nun. Sani didn't know why she wasn't one now, but she did know that whatever the reason, Ms. Fabiola felt deep shame about it—and anger.

"Yes, ma'am," Sani said, rising and speaking for the group.

Fabiola smiled, but something in her eyes suggested that she had concerns about Sani. She looked at her a little too long, her lower lip curling under just slightly, before leading the way back to the heavy door she'd come from. Fabiola ushered them into the office, where Ms. Wilshire sat at a large desk, and closed the door behind them.

"Sit, sit, please, children," Ms. Wilshire said, the big smile on her face somehow not quite matching a strange look in her eyes. Like Fabiola, her gaze hung on Sani for an extra beat, and Sani felt her nervousness turn to fear again.

They took their seats—Sani the middle of the three, still holding Mary's hand—in high-back cushioned chairs that had been placed in front of the large desk. Ms. Wilshire leaned in, still smiling that strange smile.

"Can I get you anything? Some juice or some water, perhaps? Some iced tea?"

"No, thank you, ma'am," Sani answered for all of them before Amede could ask for something. She just wanted this to be over as quickly as possible.

"Okay then. You are quite a leader, Sani. Amede and Mary are lucky to have you here. You all came together from Mount Hope in Pepillo Salcedo, right?"

"Yes, ma'am. We were taken from our bus on the way home to Pepillo Salcedo from school at Mount Hope, but the school is actually in El Copey."

"I see," Ms. Wilshire said, but her smile turned saccharine. Perhaps she didn't like that Sani had said they were *taken*, but that was the truth, wasn't it? Or maybe she just didn't like to be corrected. Sani pushed aside a few trees in her wall and took just a little sneak peek into the woman's thoughts . . .

Athaliah is right about this one. She's dangerous . . .

She snapped the trees back in place and felt her pulse quicken. Sani decided to be more what Wilshire wanted.

"I'm so grateful to be here," she said, wondering if her own smile had the same fake sweetness as Wilshire's and praying that was not the case. "This is the most beautiful place I've ever seen in my life . . ."

"And the food is amazing," Amede chimed in, as she hoped he would.

"I can't believe I have my own bedroom," Mary added.

Perfect, Sani thought to herself.

"Well, I'm so delighted to hear you are all happy here. It can be an adjustment for some, coming to a new place," Ms. Wilshire said, holding steady on Sani's eyes as she spoke. "So, no complaints then?"

"Oh, no, ma'am," Sani said.

"I love it here," Amede said.

Mary remained quiet.

"Well," Ms. Wilshire said, rising and standing behind her desk, her hands folded on the back of her big leather chair. "I couldn't be any happier to hear that. I'm meeting with all the new kids today, to be sure that no one has any concerns or questions—that no one has any regrets. We're here for you kids. It's our reason for everything we do, to give you a better life. Do you believe that, Sani?"

"Yes, ma'am," Sani answered, a little too quickly, maybe.

Ms. Wilshire nodded, but Sani saw her lips purse, making her chin into a relief map of wrinkles.

"Well, I hope you will come to me if there is anything you need, or if there is anything that worries you. You see, we find that if one child has adjustment issues, it can ripple over to the other kids, causing a real problem across the whole campus. One child with regrets or fears, or a child who thinks they shouldn't be here for whatever reason—well, that can become like a cancer here at Amour et Espoir. Do you know what a cancer is, Sani?"

"Yes, Ms. Wilshire," Sani said, and her voice trembled now,

but she felt a rage rising that she knew she needed desperately to control. Bad things could happen if she couldn't control her rage, and she had Mary and Amede to think about.

And Granmè.

"Her mama died of cancer," Amede said.

Sani shot him a look.

"Well, you *told* me she did," he said.

"Yes, a cancer can kill everything. You know what you have to do with a cancer, don't you, children?" Wilshire asked.

They sat in silence, staring at the woman whose face had changed somehow. She no longer looked like a happy choir member, but instead like someone full of anger and fear.

"You must cut it out," she said, drawing the words out and staring directly into Sani's eyes, leaning in as she did. "And then," she continued, straightening up and smiling, the happy choir lady back again, "the rest of the body can live. I'm so sorry that they couldn't do that for your mother, Sani. But now you are here. And we will love you and care for you and make you into something very special, okay?"

"Okay, Ms. Wilshire," she said, her own rage gone and only the fear remaining. Did Wilshire mean they would kill her? Did they know something about her? About her . . . gifts? "Thank you, ma'am."

"You are welcome, dear," Wilshire said as she dropped back into her leather chair. "You kids can go now. Classes have already started, so hurry along."

The three rose, and Sani could sense that Mary, at least—if not Amede as well—felt something off in the room because they were eager to leave. They headed together to the door.

"Sani, can you stay a moment?" the voice called from behind her.

Sani's stomach turned over in a knot, and she felt her lip

tremble. "I don't want to be late for class, ma'am," she said, turning slowly.

"I'm sure," Wilshire said, gesturing to the middle chair again. "But it will only be a moment, I promise you."

Mary looked at her with wide eyes. Sani squeezed the girl's hand and gave her a reassuring smile. "I'll be in class in a moment," she promised. "Please tell Mr. Charles I'll be right along," she added, finding the name of their geography teacher in her head somewhere.

Her two friends left, and Sani returned to the chairs and took her seat, aware that her hands were trembling badly.

"So," Ms. Wilshire said, her voice and her face now becoming flat and expressionless. "Is there anything you want to tell me, Sani? Anything you want to talk to me about privately? We know you are not happy here, though none of us can possibly imagine why. We are doing everything we can to give you a future, yet still, you seem unsettled. Why is that?"

"That . . . that's not true, Ms. Wilshire," Sani stammered. "I . . . I love it here. I'm just so . . ."

"Yes, yes, yes," Wilshire said, waving her hand as if shooing away an insect. "You are just so grateful, I know. But there are some who don't believe that is true, and those people are very powerful indeed. You are not the first to have trouble . . . acclimating, my dear. Do you know what that word means, Sani—acclimating?"

"Yes, I think so," she said and felt tears stream onto her cheeks.

I just want to go home. I just want to see my granmè.

"Well, tell me," Wilshire said, throwing her hands up as if exasperated. "What does it mean?"

"It . . . it means to get used to something, doesn't it?"

"It means to become settled in, to accept where you are, and to embrace it. It means adapting to change. Here, it means being grateful for all we do for you. Not *saying* you are grateful, Sani," the woman said, folding her hands and her smile becoming wicked, "but *being* grateful."

The woman leaned back in her large chair. Sani stared at her hands, watching a tear drop onto her fingers. She heard a jingling sound and looked up to see Ms. Wilshire ringing a small handbell she had picked up from her desk that Sani had not even noticed before.

"As I said, you are not the first to have trouble acclimating, Sani," she said, a wicked smile on her face and a little sliver of orange light flickering in her eyes.

Behind Wilshire, in the corner behind the desk, a door opened. Two girls walked out, the first carrying a silver tray with a teapot and two cups. The older girl was perhaps Sani's age, maybe a year younger, and the second was maybe seven or eight. Both wore simple, faded dresses and Sunday dress-for-church shoes. She guessed, from the look of them, that they were sisters.

Sani felt a wave of terror wash over her.

Both girls stared blankly ahead and moved in slow, shuffling movements. The older girl, the one carrying the tray, approached the desk and slid it into place beside Ms. Wilshire. Then she shuffled backward, hands folded in front of her. She didn't so much as glance at Sani, but once she was against the wall, she stared down at her feet. Her sister stood in an identical pose, hands clasped in front of her, eyes staring blankly at the floor.

Sani wanted to scream, to run from the room, but she knew she couldn't. The blank look in the eyes, the dirt on the shoes—

Dirt from the grave . . .

"Are you sure you wouldn't like some tea, dear?" Ms. Wilshire asked, smiling at her.

Sani shook her head, unable to answer, and felt a tear spill out of her left eye onto her cheek.

"Just one," Wilshire said flatly, without looking at the little girl.

The younger girl poured a cup of tea, her movements slow and robotic. Then she set the teapot down, shuffled backward, and stood beside her sister, eyes fixed on the floor.

"Mirlande?"

The older girl took a single step forward, hands still in front of her, eyes still on the floor.

"Yes, ma'am?" she said, her voice even, devoid of feeling.

"Would you say that you were happy when you got here?"

"No, ma'am," the girl said.

"Were you cooperative?"

"No, ma'am."

"Were you well acclimated?"

"No, ma'am," she said again, her voice never wavering from the flat note of submission.

"Are you cooperative now, Mirlande?" Wilshire asked, taking a sip of her tea and then returning the cup to its saucer. The director of Amour et Espoir never so much as glanced at the sisters behind her, instead holding her gaze steadily on Sani.

"Yes, ma'am."

"When did that start, Esther?" Wilshire asked, her lips curling up again in the corners as the older girl dropped her head and now her little sister looked up with emotionless, lifeless eyes.

"After we died, ma'am."

"After you died?" Wilshire asked, a full smile on her face now, apparently amused.

"Yes, ma'am," the girl called Esther said. "After we died, and the Calypso woman bring us back to serve her. After we be made to serve her."

"Are you happy now?"

"No, ma'am," the girl said more softly. "But now we gots no choice."

"Thank you, girls, that is all."

The sisters shuffled back to the door and disappeared.

"You see, Sani, there are many ways to help you acclimate to your life here. You must decide which suits you, but we will find one that works. Do you understand?"

"Yes, ma'am," Sani said, realizing how she sounded like the sisters—the zombies that served Ms. Wilshire now. "I'm happy here, I promise. And I can cooperate."

"Good," Ms. Wilshire said, taking another sip of tea before placing it back on the tray again. "I'm glad we understand each other." She rose, moving behind the desk. "Be sure and tell the others how much you like it here, Sani. You are a born leader. It will matter to them a lot."

"Yes, ma'am," she said, wiping tears from her wet cheeks and looking at her hands. "I promise I will."

"I know you will, Sani," Wilshire said with a long, put-upon sigh. "I hate to have to show you these things, but I just want you to understand. I'm sure we will get along famously now."

"Yes, ma'am," Sani said. She wanted to leave—to sprint from the room and never stop running. She could smell the earthy dirt odor of the girls lingering in the air.

"Run along to class now, Sani," Wilshire said. "I'm afraid I've made you quite late enough."

Sani rose and nodded, her nod almost a bow, and walked quickly to the door, resisting the urge to run.

Did Ms. Harper know about this? She didn't think that was possible—Harper seemed so sweet, so sincere. But Harper suspected something dark was going on here, didn't she? And it was Sani's thoughts that had betrayed Harper—it must have been. Sani had to keep herself inside now.

She didn't want to be killed.

But if she was, she most certainly didn't want to be raised back again to serve as a slave—a zombie slave.

Sani had to be more careful.

"Have a lovely morning, Sani," Ms. Wilshire called out from behind her, her voice light and songlike.

"Thank you, ma'am, you too," she called over her shoulder, not looking up at Fabiola as she jogged from the office lobby.

CHAPTER TWENTY-TWO

AUBERT, PORT-DE-PAIX

HAITI

1605 HOURS LOCAL

Jed slowed the truck, checking behind them for the sixth time, before making the right turn onto 1st Rue Chalet. By this point, a mile into Port-de-Paix, the "highway" was little more than a poorly paved city street. The closer they came to the city, the more his fear for the missing children and his sense of urgency grew, and he had been unable to resist a detour for an ISR run at Amour et Espoir. Gayle hadn't even questioned the decision, instead nodding eager consent to the plan. Like him, she must have felt the pull.

ISR—Intelligence, Surveillance, and Reconnaissance—was a staple of work for a Navy SEAL. The big hits, killing bad guys, and extracting high-value targets from enemy locations—that was the side of the work shown on TV and in movies. But every mission was earned through the sweat—and often blood—from hours and hours of tedious and equally dangerous missions to gain the intelligence needed to make those hits possible. And on this ISR run in an SUV, on a dusty road in Haiti—with just a CIA intelligence analyst instead of a small team of fellow SEALs—the challenges posed by the target, should the orphanage become that, became immediately obvious.

The SUV crawled slowly up the narrow street, houses crowding in on them from both sides, as the GPS dot got closer.

"Go slow," Gayle said.

She glanced over at him and blushed, realizing who she was talking to. Jed imagined that in her job of managing CIA assets, she was accustomed to giving a lot of direction. He smiled and slowed slightly, letting her off the hook.

"I can't tell on the map how close to the road the entrance to the compound is," she continued.

He nodded. Her use of the word *compound* instead of *school* was in no way lost on him. They were both in mission mode, he realized.

"Glance around at the houses," Jed said, then came almost to a stop, making a show of checking something on his phone. Then he stopped completely and leaned in to talk to her. "We're just two tourists, off the beaten path and a little lost, trying to find our rental property."

Gayle nodded and looked again at the map on her phone, zooming in but also completing the illusion. Jed let the truck begin to creep forward again.

Rue Laulier was a narrow road only fifteen hundred feet long or so, that began as 1st Rue Chalet off RD 501. It weaved north through tightly packed but large—by Haitian standards—houses on both sides, with no cross streets. Worse, Jed could see now that the road dead-ended right at a towering ten-foot iron fence with a wide gate and gold-leaf lettering announcing Amour et Espoir. He immediately spied the cameras on either side of the gate and the small shack extending through the brick wall beside the gate—a modern-looking, glassed-in structure with a green tile roof, another camera and antennae mounted to the tiles. A single thin security guard sat inside the shack in dark slacks and a white uniform shirt. If there was a heavy security presence here as Ben had suggested—possibly including Dark Ones ready for battle—they certainly were well hidden. Breaching the front gate could be done by a group of Girl Scouts with an afternoon to train.

Still—hide in plain view, right?

How many times had they hidden a SEAL platoon in plain sight? The heavy hitters and firepower could easily be inside, with a myriad of cameras there to allow for a response within seconds. There could even be snipers somewhere beyond the gate, watching Jed and Gayle right now. It wasn't like the Haitians were running sophisticated aerial surveillance, but that didn't mean they weren't being watched.

The road was so narrow that without entering the gate, it would take a three-point turn for Jed to turn around again. Jed pulled the SUV over, up onto a narrow driveway, and got out, tossing a "Stay in the truck" to Gayle. He looked up and down the street, taking in as much of the school grounds as he could, which wasn't much from this angle. A wall surrounded the grounds, edging the street, and even with his six-foot-four height, he could see very little. Through the gate, he saw a large main building at the end of the drive past the guard shack. He screwed up his face and put his hands on his hips, a hopelessly lost tourist. Then he slipped back into the driver's seat.

"Not much to see from here," he said, turning to Gayle as if he were a sheepish husband explaining he'd gotten them lost. "Long drive up to a very nice building, but little else up front. Lots of cameras for a place in the metropolis of Port-de-Paix, but a modest guard shack, as you can see, with just one dude."

He burned a mental picture of the entrance layout and the drive up to the main building, then began his awkward turn around well south of the last house before the gate, hoping that kept him out of the camera's view.

They'd also learned that there was indeed a population of adventurous tourists in Port-de-Paix because at least half of the houses on the approach to the school on Rue Laulier had rental signs and phone numbers on them, and many had Vrbo property numbers. Most also had no cars in the drives, which offered some potential for ISR if they could get eyes in the sky to confirm no heat signatures inside—if breaking and entering was not deemed off limits in their OPORD. In any case, that theirs was not the only Vrbo home listed made their on-the-fly NOC of an adventurous tourist couple easily believable.

"I wonder if we can get a better view from the east side of the compound?" Gayle said. "The map took us to the main entrance, but it looks like there's a road east of here that comes up to the other side of the compound."

"Sounds good," Jed said. "So, east on 501?"

"Yeah," she said, zooming in with her thumb and forefinger. "Make a left turn and then another left onto Rue Dalma Si less than a quarter mile east."

Jed headed back to RD 501 and turned left once, then again, onto Rue Dalma Si, which he almost missed behind a small wood-framed store with the windows and door shuttered with boards. He weaved north, and after they passed a handful of sad run-down, shanty-like buildings clustered together, some larger, nicer homes appeared as they drove toward the waterfront, most with rental and Vrbo signs outside. Jed pulled into the drive of the last home on the left, right along a brick wall that appeared identical to the one at the orphanage's main entrance. The rental sign had a sliding "Available" placard hanging from the bottom.

Jed put the SUV in Park but left the engine running. He and Gayle stepped out of the truck together and made a show of looking at the house, writing down the phone number from the rental sign, and looking around the back of the house as well. Seeing no one and glancing back at the equally vacant street, Jed scanned for cameras and then looked over the wall, where he got his first real view of the property.

Whatever evil he expected to see did not present itself. A large lake behind the rental house stretched all the way to the school property, which also had a little pond and a cluster of trees. He could see the school now much more clearly—a brick, green-tile-roofed structure that was modern, clean, and very well maintained. Behind it sat a large complex of sports fields rivaling most American high schools, fields that were filled with children: one soccer field with high school–aged kids and another with younger kids. Beyond the fields, he saw two separate playgrounds, far nicer than he'd expect for an orphanage in the poverty-stricken country of Haiti. The rear of the school had a trellis-like enclosure with picnic tables and a large wall covered with what looked like an LED movie screen. The children on the fields were dressed in sports uniforms, and those on the back patio were in the school's uniform: dresses for the girls and khaki slacks with blue shirts for the boys.

Signs of the evil he believed lurked inside were completely absent from the scene he beheld. And there was nothing in the children's behavior to suggest this was a ruse. The kids seemed happy, laughing and playing, the little ones literally squealing in delight as they ran around.

He made mental notes of the general layout—unnecessary since they would get far, far more detailed information from satellite passes and construction records soon enough, when Ben was able to get satellite tasking.

Jed had been searching for something hinting at whatever nefarious thing the Dark Ones might be up to inside. Instead, he saw a school nicer than the one he'd attended as a kid in Murfreesboro, Tennessee—and kids who seemed happier than any children he'd seen since arriving on the two-nation island.

"I think this is nicer than my school," Gayle said, as if reading his mind.

"Yeah," he said. "They don't seem to be in much distress, do they?"

As an exclamation point on his assessment, he watched as a teacher huddled the younger kids in a tight circle, arms wrapped around one another, seemingly leading them in prayer.

"You think there are Dark Ones running that program?" Gayle asked dubiously.

"I don't know," he admitted, "but Kaprica sent us here for a reason."

Gayle nodded and slowly blinked, no doubt chasing away the images of the horror at the home of the two dead Shepherds.

"We need to see inside," she said.

He nodded his agreement. But the urgency he'd felt the last eight hours was dissipating. Whatever might be happening inside, they sure as hell didn't need to go kicking in doors, guns scanning for Dark Ones, and scaring the bloody hell out of the happy, innocent-appearing children they watched.

"We'll head to the house, get settled in, and brainstorm a plan."

"Agreed," Gayle said and climbed into the SUV.

CHAPTER TWENTY-THREE

RENTAL HOUSE
12 ROUTE DJERILON
AUBERT, PORT-DE-PAIX
HAITI
1725 HOURS LOCAL

They stopped at a less modern but still nice grocery about halfway between the school and their rental, where they breezed through the aisles and stocked up on needed supplies. It took only a few minutes more to arrive at 12 Route Djerilon, a lovely house on the coast, less than a mile from the grounds of the school and orphanage of Amour et Espoir.

Jed pulled into a half-circle drive outside the gate of the house. He slid his huge frame out of the truck, arched his back, and rolled his head, getting a satisfying crack from his lower spine and neck almost simultaneously. He let out an exhausted sigh and scanned the house they sat in front of, reflexively measuring distances to the homes on either side as well, calculating approaches for enemies and routes for escape. He grinned at the occupational hazard, but then he wasn't on vacation anymore, was he?

Jed smiled at Gayle, who raised her arms and stretched her back on the other side of the truck.

Another vacation would be nice though—with a good friend. Vacationing alone sucks . . .

This house was larger and appeared more comfortable than expected, at least from the outside, and was situated south of the busy "downtown" area they had come in through. Modern two-story construction beneath a terra-cotta tile roof, bright fresh paint, and a large yard made the house look like something from an upper-middle-class Florida neighborhood.

"Not too shabby, huh?" Jed asked with a grin.

"Not too shabby," Gayle agreed, looking over the low wall at the house that would be home for a time.

Adrenaline burned off, Jed now felt a heavy weariness descend on him.

"You must be exhausted," Gayle said.

He smiled at her. She had offered twice to take a turn at the wheel, and it wasn't chivalry that made him turn her down. He just loathed riding shotgun and never could sleep while traveling—perhaps another throwback to his time in the Teams when traveling was preparation for combat—so he imagined the hours in the passenger seat would be wasted sleep time she could at least enjoy. The reason was also tactical—he knew he was well trained and experienced at functioning without enough sleep but didn't know if the same would be true for her.

"I'm good right now," he chuckled, opening the tailgate to the SUV, "but give me two minutes in a comfy chair or couch and it'll come crashing in on me."

He pulled their bags—his over-the-shoulder duffel and her

roller bag—out of the rear of the SUV and slung a backpack over each shoulder. He also scooped up the large plastic bags of food they'd picked up at the market. Once he'd looped eight bags around each wrist, he looked up and saw Gayle laughing quietly and shaking her head.

"What?"

"I can carry some bags, Jed," she said with a chuckle. "We're teammates, right?"

"Right," he said with a sheepish grin.

She took three bags off each of his wrists, lightening his load. Then she placed the brick of bottled water onto her roller bag and led the way from the small square parking pad. He followed her to the tan stucco house.

"Maybe I can make a pass through the neighborhood when you connect with Ben," she suggested.

"We should probably stick together," he said, then held up a hand when she raised her eyebrows and opened her mouth. "That's not me being misogynistic, but practical," he said. "I trust you completely, and you are very, very competent. But there's only two of us. We need to keep each other's backs. I don't know who might know we're here."

"Or *what*," Gayle mumbled.

Jed wondered just where she was on her journey toward accepting the impossible things she'd seen since first working with the Shepherds.

"Right," he said with what he hoped was a reassuring smile. "Not much of a security perimeter," he grumbled after punching in the gate code and heading toward the front door.

"More than most of the houses, I guess," Gayle said. "We're not in a FOB in Iraq, you know."

"True," he admitted, and he wasn't that concerned, actually. With or without a wall, it was going to be hard to breach this house undetected, especially once the rest of Joshua Bravo was here. God have mercy on anyone breaking into a house full of former SEALs, Green Berets, Marines, and CIA operatives.

The cool of the air-conditioning was clean and refreshing, and the home was neat and well organized. No, it was more than neat: It was immaculate. He decided to ask Ben later if this was really just a Vrbo or an established safe house the Shepherds controlled—or perhaps those of one of their informal "partner" agencies in the federal government, like the CIA, that seemed to support them frequently. He wondered again just how many assets Trinity Loop had inside the military and government agencies—both in America and abroad.

A large kitchen with a pass-through bar waited ready to receive the groceries, so he added his bags to the ones Gayle had laid out. She scoped out the large open living area and then stood at the sliding glass doors, looking out onto the surprisingly spacious backyard that even included a small pool with relatively clean-looking water.

Jed felt exhausted, but at this point he figured he'd be better brainstorming with Gayle, eating a good meal, and then getting any intelligence updates from Ben before turning in for a good night's sleep. He had been reassured by his cursory look at Amour et Espoir that nothing horrible was happening immediately, so fresh, rested eyes and heads would be the best plan forward. Tomorrow, they'd begin digging in earnest.

"I'm going to take a quick shower, and then we can do some brainstorming, okay?" Jed asked.

"I'll join you," she said. Her head snapped around, and she looked at him in horror, her face turning a deep crimson. "No. Not . . . I mean, I didn't mean I would *join you*, join you. I just meant I'll shower too . . . I mean, my own shower, like, in my own *private* bathroom."

She squeezed her eyes shut in embarrassment, then shook her head and looked out the window again.

"Of course," he said with a chuckle. "I knew what you meant, Gayle." He found himself strangely delighted by her discomfort. There was a spark there—for him, at least. But that would have to wait until this was all over. "You pick your bedroom," he said.

She grabbed her bag and hustled past him, heading up the stairs.

There were a total of five bedrooms in the house, four upstairs and one down. The downstairs master had its own bath, and there were two additional full baths upstairs. This would be an absolute luxury compared to any mission he'd ever done as a SEAL or a Shepherd.

Gayle chose one of the three rooms with two double beds, assuming no doubt she would double up with someone when the rest of the team arrived. Jed took the downstairs master, for now at least, not because he needed a king bed, but because he wanted to be on the ground floor should anyone try and breach the house—especially now while it was just the two of them.

The very long, very hot shower—which he turned to ice-cold at the end—did exactly what he needed it to do, and twenty-five minutes later, he was awake, refreshed, and wearing clean clothes—athletic shorts, flip-flops, and a Bonefrog Coffee T-shirt. Gayle, to his surprise, was already at the dining room table, laptop open, intensely studying something. She had a glass of lemon water beside her.

Jed set the pistol she'd given him in Santo Domingo on the table, grabbed a water for himself, and then slid into the seat beside her. His stomach growled, but he worried once he filled it, it would be impossible to put sleep off much longer.

"So, this is crazy," Gayle said, looking at him over a pair

of glasses he'd not ever seen her wear. The readers were low on her nose and, with her young and pretty face, gave her the appearance of a little girl playing grandma dress-up. She looked adorable, frankly.

"Whatcha got?" he asked, sipping his water and wishing he'd not been too lazy to cut a slice of lemon.

"So, did you know that zombies are real?"

"Don't be ridiculous, Gayle," he said but leaned in, intrigued. "Only God has the power over life and death. I'm pretty sure Jesus and His followers are the only ones who can raise someone from the dead."

"And I agree completely," Gayle said, looking back to her laptop. "It's more complicated than that, though. There are medical, pharmacological, social, cultural, and psychological forces that all come into play."

"I'm listening," he said, fascinated by the idea and by her enthusiasm.

"I found this article from 2017 in *Harvard Magazine*," she said, and he raised his eyebrows. He'd expected her to say the *National Enquirer*. "It's about a Harvard scientist who studied the zombie phenomenon. He was an ethnobotanist, and he'd been asked . . ."

"Hold up there, Professor," Jed said with a laugh, but in fact he felt way out of his element. "I know all the CIA operatives are Ivy League brainiacs, but you can't just drop terms like *ethobotanist* on a door-kicking frogman without some explanation."

"*Ethno*botanist," she corrected. "It's someone who studies both the biological and cultural aspects of native medicines, usually looking for some Western medicinal application. The guy in the article, Dr. Wade Davis, worked at the time for a professor at Harvard who discovered the key ingredient still used in modern anesthesia by studying the poison used in blow darts in the

Amazon. Really cool stuff. Anyway," she continued, returning to her computer, her face basked in blue light from the screen. "This Dr. Davis came here to Haiti in the early '80s, when he was a graduate student, at the request of his boss. There was a big stir about the zombie legends because they had discovered the first person claiming to be a zombie who had actual proof of his death recorded . . ."

"What kind of proof?" Jed asked skeptically.

"Well, he claims he was killed by a Voudou priest who poisoned him with what he called 'zombie powder.' He was admitted to the hospital with abdominal pain and fever and died shortly after. He was declared dead by hospital physicians, including one American physician, and kept in the morgue for a time. He was then buried. His funeral and burial were attended by his family, including his sister. The man's name was Clairvius Narcisse, and he reappeared in his village almost thirty years later. He found his sister and shared intimate, personal things only Narcisse could have known. He claimed to remember dying—remembered being pronounced dead and his sister crying at his bedside. He remembered things she whispered to him right after his death. He remembered the morgue, the coffin and viewing—even the dirt hitting his coffin when they buried him. All of it."

She stared at Jed, fascinated and looking for his reaction.

"And then?" Jed prompted, totally sucked in now.

"He claims the Bokor—that's the term for the Voudou high priest—dug him up. The Bokor told him he was now a zombie slave, and he sent Clairvius to work in the cane fields with other zombie slaves. When their master died, he claims that the Bokor's death set him free from the zombie control, and he returned home."

"Well, that's ridiculous," Jed said. "I mean, right?"

"Sure, if you look at it from a raising-someone-from-the-dead point of view. But he found a culture where nearly everyone believes in this. While Clairvius is the only zombie Dr. Davis actually interviewed, his research uncovered literally hundreds of stories just like Narcisse's, from family members and friends of zombies. He believes the practice is very widespread, or was at the time of his work, and that fear of reprisal from the Voudou priests and priestesses keeps people quiet. This Dr. Davis studied the phenomenon and even was able to find a Bokor who produced what he claimed to be a zombie powder. Davis states, in the Harvard article, that the powder was made of bones and parts of frogs, toads, and fish, but that when he analyzed the powder, he found that many of the substances could, indeed, produce a deathlike state. The article claims that the drugs in the powder, especially a drug called"—she leaned in over her computer a moment—"tetrodotoxin, can produce a super low metabolic state—like a crazy slow and weak heartbeat and undetectable breathing—where someone could very much appear to be dead. They would be completely paralyzed and unable to speak or move, not even their eyes. Their pulse would be faint to the point of undetectable, their lips would turn blue . . ."

"They would *look* dead . . ." Jed pulled at his beard and then took another long sip of water, wishing again for lemon and eyeing Gayle's glass with envy.

"Yes," Gayle said. "And even worse, they would be fully awake and aware. They could, just as Clairvius Narcisse claimed, hear people around them. They could remember a funeral. They could even remember being buried."

"That's horrible. But it sounds dangerous. I would think some people would die from the drug or suffocate in the coffin."

"Davis thinks many do," she said. "What a horrible way to die," she added, putting a hand over her heart and closing her eyes. "But he also believes that enough of these people survive long enough to be unearthed as the drug wears off but before they run out of air in the coffin. Then, because they live in a culture where they already believe in zombies, they would *believe* they were the undead—raised from the grave. The article claims Davis worked with psychiatrists and psychologists who confirmed that under those circumstances, it would be likely that the 'zombie' would obey their master, because they would believe they had no choice."

"And this Davis—and the Clairvius Narcisse guy . . . these are real people?"

She turned the computer screen toward him, where a man sat on a headstone in a blue shirt and white pants on the cover of a 1986 issue of *Harvard Magazine*. The headline on the cover read:

ZOMBIE

Clairvius Narcisse (right), raised from the grave,
led ethnobiologist Dr. Wade Davis to probe
the secrets of Haiti's "Living Dead."

"That's crazy," Jed said, his eyes now wide in fascination. "But it makes so much sense with everything that's happened. The mother I met in Santo Domingo, the mother of the missing girl Emelin, she said her daughter was afraid of being turned into a zombie. I remember thinking the mom really believed it—was terrified of it, in fact."

"Well, rightfully so," Gayle said, leaning back in her chair and placing her glasses on her computer keyboard. "I can't even imagine how horrifying that experience would be. No matter what you did or didn't believe, to be awake while you're buried alive, paralyzed . . ."

"That's just horrible," Jed said. He headed to the kitchen

to get a frigging slice of lemon. "And a powerful tool to control people, at least people who believe in the living dead. But why?"

"Davis says these Bokors become very powerful in their communities, acquiring property and wealth from their victims and an army of slaves to work their land. Most Haitians incorporate at least some elements of Voudou into their religion and lives," Gayle continued. "When this article was written, it was reported that eighty to ninety percent of Haitians believe in zombies. But in Haiti, they believe that zombies don't go around attacking people or eating brains. In their culture, the fear isn't of being killed by zombies, it's of *becoming* one. Of being made into an undead slave to a Voudou priest or priestess."

Jed paced in the kitchen, aware that his stomach was growling. Then another thought made his stomach turn over, and he had an urge to dash over to Amour et Espoir right then, kick in the gate, and scour the school for young Emelin.

"Imagine the powerful control you could have over a child if you convinced them they were a zombie," he said, his voice a harsh whisper.

"Jed, you don't think . . ."

"I don't know," he said. "But if so . . ."

Gayle closed her eyes, and Jed imagined the horrible images of the fallen Shepherds that likely filled her mind.

"I know. You're right. And those kids laughing and playing on the soccer fields certainly didn't look like they thought they were zombies . . ."

"Or that they were captives afraid of becoming zombies."

He nodded to her. "This is good, though," he said. "We need to understand as much about the culture as we can, because you can bet the Dark Ones will leverage the religion and superstition into power for themselves."

"I'll reach back to Langley as well and see if there are any agency assets we have in country that I can leverage for support. At a minimum, we can have them do a deep dive on the school and any connections to it—owners, operators, investors, government connection, that sort of thing."

"That would be great," Jed said. "I know Ben is reaching out to all partner agencies, but a request from you is probably going to move faster."

"I'm starving," Gayle said with a sheepish smile.

"Me too," he said. "I'll cook."

Jed opened the fridge, which Gayle had filled with the spoils of their grocery run. He looked at the sliders.

"You're looking for a grill, aren't you?" she said with a chuckle, rising from the table to join him in the kitchen.

He laughed. "Guilty," he confessed. "We have some steaks, some ground beef, some chicken, and the fish . . ."

"I'll cook tonight," she said, reaching past him and pulling out the chicken and several bags of vegetables. "Chicken marsala okay?"

His mouth literally watered.

"For sure," he said. "I'll put together a salad for us."

"Perfect."

He watched her work, preparing a pan and the chicken, as she shared more of what she'd learned about Voudou in Haiti, information she had gathered in just ten minutes or so while he had lingered in the shower.

She was an amazing woman.

CHAPTER TWENTY-FOUR

MIDDLE SCHOOL GIRLS' DORMITORY

ROOM #316

ST. GEORGE'S ACADEMY

0422 HOURS LOCAL

Sarah Beth shivered.

Her feet were cold.

She looked down and was surprised at how ghastly they looked—pale gray and corpse-like. She noticed, for the first time, how prominent the veins were on the top of her feet. Mesmerized, she watched them move like little blue worms under the skin.

This isn't real. I'm dreaming, she thought and pinched herself to wake up.

But she didn't wake.

The long, thin cotton nightgown she wore hung to mid-calf. The lace lining the bottom, probably once fine and delicate, was in tatters. She did not remember putting this outfit on. In fact, she did not remember owning any nightgowns at all. She'd gone to bed in fuzzy pj pants and a *Guardians of the Galaxy* T-shirt.

So, why am I wearing this?

The ancient stones she stood upon drained her body heat. She didn't know why she knew the stones were ancient, but she did. This place had witnessed much suffering, enduring the malice of both men and time. To *endure*, that was the nature of stone; its *raison d'être.*

I do not speak French, so how can I think in it?

She wanted to leave. To go back to St. George's, back to her time, but she could tell that she needed to see something—something important—before she could leave. Was God showing her something? Or was it someone else?

What is this place? Where am I?

The stones seemed to answer her.

"This is a faraway place. A secret place. A forgotten place. A place for the dead . . . Look up and see for yourself."

Was this just a nightmare then, or was this the Holy Spirit sharing what she needed to see?

Sarah Beth raised her head and gasped.

She stood in a tunnel of bones. Skulls, hundreds of them, the color of weathered parchment, rose from the floor, stacked with different types of bones, to form the walls of the corridor. It appeared that someone had ordered the bones arranged in an intricate and meticulous pattern. To make art. Sadistic, terrible, disturbing art that extended down the dimly lit tunnel as far as she could see.

"Do you know where you are now?"

"No," she whispered.

The stones spoke again, repeating themselves.

"You're in a secret place. A forgotten place. A place for the dead . . ."

"An underground catacomb?" she asked, the word coming to her despite having never spoken it before.

"Yes . . . Are you afraid?"

She nodded. "Very afraid."

"You should be . . ."

Hugging herself, she turned and glanced behind her. Lit by torchlight, the tunnel looked the same in both directions, bones as far as the eye could see. She'd never seen an actual torch before—the kind shaped like a club topped with a real flame and resting in an iron holder on the wall, like what you see in movies and castles—but here one was. She shifted her gaze to the closest flame and watched it dance, enchanted by the light, the heat, and the movement.

"Don't stare too long," the bones warned. *"This is no place to linger, little girl."*

"This way," the stones coaxed, and she knew without asking which way they wanted her to go.

She turned back and forced herself to walk. A catacomb of bones should surely have a stench, but she smelled nothing foul here. In fact, this place had no odor at all. She bent her nose to smell her armpit, expecting the familiar scent of her rose-blush deodorant, but she smelled nothing.

How was it possible?

"Do not linger . . . do not wonder . . . this way."

She pushed the question from her mind and walked, silent on bare feet, down the tunnel of bones. A row of skulls, arranged in a line at eye level, watched her with their black, hollow eyes, their jawbones missing, making it appear that they were laughing. Every one of them. Most of the skulls had smooth foreheads, but some had holes punched in them, and she shuddered at the thought of what had been done to those poor people.

The bones laughed. *"How else to get a demon out?"*

"I just want to wake up," she murmured, shivering and hugging herself as she padded toward the unknown. "Please let me wake up."

"Not yet . . ."

The torches flickered and crackled as she walked past, casting her shadow on the opposite wall where the bones distorted her form into something grotesque. She didn't know why she was here or whether this dream was a vision or a nightmare, but she felt compelled to walk, compelled to learn what the stones wanted her to know. Eventually, she could make out an arched opening in the wall of bones on her right, the first intersection she'd encountered in this place. Cautious and afraid, she tiptoed toward the opening. As she got closer, she heard voices . . . chanting or humming in unison.

It wasn't a song, she realized, but it did have a rhythm to it.

Every fiber of her being told her to turn back, that this was a very dangerous place, but the stones wanted her to see. The bones insisted she continue. With a shuddering exhale, she crept up to the edge of the opening and peeked around the corner, where she gazed into a massive round chamber, with a domed ceiling and a heavy stone chimney opening at the apex. Below the dome, a tepee-shaped pyre of wood had been constructed. In the center, she saw three men dressed in the black robes of clergy, large crosses hanging from chains around their necks, bound to a center stake, their eyes wide in fear. The baritone chanting continued echoing, louder now, but she still could not see where it was coming from. Heart pounding in her chest, she tiptoed into the chamber. Once inside, she saw another arched opening in the wall on her right, leading to another chamber.

This room was where the chanting came from.

Defying all logic and sanity, she kept going.

In her peripheral vision, she spied movement and turned to look at the pyre. One of the priests met her gaze with desperate, pleading eyes. His hands were bound, but he gestured with his head for her to leave.

"Go. Run. Flee," he mouthed.

She shook her head and turned back toward the chamber entrance where the chanting, which seemed to be reaching a crescendo, continued in full force. She crouched low and, upon reaching the arched opening, peered around the corner. Inside she saw a large round wooden table with cloaked figures seated around it. She counted thirteen in all, their faces bathed in shadow from their hoods, but their eyes glowing amber with rings of fire.

Dark Ones, her mind screamed, *and powerful ones at that.*

Like a dark planet, she could feel the gravity of their combined malice. She could hear the chaotic chorus of demons bound within these dark warriors as they bellowed and roared for blood.

What is this? she wondered.

The bones laughed at her.

"That is the wrong question."

When is this? she thought instead, epiphany striking her.

The stones approved.

"This was the last gathering . . . the last Dark Rising."

"What are they doing?" she whispered.

"Choosing . . ."

She was about to ask what they were choosing, but the question was answered for her when the chanting came to a sudden and abrupt end. One of the robed figures stood and walked to a stone altar. He picked up a heavy necklace, fashioned from skulls and bone. Squinting, she could see that each of the skulls on the necklace had a hole in the forehead, and they were connected by links of black iron. The figure, eyes pulsing with flame-colored rings, carried the necklace back to the table and stopped next to one of his brethren.

"Rise, Dark Prince," the standing figure said to the other.

The seated figure stood and bowed his head to receive the necklace. Now chosen, he turned and addressed his assembled dark brethren. When he spoke, the oily, serpentine voice made her gasp.

Victor . . . but how? He's dead. We killed him . . .

She tried to back up, tried to turn and run, but the body she inhabited wouldn't let her.

She wasn't in control.

This was her dream, but not her life.

I'm in the past, she realized. *This happened to someone else, hundreds of years ago.*

She squinted once again, trying to better make out the details of Victor's face beneath the hood. This Victor was a younger version of the one she'd faced in the halls of St. George's, which confirmed her hunch. She stilled her breathing and listened as the hooded figures resumed chanting in a language she did not know. *It's Latin,* she thought, then realized she did, in fact, understand many of the words.

I'm witnessing a ceremony. An ascension.

They were chanting to honor their master—the devil—and recognize his new demon general on earth. The assembled Dark Ones had chosen Victor for this role, and Victor would lead them in battle against God and the Shepherds. She could feel his pride, his thirst for blood, his hunger for power, and his desire for vengeance.

Now I understand, she thought and turned to look over her shoulder at the three holy men bound to the pyre.

They were to be sacrificed . . .

Victor's gift to his Dark Master.

Sarah Beth's chest felt suddenly tight as she remembered her final battle with Victor and the memories he shared—memories of his mother being convicted of witchcraft and drowned. She could feel Victor's hatred for these men of the cloth and his satisfaction at being able to pass judgment and sentence them to purification by flame in the name of his master.

A powerful compulsion to escape consumed her, and this time her body heeded the call to flee. Holding her breath, she retraced her steps through the sacrificial chamber toward the hall of bones. As she did, she glanced at the three priests bound to the pyre. The closest man to her, the one who'd begged her to flee before, nodded with approval.

"Go with God," he mouthed, and she saw that his whole body was trembling with fear.

She did not want to watch what happened next.

She did not want to hear the screams.

She hurried, but still pranced on tiptoes to not make noise. She turned left into the hall of bones just as one of the priests began to pray loudly. He was probably making a distraction, drawing the Dark Ones' attention so they would not see the waif of a girl fleeing the chamber. Once in the corridor, she took off running. Fear clawed at her—like meat hooks trying to drag her back—but she did not look over her shoulder.

The stones were satisfied.

She'd seen what she needed to see.

The bones stared at her as she ran by with their lifeless, hollow eyes full of judgment and pride.

"This is no place to linger, little girl . . ."

Behind her, screams reverberated from the sacrificial chamber. Terrible, awful screams of pain and agony as Victor lit the pyre.

"It's time to go, child. Time to leave!"

Sarah Beth sat bolt upright in her bed, screaming. Her two roommates jerked awake. Elizabeth flipped on her reading lamp.

"I'm sorry," Sarah Beth said, catching her breath. "I'm so sorry, guys."

"Were you having a nightmare?" Elizabeth asked.

"I think that's obvious," Darilyn said from the top bunk above Sarah Beth. "What else is new?"

"Are you so self-absorbed that you've already forgotten what happened to her? While *you* were hiding, Sarah Beth fought Victor and saved us all," Elizabeth snapped, taking on the queen bee of eighth grade like Sarah Beth had never seen her do before. "So shut your mouth, Darilyn, and cut her some slack."

"Sorry. You're right," Darilyn said, not even trying to clap back. "Are you okay, Sarah Beth?"

"Yeah," she said, slowly nodding as the nightmare's imagery began to dissolve from her conscious mind and the feeling of being in the catacombs faded away with it. She swung her legs out of bed.

"Where are you going?" Elizabeth asked as Sarah Beth put on her slippers and headed for the door.

"To find Corbin," she said, her mind already working the problem. "I think something *big* is about to happen."

CHAPTER TWENTY-FIVE

PALÈ NANM PÈDI YO (PALACE OF LOST SOULS)

ROUTE AMANI-Y BEACH

OVERLOOKING BAIE DE SAINT-MARC

THREE MILES EAST OF SAINT-MARC, HAITI

1937 HOURS LOCAL

Madame Athaliah watched the thin, athletic woman she had come to call Calypso enter the room, moving with a fluid grace that was a perfect metaphor for the powerful warrior she had become. Like Calypso from Greek mythology, the woman's jealousies and appetites had made her stronger and had been the perfect tools to grow her into the powerful Dark One she was now becoming.

And like the mythological Calypso, her greatest power remained her ability to move undetected among the sheep from whom the Dark Ones now pilfered their young victims. The unanticipated battle with the Shepherd who had appeared in Santo Domingo had been the one exception so far—and it was an exception that was proving increasingly problematic. Since her first encounter with him after the failed attempt to take the boy in Santo Domingo, Calypso's obsession with the powerful Shepherd was yet another mirror of the mythical Calypso, daughter of the Titan Atlas, whose fall could be linked to her obsessive love for Odysseus.

"Yes, Manbo Athaliah?" the woman said, her slight bow only modestly tempering her hubris.

Athaliah paced around her large desk, hands clasped behind her back, her smart, expensive shoes echoing her steps on the hardwood floor of the den.

"I am concerned, Calypso," Athaliah said as she approached.

The woman stared back, unafraid but with her own version of deference in her dark eyes. Calypso might be arrogant, but she was not reckless. She was confident but not unaware of the power that Athaliah held over her.

"While I agree that killing the Shepherd agents in the Dominican Republic was necessary," Athaliah continued, "I would have preferred it be done in a less dramatic and flamboyant way. It draws much attention at a rather dangerous time for us."

"I had thought that it sent a message that would strike fear in those who found them," Calypso said, chin up. "Fear has always been our most powerful tool in Haiti and Dominican Republic."

"Perhaps you are right." Athaliah nodded, needing to correct her lieutenant but not rein her in too tightly. "But unfortunately, fear will not be the emotion stirred in the Shepherd who found them. Rather, it will solidify to him that it is the Dark Ones who are involved. It strengthens his resolve to find the child, I'm afraid. It brings attention to us at a most inopportune time."

"Or brings him right to us—into a trap we can spring, Manbo," Calypso said, this time averting her eyes to the floor.

Very good. She is learning. She is growing.

"Is this from my mind, this idea, or from your own imagination?"

"The two are becoming harder to separate, if I may be honest."

"You may," Athaliah said, suppressing a grin, "and I agree. I, too, have thought that your actions outside Santiago de los Caballeros might well provide an opportunity. But this does not change that your actions, decided independently, were poorly thought out. In the future, you will check such things with me. Do we agree on this?"

"Of course," Calypso relented.

It was enough for now.

"What is it you think you will do, should the Shepherd find his way to us?" Athaliah asked.

A grin spread across Calypso's face, and her dark eyes flashed with orange light. "Take him, of course. Use him, perhaps. Kill him, for certain. It would be an amazing experience to feed on him . . ."

Manbo Athaliah paced away again, turning over the problem, and possible solutions, in her head. "The timing is unfortunate. As is the fact that I can't seem to find a thread to this man—this Shepherd. He has something more than most. He reminds me of their leader, of Ben Morvant, whom I have sought for several years. There is some powerful protection around both. Could I penetrate it, we could find him more easily."

Athaliah stopped at her enormous black lacquer desk, leaning her hands on the polished surface and staring at her travel binder with her itinerary—a reservation at the Four Seasons Hotel George V, Paris—and her passport, a US passport she had acquired easily under the name Margaret Meadows.

"I can find him," Calypso said. Athaliah turned to look at

her best warrior, who still grinned with an animal hunger. "I left a trail for him to follow," her lieutenant added.

"To me?" Athaliah felt anger rising and, for a moment, entertained the idea of using her growing power to kill the woman in front of her right then.

Calypso perhaps sensed this, her eyes again looking down and the timbre of her voice changing.

"Of course not, Manbo Athaliah," she said softly. "I left a trail to Amour et Espoir. I left the woman clinging to life and with the trail to Port-de-Paix in her head. It will be enough to bring the Shepherd and his woman to me there."

"And begin the trail to me," Athaliah exploded, whipping her hand backward toward Calypso, who, to her credit, didn't so much as flinch. Athaliah's clawlike nails scathed across the cocoa skin of Calypso's right shoulder, blood bubbling up from the three parallel wounds. The blood trickled down Calypso's arm and the back of her right shoulder, where the tattoo of a crab matched the dolphin tattoo on her left shoulder—both nods to the Greek Calypso for whom she was named. "Surely you see how this will connect us—connect me?"

"Of course," Calypso said, looking at the blood flowing down to her elbow and smiling, her eyes closing with apparent enjoyment. "But before they can make such a connection, I will have them. Already I have my soldiers and servants in Port-de-Paix watching their every move. And even if they make the connection to you before then, the knowledge will die with them. He is a Shepherd, not a Watcher. And he is alone without his team. He travels with a woman, a girlfriend perhaps, but no teammates. Long before he is a threat, he will have watched her die."

Athaliah smiled. "And then what?" she asked. She found herself curiously aroused by what she imagined Calypso had in store for the Shepherd.

"I will enjoy him and then kill him—which I will enjoy all the more. I will use the power of the Voudou."

"He will not be converted, my precious," Athaliah said, smiling sadly at the truth and running a finger gently across the sharp angle of Calypso's jaw.

"He will not need to be," Calypso said, her grin now growing vulpine. "When the magic wears off, he will already be dead and buried. He will breathe his last in the grave knowing we defeated him with the power of darkness and that his life has been a lie. If the Shepherds ever find him at all, it will be only his corpse."

"You can't raise him, Calypso," she reminded her again, just making sure.

"And I don't want to," Calypso said. "He would make a terrible servant. But I will very much enjoy his death."

Athaliah nodded, satisfied. The death Calypso had in mind would send a symbolic message to the Shepherds that their power—so successful against the archaic power of Victor—would prove impotent in the new order she envisioned.

"I must leave now to make it to Paris in time," Athaliah said. "It is another reason that this timing is so terrible, Calypso. But this meeting is important and decides many things for us. When I return, I want the problem with the Shepherd resolved." She picked up her travel folder, closed it, and slipped it into her leather satchel-style briefcase. "If you can take the Shepherd alive as you hope—which I very much doubt—bring him here. Leave him alive until my return. It would be very interesting indeed to see what we might be able to learn from a live Shepherd."

"As you wish, Manbo," Calypso said. "So long as I may dispose of him as I planned after."

Athaliah gave her a long, hard look. "If I choose to allow it," she said, reminding the woman of who commanded whom.

Athaliah slipped the satchel strap over her shoulder. Her most trusted lieutenant surveyed her, a pout of sorts on her face.

"I am surprised you are attending the meeting in Paris. None of the men vying to ascend in the Dark Rising are your equal. That you would provide counsel to lesser than yourself is confusing to me."

"I don't need to explain myself to you, Calypso," she admonished, but gently this time. "Either way, you serve me. But"—she placed a hand on Calypso's bleeding shoulder, the warm, sticky blood electric under her fingers—"as I trust you will be loyal to me, I will let you in on a little secret."

Calypso's eyes raised in surprise.

"What is that, Manbo Athaliah?"

"Whoever is chosen for the Dark Rising will learn the real truth far too late," she said.

"What truth?" Calypso asked, clearly mesmerized by the words.

"That whoever ascends will really be working for me, of course," Athaliah said. She looked at the dark blood on her fingers as she pulled her hand away. She turned her fingers over in the light, seeing the glistening blood shimmer, then one by one licked the blood from them. "It is I who have, and will continue to have, the real power. The ceremony of the Dark Rising is, in the new world we live in, no longer anything but a lie—a ruse to allow me to counsel the new leader. It will be I who makes the real decisions. And by the time they realize it, I will already be in charge. It is as the Dark Prince would want—power grown out of lies and betrayal. It's perfect, don't you think?"

"Yes," Calypso breathed, looking at Athaliah now with something much larger than just deference.

Reverence, perhaps.

As it should be.

"I look forward to meeting this Shepherd when I return," Athaliah said. "It should prove a very interesting conversation indeed."

"It will be so," Calypso said. "I will see to it."

"I know you will, Calypso." She headed for the door and added, over her shoulder, "Happy hunting, dear."

Then she walked down the long marble hallway toward the grand entrance of the estate home she had built atop the foundation of the shack her parents had raised her in. The same home that they had been in for generations, since the time of her great-grandmother—also named Athaliah—a woman who had been dragged out of the small house to be tried and executed as a witch.

Executed for what she was—a Voudou priestess.

Never again. Money and power in place, Athaliah fully intended to show the world what real power was. Voudou was never meant as a dark force. It was a blending of faith in God with knowledge of the spirits of nature—a tying together of the old and the new. But with help from the right forces, the power of Voudou could be magnified. That power became real by allegiance to the Prince of Darkness.

And soon that power would be hers.

CHAPTER TWENTY-SIX

HIGH SCHOOL GIRLS' DORMITORY

ST. GEORGE'S ACADEMY

0502 HOURS LOCAL

Standing in front of Corbin's dorm room, Sarah Beth tried to work up the nerve to knock. She'd been loitering for over a minute, second-guessing her decision to wake the older girl. *Funny,* she thought, *I've faced down Victor but I'm afraid to wake up a high-school sophomore.* Grinning at the absurd reality of the thought, she went to knock.

Just then the door opened, and her knuckles whiffed in the air.

"Hi," Corbin said, grinning at her with bedhead and still dressed in her pajamas.

"Hi," Sarah Beth whispered back. "Did you know I was standing here?"

"I woke up and had a feeling you needed me."

"That's weird and kinda cool."

"My roommate is still asleep. Let me step out," Corbin whispered, joining Sarah Beth in the hall.

"Can we go to the White Room? I'd rather talk to you there."

"Sure," Corbin said, and the two girls set off together toward the Watcher Sanctuary.

"I'm sorry to wake you up early, by the way," Sarah Beth said, feeling a little guilty about dragging Corbin into this.

"It's totally fine," Corbin said. "We're partners in the SMU now, so this is, like, what we do."

Sarah Beth liked hearing that. Corbin didn't seem mad, or annoyed, or anything, which was great. It would kind of suck if she had to always worry about bothering her with Watcher stuff.

The halls were totally quiet, and they didn't pass any staff as they made their way to the White Room. Accessing the Sanctuary, the larger space that contained the White Room, was probably the coolest secret in St. George's, and every time Sarah Beth entered it, she felt like a secret agent. The entrance to the Sanctuary was disguised as a small sitting room painted and decorated entirely in white. To somebody not in the know, it looked like a waiting room. But in reality, the little room was a huge elevator that would only operate for authorized personnel. The two girls rode the White Room elevator and found the entire Sanctuary complex predictably deserted at this hour. They walked over to one of the comfortable leather sofas and plopped next to each other in mirror-image positions with legs curled up.

Without holding back and while it was still fresh, Sarah Beth told Corbin everything she could remember about her dream. When she finished, Corbin had a perplexed look on her face.

"What do you think?" Sarah Beth asked.

"I think you had a nightmare, but at the same time, it also sounds like a vision because you said you felt like it wasn't your body. Like you were seeing through this girl's eyes."

Sarah Beth nodded. "It definitely felt that way. I couldn't

control where I went or what I saw, so that part was more like a vision than a dream."

"And you said you saw Victor when he was younger?"

"That's right."

"So that means that this girl, whoever she was, would have to be dead now. Because what you described happened hundreds of years ago."

"I know, and that's what's freaking me out. How can I have a vision if the person is dead?"

"I don't know. It's never happened to me."

Corbin reached out and gave Sarah Beth's hand a comforting squeeze; then an impish smile spread across her face.

"What's that look for?" Sarah Beth said.

"I wonder if we can figure out who the girl was and exactly when this happened?" Corbin said, brimming with enthusiasm. "I bet there's something in the history books about the three priests who died that day."

"Probably."

"And you said that you think the girl was French because you had thoughts in French and could understand Latin words, right?"

Sarah Beth nodded. "Right."

"Well, probably the most famous catacomb in the world is located in Paris," Corbin said.

"Really?"

"Yeah, it's literally, like, right under the city."

"Whoa, that's crazy," Sarah Beth said, wondering how a place as creepy and weird as the one in her dream could possibly be located under a city as posh and modern as Paris.

"Paris is a very old city, and it wasn't always as refined as it is today," Corbin said, probably reading her thoughts. "Lots of European cities are built upon older and older versions of themselves. There are Roman ruins under Paris too. I'm pretty sure the catacombs have been around for a long time, but let's take this on as a research project. Finals are over, so what else have we got to do? Maybe we make this our first Watcher SMU assignment."

Sarah Beth felt herself practically beaming at the idea. "Let's do it."

They spent until breakfast researching and trying to put the puzzle pieces together. Corbin's hypothesis about the catacombs being ancient turned out to be pretty much spot on. Before becoming a massive tomb, the Paris catacombs were underground limestone quarries dating back to the thirteenth century, where stone was harvested for construction of the growing city.

"Okay, Sarah Beth, check this out," Corbin said. "Basically, what happened is the quarries were so old that people forgot where they were, and as Paris grew, it expanded over the abandoned mines. They rediscovered them when cave-ins and sinkholes started swallowing up buildings. The mines and tunnels are huge with, like, one hundred and twenty-five miles of tunnels!"

"That's crazy, but this is even more insane," Sarah Beth said. "There was this massive graveyard called the Holy Innocents' Cemetery, where these two big Paris hospitals buried all the people who died. It got so nasty that they had to close it, but they didn't know what to do with all the bodies. So, they decided to put them in the catacombs."

"Gross," Corbin said, screwing up her face.

"Guess how many corpses they moved underground?"

"I don't know, how many?"

"Guess," Sarah Beth said, insisting.

"Fifty thousand."

"Nope—*two million*."

"No way!"

"Yes, way," Sarah Beth said. "Isn't that crazy?"

"So crazy . . ."

This is how it went for a couple of hours until hunger motivated them both to bail on the Sanctuary and head down for breakfast. As soon as they had their trays and were sitting together in the cafeteria, the discussion continued.

"Do you think that the catacomb I visited in my dream is the same one that all the tourists of Paris visit today?" Sarah Beth asked while eating her yogurt and banana.

"Could be," Corbin said in between bites of her oatmeal, "but the catacombs are friggin' huge, so it's possible the place you saw is not part of the tomb open to the public. It could be anywhere in Paris."

"Why do you think she wanted me to see it?" Sarah Beth said.

"You mean the girl in your dream?"

"Yeah."

"Well, she's dead, so I don't think it was her. I think it's the Holy Spirit who gave you that vision."

"Right, yeah. What do you think the Holy Spirit wanted me to see?"

Corbin wrinkled her nose like she did sometimes when she was thinking. "Obviously, Victor . . . and the three priests . . . and the fact that it was a ceremony . . ."

Sarah Beth's gaze went to the middle distance as she tried to remember the exact words the stones had used . . .

"I think I might understand," Sarah Beth said, refocusing on Corbin.

"Tell me."

"It's called a *Dark Rising*," she said and felt a shiver chase down her back. "I think it's the ceremony where the Dark Ones choose their leader. In my vision, I was seeing the time when they chose Victor."

"Oh, no," Corbin said, and Sarah Beth watched the color drain from her face.

"I think the Dark Ones are about to choose their *next* Victor," Sarah Beth said.

"That's bad," Corbin said. "Really bad. We have to tell our Keepers about your dream, and they need to tell the Shepherds."

"I agree," Sarah Beth said.

"But first, there's something I want to try—if you're up for it, that is?" Corbin said, dropping her spoon in her bowl and tossing her napkin on top.

"Sure," Sarah Beth said. "What do you want to try?"

"I want you to take me there, to the place you saw in the catacombs."

"I don't know how to do that. It was a dream. It happened probably a few hundred years ago," Sarah Beth said, taking her last bite and moving her trash onto her tray.

"That's not what I mean. I want you to project us to the location as it is today," Corbin said. "I have a hunch I want to check out before we brief our Keepers."

"Okay, I'll try, but I can't promise it will work."

"Certitude, sister," Corbin said with a grin as she grabbed her tray to leave. "You got this."

They headed back to the Sanctuary, passing plenty of kids on the way this time, and got a handful of jealous looks as they opened the door to the White Room. Three minutes later they were back on the big leather sofa. Sarah Beth stared up at the statue of Saint George, the dragon slayer and school's patron. The bronze spear, the same spear which Victor had used when he tried to kill Corbin, had been returned to the marble warrior's hands . . .

"I still can't look at it," Corbin said, and in Sarah Beth's peripheral vision, she saw her friend shudder.

"That night feels like it happened to someone else," Sarah Beth said as a flashbulb memory of Corbin lying impaled and purple lipped on the floor popped into her mind. "I'm not quite ready to deal with it yet . . . I guess I kind of compartmentalized it."

She'd heard Pastor Dee and her parents use that word a lot lately, *compartmentalize*. She knew it was how lots of operators, like Uncle Jed, dealt with the horrible things they'd seen or with things they'd done themselves. Every kid in the school was undergoing mandatory counseling in the aftermath of what had come to be known as the night of the Dark Fall. Sarah Beth knew that both she and Corbin were probably dealing with some version of PTSD, but a part of her was afraid to admit that, because what if admitting it meant having to relive that night over again?

"Yeah, me too," Corbin said. "But at least you can look at the spear."

"Only because I didn't get stabbed by it," Sarah Beth said and turned to her friend. "If I had gone through what you had, I can't even . . ."

"Enough about that; let's try to project to the catacombs," Corbin said with a hesitant smile.

"Give me your hands," Sarah Beth said.

Corbin reached out, and Sarah Beth took the older girl's fingers in hers. With a deep breath, Sarah Beth closed her eyes. She'd not projected since that night when Victor's army of Dark Ones attacked St. George's, and she was nervous.

"Do you remember how to project?" Corbin said, reading her thoughts.

"Not exactly," Sarah Beth said. "I had so much adrenaline last time. I was in total fight-or-flight mode. My mind was in a super heightened state—I haven't felt that way since."

"You did it," Corbin said, "which means you can do it again."

"But I've never actually been to the catacombs. How do I find them?"

"But you *have* been there," Corbin said, coaching her, "in your dream. For me, it helps if I try to imagine myself standing in a particular spot looking at a specific thing."

"Okay, I'll try."

Sarah Beth said a little prayer for help and guidance. Then, feeling suddenly more confident, she let her mind's eye look where it wanted. To her surprise, it went to a particular skull in the hall of bones—the first skull she'd seen, the one with a hole punched in the forehead. She remembered how its black eye sockets had seemed to bore into her. The next thing she knew, she felt a wave of vertigo and a shift. Her spirit untethered itself from her physical body, and she suddenly stood in the corridor of bones from her nightmare.

"Whoa," she said, having forgotten how weird and cool the feeling was. She spun in a circle but found herself alone. "Corbin?" she called.

"You need to bring me into your headspace," she heard the older girl say, Corbin's voice millions of miles away. "You're locked down as tight as the SCIF, sis."

"Oh," Sarah Beth said and opened her mind to her friend.

She heard a muffled pop, and a glowing Corbin now stood beside her.

They grinned at each other, and Corbin said, "You did it!"

"I did, didn't I," Sarah Beth said, then scrunched up her face as she gestured to the hall of bones. "This place is creepy, huh?"

"Super creepy," Corbin said, scanning the row of skulls extending off into the distance.

As had been the case in her vision, the corridor was lit by

torchlight, only these torches looked different. They weren't burning tar and reeds or whatever ancient torches burned; instead, the flame looked steady and blue, like a gas fireplace.

"This way," she said and took Corbin by the hand to lead her down the deserted hallway toward the alcove where she'd seen the sacrificial pyre.

"Why are you tiptoeing?" Corbin asked, grinning at her.

"To be quiet," she said, but then laughed as she realized that her spiritual self didn't physically interact with matter. Yes, she was "walking," but that was out of habit—a sort of muscle memory that persisted while projecting.

"No one can see or hear us," Corbin said. "You know that, right?"

"Yeah, I just forgot," Sarah Beth said.

She hoped Corbin was right, because what if they weren't alone? Thankfully, she didn't hear any chanting. Hopefully, that was a good sign.

It didn't take long before they reached the arched opening in the wall of bones.

"This is it," Sarah Beth whispered, stopping just before the opening.

Corbin nodded, which Sarah Beth took as the go-ahead to enter.

With her actual body thousands of miles away, Sarah Beth took a deep breath, then rounded the corner with Corbin beside her. Just like before, in the center of the round chamber, a wooden pyre had been built, only this one was unfinished and appeared to be under construction. Long cordwood sat in several stacks nearby, ready to be added.

"That's not a good sign," Corbin said.

"Agreed," Sarah Beth said.

She turned toward the entrance to the other connecting

room, the one with the big wooden table where the thirteen Dark Ones had chosen Victor in her nightmare-vision. Just as before, the same table occupied the middle of the room. She counted thirteen vacant chairs, evenly spaced and arranged around it. Beyond, the same stone altar she'd seen before held the necklace of bones on a cross-shaped iron display.

"Let's go in there," Corbin said.

"Are you sure?"

"Yeah," her friend and teammate said.

"Okay . . ." she answered, and they walked into the gathering chamber together.

Once inside the room, Corbin released Sarah Beth's hand and walked over to look at the disturbing necklace of skulls—skulls with holes punched in their foreheads.

"Do you think these skulls belonged to Dark Ones?" Corbin said, turning back to look at Sarah Beth, who had stopped halfway into the room. She felt a disturbing energy from that necklace and didn't want to get any closer to it.

"I know they did," Sarah Beth said. "And I think they died during attempted exorcisms."

"That's what I figured when you told me what the *bones* said."

Approaching footsteps, hard-soled shoes on stone, sounded behind them.

"Someone is coming!" Sarah Beth hissed, feeling panic grow inside her chest.

"They can't hear us, Sarah Beth," Corbin said. "You don't have to whisper."

"Right, sorry." She whispered anyway, unable to help herself as she turned to look back into the sacrificial chamber.

A man, a very tall man, dressed in a dark suit, entered the sacrificial chamber along with a shorter man dressed in grubby work clothes. The tall man had a distinguished bearing, with a handsome face and a full head of salt-and-pepper hair. He stood very straight, like Ben Morvant did, and exuded tremendous confidence and power . . .

Dark power.

The tall man said something in French to the worker, and the shorter man nodded repeatedly and answered in French. Sarah Beth couldn't tell what they were saying, but she could tell from the worker's body language that he was intimidated and frightened by the man in the suit.

Sarah Beth glanced at Corbin, who met her gaze with wide, scared eyes of her own.

The man in the suit said something else to the worker, then turned from the pyre and strode straight toward Sarah Beth and Corbin. Reflexively, both girls scampered out of the way. The heels of the man's dress shoes clicked loudly on the stone floor as he moved with purpose from the sacrificial chamber into the room with the round table. Once inside, she watched him make minor adjustments to the spacing between the thirteen chairs around the stout wooden table. And with each stop, he placed a cut gemstone—rubies, Sarah Beth thought—on the table where a dinner plate would go. The gems were huge, about the size of a gumball, which Sarah Beth guessed made them very valuable.

That task completed, the suited man walked to the skull necklace and stood before it. Then he got on his knees and began chanting something in what Sarah Beth guessed was Latin. Unlike in her nightmare-vision, she couldn't make out any of the words. Now it made sense why Latin was a foreign language option at St. George's.

"Who do you think he is?" Corbin said.

Sarah Beth was about to answer, but the kneeling man abruptly stopped chanting and whirred to scan the room.

"Don't worry, he can't see us," Corbin said, but the Dark One's gaze seemed to settle on them.

"Are you sure?" Sarah Beth whispered.

"Pretty sure . . ."

The Dark One's eyes suddenly flared like twin rings of fire, and he rose.

Sarah Beth yelped and jumped them into the hall of bones, landing at the exact spot they'd entered the catacombs minutes ago. "I think he could see us," she said through a gasp, looking at Corbin.

"But we're projecting. That's impossible."

"Then he heard us. I mean, you saw what just happened. He stopped chanting and marched right toward us."

Corbin nodded but seemed unconvinced.

"We need to get the heck out of here," Sarah Beth said.

"Not yet. First, we need to try to figure out where we are," Corbin said and turned down the hallway in the opposite direction from the two chambers. "Let's go."

They ran down the hall of bones, past the farthest point Sarah Beth had gone in her nightmare-vision. She was in new territory now with no idea where they were heading, but that didn't matter. All they needed to find was a way out.

"There," Corbin said, pointing to a cutout in the left wall about ten yards away.

They vectored toward it and a second later saw that the opening led to an unmarked, ascending staircase.

"Should we take it?" Corbin asked.

"Definitely," Sarah Beth said and glanced over her shoulder to see if the Dark One in the suit might appear behind them.

The sound of rapidly approaching footsteps echoed in the corridor. She couldn't see him, but she felt him closing in. Nerves tingling, she ducked into the alcove and headed up the long, steep set of stone stairs. At the top of what had to be a two-story staircase, they arrived on a landing and were met by a closed metal door with a massive padlock attached.

"Now what do we do?" Sarah Beth said, grasping at the door handle and watching her hand pass through the metal.

"We go through it," Corbin said with a no-nonsense look.

Sarah Beth nodded, felt her distant body take a breath, and she charged forward headfirst into the stout metal door. She felt nothing, absolutely nothing, and the next thing she knew, they were both standing on the other side grinning at each other.

"That was incredible," Sarah Beth said.

"I know," Corbin said, while scanning the room they'd entered. It appeared to be a cellar of some kind, filled with wooden crates and cardboard boxes. "Come on, this way."

Sarah Beth chased after Corbin as she darted toward another set of stairs, this time concrete steps with worn steel tread caps on the leading edge. Behind the girls, Sarah Beth heard metal rattling against metal, which she decided had to be the Dark One unlocking the padlock on the previous door.

"I think he's chasing us."

"Hurry," Corbin said as she disappeared through another locked door at the top of the flight.

Sarah Beth ran through the door after Corbin and emerged into what looked like somebody's house or apartment. There was a small yellow couch with a blanket left on one arm beside a pillow, like someone had slept there recently. She couldn't smell anything, of course, but she suspected that if she could, the room would smell musty.

"This way," Corbin said and dashed toward a door with a window that led outside.

Sarah Beth followed, and they zipped outside into a courtyard between two buildings.

"Now we just need to find the closest street corner so we can see where we are," Corbin said.

She ran through the iron gate blocking the courtyard from the cobblestone alley just beyond. Once in the alley, they ran to the closest intersection.

"You remember Rue des Thermopyles, and I'll remember 89 Rue Raymond Losserand," Sarah Beth said, looking up at the street names on royal-blue placards affixed to the side of the corner building.

"I got this," Corbin said, tapping her index finger to her temple. "I'll sketch it."

"Oh yeah, I forgot," Sarah Beth said, remembering Corbin's super sketchbook of wonders. The girl pretty much had a photographic memory.

"Time to go home," Corbin said. "See you back."

Corbin disappeared, and Sarah Beth was left alone on the street corner in Paris for a moment before she too let go—releasing the tension like a stretched rubber band—and her spiritual self snapped back into her body.

With a gasp, she opened her eyes to find herself sitting on the sofa in the Sanctuary, facing Corbin, who was still holding her hands.

"Dude, that was insane," Corbin said and let go of Sarah Beth's fingers, which were totally sweaty now.

"I told you that place was creepy."

"There's definitely something big about to happen. I think you're right, Sarah Beth, about the Dark Rising. We need to tell our Keepers what we saw, like, right away."

"Definitely," Sarah Beth said.

"You all right? You're literally shaking."

"Just the adrenaline," she said and scooted off the sofa. "C'mon, let's go find Pastor Dee."

CHAPTER TWENTY-SEVEN

OFFICE OF THE DIRECTOR

SHEPHERDS NORTH AMERICA

TRINITY LOOP COMPLEX

WEST OF NASHVILLE, TENNESSEE

0723 HOURS LOCAL

Ben Morvant flipped through the pages—copies, but full size and rich in detail—from Corbin Worth's sketchbook. He marveled at the depth and scale of the images. When the talented girl inevitably lost her abilities, which happened to all Watchers when they became young adults, she had a bright future as an artist. He could feel the emotion of the place, the terror that she and the Yarnell girl must have felt there.

Then he thought of poor Corbin with the spear of Saint George sticking out of her chest after the attack on the school . . .

He closed his eyes tightly.

He had learned long ago that it was not his place to question God's purpose. He knew beyond a shadow of a doubt that the spiritual gifts God placed in people were always accompanied by purpose. He believed God equipped the gifted with the strength they needed to answer the call He gave them. He'd seen it often enough in his own life.

But they're just children . . .

He sighed and leaned back in his chair, dropping the sketches and reaching for his coffee. His thoughts turned to his son, Jason, and the powerful gifts that still grew in the boy. Was Ben truly nurturing those gifts to God's yet unrevealed purpose?

Or am I hiding him, keeping him safe, from a future God is already trying to reveal?

He'd felt the pull to allow Jason to engage with the Watcher team at St. George's, even if they decided to continue to homeschool him. But Jason's gifts were more complicated than St. George's was prepared for.

Or at least that's how I rationalize keeping my son close . . .

He glanced at the phone that chirped on his desk, sighed again, and reached for it.

"Morvant."

"Ben, it's Damien Gough. I think we have something. A location—I think we found the location."

Ben sat up in his chair, glancing at his watch. It had only been two hours. He marveled again at the amazing team God had assembled here in West Tennessee.

"Tell me," he said to his head of conventional intelligence and signals analysis, glancing again at the horrible images in the sketches.

"Well, the cross streets that the Watchers found and the description of the courtyard were pretty easy to nail down, of course. The building is typical Paris, with apartments over top of businesses on the street. Based on the sketches, we believe the girls came up from the catacombs into a basement apartment in a building containing a restaurant called Aux Fruits de Mer. It's about a half mile south of Church of Saint-Sulpice in the Pont du Garigliano district south of the Seine. We're working with the intel shop for Shepherds Europe, and they're pretty intimate with the catacombs of Paris. Most of them are inaccessible and many are unexplored. This particular set of tunnels corresponds to an area closed by the French hundreds of years ago . . ."

Ben saw it in his head suddenly—a vivid image of three priests screaming in pain as they burned to death in a large stone room. The black smoke rose into a chimneylike space above. They were surrounded by a dozen men in dark, hooded cloaks. He recognized the glowing eyes of the man in the center.

Victor . . .

He had no idea why he could suddenly see it so clearly when during the last few days his ability to find and follow threads had felt completely out of reach. Perhaps it was a thread from the girls themselves, opened up by the sketches and the description.

"That was Victor's Rising," he mumbled.

"What's that? Sorry, I couldn't hear you well, boss."

He realized the phone was now dangling in his hand.

"Sorry," he said. "I believe that incident—the killing of the priests—may have been Victor's ascension so long ago."

"That's what the Watchers believe also. Did you speak with them again?"

"No," he said. "But I want to. Let's get a briefing here at Trinity with the Watchers and their Keepers, as well as our liaison, Rachel Yarnell."

"Ben, from what Sarah Beth described in her vision, it seems likely that they're planning another ceremony—another Dark Rising."

"They're picking a new leader," Ben agreed. "A new Victor."

It made sense now—the chaos he'd been feeling and the same weird, chaotic dreams and visions the Watchers described.

It wasn't a diminishing of his powers. It was *actual* chaos. Many evil men and women would be vying for more power as they served the devil. He knew of a few people, mostly in Europe, who *could* be contenders, but the Shepherds had no hard intelligence on which would be the most likely candidate. The Watchers had uncovered nothing substantial about the plans for the Dark Ones' network after Victor's demise—not until this. They were operating in the blind, it would seem. There were no organized threads because until a clear leader emerged, there was no clear structure and thus no clear plans.

But then who's running the operation Jed stumbled on in Haiti?

That question would have to wait for his attention. Jed would handle it for now, and he'd have his team with him in another couple of days.

"Damien, coordinate with Julia Nesbitt to get the Watcher team and your intel team together in the next hour in the SCIF planning room," he said. "We should have Shepherds Europe streaming in as well. We need to pull together a short-fuse operation in Paris. We need staging areas, infil and exfil, medical contingency plans, fires—the whole works."

"You want me to divert Joshua Bravo here to Trinity or get them headed to Paris?" Gough asked.

Ben gritted his teeth. Joshua Bravo was the elite direct-action team, so the question made sense. But Jed needed the team in Haiti to support whatever he had going on, right? Plus, the hit in Paris would be high stakes, but in the end, it was a straight-up strike mission. The number of HVTs certain to be present meant they needed a large number of talented operators, but every platoon in the Shepherds was capable and qualified for the mission. If Joshua Bravo was being redesignated as their SMU, then the mission in Haiti—with not only the need for intelligence gathering but, more importantly, the need for autonomous decision-making if the head shed was out of pocket in Paris—meant Jed's team needed to be down south on the island nation.

And Ben would *personally* be out of pocket since he fully intended to lead this Paris strike mission himself. Because this Dark Rising was something that hadn't happened in three hundred years. If ever there was a purpose for his unique gifts, it was this.

"No," he answered finally as Gough waited patiently for his reply. "Get me all three platoons from Gideon Squadron. And we need a mobile TOC, so let's prep the big jet. Have Jack Stewart coordinate that as well as any air assets we need in Paris. I'll get with David Yarnell ahead of the brief and get him to Haiti to join his team there."

"Mobilize the Watchers with the mobile TOC to Paris?"

"No," he said. They only rarely moved the Watchers forward, but it was far from unheard of. Still this—this was something much bigger than anything they'd done before, at least in his generation of Shepherds. There was no way he wanted the children on the ground in Paris.

Just in case . . .

"We'll have the Watcher team operate from the TOC at St. George's," he said. "Corbin and Sarah Beth will take the lead, but I want two other teams as well, as check and balance. For something this big, the Dark Ones will pull out all the stops to subvert our intelligence. And we need Corbin and Sarah Beth available here for Joshua Bravo, too, should that operation accelerate. With any luck, we can have this Paris hit over in twenty-four hours. I want to be wheels up in three."

"You got it," Gough replied. "See you in the SCIF in an hour."

Ben clicked off, then dialed a satellite phone number from memory.

"Hey, boss," Jed's clear, strong voice said.

"You sound better," Ben said.

"Rested," Jed said simply. "Getting me an update on the team movement?"

"I'll have that for you shortly, but I wanted to get a sitrep from you, actually."

"Well," Jed said, and Ben could picture Jed pulling at his beard like he did when he was thinking things through. "We're gathering intelligence at the moment. Today, we'll leverage assets Gayle is trying to uncover through her, um . . . business connections in the area. We've begun ISR on the school, but so far what we've seen has brought the urgency level down just a notch."

"Explain," Ben said. He needed to make sure this operation was under control and then shift his attention to bigger issues in Europe.

"Well, we're not really sure. We *had* believed that the site might be where the kids are being taken," Jed said. "Or at least that it might be one such site. We don't see any evidence of that yet, but we really need a closer look. We're crafting a plan to look inside. Maybe this is a site the Dark Ones want to hit, instead. We just don't know yet. Ben, the numbers appear to be pretty large, but it's hard to really get a firm handle on it because there's so much human trafficking going on down here already. But we do see an unusual pattern beginning to emerge, like I described. There is a definite targeting of very specific children, but we can't seem to find any connection. I'm hoping Gayle's . . . corporate connections . . . might help unravel that part. In any case, our initial observations don't seem to uncover any emergent threat to the kids at the site here. We're going to be able to dig deeper when we get Joshua Bravo in place, but I'll need some Watcher support as well."

"You'll get it," Ben assured the leader of his new Special

Missions Unit. "We have some things to deconflict, but we'll have support for you."

There was a long pause as Jed read between the lines.

"Anything I need to know about?"

"No," Ben said. They were on one of the most secure and heavily encrypted networks in the world, but there was no way Ben was discussing anything about Paris. The stakes were just too high to take any chances. And, in any case, it served no purpose to distract Jed with a mission he would not be involved with while he was on task in Haiti. "But we'll get it squared away."

"Okay," Jed said, his voice suggesting a hunger for more information, but an acceptance that it wasn't coming anytime soon. "Would love to have the Watchers assigned to the new model of my team, if possible."

Of course he did. The relationship with the two girls aside, Corbin and Sarah Beth were the most gifted Watchers they had. And working together with Joshua Bravo, the two girls took the Watcher mission to a whole new level.

Which is why I need them for my operation in Paris.

"We'll do our best," Ben said, knowing his answer would only raise more flags and questions for his operator. But Jed was too professional to press. "I should have them available in the next twenty-four hours or so. And I'll have David en route to you later today."

"Oh, that's great," Jed said. "We can use him here for sure."

"Stay safe, Jed," Ben said, glancing at his watch. He had a lot to do. "Stay low until your team is there and keep me in the loop."

"OPORD?" Jed pressed a bit.

He wanted to know just how much autonomy his new SMU really had, perhaps.

"You have operational autonomy and authority here, Jed,"

Ben answered. That had always been the plan, right? They intended to train the new paradigm heavily over the coming weeks, but circumstances had changed. Even so, he trusted not only Jed but the entire team. It would be trial by fire. Having the assets of the CIA available through Gayle and the spiritual guidance of David in place helped a ton, but Joshua Bravo was the most capable team for this autonomous mission—especially with Jed, and his gifts, at the helm. "I trust you, Jed. Lean on David and be in prayer for guidance from the Holy Spirit."

"Always," Jed said, his voice betraying a growing curiosity.

"I need to go, Jed, but keep me looped in as needed."

"Wilco, boss," Jed said, and then was gone.

Ben replaced the phone receiver and took a final swig of his cooling coffee. He would head to his equipment cage and square away his kit, weapons, and gear before the brief. Then he'd connect with Lou Garrett, the head of Gideon Squadron, and his three platoon leaders. The sooner he got them thinking through the assault plan, the better.

He reached reluctantly for the phone again.

First, he needed to let Christy know he would be deploying . . .

CHAPTER TWENTY-EIGHT

CITATION LONGITUDE TAIL NUMBER HH 2C1114

TAXIING TO ASTONSKY FBO RAMP FROM RUNWAY 25

PARIS-LE BOURGET AIRPORT

TEN KILOMETERS NORTHEAST OF DOWNTOWN PARIS

LE BOURGET, FRANCE

1412 HOURS LOCAL

Athaliah raised an eyebrow and reached for the satellite phone on the polished table separating her plush leather seat from the empty one across from her in the cabin of the luxury, long-range business jet currently taxiing to the gate outside of Paris. No number popped up and no name or identifier.

Which told her exactly who it was.

"Yes," she said, rising from her seat and packing up her briefcase from the seat beside her. "We're taxiing to the ramp now. We just landed. Please tell me that the car is here and waiting for me."

"We have a problem," her soldier in Paris said in clipped English heavily accented by his French roots. Viden was more than just her man in France, he was part of her inner circle and an important player for her plan to work. He was a Dark One possessed by several demons and a very powerful force indeed.

"What?" she asked, dropping back into her seat. She needed the Rising to happen on schedule. She had her people in place. She had her two pawns moving on the board. It was now or never. If that asshole ascended, she was out of any position of power . . .

"There has been a breach."

"A breach? What kind of breach? I would have sensed it . . ."

"Not this. There was a . . . presence. Watchers from the Shepherds were inside the temple."

"You saw them?"

"I felt them . . . and heard them, I think."

"Heard them?"

There was a long pause. The man was her confidant and her most trusted soldier, but he knew the stakes. And he knew what would happen if he failed her.

"They were here. Not physically, but I assure you they were here. I pursued them, and I know they were here."

"What did they see?"

"Enough. We were preparing the chamber. It will not be difficult for them to figure out what is going on. Ben Morvant . . ."

"Is in America. The Watchers are talented and gifted, but in Europe, I believe them less of a threat."

"I believe these Watchers *were* Americans. I could sense their conversation."

"How sure are you?" she asked.

There was a short pause as she imagined Viden weighed the risks of being wrong.

"Very."

She felt her heart sink. Was it possible? Did the presence

of the Shepherd in Port-de-Paix mean that they knew about her, perhaps even of her plans? Was this Jedidiah Johnson the advanced team? What had she missed? How could they have found her?

"Manbo?"

"A moment," she snapped.

If they thought she was part of the Rising, then surely they would have sent more than a single Shepherd and his woman. No, it was as Calypso had said—it was a single operator in the wrong place at the wrong time. He was in search of a missing child, and soon he would no longer be a problem. And if Ben Morvant suspected her involvement with the Dark Ones, but especially with the pending Rising, they would have taken her already. She had slipped beneath the Shepherds' radar—just as she had remained in the shadows of the misogynistic fools who believed they would control the Dark Ones. Until the Rising brought a leader to power, the chaos would continue, and the Dark Ones would be ineffective in their mission to disrupt God's plans for His people. No, it was a horrible coincidence that they were here in Haiti, somehow.

But if the Shepherds now knew about the Rising . . .

"This is unfortunate, but we may be able to turn it to an advantage," she said, and a grin spread on her face.

"How?" But the voice told her Viden suspected at least part of the plan.

Should she just let the assault unfold? If the Shepherds wiped out the entire cabal, then could she perhaps fill the void . . . ?

No. No, that would not work. She still had too little recognition to rise in power, even from such ashes. The Spaniard and the Frenchman were surely claiming her insights as their own. No, she rose best on the backs of others. She would preserve the cabal, allow the Rising to occur, and rise *with* the new leader—pulling the strings and wielding the real power. Her time was coming, and her own Rising was beginning, but she must be patient.

"Set a team in place," she said finally. "In the catacombs but far from the temple and out of sight. And stage the main assault force in the buildings around the restaurant. We'll ambush the Shepherds when they come, and we'll kill them all."

"There will be others . . ."

"It won't matter," she said, the rest of the plan crystallizing in her mind. "We will hurt them, and by doing so we will establish our relevance for the leadership of the Dark Ones. I will notify the leadership and, when proved right, establish myself as a valuable asset to whoever it is that ascends. Then, I will have the ability to control that person even more." The last thought brought a larger smile to her lips.

"Shall I wait for you to contact me?"

"No," she said, snapping her fingers at the man at the forward galley of the plane. He hustled toward her. "Begin to assemble your teams immediately. Morvant's Shepherds may well be on their way already. I will spend the next hour notifying the dark brotherhood of what we have uncovered and our plan. I'll begin with the German, who will oppose me almost certainly."

"Then why . . ."

"Because in doing so, and being proved wrong, he will emasculate himself."

"It will be done. And the Watchers?"

She thought a moment. She was growing her operation to destabilize the effectiveness of the Watchers, but she was a long way yet from success.

"We will rely on the chaos in their network of threads. And leave some bait so they have something to follow."

"Bait?"

She sighed. She seemed the only one left that saw the long game. She'd read the book. They lose in the end. It was about power in the moment, in the now. Unlike so many who rose to power, she didn't believe they could defeat God. But they could certainly scatter many, many of his sheep along the way and enjoy the power of the now.

"Sacrifice someone, Viden. Likely, it will need to be several people—a small team even. You need to have the Watchers find a thread and lead them to the bait. Then, the real assault team can fall in and destroy them."

"It will be done."

And he was gone.

The man from the galley, the servant from her estate, knelt in the narrow aisle of the luxury corporate jet, head down, eyes on the floor.

"I will need a meal," she said.

"Yes, ma'am."

"Send the car to bring me something delicious. I will eat it here on the jet, so have the pilot leave the power on. They may go and file a new flight plan. We will be heading out again very soon."

"Home?" he asked in a voice that suggested he'd rather be almost anywhere in the world.

"Yes, home. But I will need a few hours here in Paris before we depart," she said. She wanted to be sure she didn't lose her signal during an important series of phone calls. "And we may wait on the ground for a time at the refueling point."

"Tenerife," the servant said.

"Yes, fine. We will spend time on the ground in Tenerife. I don't know how much, so they should file their plan that far only for now."

He gave a deferential nod, then rose and headed for the door.

"I want lamb," she said, smiling at the symbolism that would make it all the more delicious. "And a very good bottle of wine."

"Yes, ma'am."

"Something not French," she added, lifting the satellite phone again to make the first in a long series of calls.

Then she would turn her attention to these troublesome Watchers. Victor had been able to penetrate the minds of the enemy at times, and her own powers were growing. Perhaps she could cut the head off that particular snake—temporarily, at least—all on her own.

CHAPTER TWENTY-NINE

WATCHERS TOC

ST. GEORGE'S ACADEMY

1640 HOURS LOCAL

Rachel Yarnell stared in amazement at the bustling activity in the TOC. She'd seen the space before, during the orientation to her new position, but it had been all but empty then. The two students and their Keeper who had been present had been eating lunch in the corner and laughing during that visit.

This was something entirely different. The energy of the space was palpable, a gentle buzzing of electricity.

She wondered if everyone who came here could feel it or if it was because of her connection to her daughter. Or was it something else? Rachel felt an awakening of some long-dormant feelings recently that felt heightened here in this space. *Senses* she had once had.

She stood instead of taking a seat, her own buzzing energy making sitting still impossible, and in any case, she was unsure exactly what it was she was supposed to be doing. She knew it wasn't worrying about her husband, who had left suddenly just before she'd been called into the St. George's TOC from her office. He'd made the drive over just to kiss her goodbye, a very David thing to do, but she'd been summoned here before he'd had a chance to share much about what he would be up to. She wondered if, now that she was part of the team, he'd be sharing more of the top-secret details of his travels. He'd been generous with information since they'd slid down this bunny hole behind their daughter, but she always wondered what there might be that she *didn't* know.

And now, it could work both ways.

Because the briefing they had received just a while ago about what was going on was chilling and frightening but also very, very exciting. That she could play some small part in a covert operation to prevent the next Victor from rising to power? Well, that was unbelievable and thrilling and terrifying and—too many other emotions to contemplate. Perhaps mostly she felt like a fish out of water. She'd never had the chance to grow her gifts like Sarah Beth was doing now. It wasn't jealousy that she felt at that thought, but a deep regret.

But admiration too. She glanced over at the daughter she was so very proud of and felt a smile spread over her face, despite the weight of the mission they were part of. She was glad that Sarah Beth had an outlet and purpose for the gifts she'd been given.

If only . . .

Rachel chased the pointless thought away.

Being here in the TOC, watching her daughter work beside Corbin and Pastor Dee, allowed her to see her daughter in a new way. She'd been protecting the little girl whose safety and happiness were her responsibility—a responsibility she took very seriously. But the Sarah Beth who was leaning over something at her workstation with Corbin wasn't a little girl at all. She was a young woman. Emphasis on *young*, to be sure, but Rachel realized that she saw Sarah Beth now as so much more than she'd imagined possible. The insightful questions she'd asked in the briefing alone had given Rachel pause . . .

"It's a little overwhelming to watch the first time, isn't it?" She turned to see the serious but smiling face of Jean-Baptiste Allard. "I'm sure it's much more so when it's your own daughter involved."

"It's a lot," she agreed. "But it's amazing. I'm just so glad to be part of it." She glanced again at her daughter, who, catching her eye this time, gave a little smile and waved like a fourth grader from the stage of a school play. She waved back. "It's good to see her this way. I think it helps me understand, but it also helps to see her differently. It's too bad that other parents can't come here to see this too. I think it would help so much with the worry and anxiety."

Allard nodded. He seemed to really consider that for a moment.

"What an interesting thought," he said. "I wonder if we should pilot a program like that. Some sort of limited read in that would allow for observation of the work we do here. I bet you're right—it could allay many worries for parents. I'm sure what they imagine is far worse than the reality of the work we do."

"I promise that's true," she agreed.

Though, of course, nothing in any of their wildest dreams could have approached the horror of Victor's attack on St. George's. There would be no children enrolled here at all if such a thing could have been imagined. Whatever happened or didn't happen in the TOC could never compare to Sarah Beth confronting Victor, or to her closest friend at St. George's taking a spear to the chest.

She shuddered at the thought and then chased *those* demons away.

"Perhaps, after this operation, we should meet to see if you could help us with something like that—a pilot program. It's outside of your area of responsibility, of course, as the Shepherds' liaison, but . . ."

"I'd love to," she said.

"We'll circle back on it over the summer, okay?"

"Sure," she said.

The largest of the screens on the wall of LED monitors—many dark and several on various cable news streams—flickered to life. Everyone turned to face it when the image of Ben Morvant appeared. A hush settled over the room as they all focused on the head of Shepherds North America, though Rachel noticed that buzzing energy remained.

Now we get into it.

She turned to Allard, but he wasn't facing her at all. Instead, he stared at the screen, arms crossed on his chest and face tight with anticipation.

"Did you say something?"

"What?" he said, clearly confused.

She waved a hand, shooing the conversation away.

"Watchers, I just want to thank you for your hard work and support," Morvant said from the screen.

Rachel realized he was dressed in a military-style shirt and vest, like the one Jed had been wearing that night at St. George's. She knew Morvant had been a Navy SEAL, but seeing him in combat gear felt strange and new, even though it shouldn't have been. Still, she didn't really think of him that way, for some reason. This was a different Ben than from their backyard barbecue.

"This is an opportunity for us to do something amazing, and I have no doubt God has placed this in front of us for His purpose," Ben said. "Remember, whatever God calls us to, He equips us for, so don't let the enemy whisper lies to you about what you can or cannot do. You are what He says you are; you are here, called to His purpose. Hooyah?" he asked, a phrase Rachel thought was a Navy SEAL or Army Ranger thing.

"Hooyah," Sarah Beth whooped while others replied with more teenaged expressions of enthusiasm. "Slay!" one boy hollered from a station across the room from Sarah Beth. Her daughter grinned at the boy and gave him a thumbs-up. Rachel thought his name was Daryl.

"So, listen, Watchers and Keepers. In the briefing, we divided up your responsibilities, but understand that we're imperfect and that if the Spirit leads you differently, notify your Keeper and keep us in the loop. Sarah Beth and Corbin?"

"Yes?" Corbin said, her voice brimming with the confidence of someone fifteen years the teenager's senior.

"You'll have comms directly to my team, which is running lead on the op. We're first in and last out, so have our backs."

"Always," Sarah Beth said, her voice similarly confident and mature. Rachel shook her head in amazement.

"We're moving to the infil point, based on the intel from Watcher One and Two, in about sixty minutes. Now is the time to chase any threads and see if you can get inside to get us eyes on and call fires from on the X."

"We're having a really tough time, Ben," the older boy named Daryl said, frustration in his voice. "It's like everything is just mixed up. Threads I used to pick up and follow easily now go to dead ends. I'm not sure what to do about that, but I'm finding it impossible to make my way in."

"Me too," said the slightly younger boy beside him. That boy Rachel did know—his name was Josh, and he'd suffered a skull fracture when they'd confronted Victor . . .

"It's like chaos inside," Sarah Beth agreed, pulling Rachel back to the present. "But if you're able to project, that seems to be unaffected. And we're going to try and find a thread to the man we encountered on our ISR run, but we want to wait until the last minute . . ."

"We felt like he became aware of our presence the last time," Corbin explained. "So, we don't want to tip anyone off about the assault force."

"Is that even possible during a projection?" Josh asked.

Corbin shrugged. "I didn't used to think so, but . . ."

"Not that it matters," Daryl said with a grin. "Corbin the Master Watcher and Sarah Beth the Wonder Girl are the only ones who can project in a tactical situation."

"I projected myself into a movie theater once," Josh bragged. "Saw like three minutes of the *Top Gun* movie for free."

"Yeah, you keep saying," Daryl said and rolled his eyes.

"The plan to hold off on projecting until the last minute is a good one, Corbin," Ben said from the screen, returning the conversation to the matter at hand. "But any chance to find threads into the minds of Dark Ones who might be on the X will be helpful. To that end, our intelligence team is sending names and biographical data of several people in Paris whom we believe are connected to the operation the Dark Ones have going on there. This is based on non-Shepherd source material and intelligence gathering, but we're only sending information on those we've cross-referenced as having ties. We don't want to waste time or send you on any goose chases, okay?"

Nodding around the room.

"Mrs. Yarnell, do you have anything to add?"

Rachel felt her face flush and shook her head.

"No, I'm still getting my feet under me. But I'm available to help if you think of anything I can do."

"Of course," Ben said. "Your primary role in this new job is to communicate needs and deconflict problems with meshing the programs. Right now, you're here to learn more about what the Watchers do so you can anticipate what they need and any problems that may arise." Rachel nodded, wishing she hadn't pointed out the currently superfluous nature of her job. "Watchers, the bios are coming from our intel shop to your stations now. See what you can find, but Teams Two and Three, I want you to communicate everything you find to Sarah Beth and Corbin. Corbin, you guys vet that information and pass directly to me anything you feel is relevant, okay?"

"You got it, sir," Corbin said, giving an awkward two-finger salute.

"Okay, get after it, and thank you. We'll do a comms check in about fifty minutes but hit me with any updates between now and then."

"Thank you, Ben," Allard said.

Ben nodded and then the screen went black.

"Let's get to work, Watchers," Allard said, clapping his hands. "Let's keep our Shepherds safe."

Three teams of two kids each bent over their screens and then began to chatter among themselves.

Rachel now felt even more overwhelmed by the feeling that she had little or no purpose in the room. She had exciting thoughts about how she might be useful in the future—how she could provide a perspective regarding these kids to the teams at the Shepherds, from both a maternal and former-gifted-person perspective. But none of that was in place, or even more than a germ of an idea. At the moment, she could think of literally nothing she could do to help.

I feel pointless . . .

"Your presence here is more help than you know," Allard

said, turning to her. "So don't say that. Your role will mature and evolve, but it sends a clear message to the teams that Morvant has a liaison in place just to address their needs and concerns. Okay?"

"Okay," she said, shifting uncomfortably, unsure what had led him to address her inner insecurity. Did he have gifts himself? It was her understanding that the gifts disappeared by the time a kid was eighteen to twenty. But then Morvant was an exception, wasn't he?

"Just walk the room and show your support," he suggested. "Honestly, in the tactical environment, it's about all I have to offer as well, at least once they're on mission." His smile was genuine and warm.

Rachel began a slow circle of the room, where the three teams of two Watchers and one Keeper worked, though she was unsure about exactly what they were doing. The pair in the far corner were scrolling through something on their computer screen. The boys, Josh and Daryl, seemed to be in prayer with their Keeper. She headed for where Corbin and Sarah Beth leaned toward each other, elbows on knees and foreheads almost touching. As she approached, she saw that they held hands and that Sarah Beth's eyes were closed. Corbin's were open but seemed focused on nothing.

Pastor Dee raised a finger to her lips and beckoned to Rachel.

Rachel tiptoed over to the woman and slipped into a chair beside her, taking her place at a long black table beside the U-shaped workstation that Sarah Beth and Corbin shared. The girls' station had two computer screens each and a space between where Corbin's sketchbook sat beneath other sheets of paper with notes written on them in various colors. There were also a bag of chocolate-covered raisins, a paper plate with chips and pretzels on it, and two water bottles.

"They're trying to find threads," Dee said, her voice soft but not quite a whisper, as she lifted a teacup to her lips.

"How does that work?" Rachel asked quietly, staring at her daughter in fascination. Somehow her face seemed both tense and slack-jawed at the same time. Beneath her closed eyelids, Rachel could see her daughter's eyes darting about madly. Sarah Beth clutched Corbin's hands so tightly that her knuckles were white.

Dee smiled. "It's a lot like chasing someone down through his phone or social media connections and then using those threads to listen to his conversations. Except in this case, you're inside the person's head. You're seeing what they see, hearing what they hear, and listening in on their thoughts."

"Can't they, I don't know, *see* you or whatever? They don't know you're there?"

Dee shook her head.

"Not usually, but of course Victor was a notable exception. To be honest, I can't tell you much more about what it's like. I only know what the kids have described to me over the years."

Rachel nodded. She remembered the feeling of other people's thoughts coming into her head when she was young. For her, it was like being in a room and listening to dozens of conversations at once. It had been overwhelming and confusing. The other things she'd seen, well . . .

Another thought came to her suddenly. She looked at Dee, confused.

"Wait, you said only what the kids have told you?"

Dee nodded.

"So, you've never . . . you know. You were never a Watcher?"

Dee smiled. "No, my dear."

"Oh. I just assumed . . ."

"My gift is leading these kids," Dee said. "Understanding and supporting them. I'm more youth pastor than Watcher by far. But I'm connected to these kids in a powerful way."

Rachel was about to ask Pastor Dee more about her

background when she was interrupted by a gasping scream from her daughter. She watched as Sara Beth suddenly stood up, her water bottle crashing to the floor. Rachel felt her heart sprint in her chest and rose to rush toward her daughter, but Dee grabbed her hand.

"Corbin!" Sarah Beth shouted. Rachel saw that Sarah Beth's eyes were still closed. "Corbin, get out of there."

Corbin blinked, her eyes focusing back on the Watcher TOC. She looked up at Sarah Beth, confused.

"What happened? Why did you come out?" Corbin asked. She was on her feet now, staring at Sarah Beth but still her face was just confusion.

Sarah Beth opened her eyes and sat down, then glanced over at Pastor Dee.

"You're safe, Sarah Beth," Dee said. "What happened?"

"I . . . I'm not sure."

"We were on a thread," Corbin said, addressing Dee now. "It seemed promising. Definitely someone in Paris related to two of the names on the intelligence list. I felt the darkness and heard the gross thoughts, but . . ."

"That wasn't it," Sarah Beth said, pulling on Corbin's hand until the girl turned to her. "There was something else in there. Did you feel it?"

"Something else? No, I . . . I don't think so. Sarah Beth, was there another thread you jumped on? Is that it?"

"No . . ." Sarah Beth was up again and pacing now. Rachel wanted to run to her, to wrap her arms around her, but Sarah Beth no longer looked frightened. Instead, she seemed intrigued—almost fascinated. "No, I was on the same thread. I was in there with you. And it wasn't the gross thoughts or any of that. I've seen way worse."

"So, what?" Corbin said.

They both sat now, and Rachel struggled to wait while her little girl pursed her lips in thought.

"There was something in there with us. Something else on the thread and inside the target."

"Another Watcher?" Corbin asked, gesturing at the other two teams. "Is that it?"

"No," Sarah Beth said, shaking her head. "No, there was something on the thread all right. But it wasn't one of us."

"How do you know?" Pastor Dee asked. Her voice held no judgment or doubt. Rather, she seemed fascinated. Rachel got the sense that whatever was going on wasn't something that had happened before.

"Because," Sarah Beth said, her voice confident and sure, "whatever this thing was, it was hunting us."

"Hunting us?" Corbin asked.

"Yes."

"Did it find you?" another voice asked.

Rachel turned to see Allard behind her, unaware he had come over.

Sarah Beth paused a moment. "No," she said.

"Are you sure?" Allard asked. "If it found you, we need to let the Shepherds know they may be compromised."

"I'm sure," Sarah Beth said. "But we still need to tell Ben. If something is hunting us, that's still a bad sign, right?"

"It is," Allard agreed. "But one thing at a time. If we can stop this Dark Rising, we will prevent the next Victor from rising to power and will eliminate the infrastructure of the Dark Ones' leadership in a way we've never done before. We need to be sure that we're not compromised. Then, we support the Shepherds and this operation and get the mission done."

"So we don't tell them?"

"No, of course we tell them," Allard said. "Let Ben know

right now, in fact. In the meantime, you and Corbin stay off the threads. We'll have the other teams continue to share what they can about the thread you were on."

"But if they're hunting the Watchers . . ." Sarah Beth protested.

Rachel watched Corbin take Sarah Beth's hands again. "They're not hunting the Watchers, Sarah Beth," Corbin said. "They're hunting *you*."

"Who?" Rachel blurted, feeling an overwhelming need to protect her little girl.

Corbin shrugged.

"I don't know, Mrs. Yarnell," she said. "But I was there too and felt nothing. It could be that it's from our projection earlier. We sensed someone was aware of our presence then. Maybe that someone got, I don't know, dialed in on her and not me. But if it was all of us they were looking for, I think I would have felt it too."

"That makes sense," Sarah Beth said, and Rachel was amazed that her daughter seemed far less disturbed by the thought than she did.

"We have a half hour before the Shepherds start their infil," Allard said to the whole room, and Rachel saw that the other two teams were watching them. "Teams Two and Three, Corbin will give you what she can on the thread they were following. Sarah Beth, do your best to describe everything you can to Mrs. Yarnell and your Keeper, and they'll convey it to the Shepherds. If Ben agrees, then we will hold you back until they breach. Then, let's see if you can project back into the catacombs. Are you okay with that?"

"Absolutely," Sarah Beth said.

"I agree," Corbin said, patting Sarah Beth on the back and then heading across the room to the other two teams.

Sarah Beth moved to take a seat between Pastor Dee and Rachel, who could no longer resist and took her daughter's hand and squeezed it.

"It's okay, Mom," Sarah Beth said with a smile. "This is what we do. Everything is fine, I promise."

Rachel smiled and then chuckled.

"What?" Sarah Beth asked, then smiled herself. "What's funny?"

Rachel felt another wave of admiration, love, and maybe just a twinge of jealousy. "Sometimes it's like I'm not sure who's the mom," she said and winked. "I'm fine, and you are absolutely amazing. Now," she said and accepted the pen and leather notebook from Dee, "tell me what you saw and felt and exactly what you think it means."

"I have something," Daryl called from across the room, all eyes turning to him. He smiled and gave a thumbs-up. "We followed one of the threads, and it took us to a Dark One inside the catacombs. There's a small team of six shooters in two teams of three on twin tunnels leading to some sort of, I don't know, like a big creepy room. The man was the team leader, I think. From his thoughts, it seems like they're providing security for some very important people arriving any minute . . ."

"That's it," Jean-Baptiste Allard said, clapping hands together. "That's what we needed. Josh and Daryl, stay on that thread and relay it to Corbin. Sarah Beth, stay off threads entirely until after the breach, then you and Corbin can project together and call fires." The head of St. George's seemed to practically glow with enthusiasm. Rachel realized she liked the guy a lot. "Brief Spear, Corbin. It's time. We've got 'em, I believe!"

Sarah Beth turned from her mom, taking a seat back at her workstation. "I'll describe it all to you later, Mom," she said, her voice excited now. "I gotta get to work on this."

She watched her child lean in, talking in a low voice with Corbin.

Rachel had to admit she still felt a little jealous. But that embarrassing emotion was buried deep beneath another, more powerful emotion.

Pride.

CHAPTER THIRTY

ALLEY BEHIND CAFÉ AUX FRUITS DE MER

CORNER OF RUE DES THERMOPYLES AND RUE RAYMOND LOSSERAND

PARIS, FRANCE

0037 HOURS LOCAL

Ben Morvant crouched beside the sliding door of the large and boxy Citroën HY van. From the outside, the van looked like any other converted food truck, the type seen all over Paris, complete with advertising and menus painted on the sides. Inside, however, it was a spacious, up-armored tactical vehicle his counterpart at Shepherds Europe had secured for the operation. An identical truck sat in place eight blocks east, where another catacomb entrance had been found by the local intelligence teams.

Ben felt an energy and purpose just as he did every time he kitted up to join the fight. The transition from combat-wounded SEAL to head of Shepherds North America had not been easy—nor had moving from door-kicking SEAL to the head shed, where his role was one of leadership and strategy most days. The last time he'd felt called to be at the tip of the spear had been following Jedidiah Johnson around Nashville and then into the mountains in search of a young kidnapping victim—the girl who was now the most gifted Watcher he'd ever seen—before Jed knew anything about God's calling for his life.

Ben's hands flew across his kit, time having in no way dulled the muscle memory of the ritual. He still qualified in the high-tech kill house on Trinity Loop every few months as well, both alone and with other Shepherds, to keep his skills sharp.

"Spear One, this is Watcher One," Corbin's voice came in his earpiece.

"Spear One."

"Nothing new to report, but we found very little to follow other than Watcher Three's thread. There are a half dozen guys—older guys in suits—in the large chamber room now. No luck finding the thread we were following before—the man named Viden, who we are sure is a Dark One—and everything else is weirdly quiet. Do you want me and Watcher Two to go in before you commit?"

Ben thought a moment, looking beside him at Jeremy Turner who led Gideon Alpha. Bravo was at the other catacomb entrance beneath a shoe store, and Charlie Platoon was the QRF, with the European Shepherds in reserve, between the two locations a quarter mile to the south. The bulk of the force mobilized by Shepherds Europe would be hitting several HVTs they had identified as part of the Dark Ones' operation in Paris before they could squirt and disappear—which would happen quickly when word got out about Ben's hit on the Rising. Both infil sites had sniper teams in place as well, to guard against any enemy QRF.

"No," Ben said finally. "Not yet. Exfil Watcher Two for now. Once we're inside the catacombs, we'll pull the trigger on your projecting infil, okay?"

"Roger that, Spear One," Corbin said.

Ben looked at Turner and nodded.

"Chapel, Spear One—Spear is go," he said, alerting the TOC that they were heading to the entry point and signaling Bravo to begin their breach. Then he spun a hand over his head and led the other six operators across the dark alley to the closed back door of the café. Ben took a knee beside the heavy door, scanning his sector toward the corner of Rue Raymond Losserand as one of Turner's operators pressed a small breacher charge onto the door by the handle and lock. Ben squeezed his eyes shut to protect his night vision as the dull *whump* signaled the modest blast. He turned back to the door and surged forward—one operator to his left clearing the corner as another cleared right. The green beams of IR light crisscrossed the empty storage area behind the café's kitchen, glistening in the smoke and dust from the breacher charge like a weird Christmas light show.

The small room and the kitchen beyond were empty.

One Shepherd remained at the door, watching for anyone coming from behind them, but just as Ben's mind shifted from the empty room to the potential threat at their six, a soft "Alley still clear" came into Ben's earpiece from former Naval Special Warfare combat medic Gabriela Ortiz.

"Spear Nine, secure the door and fall in with us," Ben said, leading Turner through the kitchen and then scanning the empty dining room for missed tangos.

Finding none, they returned to the storeroom to find Spear Three snipping a padlock off an ancient black metal door. Ben caught the lock in a gloved hand before it clattered to the floor as Five pulled the door open and Ben pressed left, scanning the small space behind it for a waiting ambush.

The open door revealed a simple dirt-and-stone landing that descended immediately into darkness, rendered gray green in his night vision. A dank, musty smell drifted out to meet them as Ben now took the lead, clearing cautiously down the steep stone stair. Twin beams of IR green targeting lasers joined his as fellow operators descended the narrow staircase behind him, scanning over his head from a few steps above. The air felt heavy and wet. He heard the soft dripping of water into a puddle somewhere up ahead. The walls were the same dirty stone as the floor and ceiling.

They reached the bottom of the stairs, a much deeper descent than he'd expected, and he took a knee, scanning to the left as the operators fanned out around him in the tunnel, the ceiling low but the walls much wider apart than he expected. A chill made him shiver—not from the three neat rows of skulls embedded in the stone wall, but from the temperature that seemed to have dropped fifteen degrees or more.

"Clear," Turner announced after scanning behind them to the right.

Ben was up, moving slowly forward in the dark wet of the tunnel.

"Chapel, Spear Alpha is Bethlehem," Ben said softly into his boom mike, announcing they had made the first checkpoint—the entrance into the catacombs. His next call would be an intersection of two tunnels a quarter mile away, their initial point for the approach to the chamber Corbin had sketched, which was just a hundred yards beyond. The call sign for that checkpoint was Nazareth, and they would call Calvary at the final chamber. Mission complete would be Jerusalem.

"Spear Bravo is Bethlehem," Tyson Young, the former Ranger leading Bravo, announced, indicating they were also in the catacombs.

Ben moved forward slowly and quietly, the pointy tip of an arrowhead formation. He felt his heart quicken not with fear or dread, but with excitement and purpose. He blinked, his mind filling now with a strange murmuring, like he was overhearing people at a party two rooms away—clearly voices, but too indistinct to make out. The voices were in his head, not in his ears, but they confirmed one thing: His team was not alone in the catacombs. As he crept forward, he momentarily considered asking Sarah Beth and Corbin to try and project and clear the way but dismissed the idea. If there really was a Dark One here who could sense their projection into the catacombs, they risked tipping their hand too soon.

He would wait until they made it to the Nazareth checkpoint and then ask for them to do a projecting ISR pass. Until then, he decided blind was better if it meant they were also quiet . . .

CHAPTER THIRTY-ONE

WATCHERS TOC

ST. GEORGE'S ACADEMY

1905 HOURS LOCAL

Sarah Beth looked up at Corbin, who gave her a tight smile, and resisted the urge to get out of her chair to pace. She felt her mom's eyes on her, which was a distraction all its own, but what stressed her most was the nothing. She'd been in the Watcher business only a short time and still considered herself a rookie, but never so far had she been asked to just sit and wait. She couldn't chase threads because it felt like someone was hunting her—*her* specifically. She couldn't project because—well, same reason. And she couldn't even hear the calls from the TOC right now because Dr. Allard and her mom were monitoring those comms to keep them from being a distraction.

The real distraction is the nothing. Listening in on the comms would calm me . . .

She sighed.

"It's just the worst, right?" Corbin asked with another smile. "I'll do anything they ask us to do, just don't ask us to do . . ."

". . . nothing," Sarah Beth said in unison with her friend and teammate, and both girls laughed softly.

"Spear Alpha is now at checkpoint Nazareth," Dr. Allard announced to the room. His very not-at-all-tactical way of making the call annoyed Sarah Beth more than it should have, but at least the nothing was about to end. Allard held a finger to the headphone over his left ear, listening, and then nodded as if everyone could hear what he heard.

"Why is the radio so sketchy?" her mom asked, looking up at the head of St. George's. "It seems broken up. I can hear the ops center or whatever it's called . . ."

"The TOC," Sarah Beth interrupted, feeling very irritated now.

"Right, the TOC, but then Ben and his Shepherds are broken up."

"They're in the catacombs, far underground," Corbin said, just as Sarah Beth had the same thought. "We should keep Watchers ready to relay comms if needed. Dr. Allard, can you put comms back on the speakers? That would help us a ton at this point."

He nodded and tapped something on the laptop on the table beside him.

The speakers came to life with the calm and much-more-tactical voice from the Shepherds TOC aboard the jet in Paris.

"Say again, Spear Two," the female voice said softly. "You are broken up."

"Sp . . . ooh . . . azareth . . . ready."

"Chapel copies Spear Two—Bravo is Nazareth and ready. Be advised your comms are barely readable."

"Chapel, Watchers are standing by to relay," Allard said, but Ben Morvant was way ahead of him.

"Sarah Beth and Corbin, do you read me?"

The voice in her head was as clear as if it came over the comms—clearer, actually, even on the best day. It was as if Ben stood right beside her. No other adult could communicate with her like that—not even Uncle Jed.

"Loud and clear, Ben."

"Go ahead and project; see if you can guide us and call fires. Just stay here in my headspace and tell me directly, then I'll relay."

"Okay, Ben," Corbin said in her head—in *their* heads, Sarah Beth supposed.

She looked at her friend and took her hands.

"Ben has contacted us and asked us to project," Corbin announced.

"Very well," Allard replied.

"You ready for this, sis?" Corbin asked, her face all business now.

Sarah Beth resisted the need to look over at her mom, whose eyes she felt burning a hole in the side of her head.

"Always," she said, closing her eyes.

The transition was easier than when she and Corbin had projected to the catacombs before. This time, Sarah Beth simply blinked and materialized inside the tunnels. She was right beside one of the Shepherds who crouched low, leaning forward on his rifle with legs churning as he moved swiftly down the tunnel. She didn't think about moving along with them but did anyway, as if caught in the eddy of their movement, drafting off whatever it was that spilled over from their physical world into her spiritual one.

"Corbin, are you here?"

"Yeah, I'm with the other half of the team."

Sarah Beth wondered if that was on purpose or if God had somehow worked it out for them.

"Ben, we're here—it worked. I'm right beside one of your operators in the tunnel—I can see you just up ahead. We're going to go ahead and see what's up there."

"Roger, Watcher One and Two."

Ben's voice was so clear that she looked over at him, surging down the dark tunnel. He didn't return her glance. Everything was new to her, of course, but projecting like this most of all. It felt cool and creepy at the same time.

Sarah Beth sped up and soon approached a glowing light which she knew spilled over from the room outside the main chamber. Just as she slowed her approach, she heard Corbin.

"I've got four shooters spread out in an eight-foot recess full of bones past your side of the entrance, Sarah Beth, so check your side."

"Okay . . . Hold on . . ."

She slowed, then stopped completely. The tunnel turned to the right, and as it did, it widened, the glow becoming brighter, though she seemed able to see in the dark just fine. There was an opening in the wall to her right, an arched opening like a giant fireplace, and she peered in to see four men, all with glowing orange eyes, armed to the teeth and dressed in black.

"Four on this side too. Did you hear that, Spear One? There are two teams of four shooters on either side of the entrance to the chamber. Security, I guess."

"Understood, Watcher Two," Ben's voice said from all around her. *"Go inside and get a head count and layout of the men in the chamber and tell us what they're doing."*

"On it already, Spear," Corbin answered. *"I'm in the room just outside the chamber and there is one additional armed security guy here. You coming, Sarah Beth?"*

"Spear Two, One—hold Bravo short. We have new ISR

incoming," Ben said out loud. Apparently, the radios worked between the operators even if the signal couldn't reach the TOC.

Sarah Beth rounded the corner of the arched opening to the outer room they'd seen before. This time no priests were screaming in pain as they burned to death, but there were three empty small tree-sized stakes in the ground marking the spot where those deaths had happened—whether for historical purposes or in place for a fresh set of sacrifices, she didn't know. Sarah Beth saw Corbin beside the entrance to the chamber, and beside her stood a man with a machine gun, clearly oblivious to their presence.

She joined Corbin at the door. Her friend smiled.

"Ready?"

"Ready . . ."

This was the only opening they'd encountered with a door, a heavy, strangely shaped door that reminded her of a dungeon. It didn't matter—she followed Corbin, and just as they'd done last time when they met the door at the top of the stairs, they dissolved through the metal like it wasn't there at all.

On the other side, Sarah Beth's eyes widened, and she felt her pulse pound in her temples.

The men in the room weren't dressed in black robes, and they weren't the old men she'd expected. There were thirteen people in the room dressed in black tactical gear, armed with assault rifles and machine guns, grenades hanging from their vests. Each had a black helmet, just like the Shepherds wore, with the night-vision goggles affixed to the top.

This wasn't a meeting at all.

It was a trap . . .

"In more ways than one, my dear," a man's voice said in her mind.

She looked over to the head of the table, where a muscular

man—dressed in black like the others but without a helmet, a machine pistol slung on his chest—seemed to stare right at her. As he did, the orange glow in his eyes flickered and became a red flame. He smiled like he saw her. But that was impossible, right?

"You'll find very little is impossible in the world of spiritual warfare, girl."

"Sarah Beth, what is it?" Corbin asked from beside her, but Sarah Beth was already stepping in front of her, instinctively, to take the bullets that must be coming.

"He can see me!"

"Ah," the Dark One said, an evil smile spreading across his face, his dark lips parting to reveal perfect white teeth. *"You have someone with you, do you? No matter . . . the trap is set."*

He moved slowly around the table, moving toward her . . .

"Ben! Ben, it's a trap! It's an ambush . . ."

She was moving backward now, trying to pull Corbin with her.

"We have thirteen Dark Ones—heavily armed and waiting for you in the chamber room," Corbin said. *"Get out!"*

"Corbin, it's Daryl," a new voice, the teenage Watcher back in the TOC, said in the air around her.

The Dark One still came, slowly, steadily, smiling as he did, his eyes now red fire.

"Tell them it's a trap!" Daryl's voice continued. *"It's an ambush. There are two teams of eight Dark Ones each entering the tunnels behind the Shepherds. I fell onto a thread from the profiles and . . . and . . . I don't know where they came from! They must have entered the tunnels from farther out, but they're moving in fast. They're coming in behind them . . ."*

Fear consumed Sarah Beth now. Fear of the Dark One, who, impossibly, still stared at her as he approached. And terror at what was coming—terror that the Shepherds were about to get wiped out.

She felt a real, physical hand grab her wrist.

"Sarah Beth!"

Sarah Beth opened her eyes and stared at Corbin, who sat across from her in the chair at their workstation.

"Wait," she shouted, louder than she meant to.

The room went silent as eyes turned to her.

"Ben, it's Sarah Beth. I mean, Watcher Two. You have teams of eight in each tunnel coming in behind you. Eight Dark Ones behind Alpha and another eight behind Bravo, four more ahead of each team in the rooms along the tunnels just before the chamber, and then thirteen—no, fourteen with the guy in the outside room—fourteen bad guys waiting in the chamber. We led you right into a trap . . ."

"Sarah Beth, we have to go back in," Corbin said, her grip tightening on her wrist to where it became painful. "We have to go in now."

"We can't," she said, her voice trembling with fear. "Corbin, he can *see* me . . ."

Her mom was out of her chair now and coming to her.

"What's happening? Who can see you, Sarah Beth?"

"Sarah Beth," Corbin said, and she looked up into the eyes of her friend, her mentor, her *teammate.* "Ben hasn't answered us. We need to go back."

"I can't," she said.

"You can," Corbin said. "Listen to me, Sarah Beth. He can see you—fine. It's scary, but so what? He can't hurt you. We're not really there; we're here. He can't touch you physically."

She looked over at her mom, whom Pastor Dee held back with a gentle hand on her arm.

Sarah Beth turned back to Corbin.

"What if it's like where if you dream that you're falling and don't wake up before you hit the ground, then you die in real life?"

"That's just an urban legend, first of all. And second, it's not like that. In real life, you're here. You're safe in the TOC. He can scare you, but he can't hurt you. Now, come on—the Shepherds need our eyes or they're going to get slaughtered . . ."

"You're right," Sarah Beth said, squeezing her eyes shut a moment and mouthing a little prayer for strength and courage. She popped her eyes open. "Let's go."

"Sarah Beth," Corbin said, just as she was closing her eyes, and Sarah Beth looked up at her friend again. "Maybe we can *use* the fact that he can see you. Maybe we can do more than be the eyes for the Shepherds. What if we can lure some Dark Ones in the wrong direction?"

"What? Wait," Sarah Beth heard her mom say from behind her. "Corbin, Sarah Beth, that sounds dangerous. Dr. Allard, tell them . . ."

Sarah Beth ignored her mom and smiled. "I see where you're going with this," she said. "Let's go . . ."

She closed her eyes, took Corbin's hands in hers, and her mom's words of protestation faded away.

"Spear One, we're coming. We're gonna help you get out of this . . ."

CHAPTER THIRTY-TWO

CATACOMB TUNNELS

LESS THAN A HUNDRED YARDS SHORT OF THE CHAMBER

0114 HOURS LOCAL

Ben Morvant tapped his gloved finger on the trigger guard of his custom assault rifle, cursing himself for not somehow seeing this contingency. He had just led Gideon's Alpha and Bravo teams to their deaths. How had he not seen this—sensed it? And with no Dark Rising, who the hell was calling the shots? He'd let the fact that the Dark Ones were in chaos, without a leader, lull him into overconfidence, and his hubris was about to have a very high price.

"Bravo, hold fast one moment," he called.

They could turn now and fight their way out against the Dark Ones who were flanking them from the two entry points, knowing that another group of shooters would join the fight in each tunnel at their new flank the moment the shooting began. Maybe they could fight through before they arrived, but not likely.

He closed his eyes.

"Watcher Three, it's Spear One. Do you read me?"

"Yeah, it's Daryl— I mean, Watcher Three . . ."

"Tell the TOC to have Gideon Charlie form two teams and head to both entrances to the catacombs. Descend into the tunnels and then hold at the entry points until I say, but be ready to enter the fight."

"On it, Spear."

There were no good options, but having Charlie ready to flank the assaulters coming up on them was something at least.

"Spear One, we're coming," Sarah Beth announced suddenly. *"We're gonna help you get out of this."*

"What do you have in mind, Watcher Two?"

Corbin—Watcher One—filled him in instead.

"We think we can lure them into a side tunnel and away from the team," she said in his head.

"Where is that tunnel?" he asked.

"Behind the chamber."

It just might work.

But they had a bloody battle ahead of them first, even with the possible exit strategy. But having the girls helping them might make the difference and keep the additional shooters off them long enough.

"Two, this is Spear One," Ben said in his boom mike. He briefed Tyson Young, Bravo Team's lead, on the new plan. "Move now and engage the fighters flanking us from the tunnels."

They just needed to push them back past the branch points of the crossing tunnels to open a path to escape. Once they pushed them back, Ben could lead the team into the empty tunnels and find a way out.

He sent a message to Daryl, instructing him what to pass on to Charlie's split team, then led Alpha down the catacomb tunnel the way they'd come, pressing into the walls as best they could to keep the center line of fire clear. On night vision, the eerie row of skulls near eye level stared at him as he passed, grinning at his situation. Ben did the math quickly. They were evenly matched, roughly, with the eight shooters they approached now. But if the Dark Ones behind them from the chamber split into two equal teams, they would have the four fighters from the original group plus now *seven* more—eleven more shooters moving in behind them the moment gunfire erupted in the tunnel.

Unless Corbin and Sarah Beth's plan worked.

And he had ideas about how to make it more deadly for the enemy if it did. Because God gave gifts with purpose, and he'd received more than his fair share . . .

He saw no motion up ahead as the tunnel bent left, but the turn restricted his range of view. He held a hand up and took a knee, the other operators scanning their sectors forward and back, he knew. Ben let out a long, slow breath and closed his eyes.

He reached out with his mind, searching for a thread in the space around him. He couldn't project like Sarah Beth and Corbin could, but he was damn good at finding threads and letting those thoughts in through the filter he'd built in his mind.

"We'll be able to kill them all. We'll come up behind them and slaughter them. We will fill the tunnels with the blood of the Shepherds . . ."

Ben could see through the Dark One's eyes, but it didn't help him much. From the stairs of the café to their position now, the tunnels looked pretty much the same—stone floors, arched ceilings, and walls of stacked stone with rows of skulls blended in on both sides, millions of dead forever entombed beneath the city. He wanted to know if the inbound shooters were past the intersections of the other tunnel but couldn't tell. He surged forward, assuming that, if not, they would be soon.

His team was only minutes from a cross fire that would cut them to pieces.

"Pick it up, Alpha," he whispered into his boom mike, his voice amplified in the earpieces of the Shepherds. "PEQ-4s off."

The view he had through the eyes of the Dark One definitely suggested the bad guys were on NVGs. So having his own team use their green IR beams would give away the Shepherds' position. With his left index finger, he clicked the IR designator off and switched to the floating red-dot holographic sight. He surged forward, thighs burning, and moved to the center of the catacomb tunnel.

Ben kept the view from the Dark One's eyes in his mind as he pushed forward.

"What is that? I hear them . . ."

This was the demon-possessed man's thoughts, and Ben sensed his fear. He moved his finger inside the guard, putting gentle pressure on the trigger.

"Then we will finally bathe in their blood," the demon inside the man answered his host.

Ben's mind's eye suddenly saw a crouched operator coming around the gradually sloping turn of the tunnel. He realized he was seeing himself through the eyes of the Dark One, and he squeezed his trigger, letting loose a shot as his brain shifted from the gifted sight to his real eyes and adjusted his aim, dropping the floating red dot onto the face of the Dark One and squeezing twice. The man pitched backward onto the ground, and Ben could feel the terror and pain engulf the dying man just as Ben snapped out of his head.

The tunnel lit up now with tracers and muzzle blasts from both sides, and Ben shifted back to the left, took a knee, and continued to fire.

"Now, Watcher One and Two!"

"We need them back past the intersection," he ordered with his voice this time.

He led the Shepherds, surging forward, knowing that with the shooters now coming from the chamber behind them as well, they were almost out of time . . .

CHAPTER THIRTY-THREE

CATACOMB TUNNELS

OUTSIDE THE DARK ONES' CHAMBER

PARIS CATACOMBS

"Let's go," Corbin said to Sarah Beth in the Sanctuary TOC, and Sarah Beth gritted her teeth and nodded.

They projected to the outside room of the chamber where the same single shooter paced now, like a caged animal at a zoo, wishing it could get through the glass wall to devour the child looking at it. His eyes glowed with fury, but as before, he did not seem to see her.

The door to the chamber burst open, and Dark Ones began filing out.

"The Shepherds are in a cross fire. Split into two groups and join the fight. Kill every one of them . . ." The voice from inside the chamber was familiar, and Sarah Beth felt her throat tighten.

"Remember to pretend not to see him, Sarah Beth . . ."

She followed Corbin into the chamber, immediately feeling

the man's eyes on her. She forced herself not to look, then spoke from her projected self:

"Two of you stay here," Sarah Beth said, not looking over. *"They can't see us, so just be the eyes for the Shepherds in case some of them return. Corbin and I will lead the assault team from the tomb in the cemetery and come in behind them . . ."*

"What are you up to, little girl?"

Sarah Beth could feel the doubt that had crept into the voice of the Dark One more clearly than she heard it. She didn't dare get on his thread, fearing he would sense the ruse, and she prayed he couldn't get on hers like Victor had been able to do. She didn't know how or why this Dark One could see her when she projected, but she knew for sure this man was no Victor. That enormous and powerful evil had died at St. George's.

"Come on, Corbin. We need to make sure they don't have backups in the tunnel from Montparnasse Cemetery and clear the way for the team. Once we get them into the chamber, they can split into two teams of eight each . . ."

"HOLD ON!" she heard the man named Viden bark to his men as she and Corbin dissolved through the small black metal door at the rear of the chamber. "Form up on me. We have more Shepherds coming through the tunnel from Montparnasse. Join me and we'll kill them in the tunnels."

Sarah Beth glanced at Corbin as the girls ran up the dark tunnel, sloping slowly upward.

"It's working," Corbin told Ben. Sarah Beth remained silent for fear Viden would discover the ruse.

"We just need a couple of minutes," Ben said in her head.

Sarah Beth heard the creak of the metal door behind her, then the pounding of booted feet. The trick was to stay ahead but let themselves be seen by Viden. They would only need a few minutes. If the Shepherds could win the battle they were in, then they could escape before Viden and his Dark Ones realized they'd been tricked.

God, please let them win their fight. Please let this be enough time . . .

CHAPTER THIRTY-FOUR

CATACOMBS EAST OF THE CHAMBER

The Watchers' plan to lure the large force of Dark Ones away from the fight sounded like it was working and might just give Ben enough time to survive this ambush.

Ben fired a three-round burst up the tunnel with no clear target in sight because the curve of the tunnel kept the seven remaining Dark Ones just out of view. But the episodic fire from Ben and his teammates was succeeding in driving them back. If Ben could push them all the way past the intersection, as he hoped, then he could lead his team into the crossing tunnel, which seemed clear of shooters. From there they would have cover to finish the assaulters east of them and ambush the four others joining the fight any second from behind them.

If the Dark Ones chose to slip into the intersecting tunnel, ruining that plan, then Ben would lead his team to safety through the café.

He hoped that the Dark Ones didn't do that because after this ambush and the damage to his team, Ben realized he didn't *want* to be out of the fight safely. He wanted to engage the enemy and finish them.

Every last one of them.

To his left, he finally saw the dark gray opening to the intersecting tunnel. He grinned as he realized the Dark Ones had bypassed this turn and continued to retreat slowly back toward the café, firing in bursts to keep the Shepherds from descending on them. In the pre-op briefing, they had mapped all the tunnels, so he knew that they split again—more than once, in fact. Even if trapped in these side tunnels, they could be led by Sarah Beth and Corbin to an alternative exit and safety, though not without considerable logistic difficulty.

But that wasn't how he hoped to use the tunnels . . .

Ben shifted right, hugging the far wall and opening a line of fire into the side tunnel in case the Dark Ones had maneuvered a shooter there, his BDU blouse dragging across the row of grinning skulls, the perfect symbol of the physical and spiritual warfare they found themselves in. He swept his red dot back and forth across the wide opening to the other tunnel, searching for a target.

He found one.

He saw the weird flash of the enemy operator's optics just as he made out the silhouetted figure pressed against the left side of the tunnel entrance. Ben squeezed his trigger and simultaneously juked left, away from the direction his angular momentum tried to propel him, which would make his position predictable if he missed.

The Dark One's bullet exploded a yellowish skull beside Ben's head, just before his own bullet plowed through the face of the enemy fighter, driving him onto his back.

"Contact left, inside the side tunnel," he called, jinking again back to the right, searching for another target.

The wall behind him was torn apart by fire that could only

have come from farther down the catacomb tunnel they'd arrived from.

"They split the team—four and four is my guess. We need to take the tunnel to the right . . ."

He fired at another silhouette as Special Operations combat medic Gabby Ortiz sprinted across the wide tunnel, firing a three-round burst down the catacomb tunnel toward the café, then took a knee beside him. The Dark One he'd fired at pitched forward, but then suddenly exploded toward him at a full sprint, eyes flaring with red, fiery rage. The possessed man moved with impossible speed, jerking side to side as he and Gabby both let loose two three-round bursts. The bloody mass of a man collapsed a few feet from them and let out a scream that sent a chill up Ben's spine and reverberated down the tunnel until he was silenced by a final head shot from Gabby. The rest of the team arrived beside Ben.

"Covering fire—one burst, then two of you follow us in . . ." Ben commanded.

The tunnel was lit by tracers as he and Gabby sprinted toward the split off to the right. Seconds later, they controlled the tunnel entrance, two additional Dark Ones dead at their feet.

"Right side is clear," Ben announced, aware that his breathing came in gasps, less from the physical demands of the engagement than from the adrenaline in his bloodstream driving his breathing and heart rate through the roof. "We'll provide covering fire—come to us." Ben got to his feet, leaned into the tunnel, and Gabby took a knee beneath him. They fired alternately east until the other five Shepherds joined them.

"Two more on our side and three of you on the west side," he barked. "Be ready to engage the four coming in behind us."

A minute later, it was over. The four shooters joining the fight from the west were slaughtered by Turner's well-trained team as Ben and Gabby, together with two other Shepherds, made short work of the Dark Ones farther east down the tunnel. As they checked for any other shooters to the west, he heard the four single shots of Turner's men making sure that the enemies were really dead.

You never knew with Dark Ones . . .

A few minutes later, the seven of them arrived deeper in the tunnel and surveyed the carnage of the Dark Ones at their feet, finishing them off as well. Ben felt nothing but satisfaction as he pulled the trigger the last time, the echo of the shot punctuated by the tinkling sound of his spent cartridge bouncing off the stone floor.

"Bravo, Alpha, sitrep?" Ben said.

"West tunnel clear," Tyson replied. His voice was tight, and Ben wondered if it was from pain or something else.

"Exfil to the vehicles by the café?" Turner asked him, his voice low and tired.

"No," Ben said, swapping his nearly spent magazine for a fresh one, not needing to cycle the charging handle since he still had a round in the chamber. "We're going to finish them off."

He circled a hand over his head, then chopped the hand west.

"Bravo, move toward the center chamber again," he commanded on the comms circuit.

"Roger that, boss," came Tyson Young's answer, the voice soft, but thick with purpose. Ben had heard voices like that in combat many times, spurred mostly by a need for revenge.

And bloodlust.

Who was he to judge? They'd been duped and ambushed. It was time to finish it.

"Watcher One and Two—bring them back to me in the chamber, if you can . . ."

CHAPTER THIRTY-FIVE

CATACOMB TUNNEL

HEADING NORTH FROM THE DARK ONES' CHAMBER

Sarah Beth stopped, Corbin slowing and looking back at her from a few steps away, when they heard Ben project his request into their minds: *"Watcher One and Two—bring them back to me in the chamber, if you can."*

"How are we supposed to do that?" Sarah Beth wondered.

The projected iteration of Corbin shrugged, and Sarah Beth felt hands squeeze hers many thousands of miles away back in Tennessee.

"I don't know," Corbin said.

Sarah Beth looked behind her where more than a dozen armed men followed them, hunting the Shepherds. The man at the front, the man called Viden, stared at her with venom, but she pretended not to notice. But just as Sarah Beth felt certain that Viden could hear her, she believed that for some reason he wasn't aware of Corbin at all—at least he didn't seem to have been before. It was like Corbin was on a different frequency or something, one that Viden wasn't tuned in to.

Then she had an idea and sent the message to Corbin, knowing Viden would hear it too.

"Great job, One. Spear is heading back to the chamber to see what intel they can collect. We can head back to the TOC, I believe . . ."

It took all her will and effort not to look at the one called Viden.

But she heard him.

"Turn around," the Dark One barked at the dozen men he led. "The Shepherds are coming back to the chamber. We'll take them there."

"I thought you said they were coming from the north in this tunnel?" another demon-possessed man growled from behind the leader.

"It was a ruse," Viden answered. "They're coming to the chamber. Now move, all of you. Kill them. Kill every last one of them!"

The army of demons spun on heels and began charging south again, toward where Ben approached the chamber. Sarah Beth jogged after them, Corbin beside her, passing Viden without a glance. A wave of nausea overcame her as she did.

"We need your eyes, Watchers . . ."

Ben's voice in her head was different, but she assumed that was just the heat of battle. She let Corbin answer, still fearful that Viden could hear her.

"Spear, Watcher One—we're following a group of fourteen shooters headed back to the chamber from the north," Corbin said in their heads.

Sarah Beth became aware of footfalls echoing behind her and looked nervously over her shoulder. Viden was sprinting north now, away from them.

"Watcher One?" Sarah Beth said in their minds.

Corbin turned and looked at her, then spotted the fleeing man behind them.

Sarah Beth didn't want to speak but raised an eyebrow in the universal *Well?* symbol.

"Follow him for now, Two," Corbin said.

Sarah Beth turned and headed north, after the fleeing Dark One, nervous at being alone yet prepared to eject back to the Watcher TOC if needed.

Moments later, the tunnel behind her echoed with a cacophony of gunfire.

And then screams . . .

CHAPTER THIRTY-SIX

INSIDE THE DARK ONES' CHAMBER

PARIS CATACOMBS

Ben rose slowly, scanning over his rifle through thick smoke from the hundreds of rounds that had been fired in the closed space, the green beam of his PEQ-4 glistening in that dissipating smoke. He glanced at the Suunto watch on his wrist. After so many years of combat, he shouldn't be shocked by how little time had passed, but he was. The massive firefight that felt like it had raged for nearly an hour had taken only four minutes.

Four minutes . . .

To his right, he sensed motion, turned on a heel, and dropped his green beam between the glowing eyes of the bloodied Dark One who now rose impossibly to his feet, the dead man's rifle coming up. Before Ben could squeeze the trigger, simultaneous gunshots rang out from his flanks as Shepherds from Bravo and Alpha fired. The demon-possessed man's head jerked around before the body slid back to the floor.

Ben scanned across the carnage. "Clear," he said softly but clearly.

Several other calls of *Clear* rang out from the team.

"I have an urgent surgical," combat medic Gabby Ortiz said from behind him.

Ben felt his gut tighten like he'd taken a punch, then turned to find the former SEAL Team medic kneeling over an operator from Bravo, a former Marine named Cedric Belacort, whose face was set but whose eyes suggested he was in considerable pain.

The magic man, his teammates call him.

Ben hadn't known that before, but it came to him now, his filter still open. He had no idea of the source.

"You good, Magic?" Jeremy Turner asked as he too knelt beside the man and took his gloved hand.

"All good, boss," the operator lied. Technically, Jeremy was the boss of Alpha, but Ben knew the men were tight.

"Round went through his femur up pretty high," Gabby said grimly. "He's lost a lot of blood, but I got it stopped with the tourniquet. Gotta get him out of here."

The tourniquet was no doubt the source of the pain. Ben had been there before . . .

"Spear One, Bravo has . . ." the voice of Tyson Young cracked, and Ben felt his chest tighten, knowing what would come next. ". . . Bravo has two angels."

Angels. Radio code for dead operators—operators killed in action.

He blinked away tears.

"You good?" he asked Turner and Ortiz.

Both nodded grimly.

"We'll get you out of here, Belacort," Ben said to the wounded man. "Stand by."

He switched to his "other" comms as he headed to the outer chamber where Bravo had fought.

"Watcher Two, where is Viden?" Ben asked his Watchers. He wasn't sure how that name came to him, but like Belacort's nickname, he knew it was correct.

He felt his own impure thoughts, the desire not for justice but vengeance, bubbling to the top of his cauldron of emotions.

"I'm not sure, Spear," came Sarah Beth's voice. *"We're deep in the catacombs, but I have no idea where he's headed. It's not either of the tunnels we came in through, and he's made, like, a bunch of turns. I'm totally turned around . . ."*

"Stay on him," he ordered, rage filling him now. *"Watcher One, let the TOC know we have one urgent surgical and two angels. We're headed back to Bravo's infil point. We need immediate evacuation to the surgical cache and security for the exfil."*

"Okay, Spear," Corbin replied.

The men in the outer chamber stood grimly in a tight circle, two holding security by the arched opening into the catacombs. Two operators lay between them, side by side. Ben stopped, watching silently as Tyson Young led the team in a quiet prayer for their dead. A voice in his head, *the* voice, told him he should join them, pray beside them, but the weight of remorse and guilt crushed the voice and made it silent. He looked down at his feet and blinked.

God, please help me . . . and please forgive me.

His private prayer was interrupted by another voice.

"He's heading up the stairs now, but I don't want to get too close. I don't think he knows I'm behind him."

"Where is he?" Ben demanded, aware that his voice, even in their shared headspace, held a venom that would feel out of place to the young Watcher.

"I . . . I don't know. Hold on . . . There's light coming in now from above me . . . wait a second . . ."

"Let's move out, team," Turner announced as he led the rest of Alpha, two carrying the wounded Bravo team member between them, from the chamber. The room was heavy with grief. "They may yet have another QRF in the wings, Shepherds, so stay frosty. Wounded and angels in the middle. Charlie front and back, and the rest of Alpha and Bravo in the middle. Spread out. Let's not be lambs to the slaughter . . ."

Ben was aware that Turner, perhaps sensing his boss was occupied, had taken command, tacitly at least, of all three platoons from Gideon.

"He's gone," Sarah Beth's clear voice said.

"What? Show me . . ."

And like that, he was on a thread and with the young Watcher. He was both surprised and relieved to find that being in her headspace allowed him to see what she was seeing.

Through Sarah Beth's mind, Ben stared out at the street—busy even at this hour—along what appeared to be a restaurant and club district. Crowds moved along both sidewalks, laughing and smiling, couples holding hands. He thought to tell her to go to the corner, to get the cross street, but he knew it was pointless. They had only a vague sketch of the man from Corbin's drawings. They would share that with Shepherds Europe and with both the French GIGN and Interpol.

But for now, the man was gone.

"I can still lead you out. We both can," Sarah Beth said, her voice heavy with emotion. *"'Angels' means some of the Shepherds are dead, doesn't it?"*

Ben blinked and was back in the outer chamber. He fell in beside the last of the group, nodding to the members of Gideon Charlie who then closed in from his left.

"I'm afraid so, Sarah Beth. You did great. You saved a lot of people—both of you. Without you, we'd all be dead."

"You killed a lot of people . . ."

He thought she was just thinking out loud, rather than talking to him.

"But not enough," he thought, regretting the public thought immediately. He didn't want the Watchers, all of whom were children after all, to think of him as a cold killer, no matter how tempting hatred felt right now. The girl was not quite fourteen, after all. He wanted her to believe—to believe again himself—that God's mercy and grace were for everyone, that God loved all His children, even those who had made horrible, horrible choices. He let out a breath through clenched teeth, wanting to pray but not finding the words.

God, help me, was all he came up with.

Then he switched back to mission mode.

"Okay, Sarah Beth, you and Corbin search ahead in the tunnel to clear the way as we exfil. Once we're in the vehicles, you get back to St. George's. We'll debrief everything in the morning, but you all did very, very well."

He waited for Sarah Beth to say something, but she didn't.

Ben moved with his team west in the tunnel, toward the exit inside a shoe store not far away. He forced his mind to stay on the mission.

They were still far from home.

And tonight, home was going to be where loved ones learned of the loss of their husbands and fathers.

CHAPTER THIRTY-SEVEN

RENTAL HOUSE

12 ROUTE DJERILON

AUBERT, PORT-DE-PAIX

HAITI

0805 HOURS LOCAL

Jed woke to the smell of bacon cooking, which made him smile broadly.

Then, he scowled. By nature, and years of military programming, he was a perennial early riser, but today Gayle had beaten him to the punch. He turned his wrist to check his watch, which he habitually wore to sleep. A long day spent hunched over computers and his worry about Ben and the team had kept him up late.

Geez . . . 0805! Oh, Gayle, I was going to get up and cook breakfast for you!

He couldn't remember the last time he'd slept in so late.

Guess I was more wiped out than I thought.

He swung his legs out of bed, arched and twisted his back,

then rolled his neck. Next, he headed to the bathroom to empty his bladder, splash water on his face, and run a comb through his hair. Finally, he threw on a T-shirt and walked out to say good morning to Gayle with bare feet and dressed in the baggy running shorts he preferred to sleep in.

She greeted him with a *Good morning, sleepyhead* smile.

He smiled back. "Morning . . ."

"Would you like a coffee?" she said. When he nodded, she poured him a cup, and he settled onto a bar stool at the kitchen island.

"I never sleep this late," he said, taking the proffered mug, then added, "Thanks for this."

"You're welcome," she said and picked up a pair of metal tongs to turn the bacon sizzling in a cast-iron skillet on the stove. "When you weren't up at the crack of dawn, I knew you must have been out cold. I figured I'd let you sleep, until I got so hungry I couldn't wait anymore."

"Which is why you used the ole *I'll cook some bacon* alarm to wake me up?" he said with a grin.

"Works every time," she said, pointing the tongs at him for effect.

"You made dinner last night. I was going to cook *you* breakfast," he said, feigning a scowl. "At least let me make the eggs."

"Sure, but only if you cook them in this skillet when I'm done with the bacon."

"Country style . . . mix in the hot grease?"

"That's how Mom did 'em when I was growing up. And she'd melt in a slice of American cheese for good measure, but we don't have any."

The comment made him think of his own family breakfasts as a kid growing up in Murfreesboro. The nostalgic memory warmed his heart.

I wonder what Mom and Dad would think of Gayle if I brought her home?

Whoa . . . where'd that come from?

"What's that look for?" she said, cocking her head.

"It made me think of Sunday breakfast at my folks' house growing up. My dad used to make silver-dollar pancakes on a big skillet. I'd eat twenty or more just by myself."

"Do you have any brothers or sisters?" she asked.

"Nope. I was an only child, but David Yarnell might as well have been my brother, because he hung out at my house as much as I did," he said. "Speaking of David, I believe he's heading down here with the rest of the team. So, you'll get to meet him." David would fill him in on whatever was happening that Ben had been reluctant to mention. But, if something really big were going on, surely he and Joshua Bravo would have been looped in, right?

"We've met," she said. "Briefly, when I came to Trinity Loop."

"Oh, that's right . . ."

"Skillet's yours," she said as she plucked the last of the bacon from the cast iron with the tongs and put it on a plate.

He took a pull of coffee, climbed off the stool, and walked around to her side of the cooking island where the egg carton was already on the counter. He grabbed a bowl and started cracking.

Gayle fixed him with a squinty-eyed stare before walking around to take the stool where he'd been sitting. "I've been thinking about the Amour et Espoir orphanage . . ."

"And?" he said, dumping the eggs into the hot skillet and mixing them there instead of whisking in a bowl first. These were "dirty" scrambled eggs, so in-pan mixing seemed the way to go.

"My legend at Gospel Missions International is still active, and I say we leverage it. Our story can be that we're touring

Haiti looking to fund and resource reputable and established children's schools and ministries, and that theirs is one of the programs we're considering funding. It will give us a chance to snoop around, meet the kids, and get a sense of the place. We can probably even request a meeting with the benefactor. Just seeing how they react to our presence could be very telling."

"I love the idea," he said as he used a wooden spatula to scramble the eggs. "Look at you, going all spook and dagger."

"It's *cloak* and dagger," she said.

"I know, but I like my version better," he said with a crooked grin. "In all seriousness, we definitely need to take a closer look. I can't get Kaprica's dying words out of my head. She certainly didn't fight to stay alive just to tell me that Amour et Espoir is some beautiful, wonderful place . . ."

They dug into their heaping plates of breakfast. Jed grinned watching the small woman beside him consume her body weight in bacon and eggs. Soon the conversation turned from the school back to the chilling things they'd learned about zombies.

"It's terrifying, for sure," Jed said between swallows. "But having viewed the school from a distance, I guess I'm struggling to see where it fits into what may be going on here. I didn't see any terrified kids, did you?"

Gayle shook her head, but he could tell from her face that she shared the same worry as him. The zombie phenomenon they'd read about would be a chilling way to control young kids and would scar them forever. It seemed like just the kind of technique the Dark Ones would delight in employing.

The conversation drifted along to the more mundane, and minutes later the food was gone, his belly was full, and the dishes were drying in the rack. Jed felt more like himself. They changed clothes and thirty minutes later had set off for the Amour et Espoir Children's Home.

Jed liked Gayle's plan of showing up unannounced. How people reacted when taken by surprise was always telling. He weaved the SUV through the narrow streets, and in minutes they arrived at the front gate of the property. This time Jed pulled all the way to the gate and rolled down his window as he leaned toward the guard shack and shifted the rental SUV into Park.

A large, muscular Haitian man dressed in a white polo shirt and dark trousers stepped out of the guard shack, which was only large enough for one person. Jed instinctively did a quick survey of the guy—mid-thirties, fit, carrying himself like someone with professional security experience, and every bit of 225 pounds. The guard wore a name tag that said "Romiro" and appeared to be unarmed.

Definitely a large enough shack to house a few assault rifles . . .

"Bonjour," Romiro said, making eye contact with Jed, then looking past him at Gayle.

"Bonjour," Jed said. "Do you speak English?"

"Pretty good," Romiro said, his gaze now scanning the back seat of the SUV through the window.

"We're from Gospel Missions International," Gayle said, taking the lead and passing her GMI ID card to the man.

Romiro took the ID and studied it, comparing Gayle's picture to her face. He did not look impressed. In fact, he looked bored.

"Why have you come?"

"Gospel Missions International is a Christian nonprofit that makes investments in schools, shelters, and orphanages around the world," she explained. "Would it be possible to meet with someone from the school—the on-site director or headmaster—and take a tour?"

"Do you have appointment?" Romiro said, handing Gayle's ID back to Jed after giving it a cursory examination.

"We do not," Gayle said. "If visits are by appointment only, we'd be happy to schedule one and come back later this afternoon."

Jed liked how she handled the first obstacle by being polite and making their intention clear: They wanted to visit today.

"*Tann isit la*," Romiro said, then translated in English, "Wait here."

Jed nodded as the security guard turned to call in their request. Before the big man blocked the view, Jed scanned inside the guard shack and noted a monitor showing closed-circuit security camera feeds, a radio hanging from a hook, and a push-button safe large enough to hold handguns, if not a compact folding stock rifle.

"An interesting choice to man the front gate," Gayle said. "He's almost as big as you."

"It certainly sends a message."

"And that message is *go away*," she said. "He's coming back."

Jed turned to look at Romiro as the big guy returned with the verdict.

"Madame Wilshire will see you later," Romiro said. "Come back in one hour."

"Come back in one hour?" Jed repeated.

Romiro nodded.

"Okay, thank you," Jed said. He rolled up the window, shifted the SUV into Reverse, and executed a three-point turn to leave.

"Interesting," Gayle said as they drove away. "Not what I expected."

"How so?"

"I figured they'd either say no or tell us to come back tomorrow. But an hour . . . is reasonable. You can't do much prep in an hour besides a bit of housekeeping. Maybe she's in a meeting."

"You can do a *lot* of housekeeping in an hour," Jed said, still skeptical, thinking of all the times he'd disappeared an entire house full of terrorists in the middle of the night, leaving no trail behind, often in under fifteen minutes. "If you're a pro and properly motivated."

Gayle smiled but shook her head.

"Not in the world they're working in. I can't clean my one-bedroom apartment in an hour. And this is an entire school and boarding house," she said. "I don't know, seems like a good sign. What you see is what you get."

He didn't argue the point. "What do you want to do for an hour?"

"I don't know . . . thumb wrestle?" she said with a chuckle.

"With your little hands? I'd crush you."

Ultimately, they passed the time driving around talking and returned to the front of Amour et Espoir exactly one hour after departing. This time, Romiro was ready and waiting by the wrought iron gate, which he opened after only a cursory look in the back seat. Once inside the perimeter, there was only one way to go: a gravel road that led to a dirt-and-gravel parking lot in front of what Jed decided was the main administration and school building. The other building on the property had a very "bunkhouse" design to it, and he assumed it was a dormitory. It reminded him, for some reason, of St. George's. Or maybe Sarah Beth was just on his mind.

He parked. Just as they were getting out, a moderately overweight, middle-aged Caucasian woman appeared on the covered front porch of the building. She smiled at them, but instead of walking down to greet them, she waited on the porch for them to come to her.

"Welcome to Amour et Espoir Children's Home," the woman said, sticking out her hand to Gayle first. "I'm Ms. Wilshire, principal and headmaster here."

"Gayle James," Gayle said, shaking the woman's hand. "And this is my colleague, Jed Lewis."

Jed smiled and shook Ms. Wilshire's hand, which was squishy and cool to the touch.

I don't have time for these interlopers.

Wilshire's thought came to Jed like a breath. It had been a while since he'd had such a clear thought from someone else in his mind. It almost never happened to him around Gayle, which he realized just then. It was almost like once he started bonding and working with Watchers, like Sarah Beth and Corbin, he'd become less receptive to non-Watcher folks' thoughts. Was that because he'd closed himself off or because he'd tuned his antennae, so to speak, to listening only to Watchers? Regardless, he now knew Ms. Wilshire's outside expression did not match her inside thoughts.

"Thank you for welcoming us to your facility," he said.

"We like to think of it as so much more than a facility. For these children, Amour et Espoir is a *home*," she said, pointing to the beautiful engraved and painted placard above the front door. "See, it's in the name."

"Of course," Jed said. "I meant nothing by it."

You most certainly did. Words matter, Mr. Lewis . . .

Jed kept the smile on his face, resisting the urge to react.

Wilshire turned to Gayle. "Ms. James, let me just say how much I admire the work that GMI does. What an incredible job you folks have done bringing light into the dark places of the world."

"Thank you," Gayle said. "I'm so proud of the work, but do you know what the most rewarding part of my job is? The relationships I get to develop with all the different in-country partners who we support. It's not GMI doing the hard work, it's the folks on the ground, rolling up their shirtsleeves, not afraid of getting sweaty to help lift up the less fortunate and spread Christ's message. Which is why I wanted to stop by today and introduce myself. Amour et Espoir Children's Home is truly the gold standard when it comes to educating and providing for abandoned and orphaned children in Haiti. And for all the incredible work you've done, we recognize there are still many more children that need to be served."

"It's so heartwarming to hear you say that," Wilshire said. "Is it presumptuous of me to read between the lines and say that it sounds like GMI is considering donating to our boarding school?"

"It's not presumptuous at all. That is exactly why we've paid you a visit. I hate to use the word *vetting*, but like I said, the nonprofit world is powered by relationships."

"It most certainly is. Would you and Mr. Lewis like a tour?"

Gayle smiled and nodded. "That would be wonderful."

Jed knew when to run his mouth and when to keep it shut, so he was perfectly happy to let Gayle do all the talking and schmoozing while he followed along, playing the role of the assistant and personal security. As he did, he surveyed the site while still absorbing the occasional two-faced thought from Wilshire.

After touring the main building, which Jed had correctly surmised held the classrooms and staff office space, they toured the children's dormitory and, lastly, the playground and sports field. An enthusiastic game of coed soccer was underway, and Jed lingered a moment. He watched as one girl dodged and weaved past two defenders to find a lane for a goal shot. She kicked a bullet aimed at the upper left corner, but the ball drifted a foot too high and went sailing over the crossbar, rolling to a stop at Jed's feet. He stooped to pick it up as she trotted over to fetch it.

"Hi there," he said, smiling at her.

"*Bonjou,*" she said, stopping in front of him and smiling back. Because of his size, kids were often intimidated by him, but not this girl.

"What's your name?" he said.

"Sani," she said. "*E ou menm?*"

"Jedidiah. Do you speak English?"

"Yes, I try," she said.

"That was some fancy footwork out there, Sani. And you've got quite a leg on you too. A foot lower and that shot would have been a goal."

"Thank you. I like football very much."

In his peripheral vision, he could see Ms. Wilshire and Gayle walking back to join him.

Of all the children . . . he picks the biggest troublemaker.

Jed almost turned to look at Wilshire, the comment so crisp in his head for a moment he thought she might have said the words aloud. He forced himself to pretend he hadn't heard the thought.

"It's wonderful that you have a safe place to learn and play with friends. Do you like it here?"

Sani hesitated a split second. Her eyes darted to Wilshire then flicked back to Jed. "I am very blessed to be at Amour et Espoir," she said with a smile.

"This place is evil . . . I hate it here," Sani said in his head, her sentiment tinged with both defiance and fear.

Taken aback, Jed decided to try to push a thought of his own to Sani. He wasn't sure if the ease with which he conversed with Sarah Beth in their heads was his gift or just mostly Sarah Beth's. Maybe it would work with this girl, Sani, maybe it wouldn't, but he had to try.

"Are the grown-ups hurting you?"

The little girl's eyes went wide, and her mouth opened as

if to speak, but Wilshire cut her off with a rebuke disguised as a compliment.

"Sani is one of our most outgoing young students. She has so much potential, if only she could learn to reign her emotions in. Isn't that right, Sani?" Wilshire said.

"*Oui*, Madame," Sani said, looking at her feet.

Jed tried again with the girl. *"Are you safe here?"*

Wilshire snatched the ball from Jed's hands and gave it to Sani. "Run along now, dear, and play."

Sani took the ball and nodded obediently, but before running off, she glanced up at Jed and in that brief moment of connection, she answered his question.

"I'm scared they will kill me or something worse. They took us from Saint Fleur Orphanage in Pepillo Salcedo where my granmè works. I go to school at Mount Hope, but I'm not an orphan. I want—"

Then her thoughts were cut off, like a phone had been suddenly disconnected.

He watched her run back to the field holding the soccer ball under her arm; all the while his mind was racing at this development.

Was this girl, Sani, gifted? Was she Watcher material? They needed to dig into the orphanage she claimed to have been kidnapped from . . .

"Mr. Lewis?" Wilshire said, snapping him out of his headspace. "Shall we move on?"

"Yes, of course," he said, turning to her with a plastered-on smile. "Quite the little athlete, that one."

"Oh, yes, Sani is a child of many talents. We're so lucky to have rescued her. If you could have seen the squalor she was living in when we found her," Wilshire said.

"Is that so?" Jed said.

"Sadly, it's the case with almost all our kids . . ." she said.

Wilshire babbled the entire walk back to the parking lot, where she delivered them to their SUV.

"Thank you so much for the tour and your gracious hospitality," Gayle said, shaking Wilshire's hand.

"My pleasure," she said. "I hope the rest of your visit in Haiti is both safe and productive. Do you have a business card, Ms. James, so that we might remain in touch?"

"Certainly," Gayle said and handed the woman a card.

"Nice to meet you," Jed said when Wilshire accepted the card from Gayle.

"Nice to meet you as well," the woman replied but did not extend a hand in farewell.

Jed and Gayle climbed into the SUV and waved goodbye through the window, then Jed executed a 180-degree turn and headed back toward the main gate. Romiro was standing by with the gate open and watched them leave without a wave or a smile.

"Well, that was telling," Gayle said, looking over at Jed expectantly.

"It sure was. What's your hot take?"

"Wilshire is definitely hiding something," Gayle said. "She sure didn't like you interacting with that little girl. And you would think she would have had us interact with lots of kids to show the great work they're doing, if she was serious about trying to build a relationship with a donor, right?"

"Yeah, well, there's more. That girl, Sani, who I spoke to. She's not an orphan," he said, the words tumbling out before he could catch himself.

"What do you mean, she's not an orphan?" Gayle said.

Jed hesitated while his brain did mental gymnastics. Gayle knew about Dark Ones, but how much did she know about the Watchers or spiritual gifting? He'd certainly never told her about his gifts and was reluctant to do so now. What would she think if he told her the truth before she was ready? It had the potential to completely undermine his professionally credibility. *Oh, by the way, Gayle, I forgot to mention I can read people's thoughts.* He could even picture the creeped-out look on her face as she backed away slowly. And on the *personal* side, the outcome would probably be worse. The questions would come fast and terrible: *Can you read my thoughts? Which ones? All of them? Oh, dear Lord . . . how could you not tell me something like that, Jed!*

Gayle snapped her fingers. "Jed? Hello . . ."

"Yep, I'm with you."

"You zoned out on me there for a minute," she said with a chuckle. "I said, what do you mean she's not an orphan?"

"Sorry, that's probably just me jumping to conclusions. It's just a gut feeling, I guess," he said, "from the way she carried herself and the fact that she spoke English. How many Haitian orphans can speak English?"

Gayle looked at him strangely and chewed her lip for a moment. "More than you might imagine, especially those who are schooled. English is an important part of rising out of poverty in Haiti. What did you think of Wilshire?"

"Pretty frosty. She seemed to put up a wall from the moment we arrived. And what kind of site director doesn't offer potential donors a little schmoozing time? I mean, she didn't even offer us a cup of coffee or tea or anything. I thought that sent a pretty clear message."

"Yeah, and that message was: Get the heck off the property and don't ever come back."

"Sounds like we're in agreement," Jed said.

Gayle nodded. "Okay, I think this was the evidence we needed to keep digging. When we get back to the house, I'm going to log in to my high side and see if I can get some analyst support to run a background search on Wilshire and try to figure out who's running the parent organization as a whole. I'll also try to dig into their finances."

"Good idea," Jed said. "We'll have a couple of hours before we have to leave to pick up David at the airport this afternoon."

"The rest of the team comes in tomorrow, right? Because we may not know yet what part Amour et Espoir plays in all of this, but something is happening to children here, and Marcello and Kaprica died trying to figure it out."

"Yeah," he said grimly. But he was certain that Wilshire and the school were involved somehow, now more than ever. The girl had said that the place was evil. As a Shepherd, he knew more than a little about evil. "Tomorrow, we get the band back together," he said with a sly grin. "And that's when the real party begins."

CHAPTER THIRTY-EIGHT

CITATION LONGITUDE TAIL NUMBER HH 2C1114

CLIMBING WESTBOUND OUT OF TENERIFE AIRPORT

CANARY ISLANDS, SPAIN

Athaliah leaned her seat back and let out a long sigh. She was tired, but not tired enough to lie down on the convertible sofa at the rear of the cabin, especially not with more than one urgent phone call certain to be coming in over the next hour. In any case, it didn't serve her well to have people see her weak, much less vulnerable. She shot a glance at the large man in the small jump seat by the cabin door. The man fumbled to undo his seatbelt, unconcerned by both the still-steep climb and the still-illuminated safety sign on the forward bulkhead's screen. No, he was afraid of other, far more terrifying things.

"*Wi*, Manbo Athaliah?" the man asked as he arrived at her plush leather seat, taking a knee in the aisle beside her. "*Ki jan mwen ka sèvi ou?*"

"I need a latte," she said without glancing at him. "Double shot and dark chocolate."

"*Wi*, Madame," he said, rising and heading to the galley in a hurry.

"And Samuel?"

The man froze and turned.

"I won't ask you again to speak in English."

"Of course."

He hurried forward, and she smirked.

The satellite phone on the polished wood table in front of her chirped. She looked at the number and smiled.

"I trust you are well, Gunther?" she said, crossing her legs at the knee, beneath the skirt of her Saint Laurent suit.

"I want to know how you knew," the man on the other end hissed.

"What do you mean?" She heard the whirring of an espresso machine grinding beans for her latte.

"You know what I mean. The attack happened as you said it would. It is a miracle none of us were present."

"I would be careful using the word *miracle*, Gunther," she said. "In our line of work, it might be misconstrued."

"You know what I mean," the German diplomat growled. "I want to know how you knew."

She chose her words carefully. "The magic I use is powerful, Gunther."

There was no magic, of course. Her ability to use the children she had turned to find the threads of the Watchers was amazing, but not magic. And in any case, it wasn't her nascent dark Watchers program which had predicted the attack. No, it was the powerful Dark One Viden, who worked for her—and her alone—in Paris, who had somehow sensed the presence of Morvant's Watchers. "But do I not make it available to all? I serve the same Dark Lord as you."

It is my mind and my cunning you should fear, Gunther. Not the magic of Voudou.

There was a long pause, which she found delightful. The German's mind reeled now. Gunther knew full well that Jules Moreau, the wealthy Parisian art dealer, and Mateo Santos, who served as the UN ambassador from Spain, both sought her counsel. And, as a result, both were almost certainly ahead of Gunther in the queue for the Dark Rising. The German surgeon-turned-politician had dismissed her *schwarze magie* as *abergläubisch.* His scientific mind often hurt him when it came to the realm of spiritual warfare. She knew he had no chance at rising to replace Victor, but he might well fear that his authority and position in Germany were also in jeopardy. Victor had set up individual, autonomous cells throughout the world, and the German's cell was indeed powerful and effective. But Gunther wanted to be more, didn't he?

"Gunther, I serve the Dark Prince when I serve all of you. It was a mistake for you not to heed my counsel sooner, but no matter. How did our security forces fare in the attack? Was their ambush successful?"

"Not in the least," Gunther answered, and from his rapid breathing, she could tell he was pacing now. She could picture his ruddy cheeks shaking as he sucked air into his fat face. "The Shepherds defeated us completely. We believe they may have wounded among them, but I have dismissed the claims of our two survivors that they killed many Shepherds as lies to protect them from punishment. But their dead or wounded are academic at this point. This is catastrophic. The Shepherds have found our sanctuary."

"Then we will build a new one, Gunther. Times change. The move to Europe occurred when the Dark Ones were forced from the Baltics in the thirteenth century as the believers invaded the pagan lands. But, we adapt. We continue to fight for the one we serve."

"Where will we meet?"

Was he really asking her? She didn't think so. He was thinking out loud and looking for a way to position himself in power. But that would not happen.

The new location had already been decided.

"You will be notified very soon."

"Notified? How can you know this? You are but a confidant."

"I know what I know. Goodbye, Gunther."

She hung up, giving a little laugh and a shake of her head as she reached for the latte Samuel handed her, averting his eyes as he did. There were still some flickers of hope in those dark eyes. Samuel still hoped—probably still *prayed*—that there was a way out of his service to her. That hope would fade with time. It always did.

She picked up the phone again and pressed "1" on the speed dial.

"Hello, Manbo Athaliah," came the thick-accented voice of Mateo Santos, which she always found sexy. "I'm delighted to hear your voice. I'm sure you already know you were right."

She smiled again. Of course, it would have been far better had she learned of the attack before traveling all the way to Paris. She would have relished the honor of being there for the Rising, but more importantly, her presence, even outside the chamber, sent a message of her importance. But she'd made the right call waiting in the plane to see how the Shepherds' attack would unfold. It would be another seven hours before she arrived back home in Haiti. There was a tremendous amount of work she could be getting done. Calypso would deal with the Shepherd Jedidiah Johnson, but Athaliah needed to find a way to use the children more efficiently, especially now. While their innocence could be exploited to share things they saw with their gifts, she had not yet succeeded in turning them completely. She needed her own

Watchers to combat Ben Morvant's tactical advantage, but so far, the very few she'd turned seemed to have their gifts diminish or disappear. Ben Morvant was no fool, nor was Vincenzo, the head of Shepherds Europe. Things were getting dangerous for everyone.

"Of course, my dear. It is why I am still at my home in Saint-Marc," she lied.

"Brilliant, *mi querida*. You are truly amazing. Together we shall rule the world soon."

One of us will, my darling, she thought.

"We must complete the Rising. Are you on your way back to New York?" Athaliah asked.

"Landing in less than an hour."

"We must set the meeting for the Rising as soon as possible."

"I agree," Mateo said, and she could hear in his voice his mind was turning over the possibilities. "But the question is: Where? Everyone will be vying for a hometown advantage now that Jules has lost his. We must find somewhere everyone will agree to quickly."

"Saint-Marc," she said before taking a long sip of the perfectly brewed mocha latte. "I will host the ceremony at my estate in Haiti. It will seem neutral ground, and I will serve as hostess to all."

"It will not seem that way to Gunther Schmidt," Santos said with a chuckle. "He is quite upset."

"Yes, well, that is for you to deal with, darling. My estate in two days. It is time for your Rising."

"With you by my side as an adviser—with your powers—it is inevitable."

"Two days. I will make sure all is arranged on my end."

"Until then, *querida*."

She ended the call, took another long pull of frothy coffee, then pressed the next speed dial.

"*Mon cherie*," came the cheerful voice of Jules Moreau. "You were right, of course. Your magic is very strong."

"I serve all of you and our Dark Prince," she replied. "I trust you are well?"

While Moreau answered, she sent a text home to Haiti, to Calypso, her most trusted warrior.

En route to home. How are things going?

I know where he is.

We will take him tonight and kill his woman.

I will land in seven hours.

Your prize will be waiting.

She thought a moment about another potential problem as Moreau shared his joyful expectations about what he believed to be his inevitable Rising. She put little credence in concerns of Ms. Wilshire—who was loyal, but not terribly bright—and believed that those worries about the girl's compliance were unfounded now that she'd seen the possible consequences.

I need the girl Sani taken to the estate from Amour et Espoir.

Of course. I will send someone tonight.

She is not to be harmed.

The girl had potential. Sani's gifts were strong if she could be manipulated into using them for Athaliah. But she needed to close all strings to her past . . .

Athaliah turned her attention back to the call with Jules Moreau.

"My magic will make you powerful, but time is short. We must set the meeting for your Rising as soon as possible, my darling . . ."

CHAPTER THIRTY-NINE

RENTAL HOUSE
12 ROUTE DJERILON
AUBERT, PORT-DE-PAIX
HAITI
1927 HOURS LOCAL

For the second time in as many minutes, Jed caught himself looking at Gayle as she worked on her laptop at the kitchen table while he cut the steak. When he turned to ask David to pass him the platter with cubed veggies, David flashed him an *I caught you, dude* grin.

Jed shook his head.

Busted.

"You gonna help me assemble these kebabs, or just stand there and eat all the mango?" Jed asked his childhood-best-friend-turned-teammate.

After being estranged by Jed's life choices for a decade and a half, they were rebuilding both their trust and their bond. It felt good to be hanging out and grilling with David again. He'd picked up his platoon's TSL at the airport an hour and a half ago and, for the first time since high school, hadn't felt awkward being alone with him. Was David married to Jed's first real love? Yes. Had he been living Jed's childhood dream in the ministry—and with Jed's high-school sweetheart no less? Also yes. But Jed felt now that whatever mistakes he may have made in his relationships with both David and Rachel, and whatever jealousy he may have felt, he was now exactly where God wanted him. That peace and confidence had changed everything for him.

That, and having an actual, real relationship with the only one who mattered: God himself.

"Absolutely I am. Because if I don't, you'll make two massive steak kebabs for yourself and four vegan ones for me and Gayle," David said.

"I heard that," Gayle chimed in. "If there's no steak on my kebab, there will be hell to pay. Literally."

Fifteen minutes later, Jed had already devoured the first of his two kebabs. Despite adhering to his promise to pick last, his friends had left the two kebabs with the most meat for Jed because—well, they were the type of friends who did that sort of thing. As he drank Prestige lager and enjoyed a savory and sweet dinner, Jed told himself to enjoy the moment, a moment which reminded him of the old days when the "Three Musketeers" used to hang out and share meals just like this one. Of course, back then Rachel, not Gayle, had been the girl of the group, but the dynamic tonight had a nostalgic warmth. They laughed and told stupid jokes, mostly at Jed's expense, and enjoyed each other's company. When the meal was over, the three of them cleaned up and did the dishes before settling back at the table for Gayle to share what she'd learned through her research.

Sitting with her legs crossed, Gayle turned her laptop screen to face Jed and David.

"This woman is Athaliah Guerrier," she began, and Jed looked at a picture of a beautiful, well-dressed woman. "She is the benefactor and driving force behind Amour et Espoir Children's Home in Port-de-Paix. And as it turns out, the Port-de-Paix campus is not the only school her foundation owns and operates. There are presently four Amour et Espoir boarding schools in different locations around Haiti, with a fifth under construction," she said.

Jed studied the picture of the middle-aged Haitian woman whose striking appearance he suspected belied her age. With her high cheekbones, wrinkle-free complexion, and thick mane of silver hair, he had no idea what her true biological age might be. The photograph on Gayle's computer looked like an image from a professional photoshoot, but something told him that if he were to meet the woman, this was probably how she looked in person.

Her eyes, though . . . Those pale blue eyes seemed to pierce through him even from a picture on a computer screen.

"She has a real presence about her," Jed said, shifting his gaze from the screen back to Gayle.

"I ran an image search, and she shows up repeatedly at fundraising galas and VIP events in Haiti, the Dominican Republic, and abroad. Using some of the agency's tools, I estimate her net worth to be about fifty to sixty million dollars," Gayle said. "She's been photographed numerous times with the current prime minister, Claude Marion, with whom she reportedly has a decades-long friendship, and she is rumored to have helped launch and fund his early political career," she said.

"I thought Marion was the president of Haiti," David said, "not the prime minister."

"He's the acting president," she said, nodding. "Marion assumed the role after the assassination of Henri-Michael Etienne last year. Some say he's planning to follow the lead of other strongman presidents around the globe, who've turned the prime minister role into a puppet position with no institutional authority to function as a check or balance to his power. Other rumors suggest that Athaliah Guerrier might be angling for the position of prime minister herself. Regardless, Marion is dirty. He's got ties to the Haitian oligarchy—a cadre of Judas-investors and vampire tycoons—who use their wealth to control the government, protect narcotics traffickers from prosecution, and exploit the impoverished populace."

"And Guerrier's wealth makes her one of them?" David asked.

"I suspect so," Gayle said. "I can't find any legit business ventures tied to the Guerrier estate. I tried to follow the money, but it was just a big black hole. It might be family money, drug money, or worse."

"So, the orphanages are just a cover story?" Jed said. "Window dressing for her image?"

"Maybe, but if that were the case, you'd think she'd use them as vehicles to solicit donations from corporations and nonprofits and then skim off the top for personal gain, but that doesn't appear to be the case. As far as I can tell, Amour et Espoir is one hundred percent funded by the Guerrier estate."

"That might explain Wilshire's apathy to our visit this morning," Jed said. "Our gambit was a flop because Amour et Espoir doesn't need outside donations."

Gayle nodded.

"Hmmm," he said, rubbing his chin. "Then why kidnap kids to fill it?"

"Jed, as far as we know, those kids are orphans," Gayle said. "This is the second time you've mentioned the possibility that they've been kidnapped. Is there something you're not telling me?"

"Well, for one, the woman who approached me and started

this whole thing was a mother whose child had been kidnapped. That kid was clearly not an orphan."

Gayle nodded, but her eyes suggested she was still skeptical. "That's true," she said. "But we have no evidence at all that the people who took her—or tried to take the boy off the street the next day—had anything to do with Amour et Espoir."

"Marcello and Kaprica sent us here. They were looking into the missing children."

"I know," Gayle said. "And I also feel *that's* a strong connection. And, kidnapping orphans is no better or worse than kidnapping non-orphans. But there is something more that you're not telling me, Jed. I can tell. Earlier, you claimed that the soccer girl wasn't an orphan, but you offered nothing as to how you would know that." She leaned in now, moving her laptop aside and studying him carefully. "What are you not telling me, Jed?"

Jed looked at David, whom, as they'd driven from the airport, he'd read in on his "conversation" with the little girl Sani. At the time, Jed wasn't prepared to go there with Gayle, and he still wasn't. But maybe if David did the talking . . .

"Gayle, there are some things about our organization that neither you nor your predecessor at the CIA have been fully read in on," David said, as if reading Jed's mind. "And it's not a question of trust; it's a question of receptivity."

David's delivery was so smooth, confident, and unassuming that it floored Jed.

"I don't understand," she said, crossing her arms.

"Do you believe in miracles?" David asked.

"You mean like 'walking on water and turning water into wine' type of miracles?" she asked. "Bible stuff?"

He nodded. "Sure, along with the healing power of prayer, the power to exorcise demons, and the power to know the thoughts and feelings that live in another person's heart without the exchange of words. That is stuff from the Bible, to be sure. But doesn't scripture promise these gifts to Christ's followers? I mean, I'm not familiar with an expiration date on the promise of Matthew 10 or on the powers given through the Holy Spirit in Acts 1:8. We find it easy to believe in the miracles of the Bible when done by Jesus himself or his disciples. So why is it so hard to believe those powers persist today? That God gives spiritual gifts to those who need them to accomplish His mission even now? Why would it be hard to believe that God, who is never-changing through Jesus and the Holy Spirit, could still empower us when need be?"

She crinkled her nose at this. "I mean, since I've started hanging with you guys, I've seen freak show–worthy stuff, but *miracles* . . . I don't know."

"Well, whether you choose to believe it or not is up to you," David said. "What and how you believe is not a litmus test to work with us as a partner. What is a litmus test, however, is the type of person you are. Jed and I both believe you to be someone with an upstanding character and a noble heart."

"Thanks, I guess," she said, shifting in her seat.

"What I'm trying to say, Gayle, is that we trust you—trust you to safeguard our secrets, even secrets about things you don't believe possible. Is that secrecy something you can commit to uphold?"

"Yes, you can trust me," she said, shifting her gaze from David to Jed.

I want to believe . . .

Jed heard Gayle's voice in his head, searching for the truth behind all that he had dedicated his life to, and it took every fiber in his being not to react.

"Very well," David said. He looked at Jed, who gave him an uncomfortable nod of consent. "Certain members of our community, some of whom you have met and many more who you haven't, have the gift to read the hearts and minds of people."

"You mean, like, telepathy?" she said.

"You could call it that, I suppose . . . if having a label for it is helpful for you. But it's not some weird thing. Jesus is frequently said to have known the hearts and the minds of others throughout the Gospels, and he promised his disciples they would have the powers and gifts they saw in him, even promising there would be more they had not yet seen. So, believing the Holy Spirit can give such gifts to God's servants is quite Biblical, in fact."

"And you can do this?"

David shook his head. "No, not me."

Gayle turned slowly to look at Jed, her eyes asking the question.

Jed forced himself not to look away from her gaze, telling himself all the while he hadn't done anything wrong, that keeping this from her was in no way a betrayal. "It happens to me sometimes," he said, keeping it vague. "Sometimes I just can read things from people. And it happened this morning with Sani, who kicked the soccer ball over."

"I remember," she said. Her tone was not angry or upset but was definitely annoyed. "And what did you *read* from Sani?"

"She's not an orphan," Jed said simply. "They took her from her grandma—*Granmè*, she called her—and she's terrified."

"Terrified of what?" Gayle said, her arms still crossed but sitting a little straighter in her chair now.

"I don't know," he said. "She said she was afraid of being killed, but I didn't get any details from her. I wish I had. But she feels there is evil at Amour et Espoir."

Gayle nodded and looked down at her lap for a long moment before speaking. "Were you ever going to tell me?"

"Yes," he said, and it wasn't a lie. "When the time was right."

She shot him a look that wilted him.

"Gayle, the truth is, I was afraid how you'd react. I was afraid that you wouldn't feel comfortable around me anymore. I didn't want you to think I was some sort of kook or nutjob if I started talking about stuff like reading peoples' thoughts or feelings."

"In other words, you didn't trust me."

"No, that's not it at all. The opposite, quite frankly. My worry was what would happen if you didn't believe me or . . . weren't ready to believe me. What kind of impact would that have had on our relationship?" he said, then red-faced, quickly clarified, "Our professional relationship, of course."

He felt David's eyes on him after that comment, amplifying the awkwardness.

"I can appreciate that, I suppose," she said, finally uncrossing her arms and placing her hands in her lap. "I probably would have done the same thing if I were in your shoes. Spiritual telepathy is certainly not one of the approved means and methods in the CIA's ISR handbook."

She chuckled to herself after that, and it palpably defused the tension in the room.

"Exactly," Jed said, taking her olive branch and running with it. "We have to be careful how and when we share our spiritual ISR because the source material cannot be validated or reviewed by our partners. It's something we constantly struggle with."

The smile he got now was warm and sincere.

"There's more," Jed said. "And I think it might help with any doubts you have about what I heard from Sani."

"What's that?" Gayle asked, and he felt both her and David's eyes on him.

"The girl told me where she was from. I think that might be something we can verify, but that also might help us identify more of the players here."

"Where is she from?" David asked.

Jed could still hear the girl's voice in his head, in his memory.

"She said she was taken from the Saint Fleur Orphanage in Pepillo Salcedo," Jed said and watched as Gayle immediately began tapping away on her laptop again.

"I thought you said she wasn't an orphan," Gayle said, her voice more confused than accusatory.

"She's not," Jed said. "She lives with her *granmè*—that's her grandmother. She was abducted on the way home from a school called Mount Hope. She was on a bus, I think," he added, now seeing flashes of children hiding under seats on an old bus. He saw the boots of a man walking up the aisle before the image faded and disappeared entirely.

"So, that's something easy to vet, I would think," Gayle said, hunched over her computer.

It turned out there was not as much as you would think about the kidnapping of the girl named Sani from an orphanage called Saint Fleur. They quickly realized that child kidnappings were, as heartbreaking as it sounded, far too common to make the front page of any city newspaper in Haiti or the DR. There was, however, a mention of the event Jed had seen in his head while exchanging thoughts with Sani—three kids had been taken from a bus near the border of Haiti to somewhere inside the DR. The article mentioned Saint Fleur and the school called Mount Hope but didn't mention the names or ages of the children. The piece was all of five sentences long.

But it was enough, apparently, to validate what Jed had said.

"Her grandmother must be sick with worry," Gayle sighed. "I can't believe how little there is about this."

"Common, I guess," David said, his voice tight with emotion at the thought. "And orphans aren't treated with the same level of compassion in countries like this as they are in the US.

I bet that's how Madame Athaliah Guerrier can be so revered as a philanthropist by the people."

"Yeah," Gayle agreed. "The domestic articles about her are quite flattering. She's more than just a woman of power. They seem to love her here, and I guess I can see why."

They talked and strategized next steps for the better part of two hours, all agreeing that Madame Athaliah Guerrier warranted a much closer look. Other members of Joshua Bravo would begin arriving tomorrow, giving them a bigger and more secure footprint from which to operate, something that would ease Jed's mind. When they finally all started yawning, Jed looked at his watch and laughed.

"It's barely ten o'clock, but looks like we're all hanging on by a thread."

"I'm exhausted," Gayle conceded.

"And I went from planning a family vacation to being on a plane to Haiti on pretty short notice," David said.

Jed and Gayle's good-night, while outwardly polite and cordial, had an unspoken undertone of mutual apology. He'd hoped to steal a parting thought from her, but none came to him. But her over-the-shoulder glance and smile told him everything he'd hoped to know.

We're good . . . he thought.

"Good night, guys," she said. "Glad we have a plan. We'll probe a little and see if we find any scuffs on Athaliah Guerrier's veneer. Then when your team gets here, we'll hopefully have some intel to guide what, if anything, we do tomorrow night."

"Roger that," Jed said. Then, setting his jaw, he added, "One thing we know for sure is that little girl and at least two others at Amour et Espoir are kidnapping victims."

Gayle nodded. "But for some of these kids, even if they

were taken, they were taken from abject misery and squalor to a pretty nice life, comparatively."

"Maybe," David said. "But nothing justifies taking a child from their family."

As the only parent in the room, the pain in David's voice at the thought went a long way. Gayle nodded emphatically.

"Of course," she said. "I'm certainly not defending it."

Jed watched her head up the stairs, where she cast that one final look he was hoping for before disappearing.

He turned to David. "How's Rachel and Sarah Beth?" Jed asked. He realized he missed his adopted niece terribly.

"They're great," David said, and his face lit up as he gave Jed the rundown of Sarah Beth, her activities, and her exams. "They got something going on, though."

Jed glanced at the stairs and pursed his lips. "Any idea what?" he asked. "Ben was vague, but it sounded like something big. Is Sarah Beth involved?"

David shook his head. "Yes, I think. I don't know much, really. Rachel was headed to the TOC at St. George's when I was leaving, but she didn't know anything yet. It's something though."

"Why do you say that?" Jed asked.

David shrugged. "Lot of excitement around the base as I left."

Jed nodded. It was clear they weren't going to learn anything else until Ben or someone decided to read them in. Maybe the rest of Joshua Bravo—or whatever they would be known as once the conversion to the Shepherds' Special Missions Unit was completed—would know more when they arrived.

"Let's get some sleep, bro," Jed said. "Busy day tomorrow."

Ten minutes later, he was in bed and fast asleep.

CHAPTER FORTY

ROOM #316

WOMEN'S DORMITORY

ST. GEORGE'S ACADEMY

OUTSIDE OF NASHVILLE, TENNESSEE

2215 HOURS LOCAL

Sarah Beth slipped into bed, smiling at Elizabeth, who was on her iPad reading something or, more likely, playing a game. Darilyn was already asleep, it appeared, her breathing slow and steady, her back to Sarah Beth.

And no wonder—exams had wiped everyone out. She should be exhausted too, having added a crazy day in the TOC to exam week, but instead, she felt energized by all that had happened. That was nothing new—she always had trouble coming down after time spent in the Watcher TOC, but this was at a whole new level. Teeth brushed, phone plugged in, she pulled the covers up over her shoulders but with absolutely no expectation that she would fall asleep anytime soon. She was literally tingling with energy, and her feet rocked back and forth beneath the covers. She wished she could share her amazing day with her roommates, but that wasn't permitted. Neither Elizabeth nor Darilyn was read into the TOC operations—not yet, anyway.

After only a few seconds, Sarah Beth already felt a need to flip to her other side, the adrenaline as well as the images of violence and bloodshed from the catacombs of Paris still burned into her mind. She glanced at the clock to see that only two minutes had passed since she last checked.

She let out a long, frustrated sigh.

If only she could hang out with Corbin in the White Room for a while. They'd gorged on pepperoni pizza and buzzed with the other two teams about the operation, but then it was time to head for their rooms. Even though exams were over, it was past curfew by more than fifteen minutes. Yes, she had unrestricted access to the White Room, theoretically, but did she want to really push that—to take advantage of that privilege—for no reason other than being unable to fall asleep? Maybe she should have asked to go home with Mom. Mom would have loved that—she had been almost unable to pull herself away after gushing about how proud she was. It had been embarrassing and warm at the same time. Dad was on a trip, so Mom would have loved the company, and they could have had a girls' night, watching some movie and staying up late. Mom might have even made cookies . . .

I sure earned it . . .

She turned in her bed again.

Too late now.

Her mind suddenly filled with Uncle Jed's smiling face, and that made her smile as if his goofy grin were here with her. She didn't know if there was a time difference, but he was on vacation, right? It wasn't like he had to get up early or anything. She'd been meaning to catch up with him for days, but then things got crazy. He was someone she could actually tell about everything they'd done. He probably already knew all about it, but it would still be fun to share it with him.

She lay on her back, folded her hands on her chest, and took a long, slow breath.

Then she sent out a message on Watcher snapchat, reaching out to her adopted uncle with her mind.

"Hey, Uncle Jed! Are you up?"

She waited expectantly, a smile on her face, but after a moment or two, no reply came. She made a little *huh* sound.

"You there, Jed? I had an amazing day. It was terrifying and exciting, and I think I did a great job. I just can't sleep until I tell you all about it . . .

"Jed?"

She opened her eyes.

Maybe he was asleep? If so, could she wake him with her mind? Was it okay to do that? If she called him on the phone that would wake him, right? This wasn't really different, actually.

Finding a thread to Jed was easier than stumbling to the hall's restroom at night. At this point, the connection between them was less of a thread and more of an interstate highway. They had connected, both as uncle and niece and as a Navy SEAL and Shepherd and a Watcher so many times now, it was ridiculous. She wondered if she'd been on Uncle Jed's thread more than she had been on the phone with Mom and Dad . . .

She found it easily, slid along it like a familiar carpet in her house. If he was sleeping, she'd pop right back out.

He was sleeping, but she stayed anyway, her pulse quickening as fear of what she found in Jed's head gripped her.

The beach she stood on inside Jed's head was dark, lit only by a sliver of moonlight reflecting off the calm waters. She knew she wasn't alone, and it wasn't just Jed she felt. There was something else, a creature that she sensed just out of sight, and the presence made her stomach turn.

If Uncle Jed was on this beach somewhere, then he needed help.

Because she could feel the evil in the air like cold, wet rain . . .

She turned to find Jed, heading up the beach but glancing frequently over her shoulder, afraid of what else she might see.

But then suddenly, her world shifted, and the new vision made her scream in her mind. She was in an unfamiliar house, but the horror was what she saw in front of her. Her dad was kneeling beside a woman she thought she knew from somewhere. His hands were behind his head, and men pointed guns at him and the woman. Sarah Beth knew instantly that she was seeing the real world. She searched desperately and finally found Jed's thread again, and then she was accelerating across the kitchen and into a bedroom. A woman straddled Uncle Jed while he slept—in Haiti—whispering things to him.

What was happening?

"Uncle Jed! Uncle Jed, wake up!"

CHAPTER FORTY-ONE

SOMEWHERE FAMILIAR

Jed was back on the beach—the one in Punta Cana that he'd never been to but had seen online. Just like his other recent nightmare, he was reclining on a chaise, sipping a tropical cocktail, but he was far from relaxed. He knew something dark waited for him here.

Again.

Movement from the right caught his eye, and he turned his head. He wanted to leap to his feet. His mind was in combat mode already, but his body—at least, this lame dream body—was still in "mai tai on the chaise longue" mode. The discordance between mind and dream body was jarring and almost nauseating. A soccer ball bounced toward him and rolled to a stop in the sand beside his chaise. He sat up, far slower than his mind demanded, and scanned the deserted beach for the person who'd kicked it.

"Sani?" he called, searching for the girl from Amour et Espoir Children's Home, somehow knowing it was her.

"Here I am," a girl's voice said with a giggle from behind him.

He whipped his head around to find Sani—dressed in her school uniform but barefoot in the sand—staring and smiling at him several yards away.

"It's not safe here," he said.

"Nowhere is safe, silly," she said, giggled again, and vanished.

In the near distance, something caught his eye. He squinted and raised a hand as a sun visor over his eyes. A bulge in the sand was moving toward him and accelerating as it did.

"Oh no . . . Not again," he breathed.

He tried to move, tried to climb out of the chaise longue and run, but his body was bound with invisible straps. Puffs of sand burst skyward as the massive sand snake slithered rhythmically toward him just below the surface. In the final moment, instead of surfacing right in front of him where he expected, it dove and slipped under the chaise, only to pop out on the other side.

It exploded out of the sand, looping around him with incredible and violent speed until both his body and the chaise were completely enveloped inside massive coils. With each breath, the constrictor crushed him a little more until, finally, the serpent's head drifted into view, settling into a hover nose-to-nose with him.

Oh God, it's her . . .

The demon reptile's forked tongue flicked out and kissed Jed's lips.

Then, like before, he watched as the creature slowly changed—the serpent body contracting into a naked torso, limbs growing from her sides, as she morphed into her human form. Straddling his chest now, she glared down at him with serpent's eyes. Her lips curled in a disturbing smile, revealing viper's fangs.

"You're mine, Shhhhhhepherd," she said, her voice a whispered hiss, and pressed her mouth to his.

"Afraid not," he said, turning his head away from her violation. If this was where she wanted to battle—in some dreamscape she created—then so be it. "Maybe if you'd read the Book all the way to the end, you would know you chose the losing side."

"Not hardly, Shhhhepherd," she hissed. "Your God isn't here, in this place. And mine has dominion over far more people of this earth every day. I have chosen the power of the now over the promise of some one-day future, bending a knee to your God."

"My God is everywhere," he said. There was nothing she could do to him here in this dream she had created. Surely she knew that. But maybe, just maybe, he could learn something from her.

"Tell me, Shepherd," she said, her lower body tight around him, pinning him down. "Just what is it you hope to do? Don't you know you can't save these people? Even Jesus himself said the poor would always be with you. So, just what does your faith offer these people—these children? What can you give them?"

"Hope," he said, fear leaving him now. Despite the glowing serpent eyes, he'd seen far, far worse things during his years as a SEAL and the nightmares that followed. If this was to be a battle of words and wits, he could hold his own. "And peace. And joy . . ."

Her forked tongue flicked out, her glowing serpent eyes narrowing. "Peace and hope and joy—amid their suffering. Absurd. No wonder you are losing . . ."

"Uncle Jed!"

The voice was in his head—Sarah Beth calling out to him—but it was her urgency that caught his attention.

Urgency and fear.

"Uncle Jed!"

He turned left and now saw her running up the beach from the water. She was waving her arms frantically, her feet bare beneath fuzzy pajama pants.

"It's okay, Sarah Beth. She can't hurt me here, in this dream world . . ."

"Go away, child," the serpent woman hissed. "He is mine now. You don't want to be next . . ."

Sarah Beth ignored the woman, her eyes on him.

"It's not a dream, Jed," she hollered urgently. "Wake up! She's there, in your room in Haiti. I projected here to find you. She's there in real life. She's trying to distract you . . . They have my dad!"

Jed jerked awake to find the lithe female Dark One from Santo Domingo straddling his chest and kissing him. Free from the paralysis of his dream, he whipped his right arm around her neck and rolled her beneath him into a crushing choke hold. Instead of fighting back, she wrapped her legs around his waist and ran her fingernails down his back in seductive surrender. This only stoked his rage; he squeezed her neck with crushing force.

"Give me one reason why I shouldn't end you right now," he growled in her ear.

"I'll give you two," she said, seemingly unfazed by the pressure on her neck. "They're in the kitchen waiting to be executed."

Her words might as well have been a dagger to his chest. "You're lying," he said, but his reply lacked conviction.

"Test me and see," she said, her eyes flickering amber for a hundredth of a second.

"What do you want?"

"*You.*"

"I don't get it. You could have slit my throat. Why didn't you?"

"Because I have other plans for you," she said, her voice honey and razor blades.

Jed's mind raced through a dozen possible scenarios of how this engagement might play out, but in every case, it ended badly. She wasn't bluffing. Her presence in his bedroom alone was proof that the Dark Ones were already well ahead of them. They had known, perhaps all along, that he was here in

Haiti. They knew that he and Gayle were tracking them and that they had been to Amour et Espoir. And, somehow, the Dark Ones had ambushed him here at the safe house, without any of them seeing them coming, and had made it to his room undetected.

Whatever chaos the Dark Ones had suffered as an organization, they were apparently still quite effective and lethal here in Haiti.

Jed released her from the choke hold, and she slithered out from underneath him with serpentine fluidity. He scanned her up and down for a weapon and was surprised not to find anything on her person, not even a blade.

With a victorious smile, she gestured to the open bedroom door. "Your destiny awaits."

Jed shrugged on a T-shirt and slipped his sockless feet into the trainers beside his bed.

"Sarah Beth—let Ben know what's happening. The team is on their way. I need you."

"I should stay with you!" she protested.

"I need you to get the team. Then find me. Find my thread. It's going to be okay."

Grudgingly, he walked out of his bedroom. In the kitchen, as he'd feared, Gayle and David knelt, machine pistols pointed at the backs of their heads, in front of a pair of armed assaulters. A second pair of shooters stood in the shadows with their weapons trained on Jed. A quick glance confirmed Jed was a trigger pull away from heaven as he watched two red dots dancing the tango between his pecs.

He did the math. There was no solution, not even for a blooded SEAL like him, at least not one that ended with anything other than two dead Shepherds and a dead CIA agent beside them.

He returned his gaze to his friends, and gruesome imagery flashed before his mind's eye—a disemboweled David crucified and nailed to the ceiling while Gayle clutched at her sliced-open neck, blood streaming between her fingers.

An involuntarily shudder shook him where he stood. *Victory in this engagement is impossible. The only bargaining chip I have to play is . . . me.*

"Let them go, and I won't resist," he said, turning to look at the Haitian woman. "If this comes to a fight, you may win, but you won't have a prize to take to your master, I can promise you. If I engage, it will be to the death."

An evil grin split her face, and in that moment she looked very much like the serpent she'd been in the dream.

"You have my word they won't be harmed," she said.

Jed laughed in reply. "Your word isn't worth very much. Your side works in lies and betrayal like fine oils in the hands of a painter. After what you did to Marcello and Kaprica, I'm sure you can understand why I don't believe you."

Her eyes narrowed. "You don't seem to be in a position to make demands," she hissed.

"I disagree," he said, holding her gaze. He realized this wasn't much of a strategy. It was in God's hands. "Either they leave now, untouched, or we turn this house into a bloodbath for everyone and you lose your prize. Your choice."

"Jed, no. Please, don't do it," Gayle begged, her eyes so full of both love and fear that he almost had to look away.

"Everything will be okay," he said with a SEAL's bearing.

"That's right," the dark warrior said, putting her hand on his shoulder. "We'll take good care of Jedidiah."

Jed shifted his gaze from Gayle to David. The man's eyes told Jed that his TSL was milliseconds away from doing something incredibly brave but incredibly stupid. He couldn't read his friend's thoughts with his gifting, but he'd been in enough scrapes to do it the old-fashioned way. He shook his head.

Don't do it, bro.

David gritted his teeth but gave an almost imperceptible nod in resignation.

"Go now, Shepherd's friends, before I change my mind," the woman said. "Run away and hide where we can't find you." She narrowed her eyes and bent over, hands on her knees as if talking to children. "And I promise, we will be looking . . ."

Then she laughed, a gasp of air and a hiss through her teeth.

The assaulters behind Gayle and David gave them each a shove. At first, Jed thought Gayle was going to ruin it all and refuse to leave, but David grabbed her by the arm and tugged her toward the front door. The TSL crossed himself as he passed Jed, and they traded glances, their eyes doing the talking.

Take care of her, David.

You have my word.

Jed watched David grab the car keys from the little console table in the front foyer and drag Gayle out the door toward the SUV. As Gayle crossed the threshold, she turned.

Please, God, don't let him die. I . . . I need him in my life, her thoughts said to him.

The Dark Ones moved toward him, and Jed took up a fighting stance.

"When they're gone," he said to the woman. "Or we shed blood. Understand?"

The goons looked at the serpent woman, who nodded.

He heard the roar of the SUV engine coming to life. Tires spun in loose gravel, then he heard the truck accelerating down the narrow road.

"Sarah Beth . . ."

"Jed!"

"Can you Watcher chat with your dad?"

"Sometimes."

"Tell him to run and hide. I'll be okay until you find me and the team comes for me."

He felt young Sarah Beth disappear like vapor, and then he felt completely alone again.

His thoughts next went to Gayle. But then a hood thrown over Jed's head turned the world black, and the agony of a strike from something hard and heavy against his lower back stole Gayle away. Someone kicked the back of his knees, causing him to buckle and fall to the ground. Multiple pairs of gloved hands began to manhandle him, and zip ties were placed on his wrists and ankles.

Then he was in the air, carried like a bag of garbage, and his writhing did nothing as they moved him toward the door.

PART III

Be very careful, then, how you live—not as unwise but as wise, making the most of every opportunity, because the days are evil.

—Ephesians 5:15–16 (NIV)

CHAPTER FORTY-TWO

AUBERT, PORT-DE-PAIX

HAITI

0012 HOURS LOCAL

David could hear Gayle telling him to stop, but he kept his foot on the accelerator anyway. He was driving at a lunatic pace, in the dark and on the terrible back roads of Haiti, but he couldn't stop himself. He felt almost disembodied—like his mind was reeling in a tizzy above him while his body was driving the car.

"David, STOP!" she shouted and grabbed his right forearm, finally snapping him out of whatever bizarre discordant state had come over him.

He slammed on the brakes and the SUV skidded and fish-tailed to a stop in the middle of the dirt road. Still clutching the steering wheel with both hands, he turned to look at her.

"We're safe," she said, her voice calm and self-assured. "They're not coming after us."

"You don't *know* that," he said. "They could have sent a hit squad five minutes after we left. They lie. They kidnap. They murder. They're the epitome of evil, Gayle. You get that, right?"

"I get it," she said. "Believe me, I get it, but in this case, I'm pretty sure they accomplished their objective. They got Jed. We could have been collateral, probably should have been, but the woman leading the assault knows how Jed thinks. She knew Jed wasn't going to let them take us without a fight, and that was a fight that would have ended badly for everyone, including her and her people. That's why we're alive and having this conversation."

A sudden wave of guilt crashed down on him.

"I did it again," he murmured, shaking his head.

"Did what again?"

"Nothing. I did nothing . . . again . . ."

"I don't understand."

"Every time the Dark Ones come after someone I care about, I'm useless. When Kenny Bailey attacked Rachel in the basement, I froze while Jed saved her. When Victor kidnapped Sarah Beth, I stayed behind in Nashville while Jed rescued her. This time, the Dark Ones came for Jed, and what did I do? Absolutely nothing. Once again, Jed risked his life to safeguard ours, and I let him do it without even raising a finger. Dear God, there has never been a greater coward than me."

"There was nothing you could have done, David. Not tonight. You did the same mental calculation I did and came to the same conclusion. We were outnumbered, outgunned, and outsmarted. If you had tried to fight, they would have executed you, which would have spurred Jed into battle. We'd all be dead . . . So, I, for one, as much as it pains me to say it, am grateful that we all maintained cool heads—because right now, we're alive, and so is Jed. Which means we have a chance to regroup and rescue him," she said.

David slow-nodded as she talked him down—the logic of her words dialing down his anger but doing nothing for the angst he felt.

You're inept.

You're a coward.

You're a useless wannabe who has done nothing but ride on Jed's coattails since the fifth grade . . .

"David," she said. "Did you hear me?"

He'd heard her, but a darkness had seeped into him. Like thorny brambles strangling a farmer's bounty before it can be harvested, the dark thoughts sought to undermine and pollute all the progress he'd made these past few months. The guilt and insecurity hurt, but the hurt felt deserved.

Maybe this is a blessing in disguise.

Would it really be so terrible to have Jed out of your life? Out of your family's life?

It's obvious he wants to replace you . . . to bed your wife and raise your daughter as his own. That's what it's always been about. He plans to make a cuckold out of you. To make you a laughing-stock. To prove to everyone what you really are: a loser.

"David," Gayle said, more sharply this time. "Will you please say something?"

"Huh? Oh, sorry," he said. "You're right. Of course, you're right. We're alive and so is Jed. Our job now is to focus on rescuing him, but we can't do that alone. We don't have the training, the weapons, or the numbers . . . But the rest of Joshua Bravo is arriving soon. Once they're here, we can plan a rescue op." His mind churned as the situation became less blurry, the shock wearing off, perhaps. "And we need to let Trinity Loop know—we need to tell Ben Morvant. They'll know what to do."

He watched her expression sour at this comment, and he knew why.

"I don't know if Jed will make it until they get here, David," she said softly, tears in her eyes.

He nodded solemnly.

Exactly . . .

Dark thorns twisted and strangled his heart at the thought. It hurt . . . it hurt so good.

No! he screamed silently in his mind. *I will not listen to you. I will not abide these dark and vile impulses. I will resist. I follow the light . . . only the light.*

He reached out and took Gayle's hand. "Will you pray with me?"

She nodded.

He bowed his head, closed his eyes, and prayed—prayed with more passion than he could remember having in years. Tears streaming down his face, Gayle's hand in his, he prayed with all his might for strength, for guidance, and for the light of God to cast out the dark and the doubt and the selfish uncertainty.

CHAPTER FORTY-THREE

IN THE BACK SEAT OF A VEHICLE

During his tenure with the Teams, Jed had cuffed and black-bagged more bad-guy HVTs than he cared to count. This was the first time the tables had been turned on him, though, and he didn't like it.

Didn't like it one bit.

Sure, he'd gone through the Navy's Survival, Evasion, Resistance, and Escape training program, a.k.a SERE, but for all the pain and unpleasantness he had to soldier through, he always knew it was training. Eventually, it would end and he would get to walk away.

This was different.

I'm alone, unarmed, and the cavalry isn't here yet . . . Things are not looking so great.

The hood he wore impeded his breathing, the fabric sucking against his lips and trapping the heat from his breath until he felt like his head was stuck in a steam sauna. He couldn't see, and his wrists had been bound with heavy-duty plasticuffs, which even on his best day he had zero chance of breaking free from. The cuffs were cinched so tight that they were restricting blood flow, a tingling numbness spreading over his hands.

His abductor—the woman he'd fought in Santo Domingo and who'd invaded his dreams—sat on the bench beside him caressing his thigh. Her constant contact drove him crazy, and not in a good way. He knew this was why she was doing it—to keep him agitated and distracted. He couldn't focus, couldn't center himself, and couldn't stop wishing that she'd leave him be.

When the real torture starts, the SEAL inside said with a laugh, *you'll be wishing to go back to this, bro.*

His thoughts went to Gayle and David. He'd heard them drive away, but he had no idea if his abductor had sent a hit squad after them. This woman was more than just a warrior, she was a tactician. She'd controlled his kidnapping so perfectly it practically felt choreographed, especially the part where she let Gayle and David go in exchange for his cooperation. She'd probably set an ambush down the road to stop and kill his friends once they were out of sight. After forcing his compliance, she had no incentive to keep her promise. Dark Ones were masters of manipulation and deception.

"What's your name?" he asked, apparently surprising himself as much as her because she made a little delighted chuckle.

"Thank you, Jedidiah," she said, snuggling tight against him. "I am so glad you want to know me better. You may call me Calypso."

"Calypso," he echoed, his voice trailing off at the end.

Jed was no English major or classics expert, but as a high-school kid, Homer's *Odyssey* had been his favorite piece of mythology. In a literary twist, Odysseus's greatest foe was not a monster at all but a nymph named Calypso, who kidnapped the warrior hero Jed had identified with and held him prisoner on her secret island. Calypso loved Odysseus, but her love was twisted and malignant, and she used her powers to keep him trapped and subservient.

Will this be my fate? Will I spend my remaining days as a Dark One's captive in some sadistic, hidden prison?

"Where are you taking me?" he asked her.

"To a secret place," she said, her hot breath on his neck. "To a place where you and I can be alone, forever."

Wonderful, he thought. *She's as insane as her namesake.*

Several minutes later, he felt the vehicle slow and then transition from pavement to a dirt road. They drove for several more minutes, dipping and bouncing over ruts and ridges before stopping. He felt the driver shift the transmission into Park and heard the doors open. Calypso slid away from him, and the next thing he knew, he was jerked out of the vehicle and onto the ground. Someone kicked him hard in the gut, buckling him at the waist, which drew a stern rebuke from Calypso in what sounded like Haitian Creole. After that, two pairs of hands grabbed him under the armpits and hoisted his torso off the ground. He could have easily gotten his feet under himself and used his legs to walk, but why make it easy on them? He let them drag him, and although he couldn't see, he felt his feet passing over patches of grass, which confirmed he was outside.

They dropped him onto the ground and then strong hands rolled him over onto his back. His fight-or-flight reflex kicked in, but with the hood over his head he couldn't effectively do either. Jed forced himself to wait for the right moment to fight back—if it came at all. Fear, something Jed rarely felt for himself, swelled in his chest and throat. This felt very much like the end. He would face his death with as much courage and dignity as he could muster, but he didn't want to die. There were still so many things he wanted to experience, so many people he wanted to spend time with.

Calypso sat on his chest.

He felt her thighs squeeze tight against his rib cage and then the cold steel of a blade against his neck.

It was happening. She was going to open his throat, sever his carotid arteries, and drain his body of blood. He could probably buck her off, but she was a Dark One who fought with a strength equal to his own. In Santo Domingo, he'd struggled to block her attacks, and during that engagement, he'd had both his hands and his sight. Fighting her now, in this state, was pointless.

"Be very still," she whispered into his ear, tapping the side of the blade against his throat as she did.

Here it comes . . .

Silent prayer filled his mind, the words coming to him like a story he'd been writing his entire life.

Dear Lord and Father, forgive me for my foolishness, my selfishness, and my disobedience over the years. Forgive me for the times I doubted, for the times I faltered, and for the times I disappointed you. Thank you for the gift of my life, for the joys I experienced, for the friendships I made, for the love I shared, and most of all for the opportunity to serve you and my fellow man . . .

Unexpectedly, someone pulled the hood off his head.

He blinked, expecting to see a silver knife in Calypso's hands, glinting in the moonlight and ready to plunge. Instead, the blade was in her left hand, down at her side, and her right was open, palm up and flat in front of his face. She leaned forward with an evil smile, her eyes rimmed with orange fire, and blew hard on her outstretched hand. Her breath kicked up a cloud of powder that covered his face, burning his eyes, the fine dust forced up his nostrils and into his surprised and open mouth. It tasted of ash and pepper, citrus and copper. He coughed. His nasal passage and throat flared with an itchy heat. A sneeze reflex kicked in, but the sneeze never came, despite him wanting it to. Almost immediately he felt himself grow weak, his arms and head now heavy, his eyelids fluttering and breathing becoming difficult.

"What did you do to me?" he said, but the words he heard coming out of his mouth were badly slurred and barely a whisper.

He tried to buck her off him, but his muscles ignored the command. For a second, he wondered if she'd somehow broken his neck with her Dark One speed and strength, but that was impossible. It was the powder. She'd used a paralytic compound on him. He tried to speak again, but this time he couldn't form the words and all that came out was a pathetic *nuuuuuh*. Calypso smiled triumphantly while gazing down at him. Her eyes flashed with twin rings of flame, and he hated himself for being unable to look away.

It was just like the article Gayle had shown him. The powder was delivering the drugs to his bloodstream, paralyzing him just like Clairvius Narcisse, the real-life zombie from Dr. Wade Davis's research. For the first time in his life, Jed felt a terror he could not control.

"It is disappointing to you for it to end like this. You would have preferred to dance with me, one last time, yes?" she said, her voice smooth and almost tender. "Our battle would have been beautiful, but that is not the way. First, you must die. Only then can you be mine forever."

She kissed his paralyzed lips, climbed off him, and stood.

My heart is beating, my lungs are breathing, but nothing else, he realized, performing a self-assessment. He tried to blink, but even his eyelids weren't working. His eyeballs, however, could still move side to side, but only with great effort. Someone lit a torch, and orange light flickered around him. At the edge of his peripheral vision, he saw what looked like a concrete wing above him, and he ticked his eyes that way.

The torchlight danced across the graveyard headstones scattered around him . . .

Oh, hell no, he thought, demanding his impotent muscles heed the call to action. But his body refused to react.

"Where is your God, Shepherd?" she said, taunting him as she moved in a stalking, serpentine rhythm around him. "Why is He not here to save you?"

He wanted to curse and rebuke her, to put her in her place, but his paralyzed mouth and vocal cords kept him silent. Even on his worst and lowest day as a SEAL, he'd never felt this impotent and vulnerable.

Powerless, he followed her eyes, two glowing rings of flame . . .

She laughed with pleasure as she circled him. The blade was back in her hand now, and seeing it conjured fresh fear. In this state, she could do literally anything she wanted to him. He was a hunk of flesh for the carving . . . like a side of beef on a butcher's block.

The gruesome mental metaphor made him feel woozy.

It's not the fear . . . it's something else. Something else is happening to me.

Despite knowing that he was lying on his back, he felt like he was tipping and spinning.

She probably mixed a psychedelic in with the paralyzing compound, he realized, feeling increasingly inebriated with each passing second.

Perception and time blurred and swirled as she chanted, gyrating around him. He watched, hypnotized, as her smooth cocoa skin became a canvas where torchlight and night shadow danced.

Time passed . . .

He felt her carve a symbol into his left forearm with the

blade, the cuts agonizing and his brain screaming for him to pull his arm away.

Then she carved again, this time into his right arm, and his eyes filled with tears.

The pain was awful, but he couldn't tell if the cuts were deep enough to be mortal wounds.

After marking him, she whispered to him while he stared unblinking at the stars. Horrible things about God and man, about the devil and all he could do.

"In another life, you could have been mine, Shepherd. But it is not to be. You will not rise from the dead to serve, but you will suffer the death of a zombie. You will die in the darkness of the grave, smothered by your inadequacy and the final knowledge that the God you worship will not come to save you."

Then, abruptly and unexpectedly, she was done with him.

Her thug companions picked him up—one at the legs, another at his torso—and dropped him into a wooden coffin at the bottom of an open grave. The sensation of falling while paralyzed, of not being able to react and try to break his fall, was horrific. He landed with an immense thud that knocked the little wind he had left from his lungs and sent a reverberating shock wave of pain from his head to his heels. Whatever paralytic she'd used on him, it did little to mute or turn off his pain receptors. He could *feel* everything; he just couldn't move. Trying to recover his breath was a labor the likes of which he could not remember. His diaphragm still worked, but none of the other muscles in his torso did, making it feel like he was drowning despite being surrounded by air.

His eyes were fixed now and unmoving. The figures above him were out of focus, but then the firelight disappeared, and he was able, for a second, to focus on the lid being placed on top of the coffin.

Darkness, pure and absolute, enveloped him.

No! No! he screamed in his mind.

Paralyzed and alone, Jed began to hyperventilate in short little gasps that became increasingly more difficult. Wheezing, his pulse pounded a steady, lonely death march in his ears . . .

Until another sound joined the chorus.

The sound of dirt, landing by the shovelful, on the lid of his coffin.

CHAPTER FORTY-FOUR

PRIVATE CONFERENCE ROOM
ADVANCE AIR SUPPORT PASSENGER SERVICES FBO
PARIS-LE BOURGET AIRPORT
TEN KILOMETERS NORTHEAST OF DOWNTOWN PARIS
LE BOURGET, FRANCE
0655 HOURS LOCAL

Ben sat alone at the long, black, wood-and-glass table, staring out the window at the hangar beside the building as his team waited to fly home. Turner, the team leader for Gideon Bravo, had gone to get coffee for Ben and himself from the luxurious lounge downstairs, and the other members of Bravo—including the sniper and a spotter who had sat painful overwatch near the café when the horror show was unfolding—were in the jet, getting it ready to receive the fallen. Tyson Young was with Bravo, transporting the remains of his fallen teammates from the morgue in the Paris Saint-Joseph Hospital, with a quiet escort from Interpol vehicles for the survivors. The hospital had been the CASEVAC plan for the op, one Ben had not imagined they would need mortuary services from. Cedric "Magic" Belacort was still in the vascular ICU, recovering from several hours of surgery to repair a severed femoral artery and a shattered femur bone. Ben knew that Young had struggled with the choice between staying in Paris with his recovering teammate or escorting the remains of their other two brothers back to their families in Tennessee. There was no real decision to be made, of course. The families of the fallen needed the team leader to be there when their loved ones arrived. Tyson Young was that leader, and he and the other three survivors of Bravo would fly home with their brothers. Ben had arranged for Gideon Charlie to remain in Paris as security, in case remaining Dark Ones sought revenge against Belacort while he recovered for a few days before his own journey home.

And of course, Ben knew where he needed to be.

It had been a long, exhausting day and a half, mourning the dead, praying for the wounded, and getting updates on Shepherds Europe's operations, who had been hitting suspected Dark One safe houses around Paris while Ben had led the attack in the catacombs. They'd killed nearly two dozen Dark Ones involved in operations across Europe, but the half dozen or so suspected "big fish" had all gotten away, leaving little or no trail. Two were high-ranking government officials, which meant they would be spotted soon enough. But there were more questions than answers. How had the Dark Ones known the Shepherds were coming? Had the Rising occurred already, or had it been postponed due to the hit on the catacombs? Who were the players at the head shed–level of the Dark Ones now?

And who would be the next Victor?

Ben clenched his jaw. How much of this outcome was his fault? He had interpreted the chaos he'd sensed since Victor's death as a total lack of organization, but now he knew better, didn't he? The Dark Ones had always been highly compartmentalized, much like terrorist cells in the Middle East, working autonomously. Because of this, he had assumed that Victor's death had been paralyzing to the Dark Ones' ability to operate, but the two coffins headed to the airport right now showed just how wrong he had been.

They needed to find who was in the inner circle of Victor's remaining head shed and who the potential new leaders were. They may have delayed the Rising, but they most certainly had not stopped it. And now, the Dark Ones would likely move somewhere else—somewhere still unknown to the Shepherds.

In other words, Ben and his Shepherds were behind and running out of time.

His phone vibrated in the cargo pocket of his pants, and he closed his eyes, certain it was Christy checking on him. He wasn't sure he was ready to talk to her but knew she would need to hear his voice. Word of what had happened most certainly had gotten to her since she'd assumed the role of mother hen to the families of the Shepherds. She would be the first one to talk to the wives of the fallen and the family of the wounded Belacort.

What a horrible job. And what an amazing woman of faith that she insisted years ago on taking it.

She'd been with him from the beginning, since the SEAL Teams, and she knew all too well about loss.

Ben's phone vibrated a third time, and he pulled it out, then raised an eyebrow when he looked at the screen.

"Morvant," he said, his voice stronger and more confident than he felt.

"Hey, Ben, it's Julia," the solemn voice of Julia Nesbitt, his intel director, said. "You okay?"

"I'm good," he said, "but I'm guessing that's not why I'm getting a call from my J2? Everything okay?"

"No," she said. "David Yarnell checked in. Jed Johnson is missing . . ."

"What?" Ben rose from the table, pushing the chair back with a hip so he could pace. "What do you mean, missing?"

"He's more than missing, actually. He's been taken . . ."

As Julia described the frantic call from David Yarnell, Jeremy Turner entered the room. Ben's head pounded as Julia described the attack on the safe house and Jed's kidnapping. Jeremy read the room, set the coffees on the table, and stood motionless, arms crossed on his chest.

"Jed was on to something way the hell bigger than a child trafficking case, it seems," Ben managed finally. He closed his eyes tightly, forcing away the horrible images of what Jed might be going through. "What's the sitrep on Joshua Bravo?"

"Arriving soon, but not soon enough," Julia said. "David Yarnell and our CIA liaison are searching for Jed, but we have no real assets to assist. We're getting Joshua Bravo there as quickly as we can, but—"

"I'm diverting with Gideon Alpha," Ben said, cutting off whatever gloom she was about to share. "I'll contact Eli on Joshua Bravo en route. Send everything you have on what's happened and all the geospatial intelligence available. Task a satellite if possible and get our CIA liaison to help coordinate additional Agency assets. The Agency should be able to help since they have one of their own on the ground, but chase it up to our friend at NSA if you have to." He glanced at his watch. "I'm sending the plane back with Gideon Bravo, but get Jack Stewart on this right away. I need air to get me on the X in Haiti, and I need it an hour ago."

"Jack is already coordinating with Europe," Julia said, referring to their Air Logistics Director, former Top Gun pilot, Jack Stewart. "He's already got you a ride. He said to tell you it's a Bombardier Global and will make the trip in one hop at over five hundred knots. He can get you there in just under eight hours from wheels up. Plane will be on the ramp in a few minutes, as it's hangared there at Le Bourget. Tail number is Foxtrot-Seven-Seven-Two-One-Papa."

"Copy that, Julia," Ben said.

Eight hours . . .

"I'll get you that brief and connect with you in the air," Nesbitt said.

Ben hung up the phone and turned to Turner.

"Gideon Alpha is on mission again, bro," he said. "Get your team to pull their gear off the jet. Our ride is here in minutes."

"What's up?"

Ben sighed and shook his head. He couldn't imagine a scenario where they arrived in time to do more than clean up the mess.

Or to exact revenge . . .

"We have a missing Shepherd," he said grimly. "Jedidiah Johnson from Joshua Bravo has been captured . . ."

CHAPTER FORTY-FIVE

SANI'S ROOM

AMOUR ET ESPOIR CHILDREN'S HOME

AUBERT, PORT-DE-PAIX

HAITI

0045 HOURS LOCAL

Sani's fears about not sleeping proved both founded and unfounded. She had imagined tossing and turning all night, filled as she was with uncertainty, longing for Granmè, and terror at the images that kept filling her mind: images of the two zombie girls from Ms. Wilshire's office and the dead, earthy smell of them. She knew her grandmother was a passionate woman of faith but also a believer in the power of Voudou and zombies. Finding no stories about zombies in the Bible, Sani had quietly believed tales of zombies to be nothing more than legends from a time gone by. Now, she wasn't sure of anything. She'd seen them—the zombie girls. She'd heard them. She'd smelled them. And anyway, hadn't Jesus raised Lazarus from the dead? Hadn't He raised the Roman officer's child? If God's power could do that, might the devil also have that power?

She just didn't know anymore, and not knowing what was true felt scariest of all.

Her thoughts turned to the man who had visited the school. She'd been shocked to find that he too could see into someone's thoughts. Everything about him screamed hero and man of God, but their connection had somehow been severed before she could tell him more. She prayed with all her might he would come back and rescue them all. Because she knew for certain that the evil here was about to get worse.

And she believed the strange man, whose name she impossibly knew to be Jed, was supposed to help stop it.

If he can . . .

Exhaustion settled over her within minutes of finishing her prayer and her head hitting the pillow, wishing that she *didn't* have the luxury of her own bedroom anymore. She wanted, desperately, to be with someone—someone *alive* and familiar. Ideally, she wished for Mary or even Amede to be in the room with her, but in her wildest fantasy, Grandmè would be cuddling her on their lumpy love seat in front of the woodstove, stroking her cheeks and singing to her in French . . .

But sleep took her easily.

Which turned out to be unfortunate.

Nightmares consumed her almost instantly. She dreamed of the zombie girls, but she wasn't afraid of them. Her fear was *for* them. At least until, in her dream, Madame Athaliah ordered the zombie sisters to capture and bring Sani to her. The Voudou priestess then sat on a gravestone, laughing as the zombie girls chased Sani around a dark, wet graveyard. Sani dreamed of being buried in a casket. She dreamed of standing beside Ms. Wilshire's desk, staring at her gray and dirty feet as she told a terrified child her own story of obedience.

Most terrifying was the dream that interrupted the nightmare—images of shadowy men sneaking about Grandmè's house with murder on their minds. Before she could open the back screen door to their tiny house with a shaking hand, Sani heard a scream, her heart raced, and then she was whisked away to another dream.

In this one, she sat on her bed at Amour et Espoir, feet dangling over the edge, still in the soft, cozy pj's she'd been given when she arrived.

But she wasn't alone anymore.

"It's going to be okay," the girl said, flashing Sani a sad smile and taking her hand. She was pretty, younger than Sani by a couple of years, but spoke like she was older. Sani suddenly recognized her—the girl from the plane.

"You came to me—inside my head—when Madame Athaliah visited the school. That was you, right?" she asked.

"Yes," the girl said, her smile turning warm. "I'm Emelin."

"I remember you from the plane. Are you really here?" Sani asked, her voice low and soft.

"Yes and no," the girl said. The hand in Sani's certainly felt warm—and real. "I'm here, but like before when I came to you in your mind—and in your heart. I am here in spirit. It's easier now, with you asleep. I don't know why but for me it is."

"So," Sani said slowly, drawing the word out. "If you're here in my head or my dream or whatever, then where are you *really*?"

The girl looked down at her hands, her smile fading.

"I'm not exactly sure," she said. "I'm in, like, a mansion somewhere. We're near the ocean—I can even see it from the windows in the back. But I don't know where. I know I'm very, very far from my mama." Emelin's voice cracked at that, but then she shook her head as if the sadness were an annoyance. "We only have a minute, I think. They check on me often. I'm at the mansion with Madame Athaliah."

The sound of the name again gave Sani a chill. She believed it was Madame Athaliah—*Manbo* Athaliah—who was really behind the bad things she felt happening at Amour et Espoir, not Ms. Wilshire—that Athaliah was the one who had created the zombie girls. She felt certain that was true. Wilshire was cruel and dangerous, but not powerful. She was no Manbo . . .

"Yes," Emelin said. "You are right. I don't know who this Wilshire is, but Manbo Athaliah is the truly powerful one."

Sani looked at the girl and felt fear growing again.

"What can I do?"

Emelin shook her head.

"Nothing—not yet, at least," she said. Then she found a smile again. "Remember we are stronger together—God's children are always stronger together, Sani. And soon we will be together."

The words filled Sani with dread rather than hope. Emelin was with Manbo Athaliah. Sani didn't want to be there at all.

"Yes," the girl said, again taking the thought from her head. "I am and you will be too. They are coming for you. They will be there very soon, in fact. I'm telling you not because there is anything you can do but so that you know I am waiting for you, and so you know that we will be strong together. Don't run away because they will find you, and don't resist because they will hurt you. Go along quietly, and they will believe they can control you."

Sani felt herself shaking with fear now, unsure if she was actually awake and on the side of her bed and Emelin was just an illusion or vision, or if she was asleep and Emelin was in her dream. But she knew that, either way, this was real—that everything Emelin said was true.

And she knew she didn't want to leave and go to a mansion

with Manbo Athaliah. She didn't want to leave Mary and Amede behind. They needed her, but she needed them too . . .

"They will be all right, Sani."

"Can they do it, Emelin?" she asked. "Not Amede and Mary. I mean the bad people. Can they control us?"

The girl shook her head, a fire of defiance in her dark, pretty eyes.

"No, I don't think so, Sani. We are children of the one true king."

"Can they hurt us?"

The girl shrugged.

"Maybe," she conceded. "But God is with us—like Shadrach, Meshach, and Abednego. Or like Daniel in the lions' den."

"Okay," Sani said in a trembling voice. She loved those stories from the Old Testament, and hearing Emelin talk about them did give her hope. She looked at the small girl beside her, but Emelin turned away suddenly. In the dark of the dream, Sani had no idea what had startled her. She felt her own dread grow immediately. It could only mean one thing.

Emelin spoke again, her voice low and tight. "They're here . . ."

And a knock on the door made Sani jump just as Emelin disappeared, dissolving into the ether . . .

Sani opened her eyes and sat up in her bed.

"Yes?"

"It's Ms. Wilshire, Sani," the harsh voice said. "I need you to pack your bag and come downstairs, please. You are going to a new home—a beautiful home that you will love."

"Why?" Sani asked, but she knew whatever lie the woman told wouldn't matter.

"Because I said so," Wilshire said. "Come along quickly. People are waiting for you."

Sani turned on the light, not at all surprised to see she really was sitting on the side of her bed completely alone.

She began to dress. Just as she got her clothes on, the door opened. Wilshire rolled a real suitcase, on wheels with a handle and everything, over to her from the doorway.

"Pack everything, Sani," she said with her saccharine smile. "You won't be coming back."

"Can I say goodbye to Mary and Amede?" she asked hopefully, her voice cracking and a sob forming in her throat.

"No," Ms. Wilshire said. "But you can leave them a note. Hurry, now. There are people waiting on you."

Sani stuffed her clothes—old and new—into the bag, then sat at her small desk and quickly scribbled out notes—one for each of her friends. She told them she loved them, which was true; that she would miss them, which was also very true; and that she would see them again soon.

She suspected that last part was a lie.

Then she folded the notes and gave them to Ms. Wilshire, who held out a hand.

"Is it a long drive?"

"Yes," she said. "But you will be flying there. Have you ever been in a helicopter, Sani?"

"No," she said.

"It's wonderful," Wilshire said, but Sani could tell immediately that the woman had never been in a helicopter herself and that she was frightened of them.

It didn't matter. Sani wasn't frightened. God would be with her, she decided, like He'd been with Daniel. And she wouldn't be in the lions' den alone.

Emelin was waiting for her.

"I'm ready," she said, taking her new suitcase by the handle. She followed Ms. Wilshire down the hall.

Any hope that the man named Jed might come for her faded away, like the tears drying on her cheeks. Because if he did return, she would be gone.

But perhaps he might still save Mary and Amede.

CHAPTER FORTY-SIX

THE WHITE ROOM

ST. GEORGE'S ACADEMY

0102 HOURS LOCAL

Sarah Beth's knees shook as she waited for the White Room elevator to take her, Corbin, Pastor Dee, and her mom to the Sanctuary. The fact that nobody was talking made it worse. She felt like they were all staring at her, even though she knew they weren't.

Why is it that in elevators, everyone stands facing the door? she randomly wondered. *Weird . . .*

Her stomach got heavy as the elevator slowed on arrival. Once she heard the chime, she opened the door to the Sanctuary—unlike traditional elevators, it didn't have sliding doors—and led her entourage inside. These three women loved and supported her more than any others in the world, and for what she was about to attempt, she would need that.

Jed had "gone offline" and was no longer responding to her Watcher snapchat attempts. They needed to find him—and fast.

Instead, she'd found her way into a weak-minded man who

had been with the woman she'd seen both in Jed's dream and then in the house where Jed had been staying in Haiti. In horror, she had watched through his eyes as the evil woman taunted Uncle Jed and then blown some sort of powder into his face, this time in what looked like a graveyard. She'd seen the fear on Jed's face—a look she had never once seen on the Navy SEAL she liked to call *Uncle*—and it had grown as they dropped him roughly into a coffin at the bottom of a grave. After, the woman turned to her henchmen, and Sarah Beth had felt herself somehow ejected from the man, just after she watched through his eyes as he shoveled the first load of dirt onto Jed's coffin.

That was the major problem. She knew Jed was in a coffin somewhere in Haiti, but his exact location was a mystery, and she had no idea how they could find him. But if they didn't get him out soon, he would suffocate and die—assuming that hadn't already happened.

No, she told herself, shaking off the thought, *there's still time. We can still save him. We're* going *to save him.*

"You've got this, Sarah Beth," Corbin said, taking her hand, "and I'll be right beside you if you need my help."

She turned to Corbin and smiled. "Thanks, sis."

"Always," Corbin said.

Sarah Beth walked with Corbin to their usual leather sofa facing the fountain statue of Saint George slaying the dragon. They let go of each other's hands and plopped down on the cushions side by side, ignoring the cushion flatulence that under normal circumstances always made them laugh.

Strange how humor evaporates in crisis.

She looked at her mom, who was wearing her worried face—the one where her lips were pressed into a thin straight line and her eyebrows looked painfully strained in concentration. Since the big "Uncle Jed talk" a few months ago, they'd not spoken about him much, but she knew that her parents cared about him as much as Sarah Beth did.

"Don't worry, Mom. I'm going to find him," she said, sensing that Mom was as stressed out as she was.

"I know you will," Mom said and flashed her a brave smile.

She exhaled and looked at Corbin.

"Your bond with Jed is stronger than mine," Corbin said, "so you'll find his thread faster than I will. But if anything happens, anything at all, I'll be standing by. You can bring me in, or I can pull you out anytime. Okay?"

Sarah Beth nodded, reclined against the back of the sofa, and closed her eyes. She let herself melt into the cushion while taking several long, slow breaths through her nose. She noticed that her trembling had stopped and that her confidence felt buoyed. It never ceased to amaze her the power that the Sanctuary, and being surrounded by people whom she loved, had on her. She'd applied this lesson—the lesson of how mighty believers could be when they were together, as one—to defeat Victor when he came for her at the school.

Love and trust were force multipliers when it came to Watchers.

Now, with her body relaxed, she slipped into the mindspace and reached out for Jed.

"Jed?" she called. *"Jed, can you hear me?"*

When no answer came, she tried again.

And again.

And again.

"He's not responding," she said aloud, keeping her eyes closed as she continued to search. "I can't find his thread. It's usually super bright, but it's like it got turned off. Do you think that means he's . . ." she said, stopping before finishing the morbid question.

"No," her mom said almost immediately. "He's not dead. I'd feel it if he was."

"Sarah Beth, there might be another way," Corbin said, taking her right hand. "I want you to try projecting."

This comment instantly snapped her out of her mindspace, and she opened her eyes to meet her friend's gaze.

"But I don't know where he is," she said, confused. "I've never been there before. I thought you could only project to places you've been?"

"You'd never been to the catacombs before, and you projected there," Corbin said.

"Well, that was different because . . ."

"Because why?"

"Because I was there in my dream," she said, feeling her cheeks flush—which was weird because she had nothing to be embarrassed about.

"I think the only thing limiting where you can project is you," Corbin said with her trademark grin. "I mean, dude, whenever I teach you something and tell you what I think the rules are, you always find a way to break those rules and do something amazing. So, I'm just saying: Why not try now?"

"Okay . . . why not?" Sarah Beth said. A nervous smile crept onto her face, and she closed her eyes again.

"You can do it, honey," she heard her mom say. "I believe in you."

"Thanks, Mom," she said and drifted back into the mindspace.

It took her a little while to relax and figure out what she wanted to try. Uncle Jed had told her he'd been buried alive, so that meant he was in a graveyard, and she knew that graveyard was in Haiti. She tried to picture Haiti and imagine the graveyard, but when she tried to project to that place, nothing happened.

Hmm, she thought. *How do I project to somewhere if I don't know the place? When I projected to the catacombs, I felt like I'd been there before, even though I was trading off someone else's experience.*

An interesting idea came to her. She wasn't sure if it would work but it was worth trying.

"Uncle Jed," she called, sending her voice out in every direction. *"I can't find your thread, and you're not answering me. I know you're hurt and weak, but I need your help because I don't know where you are. If you can hear me, try to imagine me there with you. Show me what you see. I need a visual clue . . ."*

She waited, listening, scanning her mindspace for something, anything that might be a signal from Jed. For the longest moment, she felt and saw nothing. Her chest tightened at the thought that she had failed—that her uncle Jed was gone.

Then, slowly, she realized she did sense something.

At first, she didn't notice it because what he sent her was the absence of something—a black void that hovered just out of sight. But when she reached for it, the void felt connected to Jed.

Here goes nothing, she said to herself and, with a little trepidation, projected to the black void.

Where am I?

Her projected body was horizontal and lying in complete and total darkness. She reached out her hands and didn't exactly feel, but became aware of, wooden walls very close, all around her.

Then, it clicked, and she shrieked.

Oh my God, I'm in the coffin . . . I'm in the coffin with Jed!

She squirmed, turned her head, and her nose touched Jed's cheek. She couldn't see him because the inside of the coffin had zero light—like, absolute zero. Maybe even negative light, if there were such a thing. But even though she couldn't see his face, she knew with absolute certainty that it was him.

"Uncle Jed," she said. *"I'm here with you."*

He didn't answer.

She listened. Even though she couldn't hear his breathing, she knew he was alive.

But only barely.

If the difference between life and death could be measured in meters, he's one millimeter from death, she thought.

"I don't know what they did to you, but I'm going to get you out of here." She gave him a kiss on the cheek.

And when she did, she felt a drop of wetness run onto her top lip.

"Hang on, Uncle Jed. Just a little bit longer," she said, steeling herself for what she needed to do next.

When she and Corbin were fleeing from that Dark One in the catacombs, she had learned how to project through a closed door. What she was about to try now was basically the same, except she was going to project through the top of the coffin and probably several feet of dirt. She exhaled through pursed lips and felt her actual body do it too.

Here goes nothing.

She wanted it to be instant, but it wasn't. Her hope that she might just pop up onto the ground beside the grave was shattered as she felt herself dragged painfully and slowly through the moist, cool earth. The claustrophobia, the sense of drowning in dirt, was overpowering.

Just when she thought she couldn't take another moment of it, she emerged from the fresh soil. She passed through the dirt and then landed on the ground, looking at the stars, immersed in the sounds of tree frogs and crickets trilling.

"Whoa," she breathed. She felt her pulse slow as the sensation of being buried alive—even though she was projecting—slowly ebbed. Then she rose to her feet and looked around at the graveyard.

The best thing about projecting is exotic travel without the mosquito bites, she thought as she watched bugs zigzag through her projected body.

The press of time did not ease for her as she stood on the dirt covering Uncle Jed's shallow grave. She scanned right and left and noticed that his plot was just one of several dozen seemingly fresh and unmarked graves.

Well, that's just great.

She felt someone, Corbin, squeeze her actual body's hand.

"Did you find him?" Corbin asked.

"Yes. They buried him alive, Corbin. Like, literally, he's in a coffin under several feet of dirt," she said, her voice echoing back at St. George's.

"Oh no, Jed," she heard her mom say with strain and angst in her voice.

"Great job, Sarah Beth," Pastor Dee said, speaking up for the first time. "The next step is figuring out where you are so we can send the Shepherds there to help Jed."

"I don't think he has that long," she said, her voice catching. "I think he's dying."

"I understand," Pastor Dee said, calm and collected. "We need your location. Do you see any landmarks we could use to find you?"

Sarah Beth turned in a circle. That's when she noticed it for the first time—a sedan parked, partially hidden beside a grove of trees next to a dirt road that looked like the entrance to the graveyard. Inside the cab, she saw two orange glows pulsing in the darkness.

Cigarettes.

"There are guards here. I just noticed them," she said. "Two, at least. They're smoking in a car."

"That's good information, Sarah Beth," Pastor Dee said.

"Now, can you find us a landmark? We know you're somewhere in a fifty-mile radius of Port-de-Paix based on how long he might have traveled from the safe house, but we need to narrow that down if we want to help Jed in time."

"I don't see anything," she said, turning faster and feeling panicked. "Just trees and a dirt road."

"Sarah Beth, this is Corbin. I'm coming to help you."

No sooner had Corbin finished speaking the words than her projected body was standing beside Sarah Beth.

"Hi."

"Hi," Sarah Beth said. *"I'm so glad you're here."*

"Are we standing on it—you know, Jed's grave?"

"Yep," she said and looked down.

Corbin nodded and scanned the area around Jed's plot.

"What are you doing?" Sarah Beth asked.

"All these graves look alike," Corbin said. *"I'm making a mental map of his location so I can sketch when I get back."*

"Smart," Sarah Beth said.

Corbin flashed her a little grin, then continued her scan, with her eyes eventually settling on the sedan with the two thugs. *"Are those the bad guys?"*

"I think so. I mean, who else would be hanging out here at this hour? And why?"

"Right . . ." Corbin said.

Sarah Beth could see that her friend's mind was working the problem. Corbin had worked with Shepherds on lots of ops, and she thought tactically as a result.

Which is what I need to learn to do.

"Do you have an idea to figure out where we are?"

"It's not a great one, but it's a start," Corbin said, then took off running toward the car. *"Follow me."*

Sarah Beth ran after her. When they got to the car, Corbin

projected into the sedan's back seat. Sarah Beth groaned. After the experience in the catacombs, being noticed and chased by a Dark One, she really didn't want to roll the dice again. Corbin looked at her and gestured for her to project inside.

Sarah Beth shook her head.

"Come on," Corbin said. *"Don't be a chicken."*

Why was it that being called a chicken worked, even when it was a totally stupid taunt?

Sarah Beth sighed and projected into the sedan beside Corbin. She expected the two brutes in the front seat to turn around and glare at her with glowing eyes, but to her surprise, they didn't. Their attention was laser-focused on their respective cell phones. Corbin stood up and leaned forward to look over their shoulders at the phone screens. Grudgingly, Sarah Beth followed suit.

The driver was texting, and the guy in the passenger seat was watching a super violent video. Sarah Beth glanced at Corbin, whose eyes were fixed on the phone belonging to the texting driver. After a moment, Corbin turned and whispered, *"Let's go."*

They projected out of the sedan and into the graveyard.

"What did you see?" Sarah Beth asked, not really sure what they accomplished.

"I got the number of the person the driver was texting with," Corbin said. *"We'll give it to the Shepherds' tech team, and hopefully they can hack into that phone and find out the number of the driver and geolocate it."*

"Good thinking, big sis," Sarah Beth said, wishing she'd thought of that.

"What else did you observe?" Corbin asked.

"The other guy was watching a movie or something. I couldn't watch because it was super violent."

"Yeah, what else?"

"Um . . . I don't know."

"They each had a pistol, and there was a machine gun in the back seat," Corbin said. *"Whoever has to engage these guys will want to know that information."*

Sarah Beth nodded. She realized that despite all her accomplishments as a Watcher and her face-off against Victor, she still had a lot to learn.

"Okay, let's head home. Ready?"

"Yep, just one last thing," Sarah Beth said and turned to face Uncle Jed's grave.

"Help is on the way, Uncle Jed. Be strong, for me. You can do this. I believe in you."

CHAPTER FORTY-SEVEN

AUBERT, PORT-DE-PAIX

HAITI

0128 HOURS LOCAL

David had accepted the cold reality that, when it came to gifting, God had passed him over. Jed had gifts, Sarah Beth had gifts, and he'd recently learned that Rachel did too—something she'd hid from him for nearly their entire marriage. He understood why she'd kept it from him, and he didn't resent her for it . . . at least not most of the time. But it would be a lie to say that being the lone member of the circle of four without a gift didn't bother him, because it did. Every day he had to remind himself that life wasn't fair.

Every day he had to admit that God's plan was not for men like him to question.

Every day he had to tell himself that despite not having overt gifts of the Holy Spirit, he *had* been gifted with an inner strength and resilience that others had not.

But despite this daily ritual of reaffirmation, David still felt cheated and left out.

He knew that right now, at this very moment, Sarah Beth—*his* daughter—was Watcher snapchatting with Rachel and Jed, working out a rescue plan, while he sat helpless and useless in the SUV with Gayle waiting for his phone to ring with orders. The call would come from Pastor Mike Moore, his TSL boss and Morvant's right-hand man, and David could already imagine what those "orders" would be:

"David, we need you and Gayle to go to the airport and loiter at the security office until Eli and the rest of Joshua Bravo arrive. We want you safe until the tactical team can properly effect Jed's rescue . . ."

So, when his phone rang and he saw the caller ID was a St. George's Academy line, he was completely taken aback.

"You going to answer that?" Gayle said from the passenger seat.

"Yeah, sorry." He put the phone on speaker, held it between them, and said, "This is David."

"David, it's Rachel." Her voice tense and urgent. "We know where Jed is."

"Where?" Gayle said, beating him to the punch.

"In a graveyard," Rachel said. "It's about fifty miles south of your location, in Saint-Marc. We're texting you the coordinates now."

"Wait, what did you say? In a graveyard?" he said, screwing up his face and turning to Gayle.

"I know," Rachel said. "You heard me correctly. They buried Jed alive. We think he's been drugged; Sarah Beth said he can't move or speak and that he's barely breathing."

He watched Gayle's already fair complexion go even paler in the moonlit cab of their SUV.

A text message appeared on his phone screen, and when he tapped it, a pin dropped and a route formed on his navigation app.

"Got the location," David said.

A long, uncomfortable silence hung on the line. They both, apparently, were waiting for the other to say something.

Finally, Rachel broke. "David, um, we've been racking our brains with Commander Morvant and the Shepherds on a rescue plan, but . . ."

"But what?" he said when she stopped mid-sentence.

". . . I don't know how to say this other than to say it," she said, struggling to keep her emotions in check. "Sarah Beth believes that Jed won't make it if we wait for Joshua Bravo to arrive. They're still several hours away."

Fifty-one miles, as shown on the GPS, felt like a continent away in a country like Haiti, but the map application said they could be there in eighty-four minutes by staying on the RN-5 and then RN-1 highways. And the cemetery was right beside the RN-1. It was night, with little or no traffic. They could probably cut another fifteen minutes off that by hauling ass. Call it an hour plus ten . . . maybe fifteen.

"How long does he have?" David asked.

"We think three hours tops—maybe less. And that's based on the assumption we're making about the drugs he might have been given that would keep him still and quiet and keep his metabolic rate down. If he wakes up . . ."

"Then we'll go dig him out ourselves, me and Gayle," he said, while Gayle nodded in vigorous agreement.

"Dad, there's Dark Ones guarding the cemetery," Sarah Beth said, jumping onto the call and beating Rachel to the punch. "Two guys, in a sedan, and they have a machine gun."

What could only be described as a hot flash flooded his chest and cheeks with heat.

"I see . . ."

He met Gayle's eyes. With her jaw set, Gayle pulled

a compact black pistol from a concealed holster under her shirt.

"Is that all we have?" he asked Gayle, his voice quiet and low.

She nodded.

"Listen, David," Rachel said, clearly hearing their exchange over the speakerphone mike. "Leadership here does not feel like a rescue op is something you and Gayle are properly equipped to execute. The official guidance is for the two of you to observe from a safe location and only attempt a rescue if the Dark Ones guarding the cemetery leave."

This comment stirred an exciting but disturbing mix of emotions in him as he extrapolated the subtext of her statement.

"Rachel, who's there with you?" he asked.

"At the moment, just Sarah Beth," she said.

"I see . . ."

"Dad, you're Uncle Jed's only chance," Sarah Beth said, her voice heavy with desperation. "I know you can do this. I know you can save him. I'm praying about it . . ."

"We agreed you wouldn't pressure him, Sarah Beth," Rachel said. The sound quality changed suddenly. "I've taken the phone off speaker . . ."

He did the same and held the phone to his ear. "Me too."

"Listen, I don't think this is a good idea. In fact, I think it's a terrible one, but . . . I also know that if I didn't give you Jed's location, both you and Sarah Beth would never forgive me. You're a grown man and Jed's best friend. As much as I might want to, I can't make this decision for you. But, David . . ." Her voice cracked. "David, I don't want to lose you."

But you already did, didn't you, by putting it out there, he thought with a flare of wounded resentment. *You're willing to risk my life—the father of your only child—for the possibility of saving the man who abandoned you.*

He shook off the dark thoughts, and his heart reminded him that Jed had risked his life to save Sarah Beth and Rachel on multiple occasions.

If I was the one in the coffin, what would Jed do? He'd rescue me, come hell or high water.

But you're not Jed, the dark voice inside him rebutted. *You're not a warrior. You're not a Shepherd. Do you really think you'll stand a chance against two Dark Ones?*

"Ask Sarah Beth if she's positive the guards are Dark Ones. Is there a chance they could be hired thugs?" he said into the phone.

"Hold on . . ." she said, and he heard her parrot his question. "She said she's not sure. She didn't see their eyes or see them in action."

He looked at Gayle, who clenched her jaw, clearly lost in her own thoughts. "Rachel, we're going to scope it out. I'll call you back with a sitrep, but we won't go into battle without checking in."

"Okay," she said and sounded relieved, but he couldn't tell if it was for him or for Jed. "And David?"

"Yes?"

"Please be careful. I love you so much."

He resisted the urge to clear his throat. "I love you too."

He pressed the red button to end the call, pulled up the route to the cemetery on his map application, then shifted the transmission into Drive and started to pull onto the road. They were only blocks from RN-5.

"Whoa, whoa, whoa," Gayle said, grabbing his arm. "We can't just show up, guns blazing, without a plan. We need to talk about this."

"Okay," David said, pressing the accelerator and speeding toward the highway. "Let's talk. But we need to get moving."

"First question, how much combat experience do you have?" she asked.

"None," he said, telling it straight instead of hedging his answer.

"How about weapons training? How are you with a pistol?"

"Terrible," he answered. "I went through a basic weapons course at Trinity Loop on the pistol and the rifle. I was told I would have minimally qualified to wear the ribbon in the military, whatever that means. Jed said it was more like a 'fam-fire.' I've shot a gun only one other time since then."

She nodded. "At least you're honest. That's refreshing from a man." He glanced over and she shook her head. "Sorry, I didn't mean that."

He chuckled and then leaned forward to see better out the dirty windshield, not wanting to miss the turn onto the RN-5 highway. "Yes, you did, but that's okay. How about you? How much combat experience do you have?"

"Limited. I graduated from the Farm, and I shoot pistols regularly, but I'm no Jed. I've been in a gun battle though. Once. I fired two shots."

"Yeah, well, there's only one Jed. If that's the standard we need to meet, we're dead."

"I saw something in Peru that defied logic. I saw a man leaping, running, and fighting with superhuman strength. I saw his eyes glowing the color of flame . . ." she said, her gaze going to the middle distance.

"You saw a Dark One," he said.

She nodded. "If that's what we're up against, I don't think we stand a chance."

"Agreed, but they might just be hired muscle," he said. "In which case, with the element of surprise, we could conceivably win."

"How can we find out for certain?" she asked.

"I don't know. From my understanding, the eyes are the

telltale sign. But they only show them when they want to or when the demon inside takes control of the host."

He wasn't sure how she, as an outsider, would react to this comment, but she simply nodded.

"Okay, I have an idea," she said. "Here's what I think we should do . . ."

CHAPTER FORTY-EIGHT

THE CEMETERY—CIMETIÈRE DE SAINT-MARC

AVENUE MAUREPAS

SAINT-MARC, HAITI

0232 HOURS LOCAL

The drive to Saint-Marc had felt longer than it was and passed mostly in quiet, each lost in their own thoughts—or in David's case, doubts. David hadn't contributed anything to Gayle's rescue plan. Not because he didn't want to, but because he couldn't think of anything to add or change. He'd been present for a few mission-planning and prep sessions with Joshua Bravo over the previous months, so he'd learned a little bit about tactics and methods, but not enough to make him useful.

Gayle's plan seemed as good as any, so he'd simply agreed to go with it.

His mobile phone vibrated with an incoming call in the center console's cupholder. He didn't need to look at the screen to know that it was Rachel calling. She'd called three times over the last ten minutes. He'd decided not to tell her and the crew at

St. George's what they were planning. He and Gayle had made their decision and that was that. They were going to get Jed out or die trying. David's money was on the latter. Not that he wanted to die—he was terrified of the prospect—but he needed to prove to his wife and daughter what kind of man he was. If he took Rachel's call, there was a better than 50 percent chance she'd talk him out of it.

He couldn't let that happen.

I'm not a coward.

I'm not weak . . .

He and Gayle had driven the final two miles to the cemetery with the headlights off, then parked a quarter of a mile away. They'd snuck in on foot and surveilled the sedan—parked exactly where Sarah Beth said it would be, deep inside the cemetery and near the southwest corner of the sprawling property—which still appeared to contain the armed thugs. Then, he'd returned to their SUV while Gayle stayed behind to make the distraction. Upon receiving her text, he'd repositioned the SUV successfully without the bad guys noticing. Now, he waited for the signal from her.

No one will ever know if you leave, a voice said in his head. *You can say whatever you want, and they'll believe you because Gayle and Jed will both be dead.*

"Shut up," he said.

Think how much easier and better your life will be without Jed in it—

"I said shut up!" he shouted, pounding balled fists against the steering wheel.

His phone chirped with an incoming text message. It was from Gayle:

> Setting fire now . . . get ready.

He texted back a thumbs-up emoji, checked his seat belt, and, with his foot on the brake, put the idling transmission into Drive. David glanced at the heavy metal lug wrench he'd pulled from the SUV's spare-tire kit earlier and staged on the passenger seat, suddenly overwhelmed by how inadequate it would be against real operators—or demon-possessed Dark Ones.

Then, he waited . . .

It's not too late, the voice said.

He ignored it.

All you have to do is drive away . . .

"Go to hell," he murmured, the irony of the curse not lost on him.

His phone chimed again. He glanced at the screen and saw a single word from Gayle:

NOW

David shifted his foot from the brake to the accelerator and mashed the pedal to the floor. The vehicle lurched forward while the SUV's all-wheel drive traction control kicked in and kept him from fishtailing as he accelerated toward the cemetery entrance on the dirt road. He cleared the tree line a few seconds later and barreled through the entrance, holding the steering wheel in a death grip, his hands at the "ten and two" positions.

The noise from the SUV's engine and tires alerted the two guards to his assault. As Gayle predicted, upon seeing the fire she'd started in the woods nearby, the sentries had exited their sedan to investigate. Also as she'd anticipated, one of them had taken the machine gun—which David could see well because the guy was bringing it up to strafe the SUV. David steered slightly right, pointing the grill of the vehicle at the man to run him over. He tried to press the accelerator harder, but the pedal was already on the floor.

A muzzle flash lit up the night as the enemy shooter opened fire.

Reflexively, David ducked right, dropping his head and torso below the steering wheel and dashboard as bullets shattered the windshield and slammed into the engine compartment. He felt something hot and sharp in his left calf that made him yelp, but he kept his right foot jammed on the accelerator while trying to hold the steering wheel as steady as he could.

A moment later, he heard and felt a massive thud as the SUV hit something.

Not something . . . someone.

He tried to shift his foot from the accelerator to the brake, but because of his wonky torso angle, his foot hit the side of the stupid pedal. He cursed and tried again while blindly steering with one hand. On the second attempt, he managed to brake hard for a few seconds before the SUV crashed. The shoulder strap of his seat belt, stretched fully out since he was leaning over, didn't stop him from smacking into the dash, but the lap belt kept him in his seat. The driver and passenger airbags deployed, with David splayed halfway into the passenger seat.

Pain flared in his face, neck, and chest from the impact.

He groaned and tasted blood. He tried to move and was relieved when his fingers and toes wiggled, confirming he'd not broken his neck. Ever since Christopher Reeve, the original actor who played Superman, had broken his neck and become a paraplegic, David had developed a secret paranoia that it would also someday happen to him. That's why he never rode horses, never tried out for wrestling, never rode motorcycles or did a half dozen adrenaline junkie activities where neck breaking seemed possible.

A loud crack split the night, and the driver's side window beside him exploded into a thousand chunks of glass. He turned and lifted his head to see a tall Haitian man walking toward him, a raised pistol in his hand. A second thundercrack echoed. For a split second, David thought it was the last sound he'd ever hear, but he saw no accompanying muzzle flash. The shooter's body jerked and whirled to his right. Two more gunshots rang, rounds fired in rapid succession, and the side of the Haitian man's head exploded.

David stared in shock as the freshly made corpse collapsed in a heap.

"David, are you all right?" Gayle asked, her voice tense with worry, running up to the SUV.

"I think so," he said, sitting up fully.

"Looks like you might have broken your nose," she said.

Hearing her say it seemed to make the injury real, and in that instant, he realized that his nose and forehead throbbed. It was also likely the source of the blood in his mouth because he could now feel twin rivulets running over his top lip. He gingerly touched his nose with his first two fingers and instantly felt that the shape was wrong.

"Did we win?" he asked with a feeble attempt at a smile.

"Oh yeah," she said, but as the words came out of her mouth, something caught her attention to the right.

The victorious smile she wore faded, replaced by shock a split second before a fast-moving blur smashed into her.

David sat, paralyzed with fear and shock, as the Haitian man he'd run over with the SUV just minutes earlier dragged Gayle to the ground. His left arm was twisted and bent at impossible angles, but that didn't stop him from pummeling Gayle's face with the badly mangled appendage. David heard Gayle grunt and then scream as she raised her arms ineffectively to block the blows. The man outweighed her by at least sixty pounds, and he now straddled her on the ground, his arms a blur as he beat her.

A battle instantly raged in David's mind between fear and

valor as Gayle fought for her life on her back, the Dark One savagely mauling her from above.

Five gunshots reverberated as she fired her pistol up and into the demon warrior's chest. David registered them as hits because at least two of the rounds punched holes out the attacker's back with puffs of blood, but the Dark One seemed unfazed and kept attacking.

Do something! he silently screamed at himself, breaking the stupor of his inaction.

He reached over and grabbed the long-handled lug wrench, which miraculously still sat on the passenger seat, perhaps kept in place by the airbags. Jaw set, he opened the door and climbed out of the wrecked SUV. He felt a sharp burning pain in his left calf as he put weight on the leg, but he gritted his teeth and ignored it as he stepped behind the creature on top of Gayle.

"Hey, demon freak, get off my friend," he shouted, raising the tire iron in preparation for the swing.

The snarling attack paused and the Dark One turned its head to look at David, eyes ablaze with twin rings of fire and rage. David was a terrible marksman, but back in the day, he'd been a helluva baseball player. He teed up the demon warrior's head like a seventy-mile-per-hour fastball and swung. The socket end of the lug wrench smashed into the Dark One's left temple with a resounding *crack*, and the skull and side of the face caved in. Dark blood and something more horrible dribbled down the side of the jaw, already twisted from when he'd hit the damn thing with the truck. The demon-possessed corpse turned to him and gurgled. David watched with awe and astonishment as the fire in its eyes went out.

The body seemed hesitant to fall, as if held up by some invisible thread, before collapsing into an unmoving heap halfway on Gayle.

"Get it off," she said, panting. "Get it off me!"

He dragged the corpse off her as she scrambled clear, kicking away from the horror and gore as she pedaled herself backward. Feeling a strange mix of both excitement and disgust, David stared down at the foe he'd just vanquished. His gaze ticked from the fallen Dark One to the lug wrench and back again. A savage and primal urge for violence, a compulsion he'd never felt before, swept over him. Taking the tire iron in both hands, he brought it down, swinging like he would an axe to split a log. The blow connected, breaking the demon warrior's skull nearly in half.

He swung again. And again. And again.

When he finished, there was nothing left but a headless body and a mess of gore on the dirt.

He turned to Gayle, who'd gotten to her feet and stared at him in wide-eyed horror.

"They kidnapped my daughter. They tried to rape my wife. They've terrorized everyone I've loved," he said, feeling compelled to explain the unmitigated violence he'd just unleashed.

After a long silence, she said, "C'mon, we need to rescue Jed."

He nodded and dropped the bloody wrench in the dirt.

"I hope they have shovels in the trunk of that sedan," she said as she swapped out the empty magazine in her compact pistol and returned it to her concealed holster.

"Me too," he said, turning away from the carnage he'd wrought, feeling both nauseated and proud.

I knew you had it in you, a voice said inside. *You see, David, killing is not so hard to do. It's just a matter of motivation.*

He ignored the voice and started to trot after Gayle, but his left calf felt like someone had stuck him with a hot poker and he stumbled.

"Hey, Gayle," he said, taking a knee to inspect the wound. "I think I'm shot."

She turned and hustled back, kneeling beside him to look. Blood dripped from a laceration on her forehead, and her left eye was bruised and puffy.

"Are *you* okay?" he asked as she used her mobile phone's flashlight on his calf.

"Yeah, I think so," she said, "but you definitely got shot."

"How bad is it?"

"Bullet took an egg-sized chunk out of the back of your calf. I don't think it hit a major artery, but we need to wrap it tight and keep pressure on the wound."

He nodded and slipped off his polo shirt and his belt, both of which he handed to her. She folded his shirt into a rectangular pad and pressed it against the wound. Next, she wrapped the belt around his lower leg several times and cinched it tight with the buckle.

"That should do until we can get you to a hospital." She stood and extended her hand to help him up, which he took. "Can you walk?"

"I think so," he said, half limping on the leg, which hurt much more now that his adrenaline had burned off and his mind knew a bullet had hit him. Inside the SUV, a blue light dimly illuminated the cabin, and he could hear his phone ringing. "That's probably Rachel. You go check for shovels; I'm going to take this."

She nodded and jogged toward the sedan by the cemetery entrance while he limped back to the SUV. He leaned in and grabbed his mobile phone, which was, despite the crash, still in the console cupholder where he'd had it stashed. He checked the caller ID and answered.

"I'm okay," he said, preempting his wife's opening salvo. "We're both okay."

"Sarah Beth said you've been shot," Rachel said, her voice a tight cord.

"How does she know that?"

"Because I'm there with you, Dad," he heard Sarah Beth say over the phone.

"Where?" he said, scanning the graveyard.

"She's projecting, David," Rachel said.

"Projecting?" he asked, cocking an eyebrow.

"It's something new she's been working on," Rachel said. "Don't tell me you forgot the conversation we had about it."

He was about to ask which "conversation," but he had learned a thing or two over his fifteen years of marriage. Active listening was a weakness of his, and probably the greatest source of friction in his relationships. He was a daydreamer, easily distracted, and had an annoying chorus of internal competing voices to contend with.

"Oh, yeah, I remember now," he said, fibbing to keep the peace.

"Tell Dad I'm standing on Jed's grave and I'm going to guide him to the right plot," Sarah Beth said.

"Did you hear that?" Rachel asked.

"Yes," he said and turned toward the sound of footsteps. Gayle was jogging back to him, carrying a shovel in each hand.

"I found shovels," Gayle said, her left eye completely swollen shut now.

"Tell Dad to start walking," Sarah Beth said.

"She said start walking," Rachel said before he could reply.

"Okay. I'm walking," he said and set off limping toward the center of the plots with Gayle beside him.

"Veer fifteen degrees left," Sarah Beth shouted.

He did and then put the phone on speaker.

"Sorry, that's my left. I meant right. Turn about twenty degrees to your right," Sarah Beth said. "Daddy, you're limping . . . How bad is your leg? Are you going to be okay?"

Her voice had changed, and he wondered how much she had seen. He felt another wave of nausea and blinked tears from his eyes.

God, please don't let my baby girl see what I did—what I could do . . .

"I'm fine, baby girl. It's nothing. Is this the right way?"

"Yes," Sarah Beth answered, the fear and worry lessening as he forced himself not to limp, despite the pain.

"Who is that?" Gayle asked.

"My daughter," he said.

"Keep coming . . . keep coming," Sarah Beth said. "Turn a little back to your left . . ."

"How is she guiding us? Is there a drone or satellite watching us?" Gayle asked.

"Uh . . . not exactly," he said.

"Ten more feet . . . six . . . three . . . okay, stop. Jed is in the grave that Gayle is standing on top of," Sarah Beth said.

He turned to Gayle, who looked at him with questioning eyes.

"This one?" Gayle asked, stomping her right foot. "Jed's buried here?"

"Yes," Sarah Beth said. "Now please, hurry. He's running out of air."

"Great job, Sarah Beth," David said, staring at the empty space around Gayle and hoping that he might see a glimmer or ripple in space, anything that might be his daughter.

"I'm standing right beside you, Dad," she said. "I just took your left hand."

He looked beside him and at his left hand, but he neither saw nor felt anything. Despite feeling cheated out of witnessing the miracle that was his daughter, he smiled at the empty space.

"I'm going to hang up to save my phone's battery, but I know you're going to be here the whole time with me," he said. "I love you, Sarah Beth."

"I love you too, Dad. I'm glad you're okay," she said.

He ended the call and turned to Gayle.

"Is your daughter, like, invisible or something?" Gayle asked, her expression incredulous.

"It's called projecting, and I don't really understand how it works," he said, extending a hand to her.

"Are you going to be able to dig with that calf of yours?" she asked, passing him the shovel with the longer handle.

"Even if I have to do it on my knees," he said, wincing as he tried to shovel his first scoop of dirt.

"In that case, give me that one back," she said with a grin and tossed him the short-handled one.

CHAPTER FORTY-NINE

INSIDE THE COFFIN

THE CEMETERY—CIMETIÈRE DE SAINT-MARC

AVENUE MAUREPAS

SAINT-MARC, HAITI

0254 HOURS LOCAL

A dull thud woke Jed.

Or maybe he was already awake and simply noticed it. The combination of sensory deprivation, paralysis, and hallucinogenic drugs had wreaked havoc on his mind.

As someone who'd survived the physical and psychological rigors of Hell Week and completed BUD/S training, he'd always harbored a secret nugget of pride that he'd endured the worst abuse that could be thrown at a person. But during Hell Week, he'd been able to harness his body to rage against his pain. During Hell Week, he'd still had agency over his person. The same was true of the trials he'd faced during hundreds and hundreds of combat engagements as a SEAL, fighting even after the severe pain of injury.

But this . . .

What Calypso had done to him was something else entirely. In the blackness, with no sensory or physical feedback, he couldn't center himself. More than that, he couldn't *define* himself. Untethered from his physical body, was he still Jedidiah Johnson? He felt so confused. So disoriented.

So defeated . . .

Am I still me? Have I lost my mind?

Another thud.

A scraping sound.

Then a flurry of thuds and lots of scraping. The noises were coming from the lid of the coffin.

A spark of hope blossomed inside him.

Those are shovels, he realized.

"Jed?" a familiar female voice called, barely audible. "Jed, if you can hear me, we're getting you out."

Rachel?

No . . . not Rachel. Someone else.

Gayle.

Gayle!

She's alive. She came back for me!

The frenzy of scraping and thudding continued above him as Gayle worked to dig him out. He tried to call out to her, but his dry, gaped-open mouth couldn't make a sound. His body was a dead, disconnected thing and refused to react no matter how hard he tried. He heard another voice now, talking to Gayle.

David . . . Of course it's David. He was with us at the house when Calypso took me.

His mind was beginning to wake up, and as it did, the desire to move and talk became almost overwhelming. He counted every agonizing second until Gayle finally spoke to him again.

"Jed, we've got the dirt clear," she called. "We're going to lift off the cover now."

Hurry. Please hurry . . .

He heard rustling, and a beam of silver light appeared. Then, the light chased away the shadow completely, and he looked up into Gayle's worried but angelically beautiful face.

"Oh God, Jed, what have they done to you?" she gushed and climbed into the grave with him. She pressed her palm against his forehead, then turned and lowered her cheek right next to his mouth. "His forehead's clammy, David, and I don't think he's breathing."

"Take his pulse," David said, his face appearing upside down from the head of the grave.

"Okay," she said, pressing two fingers against the side of his neck and repositioning them to try a different spot. "I don't feel a pulse. Oh no, David . . . I think we're too late. I think he might be dead."

Gayle didn't know it, but his heart *was* beating—only so slowly and weakly she couldn't detect a pulse.

I'm not dead, he screamed in his head. *I'm not dead!*

"Start CPR," David said.

He felt her shift on top of him, straddling his torso. She placed the heel of her right palm onto his sternum, put her left palm on top of it, and knit her fingers together. Then, using all her upper body weight, she performed ten chest compressions. Even though she wasn't a large woman, Gayle clearly knew the proper CPR technique because Jed could *feel* each compression. And to his utter shock, the bursts of blood to his foggy brain rejuvenated his focus and clarity. After the tenth compression, she shifted, tilted his head back to open his airway, and sealed her lips around his. Her scent, both feminine and primal, wafted into his nostrils. She smelled of vanilla and perspiration, lavender and dirt, and he savored this unexpected intimacy.

Being on the receiving side of CPR while completely lucid

was, he imagined, not something that happened often—and certainly had never happened to him. Each compression brought more blood and clarity to his brain. The feeling as Gayle blew her breath into him, inflating his lungs using her own, was so powerful and intimate that he felt tears forming in his eyes. He wanted to tell her *thank you.* He wanted to tell her how he felt about her. He wanted his useless arms to wrap her in an embrace as she poured her life into his.

She completed another round of compressions and breaths before checking his pulse again. "Come on, Jed," she said, breathing heavily from the physical exertion as she stared at him. "Come back to me."

You need to show her you're alive.

Blink, damn it. Blink.

He blinked.

And Gayle saw it.

"Jed?" she said, mouth agape.

He blinked again.

"He's alive, David. He's alive!" she called, her voice a shriek of raw emotion as she threw herself against his chest and hugged him. After a long embrace, she sat up, still straddling his midsection.

"Are you sure?" David asked, calling down to her.

"Yes, I'm sure. I saw him blink," she said. "Jed, blink again if you can hear me?"

He blinked.

"There—did you see it?" she asked.

"I sure did," David said. "Jed, can you move?"

He considered blinking but decided only to blink if the answer to a question was *yes.*

"Jed, did they drug you?" Gayle said. "Blink once for *yes,* twice for *no.*"

Good, she gets it, he thought and blinked once.

"Can you move?" she asked.

Blink. Blink.

"Are you paralyzed but still have feeling in your body?" she said.

Blink.

Jed listened to the conversation above him, frustrated that he couldn't turn his head or focus his eyes on his friends, instead listening like someone eavesdropping from another room.

"David, I know what's going on here," Gayle said, her voice grim but not surprised. "There's a Haitian Voudou ritual where they use paralytic and hallucinogenic compounds that basically put a person into a near-death state and then they bury the victim alive. Just before the effects wear off, the priest or priestess digs up the victim and brainwashes them into thinking they've died and been brought back as a zombie."

"And that's what you think they did to Jed?" David replied, his voice farther away.

"Yes," she said, "only I guarantee the Dark One who did this to him wasn't planning on digging him up."

"We need to get him out of that hole and to somewhere safe," David said. "I worry we're on the clock. Those guys we killed were probably supposed to make regular check-ins."

"Agreed," Gayle said, then her voice was closer as she leaned over him, her warm breath against his ear. "Hang on, Jed. We're going to get you out."

He blinked.

Moments later, the two of them were in the hole with him. It was disorienting, watching their unfocused figures pass in and out of his field of view, but he found that he could now move his eyes, ever so slightly, if he tried with all his might. But he could feel every awkward movement as they grabbed his arms, slid him to a seated position, then wrapped their arms around his massive chest as his head lolled to one side, Gayle whispering soft encouragement into his ear with each uncomfortable attempt to find an angle that allowed the two relatively small people to lift his 225-pound body out of the grave. He heard their grunts, felt their sweat on his skin as they struggled, all the while desperate to help them. Never in his life had he felt so useless, so powerless, so vulnerable—so *dependent.*

But who better for him to be forced to experiment with dependency on than his best friend since childhood and the woman he thought he might be falling in love with.

Eventually, they hauled him out of the shallow grave and dragged him across the ground together. Loading him into the back seat of their sedan was no picnic either, but they managed that too. Several bumps, bruises, and scrapes later, they were on their way. He lay in the back, his eyes slowly focusing on the cloth ceiling, the feel of Gayle's lap comforting as, apparently, David drove. She absently stroked his head, gently combing strands of hair with her fingernails, just like his mom used to do anytime he was sick with fever as a little boy. Instead of feeling emasculated by it, the gesture was a salve for his frayed and ragged nerves. He needed the physical contact. He wanted her reassurance.

She looked down at him.

He wanted to tell her how dark and alone it had been for him. He wanted to tell her how vulnerable and weak he felt. He wanted to tell her that her face—when she'd lifted the coffin lid and appeared to him—would be burned into his psyche for the rest of his days. He wanted to tell her that she was the most beautiful thing he'd ever seen . . .

But all he could do was stare.

"I know," she said softly with a tender smile as she ran her fingers through his hair. "I know . . ."

CHAPTER FIFTY

NEW SHEPHERDS SAFE HOUSE

EBEN-EZER BAPTIST CHURCH OF SAINT-MARC

RUE SAVANNAH

SAINT-MARC, HAITI

1532 HOURS LOCAL

Jed had let the darkness engulf him, but not before feeling the sensation of, finally, pulling real gulps of air into his own lungs. The drug was wearing off, but the psychological exhaustion of his time in the grave had taken a toll that would be with him, he suspected, forever. The gentle feel of Gayle's hands on his face and the scent of her had allowed him to at last let himself slip into a peaceful slumber.

He slept—he had no idea how long—without dreams and only vaguely aware of movement and voices around him.

But her hands on his face—he felt that each time . . .

"Jed? Bro, wake up," a male voice said, and someone shook him by the shoulders. "You're okay, buddy. You're safe."

Jed's eyelids popped open to find his friend and teammate

Eli grinning at him with a big fat dip of tobacco in his lip. He blinked twice and Eli was still there.

"Eli?" he said, his own voice gravelly and unfamiliar. Jed was unsure what was real and what wasn't. He realized his throat burned terribly. "Where's Gayle?"

"Yeah, it's me," the veteran Shepherd said. "And I missed you too," he added with feigned indignation. "Gayle James is looking over intelligence with the team. They had to practically pry her from your side, so maybe we can have a chat about that at some point?"

Jed nodded, but that wasn't going to happen right now. The powerful feelings for Gayle were still a mystery to himself.

"It's good to see you, brother," Jed said, forcing a smile.

Do I dare try to sit up? What if I can't move?

With a grunt, he raised himself onto his elbows and scooted back so that he sat up in bed with his back against the wooden headboard.

"How long have you been here?" he asked, turning to his friend and teammate. He looked around the small room. "Where are we?"

"We're in a church in Saint-Marc," Eli answered. "The boys and I got here a few hours ago. David filled us in on what happened. That's messed up. I'm sorry, bro." Eli sat down in a chair beside Jed's bed. "Ben suggested that someone keep an eye on you while you got some sleep So, naturally, seeing as how I can't resist watching a grown man sleep, I volunteered."

That got Jed laughing. Damn, it felt good.

"I'm surprised Grayson didn't arm wrestle you for the privilege," Jed said.

"Oh, he tried, but I whupped his skinny redneck ass in one second flat."

"I'm glad you're here," Jed said, holding out his fist for a bump, which Eli obliged.

"Man, I'm just sorry we didn't get here sooner. I can't stop thinking that if I'd been here, none of this would have happened."

"Don't go there," Jed said. "It's the life we all chose. Comes with the territory . . . That said, now that you're here, I think it's time to end this. I'm taking that psycho Voudou chick down."

"I hear you," Eli said. "We can definitely work that into the mission package."

"Mission package?" Jed asked, screwing up his face. "How long have I been asleep?"

Eli grinned and was about to say something when a knock shook the thin bedroom door.

"Come in," Jed called.

The door swept open, and Ben Morvant walked into the room.

"Ben? How did you get here?"

"Hey, Jed," the Shepherd commander said, then added, "Wow, you look like death."

"Is this a glimpse of my future? Zombie jokes for the rest of my days?"

"Oh, I'm sorry," Ben said with a wry grin, "did I dig my own grave with that one?"

Jed shook his head but laughed despite himself.

"Take my chair, boss," Eli said, rising from his bedside seat. "I'll leave y'all to talk in private. Besides, I'm starving."

Jed gave Eli a nod, then turned his attention to a seated Ben Morvant.

"How are you feeling?" Ben asked.

The SEAL in Jed was about to say that he was *five by*, but the look on Ben's face told him they both knew that was a lie. So, Jed erred on the side of blunt candor.

"I don't know . . ."

Ben nodded. "Good, because if you'd said otherwise, I'd put you on the next flight home. Do you want to talk about it?"

Jed considered the question, then said, "Yes, actually, I do."

Ben had many remarkable gifts, but being a good listener was probably his finest. Jed decided not to hold back and told the Shepherd commander everything—no filter, no sugarcoating things, he just let it all spill out raw and real. When he'd finished, Jed let out a shaky breath.

Instead of saying something to reassure him, Ben leaned forward, laid a hand on Jed's chest, and closed his eyes.

"Lord and Father, I ask that you let me lift this burden of trauma from your warrior servant so that he might find respite from the tempest of emotion and angst he's battling. Amen."

"Amen," Jed echoed as Ben removed his hand.

It was a simple prayer, but like Ben's counsel, it was honest, concise, and laser-focused. The relief Jed felt was instantaneous and palpable—like someone had removed a two-hundred-pound yoke from his shoulders.

"Thank you," Jed said, meeting Ben's eyes after.

"Don't thank me—I'm just the conduit."

"I know, but I'm thanking you for being here for me in my darkest hour."

Ben shook his head. "As far as I understand, Sarah Beth is the one who earned that distinction. And it's David and Gayle who saved you with her guidance. I'm just the boss who showed up late to the party."

"On a wing and a prayer, huh?"

"Something like that," Ben said and repositioned in his chair. Jed saw something else in his friend's eyes—something he didn't recognize. Where Ben's eyes usually sparkled with an almost literal light, instead he saw some sort of cloudlike darkness.

Then the moment was gone.

"Jed, I think it goes without saying that what you've stumbled into here is more than just missing orphan kids. Dark forces are at work in Haiti, but there are things in play right now, things happening in the shadows, that are even bigger still."

"Bigger how?" Jed asked.

Ben answered the question by bringing Jed up to speed on everything that Trinity Loop had been working on while Jed and the rest of Joshua Bravo were on vacation.

"The chaos that we—and the Watchers—sensed was real. In the vacuum left by Victor's destruction, the Dark Ones are working feverishly to regroup. I led an operation in Paris to take out a group of Victor's lieutenants. Unwittingly, we interrupted the next Rising . . ."

"Rising?" Jed asked, but he suspected he knew what Ben was implying before he asked. "So, they've chosen a new Victor?"

The thought that the Dark Ones had already found their next general was overwhelming—like being told you still had another six months on a deployment that was supposed to end in two days.

"We don't think so—not yet," Ben said. "We interfered with the ceremony but paid a price doing so."

"Casualties?" Jed asked. But the connection between him and Ben was strong. He knew already.

"Two dead and one wounded."

In a flash, Jed could see their faces—maybe from Ben's mind, maybe from some other source. But he also felt the terrible weight of loss on his friend and mentor.

Jed let out a long, rattling sigh.

When they defeated Victor in the halls of St. George's, he'd not been so foolish as to believe that victory won the war. The battle between good and evil, between God and Satan, had raged for thousands of years and would continue until the end times. The dark would try and separate as many people from God and His grace as possible, and God would use believers throughout the world, including the Shepherds, to be His light and bring the truth about His love and grace to as many as they could. But Jed had thought—at a minimum—defeating Victor would have earned the Shepherds a respite. He'd thought that they could take a breath while the Dark Ones licked their wounds and found a new direction. He saw now how naive that was—on all their parts. God never stopped working in the world, but evil, too, never took a rest. This was a battle that would continue until the end, the end prophesied by John in his revelation. And for warriors like Jed, they were never out of the fight.

Victor's defeat had left chaos in its wake, ironically creating a fresh opportunity for evil to exploit. The patterns and threads the Shepherds were familiar with under Victor's reign had been disrupted by his demise, and the chaos, change, and uncertainty had rendered the Shepherds less capable than before.

The irony would be funny if it weren't so bitter.

"Who might they choose to take Victor's place?"

Ben shrugged. "We have a list of Dark Ones it *could* be—like Gunther Schmidt in Germany—but it's far from complete or even accurate."

"Where and when will they try again?"

Ben sighed and rose to pace. Jed thought maybe he understood the cloud in the man's eyes a little better now. "I don't know," he said. "We'd thought the Paris operation would be a once-in-a-lifetime opportunity to wipe out a slew of potential leaders. It failed. And what you have going on here is just more proof that without the leadership, evil flourishes on its own, finding all sorts of ways to battle against God and His children."

"What can we do, boss?" Jed asked.

Ben let the pause hang in the air and took a seat, making a slight middle-aged grunt as he did.

"We let the Watchers keep looking. We prosecute with conventional ISR when and where we can and deploy our new SMU with laser-guided focus"—he gave a nod to Jed—"as potential targets emerge. This is a fight that goes all the way to the end, Jed."

Jed thought about that a moment. "You came a long way to tell me that, boss," he said, the statement a question.

Ben nodded.

"I think you were right when we spoke last, Jed. I think God brought you here for a reason. You've uncovered something dark in Haiti. Dark Ones are targeting and disappearing children. I want to save those kids, but also find out why. And"—he looked at Jed, the darkness becoming full-on storm clouds in his eyes—"we'll exact violence of action on those who would do such a thing." He placed a hand on Jed's shoulder. "And maybe some payback for what happened to you. The Dark Ones don't kidnap a Shepherd, bury him alive, and escape without repercussions."

"Vengeance?" Jed asked, his voice low and intense. That felt wrong somehow.

"Why not?" Ben said, his voice a low growl on a cello. "We've bled enough. We lost our friends Marcello and Kaprica, we lost teammates and brothers from Gideon Bravo, and we damn near lost you. Enough is enough."

Jed nodded, not sure what to say.

Ben rose.

"We have a lead I want to prosecute—a mansion compound owned by Athaliah Guerrier. Spiritual ISR indicates kids from Amour et Espoir Children's Home have been transferred there. Satellite surveillance shows a robust security presence—roving patrols and armed guards. Yes, we've been busy while you've been recovering, my friend," Ben said with a crooked grin. "My plan is to hit that compound, rescue those kids, and learn once and for all what the Dark Ones are up to in Haiti."

Jed felt a swell of precombat anticipation, but before he could get a word out, Ben put a hand on Jed's shoulder.

"Jed, as much as it pains me to say this, you need to sit this one out."

Jed's cheeks flushed with heat. "What! Why?"

Ben gave him a look that said, *Do I really have to spell it out for you, brother?*

"I'm five by, I swear," Jed said, sitting up straight and clenching his fists into wrecking balls at the ready. "The effects of the drugs have worn off, and you just took care of my messy headspace. I'm fired up and ready to go, boss."

"Jed, we both know that's not true. My heart tells me you might be more of a liability than an asset on tonight's op."

"I'm the best op—" Jed almost said it, but he caught himself, thank God.

"You're the best *what*?" Ben said, lifting an eyebrow.

Jed took one centering breath and said, "What I meant to say was that despite what happened, I'm combat-ready. I'm the team leader, and the team looks to me in these situations. What would it say about me if I stayed in bed while they risked their lives? *And* I have a connection to the principals here. I've encountered this Calypso and know her better than anyone. I've connected with some of the kids involved—the boy in DR, the mother of Emelin, and a girl named Sani, who has almost Watcher-level gifts. Please, Ben, you've got to trust me. I need this, but you need me more."

Ben pursed his lips. After an uncomfortably long pause, he said, "All right, we're briefing at the dining room table in thirty minutes. Why don't you check in with Sarah Beth—I know she's waiting to talk to you—then get dressed and join us."

"Roger that, sir."

"I think we've moved beyond *sir*, Jed, don't you?" Ben said, giving Jed's arm a pat.

"Old habits . . ." Jed said with a smile.

He watched Ben leave. The instant the Shepherd commander shut the door behind him, Jed collapsed, exhausted, against the headboard, his stomach muscles near to cramping. The truth was he wasn't combat-ready—at least not physically—and he could only pray his body would be close to 100 percent by go time.

CHAPTER FIFTY-ONE

PALÈ NANM PÈDI YO [PALACE OF LOST SOULS]

ROUTE AMANI-Y BEACH

OVERLOOKING BAIE DE SAINT-MARC

THREE MILES EAST OF SAINT-MARC CITY, HAITI

2009 HOURS LOCAL

Madame Athaliah did not believe in destiny.

Destiny meant accepting a repugnant truth that her entire life was scripted. If her life was scripted, then the choices she'd made, the sacrifices she'd endured, and the meticulous plans she'd spent years plotting and orchestrating were somehow not her own. And if her choices, sacrifices, and plans were not her own, then how could she be measured on her merits by the Dark Prince? Only the weak-minded and the fearful took comfort in destiny.

Forfeiting one's life to fate is the fellowship of fools, she thought as she toured her estate's grounds, checking every last detail.

On this point, both dark and light divinity were in total agreement.

The greatest gift bestowed upon humankind was free will. Why this wasn't understood by the masses was baffling because it had always been obvious to her. The battle that had raged for millennia between God and the Dark Prince was simply a battle to influence people's *choice.* Every soul birthed into the world was granted a divine choice. On the one hand, there was light and meekness, and on the other darkness and power. Choose the light and you will receive love, but also a lifetime of undeserved pain and disappointment. Choose the dark and you get justice and permission to fight back against those who would see you fail, stumble, and suffer. Unlike God, the Dark Prince empowered his followers to question the rules and keep their winnings. How could any player love a gamemaster who demanded they play by rules that virtually guaranteed losing? What sort of sick deity demands his acolytes be lambs rather than lions in a dog-eat-dog world?

God is a sadist.

Athaliah had learned this at a very young age.

At least the Dark Prince was honest. Life is a battle to the death, and his only expectation is that you fight. Contrary to popular belief, the devil doesn't have a problem with love. His gripe is with weakness, with passivity, with forgiving those who do not deserve to be forgiven. Athaliah had devoted much of her life to loving and caring for those whom she believed deserved it, and that had never been a problem. Take the children she'd rescued, for example. Without her, they'd be condemned to a life of poverty, hunger, filth, and abuse. As members of her flock, they would grow up as strong and capable warriors.

Like Calypso.

And Viden, who even now helped her plan for her covert ascension to power. His loyalty would be rewarded.

That is fairness—and justice.

A staccato of rapidly approaching footfalls on marble tile caused her to turn and look over her shoulder.

"Manbo Athaliah," a young devotee named Charles said in greeting. "The final delegation has arrived from São Paulo. The perimeter is secure, and the VIP is being escorted to his chambers as we speak."

"Very well," she said. "See to it that he is brought refreshments and inform him and his second that they honor us with their presence."

"Yes, madame. Right away, madame," Charles said and hurried off.

She glanced at her watch: 8:11 p.m.

It was hard to fathom that in less than two hours the ceremony to choose Victor's replacement would happen at her mansion. She'd spent nearly a decade planning and positioning chess pieces for the Rising but never thought it could happen here, at home. It made her believe that Satan might well be rooting for her and her plan.

She was not in the running for the position at the Rising, of course. No woman had ever been chosen. In fact, she would not even be allowed a seat at the table or to witness the ceremony—a fact that galled her.

No matter, she told herself, for she was the invisible hand working in the background to ensure that her chosen candidate ascended to power.

Just like the Dark Prince we all serve—I am here, in the shadows, controlling . . . everything.

That irony was simply too delicious and brought a smile to her face.

All six candidates were brutal, conniving, and despicable men—but none of them were in the same league as Victor. She had feared Victor like everyone, and unlike the others, Victor had long ago recognized her ambition. He'd understood her desire to supplant him, and he had taken steps to isolate her sphere of influence to the little island of Haiti. His longevity had forced her to be patient. Many times over the years, she'd come close to giving up and accepting the cold reality that the legion of demons inside Victor, giving him an unnaturally long life, would fuel his reign for decades beyond her own death.

But then, something miraculous and unexpected had happened. A little girl from Tennessee, against all logic, had done what centuries of God's greatest warriors had been unable to do and dispatched the most powerful Dark One on earth.

The power in the child both excited and terrified Athaliah.

Victor had also recognized the girl as a threat to him, possibly even presaging the fact that Sarah Beth Yarnell would lead to his demise. Undoubtedly, it was why he'd taken her and brought her to one of his many secret compounds. Instead of simply killing her, like he should have done, his curiosity had gotten the better of him. He'd wanted to understand her gifts, corrupt her mind and heart, and turn her into his weapon.

Athaliah might judge him a fool for such hubris, if not for the fact that she had similar desires and designs at play even now. The dark Watcher operation in Haiti was her experiment in trying to harness the gifts of the Spirit for her own exploits. At first blush, such a goal might seem impossible, for the gifts of the Spirit certainly could not be used for spreading evil and chaos. But she believed there was a gray area—a loophole, so to speak—to be exploited. With the right approach, she was confident she could tap into her children's gifts.

Like everything else, this was a question of free will.

Regardless of how her little experiment turned out, she would prevail in the end. Because every child she brought into her flock was no longer available for God to call upon for *His* purpose. God gifted for purpose, she knew, and if nothing else, her operation was keeping these gifted children off the battlefield.

But with any luck, they might become so much more. Time would tell.

All that really mattered tonight was that Victor was gone. She didn't have a crystal ball, but she'd whispered promises and veiled threats to influence all the voting members of the council. Ultimately, she'd tipped the scales by giving Jules Moreau credit for anticipating the Shepherds' intervention in the Paris catacombs. Had the Dark Rising taken place there as originally planned, all the principals would be dead, and they knew it.

Mateo Santos, with his position at the UN, would be a much more capable leader than Moreau, but he was not as easily influenced as the Frenchman. Above all else, Moreau loved indulging his vices. As a man who'd devoted his life to the pursuit of carnal pleasure, Athaliah knew he would quickly tire of the rigors and burden of command. When it came to charm, Moreau had no equal, but as a tactician, he was lost. His renowned strategic genius was a well-crafted fiction and one of Athaliah's own design. He could not reign without her counsel, and they both knew it. After tonight, she would be the one running the show, and he would take all the credit.

The arrangement suited them both fine. Theirs was a union of strengths. He brought his male pedigree, charisma, and political connections. She, with her formidable mind and dark gifts, brought the real power.

Everything was going according to plan.

Calypso had taken care of the one nagging threat—the rogue Shepherd who'd stumbled into her orbit. By the time Trinity realized their nosy, vacationing operator was dead, the Dark Rising would be over, and all the principals would have returned home to their safeholds. Her contact in the Haitian president's office would notify her of any American threats arriving in their country. And if that failed, she believed her kids could warn her of impending danger.

She smiled as she ascended the grand staircase to the second story, where the guest rooms were located. The time had come to greet each of the important guests in person and pay her respects. After trading gossip and getting assurances that the vote would go the way she wanted, she would visit Jules Moreau's suite last—to pledge her undying loyalty by sating his carnal lust.

CHAPTER FIFTY-TWO

NEW SHEPHERDS SAFE HOUSE

EBEN-EZER BAPTIST CHURCH OF SAINT-MARC

RUE SAVANNAH

SAINT-MARC, HAITI

1732 HOURS LOCAL

David found it hard to sit in the busy room, a makeshift TOC where Gayle and the Shepherds busied themselves with preparing for the upcoming mission.

Since rescuing Jed from the grave, David's headspace had been a mess. On the outside, he was all smiles and *Rah-rah, go team!* but on the inside, he was a thunderstorm. He was happy for Jed but also conflicted and annoyed. He wanted to be recognized for his contribution to Jed's rescue, but for some reason, Sarah Beth and Gayle seemed to be getting all the accolades. On the one hand, he was so incredibly proud of his daughter. Without her spiritual gifts and courage, they would never have found the grave where Jed was buried before the oxygen ran out. And if he was being honest with himself, Gayle had been the architect of the rescue plan.

But David had stepped up too. He'd vanquished a Dark One—a demon-possessed super warrior from hell—and in the process, he'd saved Gayle's life.

I did something that not even every blooded Shepherd has done . . . I killed a Dark One. And I didn't use a gun either.

In triumphing over a Dark One in hand-to-hand combat, David had entered elite company. What he'd done was laudable and worthy of praise, so why hadn't Morvant personally congratulated him or, at the very least, thanked him for his contribution and courage?

He felt a hand on his shoulder and turned to find Jed standing behind him, towering over him as usual.

"Can we talk for a second?" Jed said, gesturing with his head to an empty corner away from the table and mostly out of earshot from the others.

"Sure," David said and followed his friend away from the din.

"I didn't get a chance to before, but I wanted to thank you for rescuing me," Jed said, and before David could respond, Jed pulled him in for a crushing bear hug.

"You're welcome," David said, giving Jed's back a pat. "For a minute there, I was pretty sure we'd lost you."

"If you hadn't come when you did, I think you would have," Jed said as he released his grip.

Here comes the gushing about Sarah Beth . . .

"You know, Gayle, um, told me what happened and what you did. She said you took on a Dark One and saved her life."

"She said that?" David said, pride blossoming in his chest.

"She did," Jed said with a nod and close-lipped smile.

"What?" David said, feeling suddenly awkward.

"Ah . . . I know it's your first time killing a man, David. So, if you need to talk about it, I'm here for you."

David chuckled. "Well, I don't really consider that *thing* a man."

"Still," Jed said and clapped a hand on David's shoulder. "Violence of action can be traumatic on the psyche when you're not accustomed to it. I still remember my first time."

David nodded. "Thank you, Jed, for sharing that. I'll probably take you up on that sometime."

"There's something else we probably should discuss," Jed said, his expression hardening.

"Sure, fire away."

He's going to tell me that he needs me to look after Gayle while he goes on the op so I'll feel value. But in reality, he's afraid I'm going to ask to come along. I'm not an idiot, Jed. I see right through your little mind games . . .

"Ben doesn't think I'm ready—emotionally or physically—to participate in tonight's op. He *encouraged* me to sit this one out, in fact," Jed said in a low voice. "What do you think?"

David nodded and felt unexpectedly buoyed inside. This wasn't the talk he was expecting to have at all. Jed was asking him for guidance, something the larger-than-life operator never did.

Counseling 101: Always answer their first question with a question.

"I'm happy to give you my opinion on the matter," David said, "but the more important question is: Do *you* think you're ready, physically and emotionally, to participate in the op?"

Jed responded with a heavy exhale. "I'm not one hundred percent in either category. To say otherwise would be a lie."

"I'm glad you're being honest with yourself," David said. "If you had to put a number on your readiness, what number would that be?"

"Physically, I'm not sure. I feel like the drugs are out of my system now, but I'm concerned I won't really know until I need to be kinetic. My concern is that my reflexes and reaction time might be impacted, rather than how I'll perform cardiovascularly or stamina-wise at this point."

David nodded. He'd not considered the distinction. Having tasted combat now for the first time, he could see how reaction time would be critical for a Shepherd when facing off against any enemy, especially the Dark Ones.

"Maybe you can ask Eli or Grayson to do a little sparring with you. If they're slapping you around like a chump, I think you'll have your answer."

"Good idea, David. I hadn't thought of that," Jed said.

"Do you want to discuss the emotional readiness side of the equation?" David asked, not letting Jed off the hook that easy.

Jed looked down at his hands. "Obviously, what happened to me was pretty humiliating."

David's eyes widened in disbelief. This humility and vulnerability wasn't what he'd expected from a blooded Navy SEAL. "Is that really how you feel?" he asked, still shocked by the confession. "Because, Jed, that's not how anyone else here looks at what was done to you. Seriously, Jed, I'm relieved to hear that from you."

"I don't understand," Jed said, screwing up his face.

"Look, if I was in your shoes, the trauma of the experience would totally trump any insecurity I might be feeling about what that devil priestess did to me." David clapped a hand on Jed's shoulder. "Dude, you surrendered yourself to save us. You literally traded your life for mine and Gayle's—if that's not the ultimate expression of courage, honor, and strength, I don't know what is."

Jed slow-nodded. "Yeah, but I didn't fight back."

"Not didn't . . . *couldn't*. By choosing not to fight, you

bought us and yourself time—time that gave me and Gayle a chance to regroup and rescue you. What you risked and suffered for us is something we can never repay. I was worried about how you were handling the aftermath of being buried alive. *That* was the trauma I assumed you were wrangling with."

"Well, that's bothering me too," Jed said with a sigh. "It's not that I'm claustrophobic, and I'm not afraid of death. But to be powerless . . . completely and totally powerless, unable to even blink. That was disturbing."

"I can only imagine the hell you experienced, but you beat it, Jed. You harnessed your mental toughness and persevered. What's the SEAL mantra—adapt and overcome? That's exactly what you did."

"Thanks, David. I needed to hear that," Jed said, forcing a smile.

"Of course, and it needed to be said. But, Jed, regarding the question of whether you should sit out tonight's op, I think the only way to answer that is to be honest with yourself. In the Shepherds, we're not the military. This enemy can exploit emotional and psychological vulnerabilities that a normal enemy cannot. If in doubt, I'd stay behind."

"I understand. Thanks for the counsel, brother," Jed said.

David saw Jed's gaze tick to Gayle, who was sitting at the nearby table working on her laptop, but also patiently biding her time for her turn with Jed.

"Anytime," David said. He could practically feel Jed's anxiety recede as the big man walked over to see Gayle.

There's something budding between those two, David thought with a satisfied smile.

He'd dismissed the idea before, when the three of them had hung out in the first safe house's kitchen, but seeing how they looked at each other now, it was obvious to David there was a spark. And he was glad for it, because a romantic relationship between Jed and Gayle would definitely be a positive development for David and his family.

Do I feel challenged as both a husband and a father because of Jed?

Yes.

Should I?

Most definitely . . .

Another woman demanding Jed's time and attention would take the pressure off. And unlike Maria Perez, this new CIA liaison had been conventionally and spiritually vetted. Jed didn't know that, but David did. The Shepherds couldn't afford another Maria Perez penetrating their ranks, so Morvant had ordered the vetting before allowing Gayle continued access. Having now spent time with Gayle himself, David thought a relationship with the CIA liaison might actually be as good for Jed as it would be for the Yarnell family. She was smart, tenacious, and brave. On top of that, Jed and Gayle seemed to click.

It's time to say goodbye to the Three Musketeers, he thought with a hopeful smile. *And say hello to the Fantastic Four.*

Realizing he was staring at them, David walked to the kitchenette and grabbed a bottled water. The conflicted emotions and prideful insecurity he'd felt just moments before were now both greatly diminished. Jed had come to him for counsel, and David had given it. Instead of Jed being the one uplifting David, for once the tables had turned and *he* was the strong one.

Maybe we've finally turned the corner.

Maybe . . .

CHAPTER FIFTY-THREE

NEW SHEPHERDS SAFE HOUSE

EBEN-EZER BAPTIST CHURCH OF SAINT-MARC

RUE SAVANNAH

SAINT-MARC, HAITI

1932 HOURS LOCAL

The church on Rue Savannah had been turned over to them completely, something that Jed guessed Ben might explain one day. Jed knew he still was seeing a very small percentage of the connections that the centuries-old Shepherds had around the world—both in churches and governments. Frankly, he was content with not knowing. While he may be curious, he was a door kicker—a man of action. The big picture was for head shed–types like Ben.

The safe house was working out great. They needed the open space of the fellowship hall for high-level planning. The rest of the team—Shepherds from both Joshua Bravo and Gideon Alpha, as well as the support personnel who'd arrived with Jed's teammates—were all hard at work with an intense, special-operations energy that made Jed feel at home. The operators who would soon go out into the fight were either upstairs relaxing in a recreational room or doing gear checks of the weapons and gear staged in, of all places, the sanctuary. Some were in prayer in the makeshift bunk room.

Or maybe the bunk room had always been there. It occurred to Jed that this place felt more like a permanent, military-style staging area than a safe house that had been hastily thrown together. Another question for Ben, and another Jed was unlikely to ever ask.

He glanced at the leader of Shepherds North America and felt a tug of concern at Ben's brooding face.

He's just in mission mode, Jed rationalized.

In any case, Jed welcomed the relative quiet now that it was just him, Ben, Eli, Jeremy Turner from Gideon, Gayle, and David around the large wooden table. The six of them were crowded around one end, facing the three laptops streaming in key players from both Trinity Loop and St. George's.

Julia Nesbitt, the Shepherds North America director of intelligence, took control from the start.

"We have some new and rather vital intel to share with you, Ben," she said, looking out from the center laptop screen at the assembled.

Jed tried to determine whether her face reflected something grim or exciting. He always had trouble reading the neutral mask the intelligence director habitually wore.

"I hope it's that Athaliah is present on the compound. There is no doubt in my mind whatsoever that she is the key player in all of this," Jed said, reflexively rubbing his eyes, which were still plagued by what felt like phantom nerve effects from Calypso's zombie powder.

I'm not 100 percent. David's right about that. But my 90 percent is more than enough . . .

"Oh, she's there. But it's much bigger than that, Jed."

Everyone exchanged glances. David held Jed's eyes a beat longer than most.

"Athaliah arrived at her compound early this morning," Julia continued. "She flew into the main airport by private jet and then used her personal helicopter to bring her to the compound. But that's just where we started. We had trouble locating her for a while because our search focused on Haiti and her known associates. It was actually the team working the Paris hit who made the connection . . ."

Jed found waiting for the next bit of information unbearable, but some secret voice inside him whispered he already knew where this was headed.

"Ben, I feel this was a true God moment, getting you and Gideon to Haiti in time for what's happening," Nesbitt said, finally cutting to the chase. "We believe the Dark Rising has been relocated to Palè Nanm Pèdi—Athaliah's compound—and that it will happen tonight."

Jed looked at Ben and saw the man he'd come to love as both a brother and his leader close his eyes, his head nodding gently.

"Of course . . ." Ben said.

"What in the hell is a Dark Rising?" Gayle asked, confusion in her voice. They'd been asking her to suspend quite a bit of disbelief the last week, after all. But what she'd seen since then must surely make all of it more palatable, right?

Jed gave her a gentle smile and hoped his eyes showed he understood her confusion.

"We can fill in specific details later, but the long and short of it is that the Dark Rising is the selection and coronation ceremony to replace Victor, the . . . *terrorist* leader who led the attacks with the directed energy weapon, the attacks on us, and the recent assault on St. George's Academy."

Nice touch using the label terrorist, Jed thought as they walked Gayle into their world step by step.

"He was also responsible for the attack on the Vatican not long ago . . ." Eli added.

"And he's responsible for hundreds of other attacks over the last three hundred years," Jed added, holding her eyes.

"Wait . . . I'm sorry, did you say the last three hundred years?"

Jed nodded gently and mouthed the word, *Later.*

Gayle blinked twice and turned back to the screen. "Okay, sorry, so this is Victor's successor, and he's getting crowned at some ceremony that you thought was in Paris, but now believe is happening tonight, here at Athaliah's compound in Saint-Marc."

"Yes," Julia said, unfazed by Gayle's incredulous tone. "Ben and Jeremy were both involved in the Paris op, but let me explain how we made the connection. The Paris team searched all sorts of intelligence streams, of course, including unusual people coming in and out of Paris around the time we *thought* the Rising would occur in the Paris catacombs. One that got interest was the private jet for the president of Haiti . . ."

"Wait, you're saying that Claude Marion—the prime minister and acting president of Haiti—is involved?" Gayle asked, but Julia held up a hand.

"Not strange, actually, that he traveled to Paris. It turns out that with the wealth he has amassed from the Haitian people and the country, he does quite a bit of international jet-setting. What was very odd was that, when we dug deeper, there were only three passengers on board—two Haitians we have precious little information on . . . and one Athaliah Guerrier."

"When did she arrive in Paris?" Ben asked.

"A few hours ahead of the operation. She never disembarked, then left shortly after, connecting through Tenerife, the same way she flew in. She was on the ground at Tenerife for two and a half hours, but again never disembarked. She then flew back to Haiti. They dropped her and the other two men on the manifest at the airport in Saint-Marc, where she took her private helicopter back to Palè Nanm Pèdi."

Ben stood and began pacing. This was out of character for the laid-back head of the Shepherds, and the motion made Jed uncomfortable for some reason.

"So, that would definitely seem to connect her to the Dark Rising, I agree," Ben said, moving back and forth behind the leadership team. "And it increases the importance of the mission tonight since she is now linked directly to the Dark Ones at the leadership level, so we're all in to go get her. But that's still a long way from concluding that the Rising is happening at her home."

"I'm getting to that," Julia said, nodding her agreement. "Once we made the connection, we merged the intel teams running signals and other forms of conventional intel for both the Haiti and Paris operations. We also got help from Ms. James's office at the CIA and, of course, our Watchers program. Ben, two of the men on the list as possible successors to Victor—Gunther Schmidt and Mateo Santos—have been identified arriving in Saint-Marc earlier today with a contingent of security. There are four others—not on our radar but certainly not people expected to be traveling to Haiti—who also arrived today. The small airport at Saint-Marc has had one of its busiest days in its history, with six large corporate jets arriving almost simultaneously. I wish we had had satellite coverage over Haiti to confirm movement of all these groups from the airport to Palè Nanm Pèdi, but at least our satellite is in place now, so we should get eyes on for facial recognition of anybody standing outside we can send along. We also have conventional HUMINT trying to exploit assets . . ."

"The Dark Ones are at the compound," Ben said, leaning his hands on the table now. "You're right. The Rising is here. And I feel you're also correct that God moved us into the place where and when we needed to be."

Jed knew it too. He didn't know how—though he had an idea—but he was certain of it.

"I agree," Jed said.

"Me too," David chimed in.

"The Watchers agree as well, Ben," Jean-Baptiste Allard added from the laptop screen to the right. "They found a thread on the Dark One who detected Watcher Two on your op. We sent Watcher One in because he seems tuned to Watcher Two." Jed wondered if Allard was intentionally keeping names confidential because they were streaming the conference or because Gayle was present. "Watcher One was successful, and we can confirm that the Dark One known as Viden is present at Palè Nanm Pèdi . . ."

"And CISA has confirmed communications between Athaliah and Viden," Julia added.

"Yes," Allard said. "Watcher Two has also made contact with one of the children present at the compound."

"Tell us everything you know," Jed said. He was fine that they left names and identifiers of the Watchers out of the conversation but didn't want Gayle's presence to inhibit a free flow of information. "Ms. James is fully read in now on *all* aspects of our operations."

"Understood, Jed," Allard said.

Ben took his seat, and a grin spread across his face. He radiated more energy than Jed could remember seeing in a long time.

"Tell us everything you have, Julia. Then we'll get to work on our strike package."

CHAPTER FIFTY-FOUR

STAGING ZONE

A HALF MILE FROM PALÈ NANM PÈDI YO (PALACE OF LOST SOULS)

THREE MILES EAST OF SAINT-MARC CITY, HAITI

2142 HOURS LOCAL

Jed crouched next to Eli in the thick Haitian rainforest, waiting for the signal from Ben—though what felt like jungle only surrounded a half-mile perimeter of the property at Palè Nanm Pèdi. That didn't change the fact that the air was practically suffocating it was so hot, humid, and thick with bugs. And the foliage was so dense it obstructed his view of the ground and distance vision.

So long as I don't step on a damn snake, I can live with the rest.

He glanced at Eli, one of the first Shepherds he'd met and now his teammate and friend. The man was a beast of an operator, but with a heart as big as the sky.

Jed hadn't had the time to catch up with everyone in his squad like he'd wished, but he'd at least been able to hug it out with everyone and let them know he was beyond relieved to have the band back together. Despite coming from different locations, they'd all made it to the safe house in time for the op. In addition to Eli, everyone in Joshua Bravo—Grayson, Hyeon, Carl, Nisha, Bex, and Johnny—was rested and healthy.

Everyone except for me . . .

For tonight's raid, Jed was the OIC for the Striker Bravo platoon while Ben led the overall mission as well as Striker Alpha, which was comprised of Gideon Alpha Shepherds, the same shooters who'd participated in the failed catacombs raid. The tension in the safe house before the infil had been palpable. Ben and Jed weren't the only Shepherds looking for payback tonight. The Gideon Alpha boys were itching for a fight.

No matter what happened, one thing was certain: Tonight, blood would be shed.

"Bravo Seven is Eagle One," Carl said on the comms circuit, reporting from well ahead that he was now in position as their sniper overwatch. "Good lines on the south perimeter and all target structures as briefed."

The former Marine sniper had taken position south of the compound with lines on the front gate, main drive, the front elevation of the main house, and the southern-facing sides of the two other buildings that made up the sprawling estate. The three buildings were arranged in a C layout with the house in front and the additional quarters behind, one to the east and the other west.

"Check, Eagle One," Jed answered in his boom mike.

Not sixty seconds later, the Gideon Alpha sniper called in as Eagle Two and let everyone know he was set to cover the northern side of the compound.

Tonight, Jed and the rest of the Shepherds were kitted up in full battle rattle—including helmets with NVGs, assault rifles, body armor including Kevlar gauntlets on their forearms and neck guards for battling Dark Ones, and a kit full of extra ammo, grenades, and flash-bangs. Damn, it was good to feel like a SEAL again. In the last year, most of Joshua Bravo's missions had been of the spooky variety—with Jed and his team traveling under NOCs, dressed in civilian clothes, and armed only with concealed pistols. After a decade and a half operating as a SEAL, he felt practically naked conducting fieldwork like that.

Of all the adjustments he'd had to make to become a Shepherd, not kitting up regularly was one he still struggled with. That seemed unlikely to change after tonight, with Joshua Bravo slated to be the low-profile SMU unit going forward. But tonight, he got to be an operator—and Jed felt thankful for that blessing.

The other difference between tonight's op and a conventional SEAL op was that the Shepherds had real-time spiritual ISR support in the field. Corbin and Sarah Beth, call signs Watcher One and Two, were working "remotely" with them from the Watcher TOC at St. George's Academy. Just like they'd supported Ben's Paris operation, the two Watcher superstars had volunteered to support tonight's operation as well.

"Jed, I'm back from my surveillance run," Sarah Beth said in his head. *"I'm going to report what I saw on the radio, okay?"*

"Yes, do it," he answered. *"Where are you, by the way?"*

"Kneeling right beside you," she said.

"Cool . . ." he said, wishing he could see her. Actually, he wished he could do what she did and make spiritual scouting runs of his own.

"Striker, this is Watcher Two," Sarah Beth announced on comms from the Watcher TOC in Tennessee. "I finished my external surveillance run, and I counted ten men with machine guns moving around the compound outside. Six were walking the perimeter, two were at the front of the main house, and two were wandering around the back," she said, giving a pretty good report, in Jed's opinion, for a thirteen-year-old with no military training.

"Copy all. Great job, Watcher Two," Ben said.

The unique way that Ben interfaced with the Watcher kids was not lost on Jed. Ben treated them with respect, but he was also intentional about providing positive reinforcement. Sarah Beth and Corbin both desperately wanted to prove they were mature and grown-up, but they were still teens. Teenage insecurity and inexperience became tactical concerns on an op where the men and women in harm's way were blooded operators with decades of experience. Ben understood all of this and modulated his leadership to match the maturity and needs of the individual, whether Watcher or Shepherd.

"Watcher One, what did you see?" Ben asked, prompting Corbin for a sitrep on the interior of the compound building she was tasked with surveilling.

"Hang tight, I'm still inside," Corbin said after a beat, and Jed wondered how difficult it was to shift back and forth between her projected self and her body back at St. George's.

Jed wondered what would be next for Corbin when she "aged out" as a Watcher. Would she be able to walk away from all she'd done and been exposed to in the role? Or would Ben invite the young woman into the Shepherd pipeline in some capacity? Only God knew whether Corbin would take that step or not—but if she did, Jed suspected that with proper conditioning and tactical training, future Corbin Worth could be every bit as capable an operator as Nisha and Bex.

"Take your time, Watcher One," Ben came back.

Jed glanced at his watch. They were three minutes behind schedule, but time wasn't a major factor for this hit. Whether they prevented the Dark Rising was irrelevant, because the plan was to kill every last Dark One on the property. No quarter given, no HVTs designated to be taken off the X, especially since experience told them that was nearly impossible. When Nisha had asked what the ROE for the op was, Ben's three-word response had been cold and clinical:

"Kill them all."

Jed was fine with that. After the brutality inflicted on Kaprica and Marcello, the kidnapping of local kids, and the trauma Calypso had perpetrated against him, Jed's need for retribution was as powerful as it had ever been. A part of him worried about the dark pull he felt in his heart, but another part of him leaned into it, rationalizing it as the mental and emotional equivalent of putting his war paint on.

These people are the epitome of evil. The sooner we send them to hell, the better.

"Striker, Watcher One—I completed my scout, and I've never seen so many Dark Ones. They're everywhere, even the guards are demon-possessed. It's going to be very dangerous," Corbin said, and Jed could hear the strain in her voice.

"We understand, Watcher One," Ben said. "Thank you for being honest. Did you find the location of the principal targets?"

"Check. The principal targets are all assembled in the main dining room on the first floor. Thirteen Dark Ones are gathered inside. The room is not hardened, but it is guarded by six Dark Ones with machine guns. The high-value target from the brief, Athaliah Guerrier, is inside the main house, but she does not appear to be part of the ceremony. She seems to be waiting in an office with a man. The other HVT of interest, Calypso, is nowhere to be found," Corbin said.

Jed felt his jaw tighten at the last statement.

If Calypso's not here . . . where is she?

"Striker platoons, infil to Calvary," Ben said, directing the strike force to proceed to the next checkpoint just outside the perimeter in preparation for the breach.

"Bravo One," Jed said, acknowledging the order for his platoon. He turned to Eli. "See you on the other side. Good luck."

"You too," Eli said with a toothy grin and rose to his feet.

The plan was to split Bravo platoon into two elements that would breach the southern perimeter fence at two offset locations. Jed would lead Grayson, Nisha, and Bex while Eli would take point of his four-man squad with Johnny, Hyeon, and an augment from Gideon Alpha named Rick. With so many Dark Ones patrolling the breach, the odds of completing a stealth infil had dropped significantly. Jed dreaded the thought of a running gun battle from the perimeter all the way to the target house.

He pushed the negative thought from his mind, chopped a hand, and his element of four set out toward the target.

"Watcher Two, are you with us?" Jed asked Sarah Beth, snapchat style.

"Yep," she came back, *"but I'm going to sprint ahead. I want to make sure nobody's hiding in the bushes."*

"Roger that," Jed replied.

Her idea was proactive, heads-up thinking. Since they didn't have Predator drone coverage for this op, Grayson had deployed a quadcopter with a very expensive thermal imager twenty minutes earlier. Presently, it was in a static hover at five hundred feet about a hundred yards from the fence line. They needed all the eyes they could get for this one.

Jed turned to Grayson. "Three, you still got eyes in the sky?"

"Yup," the veteran Shepherd said, pulling a small tablet computer from his kit and handing it to Jed.

The tablet screen showed a bird's-eye view of the southern approach and about half the compound. Grayson had positioned the drone perfectly. Jed could easily see his two four-person elements moving in diamond formations on diverging vectors toward the fence line. He could also see the roving enemy sentries inside the fence.

"What's the loiter time?" Jed asked, seeing that the hovering drone's battery showed 49 percent remaining before handing the tablet back to Grayson.

"Supposed to be one hour," Grayson said, "but I don't think we're going to get that. I'd say forty-five minutes is the most we can hope for. Twenty, maybe twenty-five minutes to go."

Should be just long enough.

"Jed—there are no fighters between you and the fence line," Sarah Beth said in his mind.

"Roger that, Sarah Beth. Great work."

Moments later, all four-Shepherd elements made it to their individual positions along the fence, aided by Corbin and Sarah Beth. Jed held his four-man team twenty meters from the compound perimeter fence and called in that he'd reached the next checkpoint.

"Bravo One is Calvary," Jed said.

The other three squad leaders, including Ben, made similar calls.

"Striker, remember: The majority of the tangos we're facing are Dark Ones. They move and fight with superhuman speed. Head shots are required," Ben said.

The team leaders acknowledged with double clicks of their mikes.

Jed tensed, expecting Ben to give the order for Striker to breach, but instead, the next voice in his ear was Corbin's.

"Striker, something is wrong," Corbin said, hesitation in her voice now. "There seem to be other Watchers on the compound. One of them, a girl, is warning Athaliah Guerrier about our presence. I don't get it . . ."

Jed screwed up his face on hearing this. *Other Watchers? Helping the Dark Ones? What the hell was Corbin talking about?*

"Striker, Eagle One—we're made. Perimeter sentries are taking defensive positions," came the call from Carl's sniper nest, which validated Corbin's report.

"Eagle is weapons-free. Thin the herd," Ben barked, advancing the timeline and kicking off the op.

"Roger, Eagle is weapons-free," Carl said, answering for both snipers.

Despite their rifles being suppressed, Jed heard the muffled cracks and high-pitched whistles from the two snipers going to work. Jed gritted his teeth in frustration. Their most important advantage—the element of surprise—had just been lost. Taking the compound now would be much more deadly and difficult than they'd imagined.

CHAPTER FIFTY-FIVE

PALÈ NANM PÈDI YO [PALACE OF LOST SOULS]

After hearing Corbin confirm that the Dark Ones were assembled in the dining room of the main house, Sarah Beth felt a powerful compulsion to learn who the Dark Ones were choosing to replace Victor. With Jed and his team in position and holding at the perimeter fence, if she was quick, she could take a peek.

The Dark Rising is happening now.

And Viden will be there.

The thought of encountering him was terrifying, but she needed to see for herself what the Shepherds were up against. And maybe more than that, she needed to know if Viden would be the next Victor. A flashbulb memory of her bloody battle against Victor in the halls of St. George's appeared in her mind and made her shudder, even with her body safe back in Tennessee. If Viden was chosen, would he become as powerful as Victor?

I need to know. Just a quick peek . . .

She focused, took a long deep breath, and blinked. One instant she'd been crouching beside Jed, the next she was standing in the middle of a foyer. She scanned in a circle and, with a start, realized two Dark Ones were directly behind her—crouched and holding machine guns and ready to defend the front door from the coming breach. She gasped, but they didn't turn.

They can't see me. They can't hear me, she reminded herself.

Mustering her resolve, she turned her back on the dark fighters and surveyed the space. The entry had a grand double staircase that curved in two semicircular stairways up to a balcony above. A massive crystal chandelier hung from the ceiling, providing the only illumination in the cavernous space. A hallway, perpendicular to the foyer, extended to the right and left underneath the staircases. In the middle, under the balcony and directly at the back of the foyer, stood two massive and ornate wooden doors.

Both were closed.

She hated this part, projecting through a solid object to the other side. She wasn't sure why it still intimidated her, but it did. Maybe it just went against all the experience with solid matter she'd accumulated in her thirteen years—where running into things like doors ended badly.

But I have to do it.

She focused, took a long, deep breath, and walked through them.

On the other side, she found herself in some sort of fancy room.

A parlor, she thought, the word coming to her from out of the blue.

On her right, there were six guards with compact machine guns—definitely Dark Ones from the glow in their eyes—three on each side, flanking another pair of double doors. She knew what awaited beyond those closed doors; she knew because she could feel it. She could feel the darkness, the hate, the malice.

Behind those doors was the Dark Rising. Victor's replacement was being chosen.

This must be the dining room entrance Corbin mentioned.

Warily eyeing the unmoving, unblinking guards, she waved her hands at them, but they didn't react. Still, even if she was invisible, she couldn't bring herself to go through the doors between them, so she crept at an angle toward the corner of the wall they were guarding. She exhaled, swallowed hard, and dissolved through the wall beside the door.

She slid down the wall and clutched her knees on the floor she could not feel, making herself small. Having to hide inside a projection was almost as weird as the projection itself, but if Viden was in the room, she didn't want him to see her. Whether he could actually hurt her projected self was still unknown, and the possibility terrified her.

But it wasn't as terrifying as what was happening inside the dining room . . .

A Dark One stood at the head of a table surrounded by a dozen cloaked figures. His arms were outstretched, and the sleeves of his black robe billowed nearly to the ground. Head tilted back, his mouth hung open and the starched white shirt he wore was completely unbuttoned, exposing his bare chest.

Despite the awkward angle, she could plainly see that this man was *not* Viden.

At first, this came as a relief, but then a different thought entered her mind.

But if they didn't pick Viden, does that mean this guy is even worse?

And where was her new nemesis anyway? Was he one of the hooded figures around the table who were chanting, their voices low and deep, the words muffled and indiscernible? As she tried to identify him among the cloaked, fear snaked down her spine like icy fingers. The chanting seemed to be getting inside her head. She tried to plug her ears, but sticking her fingers in her projected self's ears did nothing.

Don't listen. Just tune it out.

Silver bowls lined the table. She knew they contained blood even before two cloaked men stepped up, dipped their fingers, and began to paint crimson symbols on their leader's bare chest. She watched in both fascination and horror as the strange symbols took shape and then disappeared into bloody rivulets that ran down his stomach.

A primal revulsion washed over her as a question materialized in her mind.

Where did the blood come from?

In her visions of the long-ago Rising, she'd seen priests burned alive. Had the Dark Ones drained their blood first?

Oh God, don't let that be what the kids are for . . .

But somehow, she knew it wasn't. She didn't know the kids' purpose here, but certainly it wasn't that.

Some things were simply too horrible to believe.

Having finished their work, the first two blood finger painters bowed, and the glow in the dark leader's eyes flared brighter, then two new figures rotated into position to take a turn. The ceremony continued as they dipped their fingers in the bowls of blood and painted their own symbols—this time on the man's face. With each stroke of crimson, the dark leader's eyes flared even brighter, the color of burning embers.

After they finished painting, a hulking hooded figure stepped away from the table and walked to the facing wall, where he removed a heavy chain threaded with skulls . . .

Human skulls . . .

. . . from a metal hook.

Iron, bone, and blood.

The words came to her unbidden, and she wondered if that was what they were chanting.

The massive servant raised the demonic necklace skyward, chanting some evil prayer over it before moving to place the ring of skulls over his master's head and onto his shoulders. When this happened, the glow in the dark leader's eyes grew with an intensity and fire she'd never seen in a Dark One before.

He tilted his back at an impossible angle, his mouth stretching open to inhuman proportions. Then, she saw figures materialize—demons, she realized instantly—and they began to funnel into the man's open mouth. One after another, demon after demon, they spiraled with speed and ferocity into the man's throat as he moaned with delight.

I can't . . . I've seen enough.

A wave of nausea consumed her as she dissolved backward through the wall. She took a moment, crouching and trying not to vomit. When the feeling passed and she'd wrangled control of her emotions, she projected back to the fence line beside Uncle Jed. On landing, she sent a message into Ben's mind.

"It's happened, Ben," she said, *"the Dark Rising, and I just watched it happen in the main house. The Dark Ones just chose their new Victor."*

She was aware that her body—reclined, safe and secure, on the sofa in the Sanctuary TOC at St. George's—was shaking. Not just shaking, she was sobbing, and tears were streaking her cheeks.

"Thank you for telling me, Sarah Beth, but it doesn't matter," Ben said, his voice heavy and dark in a way she'd never heard. *"Because we're going to kill them. Kill them all."*

The words sent a chill down her spine but also gave her a strange sense of hope.

"I'll help however I can," she told the Shepherd commander.

She shifted her attention to Uncle Jed, where he was crouched at the edge of the tree line, ready for action. If anyone could stop this new Victor, it was Uncle Jed and the Shepherds.

CHAPTER FIFTY-SIX

PALÈ NANM PÈDI YO (PALACE OF LOST SOULS)

Jed acknowledged Ben's order for all squads to breach the estate's perimeter fence and reposition to assault the main house, but he held his team in place with a raised fist.

He was eager to comply, but the order was the most aggressive and dangerous one Ben had given since Jed had joined the Shepherds. The alarm had been sounded by Athaliah's Watcher kids, and now the Dark Ones were mobilizing shooters to repel the attack. If Eagle One and Two failed to neutralize the countersniper threat, the Shepherds would take significant casualties trying to cross no-man's-land—a fifty-meter space of lawn between the perimeter fence and the main house.

These first few minutes could decide everything.

The perimeter fence, an eight-foot-tall wrought iron double-rail, was in keeping with the aesthetics of the grand estate's property. Unlike chain-link mesh, the bars were too thick to cut with bolt cutters, and sawing through would take too long. With no barbed or razor wire along the top, the plan was for the operators to go up and over. But now that they'd lost their stealth, clearing the top rail would expose every member of his team.

"Eagle One, Bravo One," Jed said, scanning the fence line and beyond for Dark One shooters digging in to defend the perimeter. "Need covering fire for Bravo elements to breach the fence."

"Bravo, Eagle One—hold, you've got two Delta Oscars sighting on the southern approach," Carl said, using NATO phonetic alphabet designators for *Dark Ones* as he often did. "They've taken cover behind the ATVs. They know my pos, and I don't have good lines but can give 'em something to think about."

"Check," Jed said and gritted his teeth.

The longer they waited to breach, the more fighters from inside the house would join the battle, making clearing the fence exponentially more difficult. Jed needed to move his team now.

"Eagle, keep an eye on the main house and secondary buildings. Drop anybody who tries to join the fight," Jed said. He was about to order his squad to reposition west to try and get a line on the Dark One behind the closest ATV when he felt a tap on his left shoulder.

"Hey, boss, if I can get to the fence line," Grayson said, crouching on Jed's left and holding up his rifle, "I can make things interesting."

Jed glanced at the veteran Shepherd's FN SCAR and saw that it was equipped with a SOPMOD M203A1 grenade launcher under the barrel.

"What's in the tube?"

"M433 high-explosive dual-purpose grenade," Grayson said. "This can level the playing field, but I can't do it from here. Odds of shooting this bad boy between the fence slats ain't too good."

Jed nodded; then an idea came to him as he thought of the

quadcopter drone Grayson had placed in an autopilot hover over the battlefield. "Gimme that," he said, reaching for Grayson's rifle. "I'll take the shot while you dive-bomb the dude with the quadcopter. All I need is a three-second distraction."

"Bro, I can take the shot," Grayson said.

"I know you can, but I can't fly that stupid drone."

Grayson grinned and swapped rifles with Jed. "Right on," the Shepherd said. He pulled a second grenade from his kit and handed it to Jed. "Better take a spare, you know—in case you miss."

Jed snatched the grenade and stuffed it in a pocket on his vest. "Thanks, Mom."

Gunfire echoed from multiple locations and tracer rounds crisscrossed like laser blasts in the night as the dark warriors and the Shepherd assaulters clashed. Jed wondered if the other three squads were making better progress over the fence than his and readied himself to sprint from cover to the fence line. He watched Grayson pull the tablet that served as a compact drone controller from his kit. He tapped at the screen, taking the drone off auto-hover, and then gave Jed a nod.

"Getting set to dive-bomb enemy shooter now," Grayson said, staring at the drone's camera feed on the tablet computer. "On my mark . . . Go."

Jed exploded like an Olympic sprinter out of the blocks. Arms pumping and legs churning, he ran in a low crouch, crossing the gap between the edge of the tree line and the fence in seconds. He half dove, half slid to a stop on his belly two feet from the fence. A heartbeat later, he was in his prone shooter's position with the barrel of Grayson's SCAR between the bars of the fence. He shifted his index finger forward from the rifle trigger to the grenade launcher trigger, took aim at the ATV where the enemy was in cover, and squeezed.

The grenade launcher kicked hard, and the projectile took flight with a *whump*.

A second later, the high-explosive grenade slammed into the target and exploded. Jed pulled the second grenade from his kit and reloaded, scanning the area around the now brightly burning ATV for targets. He watched as a glowing-eyed figure, now minus one arm, leaped atop the blazing ATV and began to strafe Jed's position with a submachine gun held in its remaining hand. Jed returned fire, but Eagle One's sniper round got there first and exploded the dark warrior's head.

"Alpha One is inside the perimeter," Ben's voice said in Jed's ear, informing the strike force that the Shepherd commander's squad had been the first to breach.

Chatter echoed on the party line, with all four Shepherd assault elements on the same channel, but the flow of information and commands was critical for the squad leaders, Ben, and everyone in the multiple TOCs tuning in. Jed's mind processed it all, his background consciousness building a mental map and status board while he dropped onto hands and knees and made himself into a human stepladder at the base of the fence.

"Bravo, fall in on me," Jed said into his mike and looked back toward the tree line to see his three teammates sprinting toward him like night shadows. He tensed all the muscles in his core and back in preparation for what came next.

Grayson arrived first, planted his booted foot between Jed's shoulder blades, and vaulted over the fence in a single fluid motion. The veteran Shepherd landed with a thud on the other side, transitioning instantly into a kneeling firing stance. Nisha followed; her plant foot landed on his middle back, and she propelled herself up to the top rail. As she pulled up, Nisha kicked her lead leg up and rolled over the top.

Knowing Bex—the shortest operator in their squad—might

need an extra boost, Jed transitioned into a deep squat and made his hands into a sling for her foot. As soon as her foot landed, he exploded upward from his squat, launching her into the air high enough that she vaulted over the fence with ease, just like Grayson. Bex landed hard but rolled out of the fall into a kneeling firing stance beside Nisha.

From the other side of the fence, Jed's trio of teammates opened fire on multiple locations where muzzle flashes from enemy shooters were lighting up the night. With Jed's height and wingspan, he easily grabbed the top rail, executed a pull-up, and flung his right leg over. He rolled over the fence and dropped low beside his squad as bullets zipped by overhead.

"Bravo One has breached the perimeter," Jed reported as he chopped a hand toward the smoldering ATV.

Tracers screamed past as Jed and his four-pack of Shepherds took cover behind what remained of the ATV.

"This is terrible cover," Grayson shouted as he fired a three-round burst at a Dark One running at them from the north.

"I know," Jed shouted back.

Carl called in as Eagle One in Jed's ear. "You've still got that second shooter to the west taking covered shots at y'all. I got no line."

"Alpha Two has breached the perimeter," the team leader from Gideon Alpha called in from the other side of the compound.

That left only Eli's squad, which had spread out west of Jed's team.

Jed glanced south to see if he could catch a glimpse of Bravo Two, but a burst of fire from the enemy drove him back.

"Gimme my SCAR," Grayson shouted over the din. "This dude needs to die."

Jed traded rifles with Grayson. "There's one in the pipe."

Grayson nodded and popped out just long enough to send

a grenade whistling into the second ATV while Jed and Nisha provided covering fire. The grenade found its mark and exploded the vehicle in a flash of fire and smoke, pieces of metal and plastic flying off in all directions. Jed kept his targeting laser hovered over where he thought the Dark One might emerge, and his instincts proved right. A mangled body with glowing eyes crawled from the wreckage, and Jed put a bullet into its forehead. He watched it through his targeting reticle until the eyes went dark.

"Eagle, I see a Dark One in an upstairs window in the main house," Sarah Beth said on comms.

"Which window, Watcher Two?" Carl came back.

"It's the second one from the end on the right," she said.

"Check."

Jed thought he heard Carl's round kick off, but with gunfire reverberating around him, he couldn't be sure.

A second later, Carl said, "Delta Oscar in the window neutralized."

"Great work, Sarah Beth," Jed said, in her head.

"Thanks."

"Bravo Two is inside the perimeter with one wounded," Eli reported with audible strain.

"But Bravo Five is in the fight," a pained voice said.

Five is Johnny's call sign, Jed thought and silently cursed. *One wounded already.*

"Bravo One, sitrep?" Ben said in his earpiece, snapping Jed back to the battle.

The plan was for Bravo element to breach the front of the main house while Ben's squad breached the rear. The call sign for being in position and ready to breach was Temple. Jed hadn't heard Ben call Temple yet, and he wondered if the Shepherd commander and his team were pinned down as well.

"We're in no-man's-land, trapped behind an ATV," Jed said. "What about you?"

"We're pinned down along the north wall of Building Two," Ben said.

Same exact problem in mirror image, Jed thought.

Infil to Temple was supposed to be stealthy, not under heavy fire.

"Watcher One and Two, Alpha One—we desperately need to know the head count and position of the Dark Ones in all structures," Ben said.

"Roger, Alpha," Corbin answered, sounding calm and seasoned. "Watcher Two will take the main house and I'll take the two secondary buildings."

"Copy that," Sarah Beth said. "On it."

"Striker, Eagle Two—all south and east Delta Oscar sentries are KIA," the Gideon Alpha sniper reported. "Alpha One and Two, I've cleared your six."

"Striker, Eagle One—you've got one sentry remaining. He's dug in like a tick at the front gate. I can keep him pinned down, but I have no line to make the kill," Carl said.

Jed was about to answer when a rooster tail of flame streaked through the night from Building Three toward where Carl was set up.

"Eagle One, RPG!" Jed screamed.

"Eagle Two, incoming," Eli shouted a split second later, warning their other sniper.

The two RPGs exploded in rapid succession but on opposite sides of the compound and outside the perimeter fence. Jed's heart skipped a beat. If the rocket-propelled grenades were on target, there was no way the Shepherd snipers would have had time to escape the roosts and avoid serious damage. The objective of the RPG strikes was obvious—by taking out the Shepherds' overwatch, the Dark Ones could flood the yard with demon warriors and overwhelm the Shepherd assaulters in the open.

Then, a second and equally dreadful thought occurred to Jed, a thought that he knew with absolute certainty to be true.

The next RPG has got my name on it . . .

CHAPTER FIFTY-SEVEN

Sarah Beth wasn't afraid as she sprinted toward the main house from where she'd been at Jed's side across the battlefield. Projecting and moving through the combat now felt more like a video game, only a thousand times cooler. Bullets zipped this way and that around her, but they couldn't hurt her. She could walk through fire and not get burned. She could run and jump and climb like a crazy person, and falling wasn't a concern. In this form, the physical laws of nature basically didn't apply to her because she wasn't really there. And with each projection, she was getting better at controlling her spiritual self and stifling her fear.

I'm not afraid . . .

She *was* afraid, however, for Uncle Jed and the Shepherds.

Just like the operation in the catacombs, this one was not going according to plan. Ben and Jed desperately wanted to breach the main house—they liked to use the word *breach* for lots of things; even hopping over a fence was breaching—but she wasn't so sure that them going into the house was a good idea. Wouldn't it be better to fight the Dark Ones out in the open, with plenty of space, rather than inside the house where the bad guys could hide?

What do I know, I'm just a Watcher.

What she *did* know, however, was that Ben needed updated ISR very badly, and that's where she and Corbin came into the picture.

"Whoa," Corbin said, Watcher snapchatting in Sarah Beth's mind.

"What?"

"I'm in Building Three and this Dark One has a rocket launcher. I gotta call it in."

But Corbin was too late.

Sarah Beth's body back at St. George's heard Eli on the radio call the rocket strike. That was the downside of projecting—neither she nor Corbin could do anything in the physical realm to help their friends. They were observers, nothing more.

Which means I need to be the best friggin' observer possible to help the Shepherds win.

And it also meant going back inside the mansion.

Mid-stride, she projected into the foyer, landing dead center of the room between two semicircular stairways and directly under the crystal chandelier. She whirled, expecting to see the two Dark Ones with machine guns crouching on either side of the front door, but they weren't there.

What the heck . . . where'd they go? she thought.

When she tried to push a thought to Jed, it sort of got bounced back to her. Outside, the battle was raging—she could hear the tense radio comms—so maybe Jed was too distracted to snapchat.

She decided she better try Ben . . .

"Ben, I'm in the foyer of the main house and it's empty," she said, finding Ben's thread and talking directly to the Shepherd commander's mindspace for the first time.

"Empty?" he came back.

"Yeah, before, two Dark Ones were hiding beside the door, now they're gone."

"They're probably set up in defensive positions to repel our breach—you know, behind cover or at an elevated vantage point. I need you to find them and report their locations. Can you do that, Sarah Beth?"

"Yes," she said. *"On it."*

Like a macabre game of hide-and-go-seek, Sarah Beth left the foyer and started looking for Dark Ones—first checking covered positions behind furniture, around corners, and in closets. Finding nothing and feeling the crush of time, she began to get frustrated.

He also said elevated positions . . .

Jaw clenched, she zipped up to the second-story balcony.

Bingo. Ben was right!

The two Dark Ones who'd been guarding the door were now lying prone on the upper balcony floor with machine guns at the ready. They were holding their weapons back from the edge of the balcony, so she hadn't seen them from below. She pulled back a little into her real body and reported on the radio so everyone could hear.

"Striker team, Watcher Two—I've got two Dark Ones with machine guns on the second-story balcony of the mansion. I think they're waiting to defend the front door."

"Check. Good find, Watcher Two," Ben replied almost instantly. "Keep searching and reporting."

"Roger," she said.

She zipped left down the hallway to check the rooms that faced the front yard and found a single shooter in one of the two bedrooms, crouched beside a window, waiting. She reversed and checked the two bedrooms on the right side of the stairs and found another sniper waiting there as well. She called it in and described which rooms.

"Great work. Now check the backward-facing bedrooms, Watcher Two," Ben said on comms.

"On it." She moved effortlessly down the hall.

Man, this house has a lot of bedrooms. It's like a small hotel.

"Striker, Watcher Two—found two more snipers watching the backyard," she reported from the TOC's radio at St. George's so everyone could hear. "One man in each room at the end of the hall on each side. So, in the corner bedrooms."

"Roger that, Watcher Two," Ben came back.

Six shooters was a lot, especially spread out like they were.

She wanted to check on Uncle Jed, but Ben had more work for her to do.

"Sarah Beth, I need you to confirm the current location of the principals for me. If we can catch them all in the same room before the ceremony is complete, it would be a tactical boon."

"Roger," she responded. She took a deep breath, steeling herself for what she knew she *had* to do . . . but desperately didn't *want* to do.

The thought of projecting into the dining room terrified her. The new Victor had been chosen and she was not prepared to face him, but Ben was right. If all the most powerful Dark Ones were still distracted and performing the Dark Rising ceremony, the Shepherds would have a chance to take them all out at once.

Just focus and be brave. You can do this.

She imagined the exact location in the corner of the dining room where she'd hid and watched the ceremony before. With a whoosh, she was back in that exact spot, wide-eyed and crouching. And just like before, twelve cloaked figures were focused with rapt attention on the man standing at the head of the table—the devil's newest field marshal on Earth and sworn enemy of the Shepherds. His lips, illuminated by candlelight, seemed to move with a snarl as he addressed his assembled lieutenants in a foreign language.

French? No, must be Latin, she realized.

The entire scene was a near-perfect reenactment of the ceremony in her vision of Victor's Rising in the Paris catacombs, but that had happened centuries ago. She felt gooseflesh stand up on her neck, back, and arms. Although the physical reaction was in her body back at St. George's, she could practically feel it in her projected self too.

Then, *it* happened.

One of the cloaked figures sensed her presence, turned, and looked at her.

Viden!

"Yooooou," he said, his voice nails and razor blades.

On that cue, all the other Dark Ones turned to face her, their irises flaring with rings of fire and hate—

Oh, no. Can they all *see me?*

Viden broke ranks and moved toward her, orange flames dancing in his eyes.

"I've been hoping our paths would cross again, Watcher," he said with unmoving lips that stretched across his face in a malevolent grin.

"You can't hurt me," she said defiantly.

"Are you so sure, little one? Does your book not have stories of chosen falling? Was Stephen not stoned to death? Was Paul not scourged? Were all the apostles but one not murdered by our dark forces?"

She got to her feet, held her chin high in defiance, and stood her ground against him. Her body was safe and sound back in Tennessee. She wasn't really here at all.

"How is it you can see me?" she asked.

"The same way you can see me, little one," he answered in her mind.

Then he was on her, and she swore she could feel his cold, bony fingers grip her arm.

With a gasp, she slammed back into her body and sat up, eyes wide, her mind and body now whole and unified in the Sanctuary. The return was so jarring that it felt like she'd been in a car accident.

"Sarah Beth!" her mom shouted, rushing to sit on the edge of the sofa cushion beside her. "Are you okay? Did they hurt you?"

"I'm okay," she said with a little involuntary shudder. She reached up to adjust her radio headset, which had slipped askew. "Scared the heck out of me but didn't hurt me. I should go back, but . . . but . . ."

"What is it, Sarah Beth?" Pastor Dee asked, her voice less emotional than her mom's.

"There's a Dark One who can see me while I'm projecting. He's called Viden, and he tried to grab me."

"Wait, he grabbed you?" Rachel asked in horror.

"Tried to," Sarah Beth corrected.

"He shouldn't be able to grab you. We need to inform Ben immediately of this development," Pastor Dee said with a worried look.

"I will," she said, "just give me a second." She exhaled through pursed lips, trying to calm herself.

"Sarah Beth, I think maybe you should take a break. We can all go down to the Bullpen—that way you can still observe everything going on—but we can let Corbin handle things from here." Pastor Dee laid a hand on her shoulder.

"No," she snapped, and the venom in her voice took her by surprise. "First of all, I'm not quitting. If Ben, Uncle Jed, and the others are willing to risk their actual bodies, the least I can do is support them while my body is safe here. And second, I know Corbin likes the Bullpen and does fine with all the noise and commotion, but I can't stand it. It's too crazy down there, and I can't concentrate. And if I can't concentrate, I can't project. I want to stay here, in the Sanctuary, with you guys."

Pastor Dee and her mom shared a look, but she knew if she just stuck to her guns, they'd back off.

When they didn't say anything, she leaned back into the sofa cushion. "The Shepherds need me. I've got to go back."

Rachel narrowed her eyes at Sarah Beth and gave her a firm squeeze on the shoulder. "Promise me you won't project back into that evil house."

"But they—"

"*Sarah Beth . . .*" her mom said with narrowed eyes and her *don't you dare sass me* tone.

Sarah Beth sighed. "Fine," she said, but as she closed her eyes, she sneakily crossed her fingers before adding, "I promise . . ."

CHAPTER FIFTY-EIGHT

A countdown timer started in Jed's head. They had five seconds—the time it would take the Dark One who'd just fired the RPG at Carl to reload and fire on Jed's squad's position.

"Put a grenade in that window," Jed said to Grayson, pointing to the shooter's window in Building Three.

There was no need. Grayson and he were of one mind: The seasoned former Green Beret was already squeezing the trigger when Jed gave the order. The M203 launcher burped and sent a high-explosive round into the second-story room from where the shooter had fired. The grenade exploded, blowing out windows and shaking the entire building, which Jed guessed might function as guest quarters.

Jed glanced southwest where Carl had been set up as overwatch.

"Eagle One and Two, sitrep?" Ben said on the open channel, beating Jed to the punch.

"Eagle Two is out of the fight," a voice said, raw and raspy. "Sorry, boss."

"Hang in there, Eagle Two," Ben said. "We'll get you out. Eagle One, do you copy?"

No reply came, and Jed feared the worst. He was about to put out his own desperate call to Carl when Corbin reported from inside Building Three.

"Jed, the RPG shooter made it out of the room in time. He's going to the next room over to shoot you guys . . . the window to the right. That's my right, your left," Corbin said, skipping call signs as the words spilled out so fast her tongue seemed to trip over them.

"Check," Grayson said, answering for Bravo as he popped a new grenade in the launcher.

"Hurry!" Corbin said. "He's done loading."

Grayson brought his rifle up, took aim, and . . .

Whump.

The second grenade punched a hole through the target window and exploded. The blast was amplified by a secondary detonation that blew up half the top floor of the building.

"You got him. I think his rocket blew up too," Corbin said a moment later. "He's . . . in pieces and on fire, but somehow still alive. Oh God . . . that's disgusting."

"Watcher One, get out of there," Jed said.

"I'm okay, Jed," Corbin said in Jed's mind. *"Fire doesn't hurt me when I'm projecting."*

"I'm not talking about the fire," Jed said, unexpectedly feeling the need to shield Corbin from the grisly horrors of combat.

"I've seen worse," she said, her voice calm and almost dismissive, like a salty, seen-it-all SEAL NCO.

"Alpha One, Watcher Two—I have visual confirmation of thirteen Dark One higher-ups in the dining room of the main house," came Sarah Beth's voice over the radio with fresh intel. "The Rising is still in progress! If you breach now, you can get them all."

"Great job, Watcher Two," Ben said with a renewed fire in his voice. "Striker, prepare to breach. Call Temple."

Jed acknowledged Ben's order, but as soon as he did, Corbin reported two new Dark One shooters repositioning to bedrooms to take aim.

"Jed," Nisha said, putting a hand on Jed's shoulder from where she crouched behind him. "This position is untenable. We will not survive if we stay here much longer."

"I know," he said. "Three, how many more grenades do you have?"

"Only one boss," Grayson said with an apologetic frown.

"Pick a window," Jed said. "And I'll strafe the other guy while y'all make a break for the front porch."

"We all go, or none of us go," Bex said defiantly.

"No," Jed said, shutting down her protest. "Mission before self. You heard Sarah Beth. The Dark Rising is confirmed in progress, but the window of opportunity will close. You guys need to breach the main house to support Alpha One, even if it means I'm stuck out here."

Grayson nodded. "I'll take right, you take left."

"One, Two—we're coming to your pos. We'll augment your breach," Eli said, reading Jed's mind.

Jed turned to Bex. "Happy now?"

"Very," she said, grinning.

"On three . . . two . . . one . . . Go!" Jed called.

With that, he popped up to strafe the left corner bedroom on the second story while Grayson put a grenade into the right one, then joined the team sprinting toward the relative cover of the porch. At the same time, Eli's squad ran the thirty yards from where they'd been sheltering to join Jed behind the ATV. Jed dropped low on their arrival and swapped magazines. His gaze immediately went to Johnny, who looked pallid, his face twisted in pain.

"Took one in the gut," Johnny said, with a note of fatality in his voice. "Musta been armor piercing because the round punched a hole through my Kevlar. But I can still shoot. I'll cover so the rest of you can infil to the porch."

Jed looked at the dark stain growing on Johnny's right abdomen. Then his eyes ticked to meet Eli's gaze, and the veteran Shepherd's expression offered the grim verdict that their teammate wouldn't make it.

A weird déjà vu flooded over Jed.

St. George's all over again. Only this time . . .

Gunfire boomed as the Dark One in the left corner bedroom opened fire on their position. The five Shepherds compressed into a tight ball behind the ATV, which would soon be as useless as Swiss cheese.

"All right, Johnny," Jed said, making the difficult call, "by your grace and against my better judgment, let's do it your way."

Johnny clamped a hand on Jed's forearm. "I know we haven't always seen eye-to-eye, Jed. But I also know that by following your lead I've become a better Shepherd, a better man, and a better Christian. I love you, man. I love all you guys—my Shepherd warrior brothers."

Jed choked back an upswelling of emotion and pressed his forehead against Johnny's as bullets rained around them.

"Father God," he choked, "give us strength, Lord. Give us courage. God, forgive us when we have failed and bless our mission. And please, protect our brothers and . . ." His voice cracked, and he squeezed the back of Johnny's neck. "And please heal our brother and keep him with us."

After *amens* all around, Johnny coughed. With blood-tinged teeth, he said, "On my count. Three . . . two . . . one . . ."

The wounded Shepherd propped his barrel on the chassis of the ATV, let out a battle cry, and unleashed fire on the dark sniper in the left bedroom while Jed, Eli, Hyeon, and Rick from Gideon Alpha kicked off a sprint toward the main house. Time slowed as Jed's boots pounded the dirt, the shots from the windows ebbing as Johnny poured covering fire on the positions from the ATV. Jed made the front porch first and glanced straight up at the windows above him, seeing the fire now concentrated on the ATV they'd been hiding behind. The others arrived on his heels, pressing into the wall beside the main door, now protected from the shooters above them.

"Sitrep," Jed said as he slammed his back to the stone wall between two windows.

"Two," Eli said, the use of his call sign alone signaling that he was uninjured.

"Six," Hyeon said.

"Nine," Rick reported.

After a pause, Jed made what he knew was an unnecessary call.

"Five? Five, do you read?"

Johnny's silence confirmed what they all knew, and Jed mumbled a short, final prayer for his fallen brother.

Roll call complete, Jed nodded and looked to where Grayson waited with Nisha and Bex in a mirror-image posture on the other side of the porch.

"Three, Four, and Eight are five by and ready to rock and roll," Grayson growled.

"Alpha One, Bravo One—Bravo is Temple," Jed said. As an experienced leader and operator, Ben would get the subtext that Bravo platoon was not only in position, but that Jed was ready to breach even if Alpha was unable to support. Ben hadn't called Temple, which meant Alpha was not yet in position to breach the rear of the house.

While he waited for Ben's reply, he called to Grayson.

"Thinkin' about changing it up and not breaching the front door."

"Agreed," Grayson called. They'd both heard Sarah Beth's report and knew the foyer would be a death trap with shooters on the balcony. "Windows for the rooms far right and left?"

Jed nodded and pulled a flash-bang from his kit.

"Bravo, Alpha One," Ben said, huffing in his mike as he called in. "Alpha is Temple. Bravo, call the breach."

A smile spread across Jed's face. They were stronger together . . .

"Bravo," Jed said in acknowledgment.

He waited for a five count, but when no answer came, he made the call.

"Striker, breach on my mark. In three . . . two . . . one . . . Go!"

Eli smashed one window while Hyeon smashed the other. Jed and Rick tossed their flash-bangs through the busted panes, and the concussion grenades went off like twin lightning strikes. A heartbeat later, Jed stuck the muzzle of his rifle into the window and blindly strafed the room with a prolonged burst while Eli did the same from his window. Then Hyeon and Rick knocked out the remaining glass, climbed over the sills, and disappeared inside. Jed and Eli followed behind.

Once inside, Jed and his squad split into pairs inside different rooms. Hyeon surged forward and cleared front and right as Jed cleared left.

"Clear," Hyeon said.

"Clear," Jed said, finding nothing hiding or moving in the darkened first-floor bedroom.

Through the wall, Jed heard Eli and Rick call their room clear as he and Hyeon took positions on either side of the closed wooden door leading to the hall outside.

"Two, One—ready to clear the hall," Jed said, his whispered voice loud and clear in their headsets.

"Ready. On your mark," Eli came back.

"Three . . . two . . . one . . . Go," Jed said, opening the door with a gloved hand.

Hyeon slipped past Jed and cleared left, which was the long axis of the hall toward the foyer, while Jed cleared right. They then methodically cleared the remaining rooms between them and the foyer, both of which were empty. Moments later, they were in position at the end of the hall.

"Alpha One, Bravo is set outside the foyer," Jed whispered into his boom mike.

A gloved hand on his shoulder announced Eli's return as the veteran Shepherd took a knee beside him. Jed turned to Eli, held up two fingers, and pointed toward the foyer ceiling in front of them where the balcony hung over. According to Sarah Beth, two Dark Ones had been staged up there. Whether they were still there now was anybody's guess.

Eli nodded and signaled to Grayson, in position at the other hallway across the foyer. He nodded back.

Good, we're all on the same page. Put rounds through the ceiling just in case and be ready for Dark Ones dropping from above.

"Bravo, Alpha One—in position to breach target room from the rear," Ben said in Jed's ear.

The X was the dining room where the Dark Rising ceremony took place. Miraculously, Alpha and Bravo squads had gotten into position on two sides of that room, which allowed them to put the entirety of Dark One leadership into a murderous cross fire.

"Watcher Two, sitrep?" Jed said, trying her on the radio this time since he hadn't heard from her, making him worry that their spiritual connection was somehow interrupted. "We could use eyes right about now."

"Copy. This is Watcher Two . . . I'm . . . I'm having trouble projecting in," Sarah Beth said, sounding flustered. "Any second, I should be there."

"Bravo, Alpha One—we can't wait. It's time. May the armor of God protect us," Ben said. "Striker, breach the target room. And take no prisoners."

CHAPTER FIFTY-NINE

THE WHITE ROOM

ST. GEORGE'S ACADEMY

Sarah Beth tried her best to project into the mansion's foyer but couldn't, paralyzed with fear that Viden would be there, waiting for her. She cursed silently to herself, then immediately apologized to God for the slip. With an exasperated sigh, she opened her eyes and sat up on the sofa.

"What's wrong?" her mom asked, tension and worry in her face.

"I don't know," she said. She hated that her voice betrayed how flustered she felt. "I can't project . . ."

"Watcher Two, sitrep?" Jed's voice said over the radio in her ear. The direct call from Uncle Jed asking her for info made her panic.

"Copy. This is Watcher Two," she said, feeling like a stupid deer frozen in the headlights. "I'm . . ." She clenched her teeth in frustration. "I'm having trouble projecting in. Any second, I should be there."

"Bravo, Alpha One—we can't wait. It's time. May the armor of God protect us," Ben said, his voice sort of angry. "Striker, breach the target room and take no prisoners."

"That's just great," Sarah Beth said and slammed her fist into the seat cushion. "I let Ben down. I failed them."

"No, you didn't, Sarah Beth," Pastor Dee said, stepping in. "Combat is messy and unpredictable, and the Shepherds are the best at what they do."

"But they're counting on me," she said, and tears spilled onto her cheeks.

She turned to Pastor Dee—her Keeper, her mentor, and her friend.

"Can Viden hurt me, Pastor Dee?"

"I don't know," Dee said after a beat.

"You don't know?" her mom said, her voice thick with outrage and fear. "Then she can't go."

Dee ignored her. "What I do know is God will be with you. Now, take a deep breath, in through your nose . . . Good, now hold it . . . Good . . . Now exhale through your mouth."

"Okay," Sarah Beth said while Dee's soft fingers made gentle backward circles on her temples.

"Now, clear your mind," Dee said. "Don't think of anything, just concentrate on your breathing and the sound of the water trickling in the fountain. Clear your mind . . . listen to the water . . . feel the breath in your chest . . ."

Sarah Beth did as Dee said. After a while, she started to get sleepy and let herself drift . . . until she felt someone's hand give the top of her knee a little squeeze. Waking up, she found Corbin sitting beside her on the sofa.

"Hi," Corbin said with a smile.

"When did you get here?" Sarah Beth said, squinting against the light.

"A few minutes ago. Pastor Dee thought it might be helpful if I came up."

"Thanks," she said.

"Easy day," Corbin said, stealing one of Jed's favorite expressions.

"I'm sorry, but I've changed my mind. I'm not comfortable with this," Rachel said, looking at Pastor Dee. "If this Viden person can see our girls, then it's too dangerous. We need to err on the side of caution. They shouldn't go back. Not until we know more."

Sarah Beth turned to her mom, her fear melting now that Corbin was beside her.

"I have to, Mom. The Shepherds need us. And to do our jobs, we might need to go back into the mansion."

Her mom shook her head.

"This time I'll be with Corbin, and Uncle Jed will be there now to keep us safe. I've overcome my fear. I need you to do the same."

Her mom did not look happy but after a long moment said, "You're asking me to trust you, aren't you?"

"Yes," she said, meeting her mom's gaze.

"Okay. I trust you."

Sarah Beth felt a surge of confidence from hearing those words.

"Then it's settled. Take my hand," Corbin said.

She reached out and grabbed Corbin's hand, both with her actual body and her spirit. The connection with her best friend instantly energized Sarah Beth.

The power of two . . .

"Ready?" Corbin asked.

"Ready," Sarah Beth said with a hopeful smile.

"Where do you want to go?"

"The foyer of the main house," Sarah Beth said.

"Okay, here we go . . ."

Sarah Beth felt an acceleration, heard a pop, and then they were standing in the foyer.

But the scene now was nothing like it had been minutes ago. Whereas before it had been empty, creepy, and quiet, now chaos raged all around her—with the Shepherds and Dark Ones engaged in a bloody battle the likes of which Sarah Beth had never seen.

CHAPTER SIXTY

PALÈ NANM PÈDI YO [PALACE OF LOST SOULS]

TWO MINUTES EARLIER . . .

Jed acknowledged Ben's order and used hand gestures to direct his teammates to their positions. They needed to clear the foyer and parlor to get to the dining room. That was where the long-term threat lay. That was the mission.

Jed predicted the two Dark Ones on the balcony would drop down and attack them from behind, and that the Dark Ones in the dining room would likely rush out. In every fight he'd had with Dark Ones, his personal strategy was always the same: attack with overwhelming speed, strength, and viciousness. Dark Ones were people, but people who'd voluntarily fused with demons to gain superhuman capabilities. The demon didn't care what happened to the host's body, so normal biological inhibitors like fear, pain, and injury did not impede a Dark One in a fight like it did everyone else.

This would be a battle beyond any he'd seen, including Iraq, Afghanistan, and the Horn of Africa.

Jed signaled for Hyeon and Nisha to take backward-facing positions at the front corners of the hallway to cover the breaching team's six and engage the Dark Ones from the balcony. With fluid, wordless efficiency, the Shepherds moved into their respective positions. They were righteous warriors with purpose, ready to risk their lives for God, each other, and all the innocents of the world who unknowingly needed their protection.

"Alpha is set," Ben said in Jed's ear.

"Bravo is set," Jed replied.

"On your mark, Bravo."

"In three . . . two . . . one—"

A heartbeat before Jed could say *Go*, however, the double doors to the dining room exploded open and a mob of Dark Ones rushed out.

Gunfire erupted everywhere as Jed sighted on the snarling face of a Dark One barreling toward him. He squeezed the trigger of his FN SCAR 16S, and the three-round burst found the target. The demon warrior's face caved in; it stumbled and came to rest at Jed's feet.

Jed did not, however, have time to shoot the Dark One trailing behind it.

Eyes burning with twin rings of fire, the second Dark One slammed into Jed and bowled him over. The hellish creature scrambled on top of him, and the blows rained down like hammer strikes as Jed shielded his face and neck from the onslaught, vaguely aware of the intense gunfire raging around him.

His instincts kicked in—not just his instincts from his years as a combat-blooded SEAL but also from his multiple encounters with Dark Ones. Defeating this creature required more than just tactical skill and training. He was fighting for his life and needed to fight like an animal.

He raised a forearm, reinforced with a Kevlar gauntlet, just in time to block a superhuman blow from the creature above him. He reached for the 9 mm pistol on his chest, but the ferocious barrage of blows kept his arms too busy to grab it. He braced for the coming pain and dropped his right hand to his belly until his fingers found the pistol grip of his specialty backup.

As expected, the dark warrior capitalized on Jed's lapse in defense and landed a blow to the side of his jaw, filling his vision with stars. Jed's hand, however, was on autopilot and angled the pistol muzzle into the torso of the Dark One. He unloaded five rounds in rapid trigger pulls at an upward angle under the beast's rib cage, targeting the heart and lungs. The devil's lieutenant shuddered and coughed, spraying blood all over Jed's face. As it reared, Jed extended his arm and fired a round through the underside of the jaw. A surprised expression flickered across the Dark One's face as a double visage formed, the demon revealing itself to Jed briefly before vacating the dying husk.

Jed bucked the corpse off and scanned for immediate threats from his six before rolling into a kneeling shooting stance. His gaze ticked to his rifle, which lay on the floor three feet away. For a split second, he thought about picking it up, but a blur to his right prompted reflexive action. Another Dark One charged him, sailing through the air like a comic book villain with teeth bared and hands outstretched.

Pop, pop, pop . . .

Jed unloaded three rounds into the crown of the demon-possessed man's head, and he landed dead at the Shepherd's feet.

"Jed, help me!"

A scream from Nisha echoed in the parlor, and he turned to see her grappling with her own Dark One. He watched in horror as it picked her up, as if planning to rip her in half like a rag doll. In a swift, fluid motion—born from thousands of hours of combat, kill house training, and range rounds—Jed shifted, aimed, and fired three bullets into the Dark One's head, exploding it like a sledgehammer against a watermelon. The partially headless demon warrior collapsed, dropping Nisha. She slammed hard into the ground, but Jed watched her roll to her knees, recover her rifle, and engage a new target without missing a beat.

With Nisha back in the fight, Jed swiveled, looking for the closest threat when an unfamiliar, malevolent voice spoke to him.

"There you are, little one . . . Oh, how thoughtful, you brought a friend . . ."

Jed scanned the melee, confused about where the voice was coming from. Was it real or had he imagined it?

"Uncle Jed, there's something you need to know," Sarah Beth said in his mind. *"There's a Dark One here who can see Watchers."*

"Sarah Beth? Where are you?"

"Thank you, Shepherd. Now I know her name . . ." the evil voice taunted.

"We're right beside you," Sarah Beth said. *"Can you hear him too?"*

"Yes," Jed answered.

"His name is Viden, and he's able to see and hear us when we're projecting."

As Jed advanced, a powerful sense of cold dread drenched his fighting spirit. The last time he'd felt something similar was when Victor had managed to get into his head and fill his mind with hopelessness and a compulsion for suicide. Was this Viden's work now? Or did it mean he was near Victor's replacement, the devil's newly minted general on earth?

"That's right, little one," Viden seethed, *"and after I kill your foolish Shepherd protector, I'm coming for you, Sarah Beth . . ."*

"And I'm coming for *you*, Viden," Jed snarled out loud, overpowering the dread with his own hot anger.

He vectored toward the open double doors leading to the dining room, where the voice seemed to be coming from. As he crossed the threshold, he spied a cloaked figure moving through the melee, approaching with confident, measured strides.

"Jed, he sees us!" Sarah Beth shrieked, her voice echoing in Jed's mind.

Jed raised his shooting arm, leveling his pistol, but the cloaked creature suddenly shifted left at an impossible speed, one foot landing against the wall a full five feet off the ground, spinning the Dark One over the two rounds Jed fired, which slammed harmlessly into the wall. Before Jed could readjust, the demon-man was airborne again, sailing through the air like a superhero.

Jed shifted and fired twice as he heard Sarah Beth scream in his mind.

Viden slammed into Jed's chest, driving him to the ground in a football tackle. At least one of Jed's bullets had found its mark, however, because blood arced from the Dark One's neck like a crimson sprinkler. Seemingly unfazed by the blood loss, Viden swatted Jed's shooting hand, knocking the pistol from his grip so violently that Jed's fingers went numb. A fist came careening toward Jed's nose, but he tucked his head just in time, and the dark fighter's hand smashed into the crown of Jed's combat helmet with a bone-crunching thud.

"When you are dead, Shepherd, the girl is mine," Viden said with no hint of concern at the wound in his neck.

Jed rolled his head the other way, just as another fist came down on him, glancing across his cheekbone and impacting the ground beside him.

"If I can't kill her here, I will come for her in Tennessee . . ."

Viden clamped a powerful hand onto Jed's throat and squeezed. Jed looked up at the face of the creature: a handsome man with dark hair and eyes of fire. A gouge in his neck below the angle of the jaw on the left poured blood down onto the pressed white collar of his shirt.

"There you are, little one," Viden snarled aloud, his gaze fixed on a space near the wall beside Jed. "Compared to what I'm going to do to you, child, death would be a mercy."

Jed hammered at Viden's forearm, but the Dark One's vice grip on his neck was absolute. As his vision began to go gray at the edges, Jed pulled his backup knife—a SOG Pentagon FX—from the left side of his kit with still-numb fingers. He thrust the double-edged spear-point blade into the Dark One's left eye. The demon-possessed man howled in pain and anger and jerked backward, releasing his grip from Jed's throat as he did.

"You're not going to be able to hurt anyone, you son of a bitch," Jed growled up at Viden, who still sat atop him, gripping Jed's torso between impossibly powerful legs.

But instead of dying, the dark warrior grabbed the hilt of the blade and pulled it out of his face in a disgusting display of defiance, gray liquid and blood dripping from the knife.

The now one-eyed Dark One spun the knife in his hand and thrust it at Jed's face, seeking eye-for-an-eye retribution. Jed barely managed to parry the strike with his Kevlar gauntlet. At the same time, he pulled his primary combat knife—a SOG bowie—from the center of his kit. With laser-like precision, he slammed the blade into his attacker's neck, twisted the hilt, then yanked it free. The half-serrated blade ripped the dark warrior's neck to shreds, severing cartilage, ligament, and bone. Then, Jed bucked with all his might, propelling the demon-possessed abomination through the air. On crashing to the ground, Viden writhed for an instant, then looked at Jed, eyes burning with the fires of hell itself. A demon double visage appeared, superimposed over the man's face, and howled.

"Your gun, Uncle Jed," Sarah Beth hollered in his head. *"It's on your left . . ."*

He scrambled, diving for it as Viden crawled toward him in supernatural-powered pursuit. Jed felt arms wrap around his legs at the knees, clawing him back, but not before his gloved fingers grabbed the grip of the short-barreled rifle. With a primal roar, he twisted left, rolled onto his side, and leveled the weapon directly at the top of the Dark One's head.

Then he squeezed, firing over and over until the grip on his legs went slack.

With a shudder, Jed pulled his right leg free and used it to kick away the corpse of the demon-man.

"Thank you, Uncle Jed," Sarah Beth's voice echoed with relief. *"I'm back in the fight now . . ."*

Jed popped to his feet and turned to check the battle in the foyer, which was now tipped in favor of the Shepherds. That's when another voice spoke in his head and his earpiece simultaneously.

"In the dining room . . . Alpha One needs help . . ."

The voice belonged to Corbin.

And Alpha One was Ben . . .

Jed sprinted, rifle up, toward the open double doors, feeling the presence of Sarah Beth moving with him.

"Oh no!" Sarah Beth screamed in his mind.

At the same moment, Corbin hollered, "Jed, hurry—they're killing him!"

Arms and legs pumping like pistons, he charged into the dining room and gasped at the scene before him: A cloaked Dark One, with a blood-drenched face and glowing amber eyes, was strangling Ben with a chain made of heavy square links interlaced with human skulls. Jed instantly knew that the abomination behind Ben was Victor's successor. Every negative emotion imaginable radiated from it, along with the evil certainty that it would be victorious tonight. Jed tried to position his holographic red dot, but Ben's purple face blocked a clear shot. Fresh blood ran from Ben's neck as the medieval iron links cut his flesh. While their master slowly strangled the Shepherd commander, three other cloaked Dark Ones savaged Ben's torso, pummeling him with their fists.

"I have risen, Shepherd," the dark general proclaimed. "You are beaten. This is now our time!"

"Hurry, Jed, he's dying," Sarah Beth said.

Jed quickstepped left in a closing arc, working hard to find the angle he needed for a kill shot. Seemingly reading Jed's thoughts, the dark commander gave an order to his lieutenants. As if of a single mind, the three Dark Ones who were mauling Ben with their fists whirled in unison to face Jed. Eyes flaring like embers in the dark, they rushed him en masse. He targeted the closest warrior first, unloading four rounds into its snarling face. As its fire went out and the body collapsed, he indexed his rifle to sight on the middle attacker and fired.

Trigger squeeze.

Trigger squeeze.

He put two rounds into the forehead of the charging Dark One, but then the weapon locked open, the magazine spent.

"Bravo, on me!" Jed yelled, calling for backup just as the third warrior closed the gap, ready to savage him.

Jed dropped his rifle and let it hang by its sling in preparation for hand-to-hand combat. While he shifted into a CQB stance, movement in his right peripheral vision flashed—it was Hyeon on a closing vector to join the fight. The creature punched and Jed ducked, barely avoiding a punishing blow to the side of his head. But before Jed could punch back, the Dark One pitched backward, its head exploding from a three-round burst fired from Hyeon's rifle.

"Hooyah!" Jed barked as he grabbed his rifle and ejected the spent mag.

As he snapped another magazine into place, Sarah Beth screamed in his head.

"On your left, Uncle Jed— Duck!"

Driven by reflex and Sarah Beth's warning, Jed dropped into a crouch a split second before a massive sledgehammer swung by a Dark One would have turned his head into Jell-O. Staying low, he pivoted to face this new threat. As he did, his thumb released the bolt of his rifle, advancing a round from the fresh magazine. He flicked his selector to three-round burst and fired, hitting the hammer-wielding warrior with a volley of bullets center mass. The Dark One roared and its eyes flashed with fire. Still in the fight, it raised the hammer high in the air, but before it could bring the sledge crashing down on Jed, its head exploded from a stream of bullets fired by Hyeon, who'd leaped onto a table to get a clear shot.

"Watcher Two, how many more?" Jed barked, his mind frantic as he needed to save Ben but the threats seemed to just keep coming.

"Your immediate six is clear," she said, *"but the rest of the team is still fighting in the foyer."*

"Copy," Jed replied as he stood and turned to Hyeon, now standing beside him.

Jed met his brother Shepherd's eyes. No words were necessary; they knew exactly what they had to do—save Ben.

The dark general was too powerful and too fast to risk taking a head shot. Dark Ones could move with supernatural speed and precision. All the demon lord would have to do was shift Ben's head into the line of fire, and a kill shot meant for the devil's new lieutenant would kill Ben instead. Which meant that Jed and Hyeon would have to defeat their foe using hand-to-hand mortal combat.

In perfect synchronicity, the two Shepherds slung their rifles and unsheathed their bowie knives. Then, like a pair of stalking lions, they split and charged on opposing vectors to attack the leader of the dark army.

The instant they closed within striking range, the dark general released Ben—who collapsed at his feet, unconscious. Not missing a beat, Satan's servant whipped the skull chain around so fast that even Hyeon's combat-honed reflexes weren't quick enough to avoid the attack. The heavy chain hit Hyeon in the side of his helmet. Jed watched his teammate's head snap to the side under the force of the blow. Like a prizefighter getting hit by a knockout punch, Hyeon's eyes went glassy, and he fell.

That's when Jed closed the gap.

He lowered his shoulder and slammed into the Dark One like a defensive end blindsiding a quarterback. Driving with all his power, Jed took Victor's successor to the ground. His full weight smashed down on the demon warrior's back as they hit the tile floor. Jed heard ribs break and prayed they weren't his. He couldn't really feel the hilt of the bowie knife gripped in his right hand as he plunged it into the Dark One's right kidney. The demon-powered monstrosity below him bucked Jed off with all the ferocity of a rodeo bull. Jed felt his body go airborne and slam into the dining room wall four feet away.

While Jed tried to recover his breath, he watched Satan's newly minted general rise and pick up his chain, seemingly unfazed and ready to resume the battle. Jed looked left to see Hyeon struggling up from a knee. He looked right and saw that Ben, face no longer purple, had come to and was getting to his feet as well. Summoning all his strength, Jed grunted and stood in defiance. As he turned to face the devil's apprentice, he noticed that he and his brothers were arranged in a near-perfect triangle surrounding their foe—Jed front left, Ben front right, and Hyeon directly behind the Dark One.

"You're all going to die," the Dark One said, his voice full of menace, eyes glowing like a bonfire.

Ben spat a glob of blood on the floor and wiped his red-tinged lips with the back of his hand. Then, he unsheathed his combat knife, pointed it at Satan's henchman, and growled, "Not tonight, devil. Tonight, we're sending you back to hell."

The Dark One laughed and began to swing his iron chain.

The three Shepherds, united in purpose and valor, charged. Jed landed the first strike, sinking his knife between a pair of ribs and burying the blade to the hilt in the demon's chest. Ben drove his own blade upward, thrusting it through the bottom of the creature's jaw. Simultaneously, Hyeon slammed his knife into the Dark One's lower back below where Jed's bowie still pierced the demon-possessed man.

The demon lord howled and swung its massive chain in a wide arc toward Jed's neck, which Jed blocked painfully with his Kevlar gauntlet. The chain instantly wrapped his forearm, and with all his strength, Jed grabbed one of the heavy square links, preventing the demon warrior from delivering another strike. Ben capitalized on the moment, stepped inside, and drove his blade into the base of the Dark One's throat. Meanwhile, Hyeon dropped low and sliced the possessed fighter's hamstring muscle.

Jed seized the opportunity, jerked the chain free from the Dark One's grip, and tossed it aside. Enraged, the demon warrior turned on Jed, but before he could attack, Ben stabbed him in the abdomen.

A heartbeat later, Hyeon punctured its kidney . . .

Arms and blades a blur, the Shepherds fought with fearless fury—stabbing, slicing, and thrusting. As they dealt one punishing cut after another, the half man, half abomination shrieked in agony but kept fighting, knowing it had lost but intent on taking one or more of the Shepherds down with it. But in this brutal melee of sharpened steel versus demon blood, they didn't let that happen. Working as one, Jed and his Shepherd brothers carved the devil's right hand to pieces . . .

And they didn't stop until its eyes went dark.

CHAPTER SIXTY-ONE

THE SANCTUARY AND PALÈ NANM PÈDI YO

TENNESSEE AND HAITI

Sarah Beth turned her back on the battle, the raw violence and gore too much to watch. She made herself small, clutched hands with Corbin, and prayed for Uncle Jed and the Shepherds to prevail.

Until . . .

Her prayer was interrupted by a faint and desperate voice calling in accented English.

"Can you hear me?" said the voice in Sarah Beth's mind. *"God's warriors? We need help. Please, help us. We are six kids in total. Please come and save us."*

"Did you hear that?" Corbin said in Sarah Beth's head, but Sarah Beth ignored her friend's question as she left the dining room and moved to the foyer, where the bloody battle was nearly done. A name came to her from the void, from God perhaps, but she knew it was right and so she blasted a question into the ether, *"Sani . . . is that you?"*

"Yes! It's me, Sani. It's me!"

"We're going to find you, Sani. My name is Sarah Beth, and we're the good guys. Where are you?"

"We're in the bunk room. We're scared. We need help," Sani answered in her head.

A part of Sarah Beth was astounded by this—that a kid she'd never met, a kid who wasn't a Watcher, could communicate with her in the mindspace. She wanted to ask questions, but that would have to wait.

"Where's the bunk room, Sani?"

"It's in the guest house. The smaller house outside the big house."

"They're in that building," Sarah Beth said, pointing to what the Shepherds had labeled as Building Two. "There was no activity and no gunfire from inside, so I never took the time to clear it."

"With me," Corbin said, gripping Sarah Beth's hand back in the Sanctuary.

Corbin projected them inside the little entryway of the guest house, then took off running toward what Sarah Beth hoped would be the bunk room. She followed Corbin to the room and cringed as she ran through the closed bedroom door. Once inside, she counted six kids, all younger than her. Three of the kids were huddled together—two girls and a boy. The other three were sitting cross-legged and unmoving on the floor, staring blankly at nothing. They looked like—well, they looked like zombies.

"Sani?" Sarah Beth said.

The oldest and bigger of the girls perked up. She scanned the room with wide eyes. "Sarah Beth? Is that you?" Sani whispered.

"Yes, it's me. I'm here, in the room, with you."

"Where? I don't see you?"

"I know. It's complicated. Think of me as a ghost right now.

Just my spirit and voice are here with you." Sarah Beth walked to Sani's side and knelt. *"And I've brought a friend with me. Her name is Corbin."*

"Corbin?"

"Hi, Sani," Corbin said, and Sani flinched. *"It's okay, we're going to get you kids out of here. We'll tell you exactly where to go. All you have to do is follow our instructions. Can you do that?"*

"Emelin, Francois, and I will do this. But the others, they will not come," Sani said.

"Why not?" Corbin asked.

"Because they are zombies. They only listen to Manbo Athaliah."

Corbin and Sarah Beth traded looks. They knew that name as the high-value target for the compound, along with someone called Calypso.

"Is this Madame Athaliah's house?" Sarah Beth asked.

"Yes. She controls everything," Sani said, still scanning desperately to locate Sarah Beth and Corbin in the shadows.

"What if you take their hands and try to drag them?" Corbin suggested.

"I told you, they're zombies. They won't move," Sani said.

Sarah Beth and Corbin traded looks a second time.

"What do we do?" Sarah Beth asked Corbin.

"I guess we wait for the Shepherds and they can carry them?" Corbin said.

"No, we can't wait. Madame is coming!" Sani said, pulling Emelin and Francois to their feet. "We need to go now."

"Okay," Corbin said. *"We'll lead you out and come back for the others."*

Sani nodded and rattled off a couple of sentences in a foreign language to Emelin and Francois, who both nodded. Sarah Beth could see they were afraid but also buoyed by the prospect of escape.

"Come on, let's go," Corbin said. *"It's time to leave."*

No sooner had she uttered the words than the knob turned and the bunk room door swung open. An older Haitian woman stood in the doorway. She wore a white pantsuit and gold jewelry, and her thick mane of silver hair was styled such that she looked like a celebrity. The woman's demeanor was bizarrely calm and soothing. Everything about her did not match the circumstances and the bloody massacre happening inside her house.

"That must be Madame Athaliah," Corbin said, only to Sarah Beth.

Sarah Beth nodded.

A second woman stepped up behind Athaliah, and she gave off a very different vibe. This woman was much younger, probably in her twenties. She wore her hair in dreadlocks, gathered and pulled back into a thick ponytail. Unlike Athaliah and her fancy clothes, this woman was dressed in tight-fitting black cargo pants and a tactical vest with a pistol strapped to her thigh. Beneath the vest, she must have been wearing a tank top because her lean, muscular arms were bare to the shoulder.

"I think that's Calypso," Corbin said in Sarah Beth's mind.

"It's time to leave, children. It's not safe here for you anymore," Athaliah said, her voice as smooth and sweet as honey.

The three zombie kids rose from the floor and obediently walked to her.

"Not you three. Go back to your seats," Athaliah said. "Sani, Emelin, and Francois: It's you three who I love the most. We're going to a new home together."

Without arguing or even the slightest flicker of emotion, the zombie kids returned to where they'd been sitting. Sani looked terrified and backpedaled, dragging Emelin and Francois into the corner with her.

Sarah Beth looked from Sani to Athaliah, wondering what would happen next.

The woman turned to her young companion and barked, "Grab them, Calypso. We need them now more than ever. We will rise from this yet."

The warrior woman's eyes glowed for the briefest of moments. "Yes, Madame," she said and stepped around Athaliah, walking toward the children. But before grabbing them, she stopped abruptly and turned back to Madame Athaliah. "Moreau has fallen. The Shepherds are victorious."

Sarah Beth immediately called to Jed. *"Uncle Jed—are you okay?"*

After a little delay, he answered, *"I'm in the fight, kid,"* which she took to mean he was alive but beat up . . . which was pretty typical for Uncle Jed.

"We need your help. The Dark One, Athaliah, is here, and she's taking the kids. I think the one called Calypso is with her."

"Where are you?" Jed asked, his voice suddenly tense.

"The spies . . . the Watcher spies are here," the zombie boy said, pointing at Sarah Beth.

Athaliah's expression darkened, and she scanned the room, but Sarah Beth could tell that this woman could not see her or Corbin.

"They've summoned the Shepherd called Jed," the zombie boy said. "Hurry."

Athaliah's eyes flashed amber, and her lips twisted with anger as she marched over to grab Sani by the wrist. "You're coming with me, right now!"

"No," Sani shouted defiantly and tried to jerk her hand free.

Athaliah slapped the girl hard across the face and then, in a move that completely shocked Sarah Beth, picked up Sani and threw her over her shoulder as if the girl weighed no more than a toddler.

"Kill the Shepherd," Athaliah said to the warrior woman, Calypso, as she marched out of the bunk room. "If you survive, I'll send for you. That is your penance for failing me the first time."

Calypso bowed her head. "Yes, Madame. I will see it done."

CHAPTER SIXTY-TWO

FOYER OF THE MAIN HOUSE

PALÈ NANM PÈDI YO [PALACE OF LOST SOULS]

Panting, Jed stared down at the bloody corpse of his enemy and watched the flame flicker and fade from the dark commander's eyes. With death, the bond between the human host and the demons inside was severed. Like a breaking dam, the legion abandoned the corpse. A parade of demonic faces—each more twisted, tortured, and haunted than the last—appeared in rapid sequence as a changing double visage over the fallen warrior's human face. Then, the hell-spawn fled in a geyser of ghostly flame exploding from the corpse's mouth while Jed, Ben, and Hyeon watched with macabre satisfaction. The horde of cowardly, vile, disloyal demons arced high into the air, made a U-turn, and plummeted headfirst into the ground, fleeing back to hell to beg forgiveness from their master for failing to usher in a new era of mayhem and murder on earth.

This Dark Rising had failed, and the trio of Shepherds stood victorious over the devil's vanquished general.

Jed sheathed his knife and resisted the overwhelming desire to spit on the body. He'd never done that to a fallen adversary. To do so felt beneath him.

Beneath the Trident.

Beneath the Crook and Cross.

But in this moment, the caustic hate he felt for this *thing* was so powerful that he—

"Uncle Jed, are you okay?" Sarah Beth's voice in his head snapped him back to reality.

The roar and chaos of the bloody melee just beyond—which had faded into the background during his battle with the demon commander—hit him like a returning boomerang. The newly ascended dark general was dead, but several of his lieutenants were still alive and battling Jed's Shepherd brothers and sisters in the foyer.

"I'm in the fight, kid," he said, still clutching the blood-soaked bowie knife in his right hand.

"We need your help," Sarah Beth said. *"The Dark One, Athaliah, is here, and she's taking the kids. I think the one called Calypso is with her."*

"Where are you?" Jed asked, his gaze ticking to Ben, who looked like he was about to collapse. He felt a new, fresh rage rising inside of him—not just for the woman who had buried him alive, but for Athaliah, who used children for her evil purposes, tearing them not only from their families but from God.

"We're in Building Two," Corbin said on the radio. "Hurry! Madame Athaliah is leaving with Sani."

Sani?

The name sent a chill up Jed's spine. Sani was the girl from the soccer field. How was Sani here? He'd assumed she'd be one of the children they would free back in Port-de-Paix once the dust settled from the op . . .

"Go," Ben said in a hoarse voice before dropping to a knee. The Shepherd commander's uniform and kit were soaked with blood. How much of that blood was Ben's and how much belonged to vanquished Dark Ones, Jed didn't know.

"I've got him," Hyeon said, rushing to Ben's side.

Jed nodded and sprinted out the back of the dining room, through a butler's pantry, through a large kitchen, and finally out a back door. He'd studied the compound layout in detail and now vectored toward Building Two. Legs churning, he turned on the speed, but gunfire from the darkened doorway of the guest house sent him scrambling for cover, suddenly aware that his rifle was still on the floor of the dining room. Not finding anything to shelter behind, he took a knee and reached for the pistol on his kit, but it was also gone, somehow lost in the melee.

His heart sank as he realized that he was charging headfirst into battle without a weapon.

The enemy gunfire stopped, and a lithe, feminine figure stepped from the shadow, her movements fluid and powerful, like a panther circling her prey.

"Look who's come back to me, risen from the dead," Calypso said in a melodic singsong voice, accentuated by her Haitian accent. She holstered her pistol and smiled at him. "I left you to die, abandoned by your God, but like a good zombie, you've come back to dance with your maker."

A smirk crept across Jed's face as he pressed to his feet. *I'm going to enjoy this.*

Her eyes flashed with glowing rings of amber as she bounded toward him, moving with the grace and ease of someone for whom the laws of gravity did not apply. Jed, despite the fire for retribution in his belly, felt sluggish and slow. He'd fought hard in the mansion and taken a beating in the process. Calypso's first kick connected with his jaw before his Kevlar-protected forearms came up to block. The blow sent shooting pain into his left temple and ear, and he tasted blood in his mouth.

"Ah, now that is just a kiss," she said while she circled him, her weight shifting onto the balls of her feet, ready to pounce again. "Don't look so angry with me, Jed."

His mind flashed to their first face-off by the fountain in Santo Domingo—her dancing like liquid and him trying to catch raindrops in the air. If this weren't a battle to the death, the whole thing would be comical—like watching a silverback gorilla trying to punch a hummingbird.

She kicked him on the outside of the thigh, and he felt a hematoma instantly form and begin to throb. He winced in pain and shifted most of his weight to his other leg.

She danced and darted, this way and that, daring him to throw a punch. When he finally saw an opportunity, he threw a jab at her nose. But she slipped it and kneed him in the stomach, roiling his guts.

"We don't have to fight, Jedidiah," she said with a seductive smile, leaping back and out of range of his long arms. "We're the same. We're warriors. But we need not use our warrior bodies only for violence."

The vile suggestion infuriated him. A surge of hot rage flooded his body as he remembered how she'd teased and taunted him so seductively in his dreams and while he'd been paralyzed and powerless.

She's the devil's seductress, this one . . .

"You and I are nothing alike," he said. "You've chosen darkness while I serve the light."

"You're so naive," she said, her expression both hopeful and angry. "I know you feel it. The pull. The yearning. Let me show you how we fit. We are a circle of black and white halves. Yin and yang, nested together. Neither of us is complete when we're alone. I am the darkness your light craves, and you are the light that gives me purpose. We need each other. I knew it when I met you. There is a place for you here, with us, Jedidiah Johnson."

He snorted an angry exhale through his nose and squared his fighting stance. "Never."

"Fine, have it your way, Shepherd fool," she hissed.

She cartwheeled and launched herself into a back handspring to close the distance between them. He chuckled at the absurdity of the move and spun, driving his right knee into her lower back to break her spine in half—but his knee didn't make contact. Impossibly, she had twisted in midair and his strike missed by more than a foot. And then she was on him, pummeling the side of his face, before darting away again. She moved around him, behind him, landing painful blows to his head and neck.

Frustrated and furious, he whirled to engage her with a combination of punches, but she somersaulted underneath his attack and popped to her feet, once again behind him. Before he could spin, she leaped onto his back. He felt her legs wrap around his torso, her arms tight against his neck guard. Calypso's hot breath slithered into his ear, causing gooseflesh to rise on Jed's arms.

She was the devil's serpent made flesh.

And with the unrelenting power and strength of a fifty-foot anaconda, she began to squeeze . . .

He felt and heard a rib crack.

Then another.

And another.

The compression was slowly suffocating him. He couldn't expand his chest to inhale, and the pressure on his neck began to starve his already weary and foggy brain of much-needed oxygen. In seconds he'd black out, but this time there'd be no finding his way back from the darkness.

It was probably just an auditory hallucination from his oxygen-depraved brain, but he thought he heard the familiar sound of an arriving helicopter.

Ben probably called a MEDEVAC for our wounded . . .

He felt her wet lips against his ear. "Submit to me, and I'll teach you what it means to be loved."

Jed dropped to a knee, unable to stand anymore.

An image of Gayle sitting across the breakfast table and smiling at him flashed in Jed's mind. It was the morning after she bailed him out of jail in Santo Domingo. He'd not consciously intended to burn that moment into his brain. There was nothing special or unique about it, but that's what made it so powerful.

Calypso was wrong. She wasn't the yin to his yang . . .

But he was beginning to feel like Gayle might be.

That was the pull he felt. Gayle was the thing he'd been yearning for. When he was with her, that's when he felt like two halves beginning to come together.

Jed reached back with both hands, grabbed Calypso's ponytail, and jerked with all his might. She yowled, and her grip loosened long enough for him to take a breath and much-needed red blood to surge into his brain.

My work isn't done yet.

I have too much to live for.

And too much love to give . . .

Harnessing all his strength, he stood. Then he launched into the air, leaned back, and spread his arms. He heard Calypso scream. She released her serpentine grip on his torso and tried to slither free, but it was too late. The mass of muscle, bone, and gear that was Jedidiah Johnson slammed into the earth, crushing the Haitian warrior beneath him. He heard a wet, gurgling grunt from her as he pressed up with his left arm. Spinning, he pulled his faithful SOG bowie knife from his kit to deliver both retribution and peace to the corrupted creature beneath him. Her face twisted in rage and her eyes flared with the fire of a red sun when she saw the blade.

"Noooo," she shrieked, a primal screech of fear and doubt from her bloody lips.

"Yes," he said simply and drove the blade into her heart.

She grabbed the hilt and tried to pull it out, but he leaned in, pressing all his weight down on the pommel.

Their faces were so close he could feel her breath on his lips and in his nose.

She smelled of earth and jasmine.

Then, she smiled, whispered something to him in Haitian Creole, and went still. He watched the glowing ember of light fade from her eyes and didn't let go until the fire was out. Jed climbed off the fallen Dark One.

A trio of Shepherds—Eli, Grayson, and Bex—were running toward him from the main house. He waved at them from his knees, too weak to stand.

"Jed, Madame Athaliah is getting away," Sarah Beth said in his head.

"Which way did she go?" he asked, realizing that the helicopter had not been a hallucination. He still heard the rotors.

"I don't know," she said, *"I think to a helicopter."*

"That way," Jed shouted to Eli and pointed toward the noise.

"Roger that, we got this, Jed," Eli said as he ran by clutching his rifle, Grayson at his side.

Bex, Joshua Bravo's combat medic, stopped in front of Jed. She powered on her flashlight and inspected Jed from head to toe.

"Where are you wounded?" she asked.

"Broken ribs . . . having a little trouble breathing," he wheezed. "But don't worry about me. Help the others."

"I've got everyone else stable," she said. "You're the last one."

"How many did we lose?" he asked, his fractured ribs aching as he spoke. He dreaded hearing the answer.

"We think three, but a couple folks need CASEVAC, so I don't know yet," she said, her hands moving over him searching for other wounds.

"Who did we lose from Joshua Bravo?" he asked, fearing the worst.

"Johnny. And Carl's still not answering. The rest of us are intact. One KIA from Gideon Alpha and two urgent surgical."

"What about Ben?"

"He's pretty beat up, but he's going to make it," she said.

Jed nodded and let her help him to his feet.

"There are some kidnapped kids in Building Two who need rescuing," he said, nodding over his shoulder at the guest house. "Sarah Beth and Corbin are with them now."

"Don't worry," Bex said with both conviction and exhaustion in her voice. "Help is on the way. We'll get them out. We'll get everyone out . . ."

Jed looked up at the red-and-green helicopter that screamed overhead now, rising into the night sky.

"They're getting away. Athaliah is getting away with Sani," Jed said, suddenly realizing he felt woozy.

"We're tracking them, Jed," Bex said, and she put a hand on his shoulder, easing him into a seated position. "We have a satellite tasked, and they'll see where she lands. We have our own air en route, and we'll put a team in pursuit. She won't get away."

Jed nodded.

It was over. The Rising had failed, good had prevailed over evil, and his team would rescue Sani and capture Athaliah in short order.

We did it . . .

CHAPTER SIXTY-THREE

THE LUXURY YACHT *POTE FÈNWA*

ATLANTIC OCEAN

NORTHBOUND

ONE AND A HALF MILES WEST OF BAIE DE SAINT-MARC

0000 HOURS LOCAL

Madame Athaliah accepted the blanket from the cabin steward. He nodded his deference and departed the way he'd come, along the starboard gunwale and into the luxurious salon. She was not accustomed to being chilly, but the night air was cool on the water, especially with the wind, as they motored along at fifteen knots. She wrapped the blanket around her shoulders. She knew the captain and whatever other crew were in the bridge of the seventy-foot yacht would be engaged in conversation about the strange woman brought aboard in the night. But the crew worked for the corrupt president of Haiti, and as such Athaliah imagined this was far from the strangest mission they'd been tasked to complete.

And far from the first woman brought aboard in the dark of night, she thought with a smile. The man did have his appetites after all.

The last hour had been one of quiet angst and mourning, made all the more difficult and confusing because of the maddening roller coaster of emotions she was feeling. She'd barely escaped with her life. The Shepherds had not only destroyed her home and everything she'd built in Haiti but also brutally dispatched over a dozen powerful Dark Ones. Relationships that had taken years for her to foster had been unmade in a single night. Worst of all, she was on Trinity Loop's radar now.

She was afraid.

Why not call it what it was?

She was not escaping from Saint-Marc or even the national police, after all. She was being hunted by the Shepherds and the full might of the American military and intelligence organizations that supported them. Her power had always come from her invisibility and anonymity, but those days were over now.

She'd faked boarding a helicopter and left two of the children at the estate so their testimony would reinforce her ruse. Then, after the decoy helicopter had been launched, she'd waited in secret tunnels built beneath the house with Sani, who she'd kept quiet by drugging the child with ketamine. Thanks to their Watchers, the Shepherds could have found Sani with ease if she'd been left conscious and broadcasting.

Athaliah had learned to hide her own threads.

When she couldn't bear it anymore, she'd descended to the water level where her emergency boat had been concealed. As she'd skillfully and quietly maneuvered the blacked-out skiff across Baie de Saint-Marc, with the girl wrapped tightly in a blanket in the small cuddy cabin, she'd waited for a Hellfire missile to evaporate her or for an American fast boat to intercept her.

Neither of those things had happened.

She'd rendezvoused with the president's yacht *Pote Fènwa* with remarkable ease and safety.

As if it were the Dark Prince's will that she escape . . .

Surely fate and divine intervention were not only for the believers, reserved only for followers of the light.

She shivered and pulled the blanket tighter. She sighed and returned for the third time to the beginning of her rumination.

What next?

She'd clearly miscalculated. Her bias about gentle Christians and their desire to always extend mercy had caused her to underestimate the Shepherds' will for victory and the lethality of their fighting skills. What would she have done differently? Nothing, perhaps. No—she would have changed some things. She would have waited to make her move until her experiment of corrupting gifted children to serve her purposes had come to fruition—or proven a failure. That she'd been warned of the attack by one of them suggested her program had potential, which was why Sani—the girl with the most promise—was drugged in the master stateroom belowdecks. And, she would most certainly *not* have arranged for the Dark Rising to occur at her beloved Palè Nanm Pèdi. She was unmasked now—completely exposed.

No, more than exposed. I'm being hunted.

So, what next?

She watched the dimly lit bow of the yacht slice through the calm Atlantic, the shushing sound of water on the hull soothing. She thought of her benefactor, the leader of Haiti. The name of the boat, translated to English as "Bringing Darkness," was an arrogant statement of his brutality, and a less than subtle nod to the dark forces the man was in bed with. But Athaliah knew he wasn't a true believer. He used a faux devotion to Voudou and the Dark Ones as a way to control his superstitious people, but he had no real understanding of the power he played with.

No relationship with Satan, like she had.

The man was a fool.

But he was now an enormously wealthy fool who had supported Athaliah in her international endeavors and the exploitation of their country. They had both become very rich, but the Haitian president was nowhere near as powerful as he believed. Beyond the shores of their poverty-stricken island, he was a man of little or no import. Did he know that? She doubted it very much.

The problem was, she loved Haiti. She felt anger and remorse at how the country and her people had been exploited and beaten down by leader after leader, and guilt that her own aspirations had in many ways supported that.

Once a slave colony, always a slave colony, she mused, *only now my people are beholden to a corrupt government run by one of their own.*

How could she leave them behind? But then again, how could she not?

Unless I want to give up everything and live in squalor like my people . . .

She'd accumulated social and political capital as well as monetary wealth. She was a Manbo, after all, a high priestess of Voudou. Her life could be good and comfortable enough without living in a mansion.

But without meaning. Without impact . . .

Another sigh.

Who was she to stand up to the Shepherds? They had just wiped out the entire Dark Council, the new leader of the Dark Order, and all the possible successors in one brutal attack. She was not part of the international network that could rise from such ashes. Her allies—Viden, Moreau, Santos, and even the pig Gunther Schmidt—were all dead now. She'd been counselor and confidant to all the power brokers looking to dethrone Victor. After this Rising, she would have been the puppet master pulling all their strings. But in a single night, the Shepherds had eliminated years of plotting, moving chess pieces, and fostering relationships with those on the Dark Council.

It was all for nothing.

The Shepherds had even dispatched Victor in Tennessee, perhaps the most powerful leader ever chosen by the Dark Prince. If they could kill Victor, who had reigned for hundreds of years, then who was she to stand against them?

But maybe that's the point. Maybe Victor's defeat and the failure of Moreau's Rising are proof that the Dark Ones have failed to evolve while the Shepherds have continued to adapt their tactics and methods. Perhaps that is why I am needed—the first of a new generation of Dark Ones to lead us into the future . . .

Manbo Athaliah raised an eyebrow and pursed her lips at the thought.

But was it a thought? Was it in her voice? Or was it a calling—a calling from the Dark Prince himself?

She closed her eyes, listening with all her mind's might, for the voice of the Dark Prince.

It is time. You are called. You have the tools and abilities that the archaic old men of the council lacked. You will grow a new, more deadly, more powerful future for us.

A sudden heat spread like wildfire over her chilled skin, chasing away the cold defeat of the night. She opened her eyes, wondering if the voice was indeed that of Satan, empowering her, or her own ambition.

Does it matter?

A wicked, hopeful grin spread across her face.

She could never return to the life from which she'd been born. She'd known from the beginning that she was destined for more than the life she'd been born into. Since her childhood in the orphanage, where she had killed the abusive fat woman running it by plunging a ceremonial dagger through the woman's left eye with her weak nine-year-old arms, she had always known she was special. She was capable of more. She was *destined* for more.

The scattered lights of the town of Gonaïves appeared in the distance, off to the right of the yacht's bow. They would be there soon. Manbo Athaliah rose from the deck chair, dropping the blanket from her shoulders. She didn't feel cold anymore. She felt warm—burning with purpose and a new perspective.

There was much to do because the next chapter in the ancient war was about to begin. With the entire council destroyed, she alone remained. No one was left to challenge her as the leader of Satan's new campaign.

The time had finally come for *her* Dark Rising . . .

EPILOGUE

MORVANT RESIDENCE

15 NAZARETH CIRCLE

TRINITY LOOP HOUSING COMPLEX

1645 HOURS LOCAL

During his fifteen years as a SEAL, Jedidiah Johnson had experienced the full range of homecomings. He'd come home a victor, his team riding high from months of sustained combat operations where they'd brought the fight to the enemy and returned unscathed. He'd come home angry and full of loss, a cloud of sadness over him and his brothers at the death of a teammate and friend. And he'd come home beaten, licking his wounds and arriving at Naval Medical Center Portsmouth with a lifetime of surgeries ahead of him, worried for his future.

But those days were in his Navy SEAL past.

This was a Shepherds homecoming and unlike any he'd experienced before.

First, despite the deep brotherhood he'd felt in the Teams, this organization—and the community of warriors and families living at Trinity Loop—felt truly like home.

Second, this homecoming was a complete and utter mash-up

of every homecoming he'd had as a warrior, both in and out of the Shepherds. The deaths of Johnny and Carl were unlike any loss he'd suffered before. His love for his fellow SEALs had been deep and true, but for some reason this was different. Perhaps it was because, as team leader, he felt more responsibility for these brothers, though as a senior chief, he'd certainly led men before. Or perhaps it was because this brotherhood held another dimension: that of their faith and the purpose it gave their mission. They were warrior brothers and sisters, but also brothers and sisters in Christ. The bonds he had here were deeper than any he'd ever shared.

Losing these two men, these two friends and brothers, had brought grief to the whole team. But, in stark contrast to the loss was the realization that their sacrifice had contributed to a victory that was nothing short of miraculous. The Shepherds had stopped the devil from promoting his chosen. They had stopped the Dark Rising, destroyed the leadership and inner circle of Dark Ones across the globe, and killed Satan's next general before his first orders could ever be given. The power of that victory validated Jed's decision to leave the SEALs to join the Shepherds and bolstered his sense of purpose as both team member and team leader. They'd won a battle in the spiritual warfare for the souls of mankind perhaps greater than any in centuries.

On the flip side, Madame Athaliah had escaped. Worse, she'd taken Sani with her. Both Shepherd and conventional intelligence agencies worldwide were scouring the planet for them, but so far, they'd found nothing but vapor. Knowing that Sani was trapped under Athaliah's influence and power was emotionally devastating.

I came so close to getting her out.

His mind didn't know which emotions to embrace and which to put on a shelf for later—grief or victory, regret or triumph?

Jed stared across the yard at where his teammates, and the brother and sisters from Gideon, were visiting and playing games. Everyone on the mission had been invited to join the backyard cookout at Ben's house. But Jed stood alone, sipping a beer, watching. He wanted to engage with his team—he wanted to be what they needed as they both grieved and celebrated—but first he needed a few more minutes alone to wrangle his emotions.

He felt eyes on him and shifted his gaze to the corner of the large deck, where he saw Gayle conversing with Ben's wife, Christy. Gayle's eyes were on him. When their gazes met, her face lit up, she smiled, and gave him a little wave. He felt a smile spread across his face, and he returned the wave.

Was he in love? Those were words he'd not come close to wrestling with since he'd approached the matter with a teenager's heart. The pull he felt toward Gayle was unlike anything he'd ever experienced. But was it real, or was it artificially amplified by the intensity of the dangerous and intimate experience they'd had on the island? They'd searched for lost children, found the bodies of Kaprica and Marcello, fought demons, hunted Dark Ones, and she'd saved his life after being buried alive. So, how much of the bond he felt was because of *that*, and how much was normal, everyday attraction?

And what, if anything, was *she* feeling?

Jed chuckled to himself and shook his head. Maybe his feelings for Gayle were no more complicated than a teenage crush after all . . .

"Confusing, huh?"

Jed was startled and turned to see Ben—his friend, teammate, and leader—standing beside him. He felt his cheeks go hot as he realized how easily Ben could mine Jed's thoughts and emotions.

"What's confusing?" he asked, pretending otherwise.

"The aftermath of combat. The aftermath of loss and victory. I don't know about you, but I feel conflicted and stretched by a legion of different thoughts and feelings," Ben said, going down a different path than Jed expected but the one he'd prefer to walk at the moment. "We both won and lost so much the last few days."

Jed nodded, his thoughts again turning somber. In his mind's eye, he saw Johnny, gasping in pain and expending his last full measure of devotion to his God and for his brothers. He pictured Carl, stretched out on the back ramp of a C-130 on a sleeping bag, his ball cap down over his eyes and a grin on his face, the image then morphing into that of the body bag containing their friend and sniper being loaded into a waiting helicopter. None of the Shepherds would ever be the same after having served with and lost these men.

Ben gave Jed's shoulder a squeeze of solidarity.

"It's interesting that the devil fights us the hardest not only at our lows but also at our highs, isn't it? And how he's even more vicious when those two things intersect . . ."

Jed's fingers went instinctively to his swollen, battered face. "I hear you," he said softly.

"And I hear you, but I'm not actually talking about the battle we raged and won." Ben's fingers tickled across the bandage on his own neck, where the surgeons had repaired the deep wounds inflicted by the Dark One's chain. "I'm talking about that battle he rages in here," he said and tapped Jed's chest over his heart. "Jed, I want to confess something to you. Not as the commander of the Shepherds in North America, or even as a fellow warrior. I want to confess to you like it says in James 5:16—as a brother in Christ."

"Okay," Jed said softly, glancing around, grateful that they were still alone on their little corner of the deck.

"Jed, Satan did a work on me during all of this. He filled me with guilt, he filled me with shame . . . but what he mostly filled me with was anger. And I let that become a thirst for vengeance, for revenge. He filled me with bloodlust."

"You're not alone feeling that way, boss," Jed said, remembering moments when he felt that thirst.

Ben nodded but let out a heavy exhale.

"I've spent a lot of hours over the last twenty-four in prayer and many others talking with Christy and with Mike Moore. I know that God has, once again, extended the unearned grace we enjoy through Jesus's sacrifice on the cross. I know I'm forgiven and have made strides to forgive myself, but . . ."

"Ben, I wonder if you're being too hard on yourself," Jed said, torn to pieces at seeing his mentor struggle. "As SEALs, we're trained to harness the emotions we experience and turn them into deadly skills on the battlefield. It's part of being a warrior."

"Yes, but this was more than that. I will always bring the fight to the enemy, and I'll always strive to be physically harder and mentally stronger than our foes," he said, paraphrasing the SEAL creed. "But our creed also called for me to control my emotions and my actions. I failed at that here, and in our work, it's even more important than in the Teams, Jed. Because here, we are allowed to hate the devil and his demons, but we must somehow find mercy and grace for the host. Because lost souls, even those who are led astray by lies and those who perform terrible sins, are still God's children."

The weight of *that* settled on Jed, and he looked into the eyes of the man he so admired. "What are you trying to tell me, boss?"

"I'm trying to tell you that, in combat, we have no choice but to fight the Dark Ones to the death, but we must never forget that with every victory, God's kingdom loses one of His children."

Jed nodded and then smiled. "Thank you, Ben. For sharing not only the confession but also the lesson."

"You should probably get out of the corner—and out of your head—and spend some time with your teammates. See where their heads are and ensure they have the support they need. As soon as we all heal up, it's back to work."

Jed nodded. Ben was right; he had a responsibility beyond himself.

"We're not quite there yet, but I promise I'll get the Special Mission Unit capable and field ready in short order," he said.

Ben laughed and shook his head.

"I think, after all this, you and Joshua Bravo are more than field ready. But"—he gave a tight smile—"we will have to transfer and train two new members, Jed. We'll need your team to go through the evolution with them and bond up. I'll need your help with the selection process. In this case, we won't be bringing in new recruits. You'll help me select from the existing Shepherd platoons. But we need to train together to integrate them."

"Roger that, sir," Jed said and realized he might even be looking forward to the training.

"No *sirs*, tonight. Just get on out there, mingle, and have some fun."

Jed nodded but accepted a big bear hug from his boss and mentor before heading off.

"Love you, bro," Ben said.

"You too."

Jed mingled. He spoke with each and every member of his team. With Nisha and Bex, who were off by themselves talking in a pair of Adirondack chairs, then with Grayson, who was pushing his five-year-old on the swing set, and finally with Hyeon, who drank a beer alone on the deck behind the house. Jed found it easy to give quiet support and found that his gifts helped unmask where their doubts, pains, and strengths were. He gave them brotherly love, Team-guy comradery, and a leader's encouragement.

The training will be good for all of us, he decided.

From the deck, he surveyed the operators and their families spread out in the yard, some playing with kids, some chatting quietly with spouses, some grazing the table covered with burgers and hot dogs, chips and snacks.

Then a tug on his sleeve turned his head.

"Hey," Gayle said, flashing him a smile that could stop traffic.

"Hey," he said, grinning like a kid.

"I've been watching you make the rounds, supporting your team. But how are *you*?"

"I'm good, I think," he said, and realized he meant it. "How are you?"

"I'm . . ." She seemed to give the question the real weight it deserved. ". . . good. Less overwhelmed. It's bizarre how easily the strange things I've seen feel normal, once you decide to just accept them."

He laughed. "Very true. Been there."

"I know," she said, and in her eyes, he saw both understanding and empathy.

"Hi, Uncle Jed!" a familiar voice said behind him.

He turned and was wrapped in an enormous hug by Sarah Beth.

"Good to see you, kid," he said, enjoying the earnestness of her embrace.

"I missed you," Sarah Beth said.

"Well, it wasn't much of a vacation, and despite my best efforts, you and I spent half of it together."

"Not my fault," Sarah Beth said, hands on hips. "Besides,

projecting into a coffin with you is not exactly my definition of fun or how I want to spend my free time."

"How about calling threats for me on the battlefield?"

"Better, but still a no for me." She laughed.

"In all seriousness, kid, thanks for saving my butt. If it weren't for you, I'd be six feet under right now . . . *literally*."

"And if it weren't for you, so would I," she said, flashing him a huge smile.

She held out her fist for a bump, which he happily obliged.

"I'd really like to have a few minutes to talk with you and your parents in private," Jed said, casting a sideways glance through the kitchen's glass door where David and Rachel were talking. He needed to see how David was coping in the aftermath, as well as how Rachel was fairing with her new responsibilities on the Watcher leadership team. And, he supposed, he wanted to hear from them that Sarah Beth was *actually* okay.

The horrors she'd been exposed to while projecting to the catacombs and to Haiti were a lot for a kid. Surely, they'd taken an emotional toll.

They have on me.

"Knock yourself out. You certainly don't need my permission," Sarah Beth said with a laugh, but then looked back and forth between them with a coy smile. "But how about later? You guys should grab some alone time first."

"I have no idea what you're talking about," Jed said, mock indignation in his voice.

"I'm almost fourteen, Uncle Jed," she said over her shoulder as she headed for the deck's steps. "I'm not a child."

Jed glanced at Gayle, eyes wide, and they both burst out in laughter.

"Actually," Gayle said after a moment, taking his hand, "I would like a few minutes to talk to you about something."

"Okay." He was taken aback by the seriousness of her tone. She led him off the deck and through the gate of the side yard. Then she turned to him.

"Are you really all right, Jed?" she asked. "I mean, what happened to you . . . What you went through . . ."

"I really am fine," he said, smiling at her. Gayle still held his hand, hers soft and warm in his.

"Good," she said, looking up at him. "It's important, because, you know . . ." She blushed and looked down at their hands. "If you weren't okay, it would be hard to know if any of it was real."

"If any of *what* was real? You mean, the demons, the Dark Ones, the battle for souls? Are you having doubts about what you saw?"

She shook her head and looked into his eyes. "No, it's none of those things," she said, and he felt himself falling into the warm sea of her gaze and the invitation for something more than friendship he thought he saw there. "I'm talking about this . . ."

She wrapped her arms around his neck, tipped onto her toes, and kissed him.

Jed pulled her in tight, closed his eyes, and kissed her back.

And in that moment, maybe for the first time in his life, all Jed's worries, doubts, and regrets just faded away.

ACKNOWLEDGMENTS

We want to acknowledge those who inspire these books—the real-world spiritual warriors who fight back the darkness every day by living out their faith. Teachers, counselors, day-care providers, youth leaders, pastors, and all the others who shine the light of their faith into the lives around them every day, keeping the darkness at bay. You are the unsung heroes. We see you, and we thank you.

GLOSSARY

BDU Battle Dress Uniform
BUD/S Basic Underwater Demolition/SEAL Training
CASEVAC Casualty Evacuation
CISA Cybersecurity and Infrastructure Security Agency
CQB Close-Quarters Battle
ESP Extrasensory Perception
Exfil Exfiltrate
FBO Fixed Base Operator
FOB Forward Operating Base
GMI Gospel Missions International
HUMINT Human Intelligence
HVT High-Value Target
Infil Infiltrate
IR Infrared
ISR Intelligence, Surveillance, and Reconnaissance
JSOC Joint Special Operations Command
KIA Killed in Action
MEDEVAC Medical Evacuation
NCO Noncommissioned Officer

NOC Nonofficial Cover
OIC Officer in Charge
OPORD Operation Order
OSS Office of Strategic Services
QRF Quick-Reaction Force
ROE Rules of Engagement
RPG Rocket-Propelled Grenade
SCIF Sensitive Compartmented Information Facility
SERE Survival, Evasion, Resistance, and Escape Training (Navy)
Sitrep Situation Report
SMU Special Missions Unit
TOC Tactical Operations Center
TSL Tactical Spiritual Leader
Wilco Will Comply